FEARSOME DREAMER

FEARSOME DREAMER

LAURE EVE

HOT
KEY
BOOKS

First published in Great Britain in 2013 by Hot Key Books
Northburgh House, 10 Northburgh Street, London EC1V 0AT

This paperback edition published in 2014

A CIP catalogue record for this book is available from the British Library.

ISBN: 978-1-4714-0083-4

1

Printed and bound by Clays Ltd, St Ives Plc

FSC

Hot Key Books supports the Forest Stewardship Council (FSC), the leading
international forest certification organisation, and is committed to printing only on
Greenpeace-approved FSC-certified paper.

www.hotkeybooks.com

Hot Key Books is part of the Bonnier Publishing Group
www.bonnierpublishing.com

*For my father, who taught me that I could be anything
I wanted to be.*

*For my mother, who taught me that I could be anything
I wanted to be, except a nurse. Because only superhumans
are nurses.*

PART ONE

The woods are lovely, dark and deep.
But I have promises to keep,
And miles to go before I sleep,
And miles to go before I sleep.

Robert Frost, 'Stopping by
Woods on a Snowy Evening'

CHAPTER 1

ANGLE TAR

RUE

Surely that was too much blood for anyone to lose.

She never would have thought that people had so much of the stuff inside them. Was it all in the blood, then, and was she seeing this woman's life draining away before her eyes? Would it stay with her for ever, this moment? Would she tell herself to remember it, to see if she could, years upon years later?

Rue clutched her arms together. The woman before her moaned. It sounded like a cat's warning.

'I need you to put your hands here for me, dear,' said a voice. But Rue stood stiff as a fence board, unwilling to accept what the voice was telling her.

'Rue, pay attention,' said the voice. It sounded calm and steady, but Rue thought she could hear a thin, vibrating note of stress and urgency underneath it.

'Hands, if you please. Now.'

Rue blinked, crumpling to her knees and moving forwards. There'd be hell to pay, her body had evidently reasoned without her, if she ignored the note of threat in that last 'Now'. She placed her hands where indicated, but the rags under her palms were already dripping onto the floor. Rue reached over to a pile beside her and snatched up clean strips of cloth, laying them on top of the soaked mess. In seconds the material bloomed wet flowers of blood. She pushed her hands against them and felt her throat convulse.

'Push hard, dear,' said the voice. 'Don't worry about hurting her.'

The groaning was the worst. It was thin and continuous, and she could feel the vibrations of it through the flesh she pushed against. The owner of the voice was out of sight, far away behind the hills of her knees. Rue was alone down this end. What if too much blood was lost? It would be her fault. How could anyone leave her alone when she didn't know what she was doing? She felt panic flit around the edge of her and tried hard to ignore it.

It seemed to go on for hours, but there was no asking if she could stop or have a rest. Her arms shook occasionally with the effort. The woman's blood had soaked into the cracks in the palms of her hands. She could hear the soothing up and down cadence of her mistress's voice at the head of the bed.

'Fernie?' she called.

The soothing voice stopped. Fernie's head appeared over the hillock of rumpled blankets and sweating flesh that made up Rue's current view.

'What is it, dear?'

'Um. My arms are tired.'

'Not for much longer. Dam Woolmaker's doing just fine.'

'When's the baby coming?'

'Not too long, Rue. Think you can keep your end up?'

Rue swallowed. 'Course.'

It was probably a lie, she thought fitfully as Fernie's head disappeared. Fern was an honest soul – she had once said to Rue that being honest made life a lot more interesting than lying – but when she was trying to calm a woman in labour bleeding out she'd be sneakier than a snake. The widow Woolmaker could die. Would die, maybe, and her baby with her. And maybe it would even take a few more hours. Rue didn't want to think about that, but thinking was about all she could do right now.

She'd never seen anyone die before.

She thought about praying to Tro to keep the woman alive. Then she thought about praying to Buc to keep him from taking her. In either case it probably wouldn't do much good, and if Fernie heard her she'd laugh in her face for believing that gods were worth anything more than a good story.

Odd what came into your head at a time like this. Here a woman lay dying, as Rue would eventually do herself. Was it better to be practical about it, as Fernie was, or did it help to believe there were powerful beings who could intervene and extend or take away life? Did that make everything easier?

'Let's wrap her up properly, then.'

Rue looked up. Fernie's hands were on her own, lifting them gently away.

'Move out of it so's I can get to her. But mind you keep a watch, for I've not taught you this yet.'

'She's . . .?'

5

'Sleeping, dear. I gave her something to sleep her for the time being.'

'What about the baby?'

'We'll see. Stubborn little thing, causing such trouble for his mam.'

Rue watched her work, watched her hands flit quickly back and forth the way they did when she was cooking or making up tonics. She was envious of the hands and the skill, but not of the woman. Fernie was gnarled and fat.

'Is she all right?' she asked.

'Bless you, yes. You thought she was going to die?'

'There was so much blood.'

'And she'll need to be making more soon enough, else she'll be in a bit of trouble. I'll admit it was touch and go there for a while, and there'll be more of that before the end. But she's strong, she'll pull through.'

'Fern.'

'Yes, dear.'

'You did something.'

'Whatever do you mean?'

Rue caught it in Fernie's voice. Faint, but there.

'She should be dead,' said Rue. 'She should, or her kit. You did something. You should tell me. I'm your prentice. I've to learn, haven't I?'

'Rue,' said Fernie, pulling the bandage tight and knotting it off. 'You've filled your head with too much fluff, so you have. There's no magic in what we do. Just hard work. You'd best to go on home to bed. We'll be needing you later again.'

'But what are you going to do?'

Fern sat back on her haunches, her work complete. 'Stay,

course. I'll keep watch on her, don't you worry. If I need you I'll send for you.'

'But –'

'Go on now. Off home.'

Rue thought about refusing. She would have with anyone else. Fernie was hard to test, though; somewhere under all that kindness and fat was a will of iron. So she bit her tongue and scrambled up from the floor. A wave of dizziness swamped her and she thought NO furiously, as if her will alone could keep her upright. Miraculously, it seemed to work.

'Your pardon,' she managed.

Fernie was looking at her speculatively. 'No matter. It's the smell of the blood, I expect. You did fine. You need some fresh air, is all. The walk home'll set you right.'

Rue took a last lingering look at the woman crouched on the floor, her face creased with exhaustion, and left.

Two miles to home, she thought, as she got outside and sucked in the night breeze. At least it's warm.

She woke in her room. She had fistfuls of bed sheet gripped in her hands, and her fingers ached from being clenched so tightly.

That one had been fairly bad.

She had dreamed of people. So many people it hurt to try and count them all. They were in a grey, listless kind of open space, with nothing much to see. At first she had thought them an everyday crowd; though bizarrely dressed. But they didn't move like normal people, instead following irregular, senseless paths.

The more she watched them, the more she realised that they were wandering; that was it. Wandering around in slow, looping circles, directionless. When she looked into their faces she saw nothing there. Their eyes were misty, filmed over.

She didn't like them. They seemed hollow.

Something was going on over her shoulder. She could feel a tingling as the skin on her back crawled in warning. She turned.

It took a moment to work out what was happening, but then someone near her dropped to the ground, as if their legs had been cut. She stared at the crumpled body. Then someone else fell, and lay without moving. She heard a series of thumps. Several more people fell.

Bodies flumped downwards. Their eyes were still open as they lay, curled awkwardly, their arms and legs at angles. The noise become louder and louder as more people crashed to the ground.

Rue stood rooted as the crowd fell, their limbs scattering the floor. Why wasn't this awful thing happening to her? What was saving her? What was different?

She recoiled at the cloying memory of it. Feeling clammy, she levered herself up from the bed and pulled strings of hair from her eyes. She had sweated the bedclothes through again.

Fernie would scold her. Fernie couldn't understand Rue's nightmares. She believed in the practical everyday of life. Dreams were for the academics and city folk, the studiers of mind, and had no place in a hedgewitch's repertoire. No one cared about dreams out here.

8

Rue peeled the blanket and damp sheet back, noticing with disgust how her nightdress clung to her in moist folds. She wondered if she had time for a quick bathe in the river before Fernie got back. Doubtless the witch would have spent the night with the mother-to-be, making sure she made it through the long hours in one piece. She hadn't been called, so Dam Woolmaker couldn't have given birth yet. Fern would expect the place to be clean though, and some tea ready.

Well. She couldn't work sweat-soaked. Fernie would smell her and know. Rue dragged the blanket from the bed, dropping it carelessly on the flagstone floor, and stripped off the sheet. She pushed her feet into raggy slippers and took her bathing cloth from behind the door. When she opened the shutters she saw that the sun was up, though it hadn't been awake for long. She took the dry slither of honey and lemon-rind soap Fernie had made her from the windowsill and pushed open the back door, shivering pleasantly as the cool air wound around her legs. As she walked, she worked at the nightdress with one hand, peeling it from her, and continued to the river naked. She would wash the thing at the same time as herself.

She looked about as she made her way, wondering if she'd see any sign of life. A shivery rustle in the heather patch to her right sounded like a rabbit. She loved rabbits, but Fernie wouldn't let her keep one, saying they weren't practical because they didn't provide anything of use. Fernie had bees, for honey and wax, and chickens for eggs, and a goat for milk, and the biggest herb garden in the area. Not that she needed them. Her profession never wanted for anything in the country.

Occasionally people offered to pay her, but as she always said, what use was money out here? Most of her payment was in food, clothes and services. Fernie never had to pay for anything at the farms or the village shops – even if the shopkeeper she visited that day had never been treated by her, he knew someday he would be, or a member of his family. So Fernie had what she wanted, and people did things for her as and when. A bit of gardening, or fixing her roof, or giving her a nice plump hen, or cheese and butter freshly churned, or cakes, mead and pickles.

As Fernie's apprentice Rue enjoyed most of the same deal, though some thought they could get away with charging her since she was still learning. Fernie set them to rights if Rue told her about it. After all, one day their children would be in Rue's care, and if they'd slighted her she'd remember, and perhaps those children wouldn't be as looked after as others.

Well.

It was politeness, anyway, at the end of the day. A hedge-witch would never refuse to treat children, no matter what their parents had done.

Rue reached the river, picking her way down the bank. Her bathing cloth deposited on a rock, she moved to the water's edge, clutching her nightdress and soap. The icy water tickled at her toes, catching her breath. She knew of old that it wouldn't do to wait as courage would fail, so she forced herself forwards, pebbles sliding under her feet. Launching herself in, she let out a mangled squeal as her body was enclosed in a freezing liquid case, and trod water furiously. Her skin protested in a bout of vicious tingling, but soon grew numb. She started to relax, ducking her nightdress under the surface with bloodless hands. She let it float before her, one hand thrust through an armhole to stop it rushing away, and scrubbed at herself with the soap.

She liked being here. Here she could pretend she was a river nymph, perhaps, or a goddess of the wild, surveying her kingdom. Out of the river and she was just apprentice witch Vela Rue, not worthy of her third adult name until she'd mastered a craft. She was a fairly good student, she supposed. Fernie would never have taken her on if she wasn't capable. Rue didn't want to be fairly good, though. If she wasn't going to be extraordinary, then what was the point of it? She could not wait her life out here, none but the villagers knowing the importance of her. She knew, *knew* in the very depths of her that she was destined for something more. Something she could do better than anyone else. Something that would make her shine and people flock to her.

She rinsed her arms, feeling a sudden hunger gripe. She should get back before Fernie did. Turning to wade out of the river, she spied something darting behind a tree and froze.

It was a person, that much she was sure of. Her mind worked. Who would hide? It had to be a boy.

'Come out,' she called. 'I can see you, silly!'

She was aware of her nakedness of a sudden. The water came up to her waist, but she was bare from then on up. Her skin was pimpled and white. She waded out hurriedly, one eye on the tree. Grabbing with one hand, she unravelled her bathing cloth and wrapped herself into its thick depths.

The morning air was mild, as it was midsummer, but she'd have to start moving if she wanted to get warmed up. The sodden nightdress in one hand left a spattered trail of water on the stones beside her. As she approached the tree, she realised she could see no shape behind it.

'Where've you gone?' she muttered, peering around the trunk. Nothing there. Maybe she imagined it. Maybe it had just been an animal.

Or maybe it had been a man, secretly watching her, some sprite man who had the trick of disappearing like that. Maybe he came to visit her at night, watching her while she slept, too. Perhaps she would think about that more later, alone in bed. She started to make her way back to the cottage.

Rue had a vague idea she was regarded as silly and dreamful by some, but she didn't care. She thought wishing for more a special quality, a quality always possessed by those who made something extraordinary of their lives. No one in the village seemed to think and yearn the way she did. No one seemed to want more than what they got. Stories of gods and fairies fascinated her, creatures of power that were not sway to mortal rules, not bound by normality. Fernie tutted when she brought them up, but if pressed with a glass of mead in the evenings, would tell Rue the stories she had heard in her own youth.

Rue reached the back door to the cottage and opened it, now glad of the chance to put on some clothes, at least for an hour or two. Come lunch it'd be too hot for much except a summer skirt and muslin shirt.

'That you, Rue?' called a voice. Rue sighed. Trust Fernie to get back before she did.

'Yes,' she responded, stopping to squeeze out her night-dress and hang it outside on the line to dry. She dressed in her room and skittered meekly into the kitchen, noting that Fernie had already made tea.

'I shall do some food,' Rue said, trying her best.

'No need,' said Fernie. 'We're for herbing now, then it's back to Woolmaker I go.'

'But . . . but Fern, you've not rested all night, I'll warrant,' said Rue. 'You need to lie down and catch some sleep!'

'She needs my help, dear, and herbs I've run out of. So to the woods we go to gather more, and then it's brew making, and I've to get back to her as soon as possible. She'll fade fast if not.'

Rue shuffled. 'That's silly,' she said at last. 'You can't treat someone when you're exhausted.'

'This is the craft, Rue,' said Fernie, massaging her craggy cheeks. 'It gets real hard sometimes and you just need to get through it. Who else'll do it? Who else can? You must learn this as soon as you're able.'

Rue poured herself a tea silently. She was hungry and herbing was dull. She sighed.

'We'll take some bread with us, to chew on while we go,' said Fernie kindly. 'And if you come across any berries, they're yours. Pick some to keep if you want, and we'll make some jam.'

Rue felt a familiar guilt stealing over her. Fernie could be very generous and fair when she had no call to be. It was annoying.

*　*　*

Rue ran her hands through the trailing leaves of a plant, peering at the dusty soil underneath to see if any blood herbs were hiding there. Fernie had said that particular family of herbs usually enjoyed keeping close to aurers, so it was best to scan across the wood floor for the telltale glimmer of golden petals and then have a look at the ground nearby.

Something flashed out of the corner of her gaze. She turned her head to see a squirrel clinging to a tree trunk near where she squatted. Its tiny claws dug into the bark, black eyes gazing at her. Then it was gone, the plump body disappearing upwards into the foliage.

'If only Tro would turn me into a squirrel,' Rue murmured as Fernie approached, her feet crackling over dry twigs and leaves.

'Tro knows you wouldn't last a day. You're far too silly a creature,' said Fernie, basket stuffed with plant matter.

'Squirrels ain't exactly the most sensible either,' protested Rue, as they made their way along the path. 'They're all nervy.'

'So you'd be if you were a squirrel.'

They tramped in silence for a moment. Bird calls pinwheeled across the dense canopy.

'Fern.'

'Yes, dear.'

'Have you ever lived outside this village? I mean, gone to other places in Angle Tar, like one of the cities?'

'Cities are full of idiots with big ideas. Big ideas get you little in return.'

14

'They learn things, though. They do them mind studies. It sounds interesting.'

'Rue, my chicklet. You have to have money to do such idle stuff. Only rich people live in cities and learn. Us folk mind our own business out here, and they mind theirs in the cities, and everyone gets along fine. No good stirring things up, it always leads to trouble. Why you asking me such? Don't want to be a hedgewitch any more, is it?'

'No,' said Rue. 'I love hedgewitching, you know it. I just wonder about other places sometimes, is all. You know them dreams I get. I just wonder what they're about. Are there other countries out in the world with weird people and everything's different?'

'You've no call to be thinking about that,' said Fernie briskly. 'Angle Tar's the only place with a civilised bone in its body. The world out there is nothing more than a load of places with people in 'em. And the people out there are neither more interesting, nor better, nor lower, than us here in Angle Tar. It's humans, Rue. We're the same wherever you go, no matter what we surround ourselves with.'

Rue sighed. They always went the same way, these conversations. But she couldn't quite believe the cynical version of the world that Fernie gave her. Not after the things she'd dreamed of. One day, she had long ago promised herself, she'd see the world with her own eyes.

She would have the truth of it.

CHAPTER 2
WORLD

WHITE

He woke to freezing, draining cold.

Out of everything that had been done to him so far, it was the cold that was the hardest to bear. Hunger was a creature whose ways he understood. His childhood had not been a rich one; hunger he had learned to deal with. A food unit might be free; credits to buy food from it were not. And life had been made harder than necessary for people like him.

Even as a child, White had been aware that there was something about him that didn't fit. The other children he knew were so unlike him that he found them incomprehensible and alien. They cared about pointless things like games he had never heard of, famous people he had heard of but couldn't muster up any interest in, and the latest holographic shoes that his family would never be able to afford.

Each time his father had suggested that White should try to get to know the other children at school, he had found the idea so absurd he would choke on it and be unable to speak. He felt bad, sometimes, because all his father needed was for him to agree, or comfort him with trying, and he would be happier. But instead, when he sat White down and told him that those children were not so different from him, that he should ask them who their favourite GameStars player was or which Life worlds they liked the best, he just looked back at his father, choking silently.

The truth was he had really grown to hate other children, and the truth was that at first they made fun of him and then ignored him totally as if he wasn't even worth their spite, and the truth was that even if any of them did like the same snack that he did, that would only make him hate them more. He didn't want to be anything like them. The idea had made him feel ill.

It was so cold, here.

Endless cold was insidious. You only got used to it for periods at a time, and to cope you carved your existence into blocks. Over this block and fine for a while. Barely even noticing it. Then it would stroke you gently over the arms and set you shivering with misery. You endured by begging each second to be the last, and when it was, you basked in the numbness, begging desperately for each extra minute, just another, and just one more, until the shivering began again.

So were his moments spent.

Back in the time pre-prison (as he liked to think of it, his entire life now firmly divided up into BEFORE and NOW), he had often thought about how he might cope if he were ever really and truly imprisoned. It was quite hard to imprison someone with his talent for escape. He had decided that the best way to cope would be to separate his mind from his body, and spend his time creating another life inside his head.

He would dream.

He was very good at that. It was part of the reason he was here in the first place.

But here and now, and just when he needed it most, his talent for dreaming had utterly deserted him. His thoughts were broken and confused, consisting mainly of thinking about how hungry and cold he was, and trying not to think about how hungry and cold he was. There was no energy left for anything else after that.

It would be easy to blame his mother for this. She was the one who had passed on the freakish abilities that had landed him in here. She was the one who had taught him about his gifts, and urged him incessantly on.

But there was no one to blame, not really, no one except himself, and the defect he had been born with that meant he could do things that others could not.

His mother had told him that there were others like them, but he hadn't yet met a single one. He had been the only one in his school, the only one in his district. As far as he knew, anyway. If there were others, they hid it better than he did.

He didn't want to hide it. Hiding meant shame. He would not be shamed.

When he was younger, there had been a popular slang thing going around; a little rebellious thing kids did as a nose-up to adults, because everyone knew that World's past had been a stupid, dangerous place, weren't they told so in school? So the other children's favourite nickname for him was 'jesus freak'. He didn't even know what a jesus was – he'd had to look the term up in Life's historical files. It had made him angry when he understood what it meant. He and his mother were *not* religious. Religion was for crazy people; everyone knew that.

He'd tried explaining this to his stupid, pathetic peers, but somehow he could never find the right way to say it, and they just laughed at him and screamed 'look at the jesus freak speak!' in the rhyming way some of the older ones liked to do.

Sometimes he had caught the looks on teachers' faces as they watched him, before they managed to lower their gaze hurriedly. If adults could react in such a way to what he was, then that meant that they felt there was also something wrong with his mother. And that meant that his mother could be wrong. And that led to thoughts he didn't want to have.

The door clicked.

He twitched, a tic he had developed in unconscious reply to the very particular sound of that door click.

He would be strong, this time. There was always another time, another chance to redeem himself. It wouldn't be like the last time, nor the time before that. But his body had chosen to deal with these visits without his input, and before he could stop it, his voice broke into its regular litany.

'Please please please,' he said in a babbling rush. Then, 'I don't know. I'm sorry. I don't know what you want.'

Good Man crouched next to him in his customary

position. His hands were locked loosely between his legs, his eyes kind.

'I'm trying to help you,' said Good Man earnestly. 'I'm the only one that can. You know this. I hate watching you suffer.'

He believed Good Man. He'd even seen tears running down Good Man's cheeks before.

'Please,' said Good Man. 'I'm begging you.'

No, no. I'm begging *you*, he wanted to say. You've got this the wrong way round. What kind of torturer are you?

'Only dogs beg,' said the other, Bad Man. He was in a corner, in his customary shadowed position. Good Man's face was earnest and sweat-streaked. Bad Man could have had the face of an elephant for all he knew – he'd never seen it. Bad Man never came close.

He hated Good Man, quite a lot more than Bad. In the earlier, more lucid days, he had wondered if it was because Good Man was real and close to him, and so gave him something to focus his hate on; or whether it was because Good Man seemed human and kind, in spite of what he was doing.

'What I want to know is,' said Bad Man from his corner, 'why don't you just leave? Why can't you just disappear, like you've done before? They tell me it's the drugs they give you, and the cold and the hunger. But I don't believe it. I believe it's instinctual, like a dog when it needs to hump something. It'll come out, and there will be nothing you can do to prevent it.'

Later, in his mind, they would pay. Later, he would run fragments of the conversation through his head and reply in the way he should have, with a cool, collected *screw you*. In his perfect version of events, there would be violence, and he would be powerful.

But here and now and out loud, he was a child again, frightened and begging.

'I can't do that!' he said, hating the plaintive whine in his own voice.

Good Man grabbed his arm, gripping it at the shoulder joint. 'Your hand is fading.'

White looked down. His wrist was very dirty, he realised. When was the last time they had washed him? Washing in this place consisted of shoving him, naked and grime-streaked, into a Hot 'n' Dry, a hideously ancient contraption that blasted dirt from you with chemically treated, moisture-heavy air. He hadn't felt the soothing, cleansing touch of liquid on his skin for weeks. It was amazing how much you could miss it.

'Your hand is fading, and you don't even realise it,' repeated Good Man, a little sadness creeping into his voice.

'I wasn't,' White managed. 'I wasn't doing it.'

'I told you,' said Bad Man triumphantly to Good Man. 'It's automatic, they can't help it. It'll be soon, you'll see.' He turned to White. 'And when you Jump, we'll track you. You remember the shiny new implant we gave you, don't you? It will track you within seconds to wherever you go. And if you Jump out of World again, we'll know.'

'I don't DO THAT.'

Good Man let go of White's wrist and hung his head. 'I can't help you if you don't want to help yourself.'

'No,' said White, knowing he was begging again. Hating himself for it.

'Listen to me. People like you need help. Why do you want to move around all over the place? It's unnatural. You have everything you need right here.'

'It's not my fault!'

Bad Man's voice drifted out from his corner.

'We know you help the Technophobes,' he said. 'We have evidence of them actively trying to recruit people like you. Just give us names. That's all we want. Names.'

'I don't know any Technophobes! I don't know anyone!'

Good Man sighed, pained. 'Why do you want to hurt people? Why do you hate us?'

'We don't hurt anyone. We don't hurt anyone. We don't do anything!' White screamed, his voice splitting. The worst thing about it was trying to make them *see*. They just wouldn't *see*. It was the despair over this, over knowing he was trapped by people who would never change their minds about him, who would always see him as a dangerous little mutant, that scarred him the most.

Good Man stood up.

'Goodbye,' he said, his voice resigned.

White woke.

He had managed to sleep for a while, after they had gone. But every time he woke, it took a moment for him to remember where he was, and what was happening. He

22

floated in nothingness, and a voice told him to enjoy it as much as he could, to soak up the blank comfort.

Then he remembered, and wished he'd listened to the voice.

Every wake day began the same. They were wake days now because he could only count his life between being awake and being asleep. There was no concept of time in this tiny, dank place. There were no windows to let in the light, and the strip lights overhead were never turned off. They glowed a pale, heartless sort of blue. The exact shade of blue, he thought, designed to drive you mad. His captors must have done studies on it. They must have tested each imperceptible shade on prisoners until they found the one that broke people the fastest.

The new implant really hurt. Of all the physical things that had been done to him, that galled the most. That they would use something as normal, as natural as the implant against him. Make him hate them more. Surely that was not what they wanted? Surely they wanted him to love them? He had already told them so. Told them he loved World. He *loved* it. That he would never leave. Could they somehow detect the lie in his voice, even when he screamed it with everything he had? Even when he actually believed himself in that moment that he said it out loud, because what was more convincing than desperation for this all to end?

The door clicked, and he twitched, and half of him was relieved that at least there would be someone in the room with him, someone he could talk to. The other half was revolted at himself, that a person could sink so low as to be grateful for the company of people whose job it was to hurt him as much as they could.

But instead of Good Man and Bad Man, there were two guards he had never seen before. They dragged him upwards and out of his room and down the corridor, presumably to the wash room and that horrific creaking machine.

It was rare that he got to leave his room, and the first couple of times he had looked forward to it, to the opportunity to look around, try and memorise the layout, in the back of his mind nurturing the hope of a daring plan of escape. But the corridors all looked the same, and nothing gave him a clue about anything, and after a while it was too hard to concentrate on anything much except trying not to fall down between the arms that gripped his. And a while after that, a small seed of fear began to sprout, a fear that told him he didn't want to leave his room any more, that it was easier just to stay in there. Safer.

They didn't go to the wash room this time. They went through a series of doors, doors that weren't even locked, and ended up in a small room, completely bereft of furniture. Four walls, one door, and nothing else.

He was stopped in the middle of the room, and handed a small bundle of clothes and a pair of soft shoes. He stripped off his dirty clothes and stood naked, hastily shaking out the nondescript trousers and tugging them on. It had been a while since he cared about being naked in front of strangers. They never looked at him, in any case, but neither did they turn away; as if he wasn't worth the consideration. The clothes they had given him were scratchy, but clean.

He was led through another door set into the side of

the room. Behind it was a woman in a chair, and a desk in front of her. She smiled at him.

'Hello, Jacob,' she said.

He stared at her dumbly. If this was a new tactic they were trying, he couldn't yet fathom it. Perhaps they thought a sweet motherly type would bring out his inner child. At least they couldn't read his mind yet. It had been gnawing at him ever since they had put the new implant in his head. What if that was what it did, somehow?

But so far, it didn't seem like it. If it had been able to read his mind, he was sure they wouldn't have had to carry on questioning him the way they had, and the operation had been a long time ago. Or perhaps it just seemed a long time ago. He had no way of knowing. He was pierced with a sudden, yearning need to know what date it was, what time precisely. His new implant could have told him, assuming it worked anything like the old one, but he couldn't access it in this place. They had blocked it somehow; or maybe it wasn't even activated yet.

The woman was looking at him with the glazed smile of someone unsure if she should keep waiting for him to say something. She seemed to decide against it, and spoke again.

'I'm afraid we don't have the clothes you came in. Regulations. Silly, really. But I hope those will do. They're not very exciting, I'm afraid.' She gave a fluting laugh.

It took him a moment, and quite a lot of effort, but his reply was worth the energy. 'Why do you think I would give a *fuck* about some clothes?'

He put everything he had into the *fuck*. His voice was

raspy. Another time he might have been pleased about that. He had always wanted an interesting voice.

Her face had dropped, and turned uneasy. She would know what it meant. It was a hot topic on Life news at the moment; the degradation of today's youth by the awful, aggressive language of the past.

He felt first a flash of guilt, then a tidal wave of fury that overrode everything else. So what if she was kind? So what if she went home to her three children at night and read them stories, and tucked them in, and always volunteered for extra civic duty shifts, and was the loveliest woman in her block? She worked here. *Here*. That made her either deeply stupid or plainly evil, neither of which he could forgive. She deserved it, and more. She deserved everything he could throw at her, which was only one hurtful word, after all. He would have done more if he could.

'Well,' she said brightly, as if he hadn't spoken at all. 'Everything is in order. You didn't have much on you when you came in, so nothing to give back. If you'd like to step through that door to your right, Jacob. Thank you so much.'

He considered saying no, and seeing how far that got him, but his legs were trembling, and he felt tired. He hadn't walked around this much in quite a while. He considered telling her that his name, as far as he was concerned, was not Jacob, which was a weak, normal kind of name; but White, a purer simpler name, a name that suited him much better, even if it wasn't the one his parents had given him. But the fight had gone out of him in the face of her bland cheeriness. It was an effective weapon.

So he went to the door and it opened up automatically for him, and beyond it was bright light, painful and fierce.

He stood, tears leaking from his eyes.

'Jacob.'

There was a vague shape beyond, but the light was still too bright.

'Jacob,' the voice said again, with a tremble. 'It's me, Cho. It's your sister. I've come to pick you up. They're letting us take you home.'

He heard the door behind him click shut.

CHAPTER 3
ANGLE TAR

RUE

The knocking was furtive enough to make Rue hesitate to answer it. If she wasn't alone she'd have no thoughts on it whatsoever. But the hour was late and Fernie was out, back with Dam Woolmaker and her troublesome baby.

Rue leaned against the lintel, fighting a compulsion to peer at the visitor through the window to the right of the doorway; not that she'd see much in the darkness. Fernie didn't like that, anyway, curtain twitching. Said it put the wind up people who'd already used all their courage to come to her house in the first place. People rarely visited, and even more rarely at night. Night usually meant the visitor didn't want anyone to know that they had gone to a witch.

'Yes?' she said, striving to sound authoritative.

'That Fernie?' came a male voice.

Rue pushed a sudden shot of nerves impatiently away. 'Fernie's out tending,' she said. 'This is Rue, her prentice.'

There was a long silence. Rue grew irritated.

'Well?' she demanded. 'Something I can help you with?'

'Don't know,' came the voice on the other side of the door. 'Don't know if anyone can.'

'Is it urgent? Someone need body help?'

'No, not like that. It's me that needs the help, but it's not body work I'm after.'

Rue felt easier. She was still unsure in emergencies, and blood, as last night proved, made her heave. She didn't want to embarrass herself again.

'Okay,' she said, unlocking the heavy door and tugging it open.

In truth, she'd been expecting a boy by the sound of that soft and hesitant voice. So it flummoxed her to see a full-grown man standing there, his hat in his hands, looking grave. It flummoxed her even more that she knew his form very well, had seen it on many an occasion striding through crowds with, it seemed, every pair of female eyes following him covetously. Til the quiet baker was well known around the village, even if she herself had never been acquainted with him beyond exchanging monosyllabic conversations on the bread she would be buying from his bakery that day.

She'd had plenty of interesting thoughts about Til when she was alone in bed, though, and now she felt, in sudden horror, as if each one were on display for him to see. She flushed, shifting on her feet. But he wasn't even looking at her. His eyes were on the ground, as if ashamed.

Say something, cretin, Rue told herself. He's waiting to be invited in!

'Come in,' she managed eventually, mortified by the simpering tone in her voice. She turned and walked further into the kitchen without waiting for him to move. Gods, the door, she thought, but was relieved to hear it close firmly. She moved to lean against the nearest countertop, taking a breath and forcing herself around to face him. At least there was something solid at her back.

'What's . . . how can I help you?' she said.

Til stood in the doorway, looking around the kitchen. His hair fell over his eyes constantly and he shook it back in an unconscious gesture that made girls sigh.

Oh Threya, you're beautiful, thought Rue, her heart fluttering like a dying bird.

Til looked at her, for just a moment. Then his gaze swept away and back to the floor, and she felt a sudden release, as if he had pinned her with his eyes.

'I need . . . something,' he said at last.

Rue waited.

She'd seen Fernie in similar situations. Patience was the key. They had to trust that whatever passed in this room would never be breathed to another living being. It was the relationship all witches offered to those in need of their services, and the first time they entered into it was tough. They had to open themselves to her, to divulge bits of their secret souls in order to get what they required, and that was hard on anyone, to trust. Rue understood that. She also started to understand the power of it. To get a piece of Til's soul? That would mean a connection between them, some control over him. She suppressed a thrill.

She watched Til struggle. 'Why don't you sit down?' she said, pitching her voice to a level she thought sounded soft and kind. 'I'll put some tea on, and you tell me what you need. You can take your time.'

She turned her back on him, busying herself. She thought

he watched her and tried to make her movements graceful. She arched her back a little more than usual, swept her hair back over her shoulders with a practised careless gesture. She heard the scrape of wood over stone as he sat down. When he started to talk she let him, concentrating fiercely on preparing the tea.

'I heard that Fernie deals with other problems than bein' sick. Soul problems,' said Til. His lovely voice was hesitant. 'I didn't . . . I didn't think of coming here. But someone told me she could fix it for me.'

She turned, pot in hand. 'Whatever Fernie can do, I can do,' she said firmly. 'I may be her prentice but I'm taught everything she knows.'

'I'm sorry,' said Til. 'I didn't mean to say nothing of you.' His huge hands came up and held his head. He looked bereft and broken. Rue felt her heart melt.

'Go on,' she said. Her hand shook as she set the pot on the stove. She glared at it.

'I wouldn't come here if I weren't desperate,' he murmured. 'Meaning no disrespect. It's just not . . . it's not done to talk out your problems with others. Women do that. They find comfort in it. Men don't, they fix it themselves. And they find comfort in that.'

Rue looked at him in frank astonishment. She had never assumed that he could be so perceptive, but chastised herself for that now. Things weren't always what they seemed. She set the tea on the table before him, wanting to see if he watched her hands as they crossed his line of vision. She took her time sitting, afraid of stumbling or looking clumsy.

'Please don't tell no one,' he said softly, startling her. This

31

close, she could see tiny flaws in his skin, the grime built up on his nose. But it was his downcast eyes that she watched; how she wished and feared they would raise up to her face. He was perfect.

'I won't,' she said. 'I won't. Promise. There's the rules.'

He sighed gently. She imagined the sigh landing on her neck, like a little moth.

'I'm sick,' he said. 'Sick with love.'

Rue watched his hand creep around the tea glass, but he didn't drink. He still would not look at her.

Her heart was bursting with hope.

'There's this woman. I can't have her, see. She belongs to someone else. And that would be that, except I've loved her for ever, since we was children. And she . . . she's been giving me hope. She looks at me, in a way I thought might be. You know. The same.'

Til paused. It was Rue's turn to stare at the tabletop. She felt a flash of dreaded disappointment, then a slow blush creeping up her cheeks. And of course, she saw so clearly now. How could he ever be interested in her? She was just a girl. He was a full-grown man, red-blooded prime. She'd be barely more than a child to him. A p'tite. He'd want a woman, wouldn't he, with curves and knowing eyes and legs that went on for ever.

Stupid men. Always want most what they can't have; get it and then grow bored of it! Rue had seen enough of Fernie's late-night visitors to know this truth. She felt anger and contempt and welcomed it. Better than the embarrassment. Easier. She struggled to keep silent.

Til had transferred his gaze to the wall. 'I've watched her

32

with other men,' he murmured. 'Years and years I've watched her go through them. Hoping she'd see me better than before. But she never did. She got married and never gave me a second thought, until now. I'm not a bad man. I'm not. I've waited my time. I've done it, years I've done it. But I know she's changed her mind now. It's my time now.' He turned to look at her then, so suddenly that he caught her gaze before she could drop it. His face had transformed; his dark, sad eyes burned. How lucky the woman who caused Til's face to change like that. His desire, like a blast of heat from a furnace. Rue could imagine just how it would be with him.

'So what do you need from a hedgewitch?' she said in a low voice. 'Don't you need to be talking to this woman to see what she wants, see whether she'll leave her man for you?'

Til was silent. She watched his arm across the table. It was close enough to hers to touch, if she reached out just a little. His nearness and maleness was overpowering; she could smell him, his essence.

'Maybe there's something you could do,' said Til. Rue thought she could hear an edge to his voice. Her anger flashed.

'If you're thinking what I think you are, the answer's no,' she snapped. 'And you should know better than to ask.'

Til looked at her in surprise. 'What do you mean?' he said. He knew and he didn't know. He was testing her.

'There'll be no getting rid of husbands,' said Rue. 'In any fashion.'

Til gazed at her strangely. She lost her fire. 'What?' she said, less boldly.

'You look so young on the out. But you're a bit older inside, aren't you?' said Til.

Rue felt a thrill in the pit of her belly. 'I've seen some things,' she said.

They both fell silent. Rue thought about the picture they made, close together at the table, bathed in velvet shadow and lamplight stripes, a secret sat heavy between them. She wondered if they looked like lovers. She wished they did. She looked at Til then, and he at her, and there was a moment, she thought. But she saw it run from his mind just as quickly as it had come and felt younger and sillier than ever.

'I feel like an idiot coming here,' said Til.

'Why?'

'I don't know what to do. Tell me what I should do. Is there something . . . maybe you could give me something to forget her. Maybe there's something for me to make it go.'

Rue hesitated. There was always oublie. A rare little plant that, handled by someone who knew what they were doing, took memories from you. But Fernie thought it more dangerous than not. Who knew what would happen? Maybe you'd forget the wrong thing. Or you'd forget everything except the one thing you wanted to, and it would grow in the space you'd created, consuming you completely.

The alternatives were also bad. Give the woman something to make her reckless, maybe reckless enough to leave her husband . . . or reckless enough to run away. Kill herself. Do wild and silly things. Who knew? It depended on the person in the end. Didn't it always? Or give the husband something that would make him sick every time he touched his wife. But that way lay bad power. Bad power always came back to you.

'Who is it?' she said at last.

Til sighed and shifted. 'Why do you need to know?'

'I can't help you without knowing everything.'

He looked at her for a long moment. Her belly rolled again. She allowed a small hope to bloom. It was stupid, she knew it.

He said a name, and her hope was squashed. Her reaction must have been too strong, because he sat back from her, looking wary.

'That . . .' She forced the explosion down, away. Took a breath. 'She's got men on a string. She knows how to play 'em. I've heard some wild stories. You must know this about her. All the girls know this about her!'

Til looked away, his expression dark. She knew she wouldn't change his mind. The lines across his face told her that.

The silence grew heavier. Rue fumbled with the right words. She wanted to help him. Helping him would forge the connection she craved. But she wanted to help him forget the woman who had a grip on his heart. No good lay that way. No good at all. Rue wanted Til for herself, but she also wanted to be unselfish, the way she should be, and with this battle raging she plunged ahead.

'Is there really no one else for you?' she said. 'Perhaps this'll pass.'

'Not these twenty years,' he replied, far away. 'And so I don't expect t'will ever leave me be.'

Rue felt smaller at his words. In comparison, her desire for Til was a passing moment, a flicker at best. How could she compete with this strength of passion? She had not even been alive for as long as Til had loved this woman.

'I can suggest nothing that ain't . . . uncertain,' she said at last. 'The best thing would be to speak to her.'

'No,' said Til. 'No. It won't do. I can't even look at her without her man giving me an eye. He won't let her from her leash long enough to speak to her alone. And if I stopped her in the street . . . people would talk.'

Rue understood that. He had been very careful so far – she'd never heard of a gossipful concerning him and the lady in question. Being careful was getting him nowhere.

He turned and shone his gaze on her like a lamp in her eyes.

'I've an idea,' she said, to break the stare. 'There's something you could give her. It's unpredictable, but in small bits it might help. And with the right timing and all.'

The bruised look left his face and it filled with hope. Rue gazed at her glass.

'It's most powerful as a tea,' she said. 'But wild. If you had it in a powder, and found a way for her to use the powder just a bit, every day. Then maybe that would work better.'

His brow wrinkled. 'Like how?'

'Put it in something only she would wear. Her creams, or make-up. Something.'

He was already shaking his head. 'How would I even get close enough?'

'Give her a present,' said Rue impatiently. Did men have

no cunning at all? 'Give it through one of her woman friends who can be trusted. Or give it anonymously. It don't have to be obviously from you, though t'would be better if at least she knew it were.'

'Why?'

'Cos if she uses it, you know she likes you,' said Rue.

She watched him contemplate this.

'What will it do?' he said, finally. His voice was lowered to a shameful whisper.

'Give her a push,' said Rue. She made a point of speaking normally. Whispering spoke of secret shame. This was business. 'If you time it right. Whenever she sees you, it'll . . . fan the flames a bit.'

Til stroked the side of his tea glass absent-mindedly. 'I don't want to hurt her,' he murmured.

Rue took a breath, ignoring a twinge of self-disgust. 'We could try it now,' she said. 'So you know what it's like.'

He was silent.

'A really small twist of it,' she said. 'Really small. Then you know what it'll feel like and whether it might work.'

He was still silent. Rue screwed herself up tight.

'All right,' he said at last. 'If you think that's best.'

'I'll be a minute.'

She got up from the table, heart hammering. When she looked back, he was staring at his glass. She couldn't tell what he was thinking. Done it now, dear, she thought. Made your choice. Carry it through. Stop being such a baby!

Rue moved through the cottage into the back workroom, sorting through the jars on the shelf. It would be plain old dagger weed, not even special enough to be named properly,

Fernie had said with a sort of satisfaction. It was a source of pride to Fernie that no one but hedgewitches knew what dagger could do, treated properly. Rue trailed her fingers over the paper labels, nervous of picking the wrong jar. Finally she found a small container filled with the familiar dried purple leaves.

Now how much to measure? Rue sorted anxiously through her mind. Measurements were of the utmost importance. How much for this? Less than usual. How much was usual? One spoon for a tea, wasn't it? But he wouldn't want to sit around waiting. Make it a half pinch. Should only be about an hour's worth, immediate effect.

Rue measured it out into a cup and looked at it. Didn't seem much. Maybe just a half pinch more. She made her way back to the kitchen. Til hadn't moved. She went to the stove and put some more water back on to boil.

'It should start working fast,' she said over her shoulder. His silence was getting on her nerves now, where before it had charmed her. 'Won't last more than an hour. If it does, you should take a really cold bath. The shock'll dim its effects quicker.'

In a moment more she had it done. She made her way back to the table and replaced his tea glass with the fresh, her fingers twitching just once in betrayal. She resumed her seat near him and folded her arms.

'Best let it steep for a moment.'

He twined his hands together and stared at the cup. Rue thought anxiously about what she should do. Should they talk some more? Would he think her too intrusive?

'Well, and so, who told you to come here?' she ventured.

38

Til looked up at her. 'Who . . .?'

'You said that someone told you Fernie could help? You don't have to say who it was . . . I'm just curious.'

Til studied the air in front of his face. 'Yeh,' he said at last. 'Something like this. Not a friend of mine. Just someone I know who . . . knows *her.*'

A friend of his woman. Rue rifled through what she knew of his love's acquaintances.

'Do you . . . have this sort of visit a lot?' Til said. He took a tentative sip of his tea.

'More than you'd suppose,' said Rue vaguely, still thinking. 'And more men than you'd suppose, and all. And always at night.' She glanced at him.

'You both must think us fools, all us who visit,' he murmured.

'No,' she said, wanting to impress him with her honesty and maturity. 'We're human too. We have wants and desires. We understand them best. We do silly things we'd do anything to take back. Witches are more human than anyone else.'

Til was looking at her strangely when she glanced up.

'What is it?' she said.

He shook his head. 'Tea's tingling me all over.'

'That's expected. Shouldn't be too long now.'

They fell silent. Rue traced a knot in the table under her hands.

'Not a talker, are you?' she said.

'No,' he said. 'Never have been. This is as long a talk as I've had for many a month.'

'I talk too much, says Fernie,' Rue said. 'My head's too full, she says. Too dreamy, I am. Always somewhere else.'

'You're proud of that.'

Rue looked at him in annoyance. 'You see a lot, don't you?'

'People don't think a baker's up to much. I listen, though.'

'Fernie says I don't do enough of that.'

Til swallowed and put his cup down. 'Why you prenticing with her?'

Rue played her fingers together, rubbing the nails against each other, wondering what to tell him.

'It's special, ain't it,' she said. 'Being a hedgewitch. You'll get to know things most don't.'

'You think you're special?'

Rue was ready to flare but heard no patronising tone in his voice. She shrugged. 'Maybe. Maybe I thought hedge-witching would tell me who I am.'

'Everyone's looking for that answer.'

'Maybe,' she said again.

Silence fell again, but it was of a richer, more compan-ionable sort. Til swirled his tea a little and drank a mouthful while she watched.

'Tell me,' Rue started. 'Do folk . . . think badly of witches? Do you think us frightful or odd?'

'No. Folk are nervy of what you can do. You know, healing and that. It's respect, is all.'

'Well. I mean, sometimes I think I get treated funny in the town.'

'By who?' came Til's voice.

Rue dared not look up. 'Don't know. Women talk about me when I walk past. Boys come up and tease.'

'That ain't because you're training in hedgewitching. It's cos you're a sauce.'

40

'A *what?*'

'A sauce. A little girl woman. You sway your hips and flirt with everyone.'

Rue looked up, outraged, meaning to give Til the fullness of her malice.

She blanched when she saw his face. His skin had gone pink and he seemed suddenly fast and tensed, as if he wanted to bound out of his chair. She had a flash of warning in the pit of her belly.

'I don't flirt with anyone,' she said, her voice faint.

Til snorted. 'Ha! It's a fact about you, Rue.'

Rue shrank back in her chair. Til was gripping the table edge, his eyes sparkling and over-heated. He seemed wrong, like he was going too fast for himself and was ready to trip over.

Grad take me . . . I've given him too much.

She stood up. So did he.

'Til,' she said. 'Til, it's the tea . . .'

He said nothing, as if he could not hear her. Her skin prickled slowly.

'It's the dagger weed,' she said, striving to sound calm. 'It was too much. I'm sorry.'

His breathing was loud.

'Til,' she said.

'Hush up,' he muttered. He moved towards her and she forced herself to hold still. Something told her that if she acted frightened she'd make things worse.

'Til, the tea is making you feel fast and hot. Right? You should sit down. You should . . . I can get you some water. T'will make you feel better.'

He gripped the tops of her arms in his huge hands and then stopped, as if unsure of what to do next. Rue felt sick.

'Til . . .' she tried again.

'Hold still,' he said, and pushed his weight down on her arms. She broke, wrenching free and running to the back door. She felt him up behind her and then his weight tugged her down. She fell awkwardly and felt his hands on her. His arms were against her thighs and her skirts were being pushed roughly up to her hips. In white-hot panic she kicked back and heard a thump and a 'whoof' sound. She turned, sliding on the flagstones, and scrambled backwards. He was winded, his legs splayed out in front of him. One hand clutched at his belly.

'I'm sorry,' said Rue, aghast. 'I'm sorry.'

Til jerked to his feet and she shrank back. With a hand still pushed against his stomach, he staggered past her and out the back door, leaving it wide open.

She sat for a moment, unbelieving. Then she struggled to her feet and peered through the door into the night. She could just make him out, travelling with speed back towards the village.

For one moment she thought of running after him, but she'd never catch up. And what would she do? There'd be no persuading him to anything. His blood was up.

It hadn't been how she'd thought it might go. It hadn't been nice at all. It had been embarrassing and coarse and frightening. She felt the slow blush of shame start to slip over her. How could she ever have possibly thought that it was a good idea?

Stupid, stupid girl.

'I didn't measure right,' she said aloud. 'That's all.'

It was no comfort. She felt cold and small, and got up to close the back door.

Fernie could be home any second. She had to get rid of any evidence and hope that Til said nothing. But if Fernie asked . . . Rue wasn't sure he would lie. She also wasn't sure what Fernie would say when she found out, but it would be awful, on that Rue could rely. She might even, Gods forbid, put Rue out of training. The worst and most damning of all fates. Rue cleaned up as she fretted, rinsing out the tea glasses and putting them back in the cupboards wet.

She'd have to go seek Til out tomorrow and tell him to keep it between themselves. It was the only thing to do.

She swept up the kitchen and straightened everything out as best she could. Thinking she heard noises of Fernie's return, she spooked and fled to her room, throwing herself into bed and trying to quiet her hammering heart.

CHAPTER 4
WORLD

WHITE

'Mama,' he said.

The weak and rounded bulk of his mother stirred a little at his voice.

'Mama,' he said again. 'Have you been listening?'

She could hear him, he knew she could; but she was jacked into Life.

Her bedroom was dim and grey, light kept at a minimum. He used to admire her for her spartan approach to decorating. He used to think that it was because she didn't need real things to see beauty. Now he understood that it was because for her, nothing could compare to the virtual reality vastness of Life, and how everything looked when she was inside it. Why bother decorating a place you hardly ever spent any time in?

'I'm back. They let me out. I came back,' he said to his mother, willing her to hear him. Shout. Cry. Move. Care at all.

Her bulbous frame rippled, but that was it. Nothing.

He pushed away his sudden revulsion and stood up.

Cho and Jospen were waiting in the kitchen. They

looked up as one. It had always been like this, the two of them working unconsciously together. He'd grown up jealous of that. Now he felt triumphant, because it made him free.

Cho had been crying.

Jospen's face was cold and empty. 'What did she say?'

'What do you think?' White replied. 'She didn't even turn her head to look at me.'

'She's in Life,' said Cho. 'If you just jacked in, you could talk to her.'

'The addiction counsellor said we shouldn't be talking to her in Life at all, Cho. You *know* that. It only encourages her. We should be trying to bring her back to reality,' said Jospen wearily.

'Oh, so we should just ignore her all the time, right? And just never say anything to her, then?'

'Cho,' came Jospen's tight reply.

Cho turned back to White. 'Please,' she urged. 'Just jack in for a minute. She's been so worried about you. She cries a lot.'

'You mean her avatar cries,' said White. 'Not her.'

'She's got worse since . . . since you've been away,' Jospen said.

'If she didn't have an implant, she'd have no way of connecting to Life,' said Cho darkly. 'And there'd be no problem.'

'CHO,' Jospen hissed, his face turning an ugly shade of red. 'She'd die without the implant. All of us would. And it's disgusting, talking about removing it like it's some sort of parasite.'

'Oh, relax,' said Cho, her voice tinged with a nasty edge. 'No one's listening in.'

Jospen pressed his lips together, incensed. Cho looked back at White, her eyes trying to appeal to him. '*You* should know what it's like for her. You should understand. You know, with your thing.'

White snorted. 'That has nothing to do with it. She managed to get addicted all on her own. She doesn't even practise the Talent any more, the way we used to. I don't even know if she has the dreams any more. She's let herself become what she is. She's disappearing into Life and letting her children rot. She's a fat, useless junkie.'

Jospen leaned across the table and cuffed him on the side of the head. His eyes teared up.

'No, no, stop!' Cho, frantic.

White waited patiently for his ear to stop buzzing. He blinked.

'What did you think that was going to accomplish?' he said to Jospen.

His brother's face was sucked inwards, his mouth reduced to a thin slash.

'Please don't,' said Cho.

'No, really. I'm interested. Tell me, Jospen. Beat me. You can do anything to me now. Anyone can do anything they like, because nothing will ever be worse than the prison. You remember what they did in there. Yes?' White's voice cracked and he waited until he was sure it wouldn't again.

'They let you go,' said Jospen. 'They couldn't find anything and they let you go.'

'Is that supposed to be a comfort?'

Jospen was silent.

'I'm still leaving,' said White. 'I'm leaving and you can't stop me. I can't think of one way you could do it.'

Jospen laughed. 'You're not seriously talking about going to Angle Tar, are you?'

'Yes, I seriously am.'

'Don't be ridiculous. It's a fantasy land you made up in your head. The version of Angle Tar you know is just a dream. It's nothing like the real Angle Tar.'

'How would you know? You've never even been to the real Angle Tar! I *have*!'

Jospen's mouth twisted.

'You should leave, too,' White tried. 'Go somewhere else, start again.'

'In case you've forgotten,' said Jospen, 'Cho is still a child. She hasn't applied for her adulthood status yet, because unlike you, she's not an arrogant little git.'

White swallowed a spike of fury with effort. 'You could take her,' he said. 'You're an adult. You could just go somewhere else.'

'I'm not going anywhere,' said Cho insistently. 'I'm not abandoning Mama.'

'Oh yes, you too, Cho. Come on, try your best!'

He felt a hand on his arm, and looked up into Cho's face. She couldn't speak; she was shaking her head, eyes bright with tears, and hiding her face. She was better at this than Jospen. White sighed and slumped, the anger fading away.

'The problem with you,' said Jospen, 'is that you have no idea what real life is like. How hard it is. All you do is fantasise the day away. And so does Mama. You're just like her, you know, even though you think you're special. Neither of you have ever actually lived in reality, have you?'

'Nobody does!' White exploded. 'This whole place is an endless dream! Everyone spends their entire time jacked into Life! People barely leave their houses any more. No one even travels any more! When was the last time anybody went to another country in World?'

'I met with friends in Germany this morning.'

'You met them in Life,' said White. 'Not in real life!'

Jospen gave him the look he always gave him when White had apparently said something so totally inexplicable, he might as well have been barking instead of speaking.

'It's the same thing, Jacob. Life *is* real life, so no one needs to move around,' Jospen said. 'You know this. Why do you want to live in the past? Transport is evil. It was killing us all, killing the world. The wars, and all the geno-cide, and the . . . the oil,' he tailed off lamely. 'You learned this at school.'

White forced himself not to reply. He wouldn't bring it up again, no matter how much he ached inside to try. He had attempted to explain it to his brother and sister many times, and it had always ended up in an argument like this.

'No more talk of leaving,' said Jospen. He had mistaken White's silence for backing down, and it made his hackles rise. 'It's ridiculous. How can you possibly hope to go and live in another place, all by yourself? How could you even look after yourself? Where would you get clothes from, and food? Where would you live? You don't know the first thing about it. You're just a child, still.'

'I'm not a child,' hissed White. It was the one thing that he absolutely despised about his older brother, the one thing that always made him react – as surely as night followed day. He knew Jospen used his age as a weapon to keep him in his place, and he knew that he was perpetuating the whole thing by reacting the way he did *every single* time, but he couldn't help it. He just couldn't leave it be. It was like a knife slammed in his ribs. 'I took up adulthood last year, and you know it, so stop always pretending that I'm still a child!'

'Why do you think they put you in that place?' said Jospen. 'They couldn't have done it if you'd stayed a child. They waited until you took adulthood to arrest you. They had to; it's the law.'

Jospen never referred to it as a prison, and always called it 'that place', as if it was a shame so great that acknowledging its actual name and function out loud would cause the universe to cave in.

How to even begin to explain his reasons for leaving here? Except that the kind of place that put you away and tortured you when you were different was a place that made him feel sick to his soul. White felt no affinity to it – it was not where he belonged – even though he had spent his life here. Because he was different, he could see things from the outside. Cho and Jospen could only see things from the inside. He shouldn't blame them for not being able to understand.

It was not a matter of choosing a country outside World to escape to. There was only one place he wanted to go, only one place in the world for him, and he'd seen it in his dreams.

Since he could remember, White had dreamed of places and people he had never seen before, and they felt and tasted different to his other dreams. They felt *more*, somehow. He couldn't explain it better than that. And until he'd started to talk innocently to other children about the things he liked to do (mainly dream), he had assumed that everyone had a separate dream life the way he did.

He used to try and tell Cho and Jospen about the things he dreamed of, when they were all children together. It had been a game of sorts. Their mother had encouraged it, to the point of scheduling time at the dinner table for him to regale them all with where he had been 'visiting' the night before. Because the places White visited in his dreams were real.

Their father had hated the whole thing. He'd wanted a family that fitted comfortably into their surroundings, not this collection of odd people that did nothing but stick out. He'd wanted normal. It was hard to see why he had ever married their mother. It was easy to see why, just after White turned fifteen, he had given up and divorced her.

When they grew older, White learned that Jospen and Cho didn't really care much for the ability that only he had inherited. He'd also been taught very quickly that he should stop talking about his strange dreams outside of the family. No one else wanted to see the world the way he saw it.

He was a problem that brought them nothing but pain. The solution to that was obvious. He had to go.

He knew he would miss them.

He would be alone for the first time in his life,

unconnected from Life, unconnected from everyone and everything he had ever really known. Only criminals and terrorists were unconnected.

He was terrified by the idea of it. Terrified that Jospen was right, and he wasn't ready to be an adult, despite being one in the law's eyes. Terrified of having to find a way to get his own food, and his own clothes, and every part of his material existence that had always been provided by Life.

They had said in prison that his new implant would be able to tell them when he Jumped out of World, and away from Life signal, in minutes. He knew there was no signal in Angle Tar, he *knew* that; nevertheless, he was scared that they would be able to track him down somehow and make him pay for escaping.

But it was better than staying here. It had to be better. He would be free.

CHAPTER 5
WORLD

FRITH

Frith pressed the knife a little closer to the throat in his grip.

The assassin whose throat he held was trembling very badly. It was an involuntary reaction, but he wasn't really helping himself. It was taking all Frith had to match his rhythm so that the assassin didn't accidentally slit his own throat on the blade.

Not yet, anyway.

'Gentlemen, this is growing dull,' he said.

The second assassin stood watching, frozen.

The first assassin screamed as Frith gently nudged his broken arm.

'Frankly, someone needs to make a decision,' he said, after the scream had dwindled to a scraping whisper.

The second assassin didn't move.

'Didn't they give you some sort of fancy laser gun, or anything?' Frith tried.

Silence.

Frith didn't recognise him. And after this, he probably never would. He was hired help. It didn't matter who he was, because Frith had a pretty good idea who had sent him.

It would be this: Frith would kill the man in his arms. Then he'd have to twist the body away from him in the shortest time possible, because the other would use that moment to attack him. The window would be small, but the other would take it. Frith might win. But then again, he might not.

Or it would be this: they would stand here, tension thrumming, until something else happened to change the game, or one of them grew frustrated and took a risk. And Frith had an important meeting to get to. A meeting he had travelled a long way for.

Right, then.

Frith lowered his blade, dragging it slowly down the body in his arms. The body in his arms felt it and tensed, preparing to run. Do something. Anything.

The second assassin watched the knife with wide, shining eyes.

Frith punched the blade into the base of the spinal column by his fist, so that the body dropped like a brick from shock.

The second assassin was on him, but it didn't take long.

The thing of it was, they were always so surprised. He knew how it looked on the outside, his skill – to them it seemed supernatural, when it was really just excellent body reading. The man's entire muscular structure was laid open for Frith to inspect, even in microseconds. His opponent's right arm might as well have developed a mouth and shouted, HELLO! I'M ABOUT TO MOVE OVER HERE!

It was powerful, the moment where he physically locked with another human being like this, both of them using everything they had and had ever known to stay alive. It was the closest he ever felt to anyone. The second assassin felt desperate, which was good.

He popped the assassin's shoulder out of his socket, and then rolled backwards and threw him over his head with a well-placed foot.

The sound of bone crunching drifted across the dank little apartment.

Frith had abandoned his knife in the fight, which in a slight miscalculation had lodged between two vertebrae of the first assassin. He tugged it out with a small grunt and crossed to the wall. At the base of it lay the second assassin.

To his credit, he wasn't making a lot of noise. You had to respect self-control, even though Frith had not so far met anyone with as much self-control as him.

The man didn't move his eyes to watch Frith approach. Just stared at the wall, lids heavy.

Frith crouched, balancing his knife carefully.

'So,' he said. 'Was there a message you were asked to deliver before you killed me?'

The man didn't answer.

Frith sat down on the floor, far away, to be cautious.

He felt a sudden, yawning loneliness.

He wondered if the man felt the same.

'No message,' said the man eventually, his voice cracked.

Frith waited. Sat. Listening to him die.

Everyone died, eventually.

He leaned his head against the wall. Resisted the urge to close his eyes, now that the adrenaline had worn off. Resisted the urge to bury his head in his arms and hide.

He had a meeting to go to.

Twenty minutes later, Frith left the main room and went into the back bedroom, closing and locking the door. He washed his hands carefully in the cracked little sink. Sat on the bed, and unwrapped the package he had brought to World with him. Held up the metallic-looking lozenge to the light, checking it for damage.

He hated the lozenge. It was an external Life implant; an invasive, parasitic machine. It was smaller than his little finger, but inside its smooth metal shell were a thousand different realities, just waiting to be set free in his brain.

He hated a lot of things about World. The implants, and the control they put on their own citizens, disgusted him. Their total, immersive reliance on Life, a world that didn't even exist, affronted him. But complaining to the Castle about their insistence on meeting in Life got him a giant bout of silence. Angle Tar wasn't connected to Life. He had to go where the signal was.

So here he sat in an anonymous, cramped room on the outskirts of Calais in what had been France, a long time ago. It was as far into World as he could manage; their public transport networks had slowly vanished with the adoption of Life. Only World police and certain government departments owned any kind of vehicle, and try asking for one of those at short notice.

He clipped the implant onto the back of his neck, grimacing as it extended its tiny needle claws and punctured his skin.

It always took a while to come alive for him, Life. External implants were a tenth as effective as the internal versions all World citizens had placed into their heads at birth. Some Life features would always be closed to him – the more immersive, fully simulated reality aspects. And he had no control over where in Life the implant took him, which was always the same place. It had been programmed that way.

The place the implant led him to was a virtual business hall. A long, low room dominated by a giant glass table, around which were arranged various chairs of height, design and size. Each attendee had insistently requested that they have their own particular type of chair at this meeting. It was almost funny how neatly this encapsulated everything that was wrong with people.

There was no fireplace in this room – Life designers couldn't even fathom the need to replicate such a pointless mechanism. If he'd had a more sophisticated implant, he would have been able to feel a gentle warmth spidering out from the walls, uniform and regulated. As it was, he couldn't feel too much. He felt a chair underneath him when he sat down. The weight of the table under his hands. Everything was slightly off, that was all. Physical senses were muffled, as if he were ill, and couldn't extend sight and sound and touch to their fullest extent.

It drove you mad, after a while. Your body constantly trying to adapt, to make sense of it. Failing. Meetings were usually as short as possible because of it. Attendees from World always scoffed at that. Of course they did. They scoffed at everything.

It would be their undoing.

'Frith,' said a polite voice at his shoulder. He turned his head.

'Mussyer Derger,' he said to the corpulent man who had appeared in the chair next to him. 'And how are things in the shipping business?'

'I do adore how you always insist on calling me Mussyer, Frith,' the man said. 'Even in my own language.'

I do it to annoy you, not delight you, you bastard.

'Politeness, alas,' said Frith, 'has always been a particular failing of mine.'

'When is our Castle friend getting here? I have another meeting in half an hour,' said a voice down the table.

'They're always late,' said Derger. 'Makes for a grand entrance. So, how long did your journey from Angle Tar take you this time?'

'Just over a day.'

Derger shook his head. 'I do think you get the raw end of the deal in this. I couldn't fathom having to move around so much. I'm sitting comfortably at home, right now, whereas you are . . .'

'Somewhere.'

'Ah yes,' said Derger, with a crinkly smile. 'Secrecy. Very well. Still, if Angle Tar would only connect to Life, you wouldn't be having to go through this every time.'

'We like our independence,' said Frith.

'Come, come. You wouldn't lose your independence. All

57

countries in World still maintain their own identities. We're a loose connection of nations, just sharing resources, that's all.'

That was such an outrageous lie, it was almost insulting.

'I think,' said Frith, 'I'll pass, thank you. I'm not sure we're particularly keen to leap into bed with the people that wiped out half our population.'

'Oh, Frith. Oh, really. You Angle Tarain and your hangups. The wars were a very long time ago now. We're all unimaginably sorry you were caught up in that. But honestly, harping on about it like it's still relevant today is what makes everyone shy away from doing business with you.'

'Yes, aren't we silly. Nevertheless, I highly doubt Angle Tar will be joining World while I'm alive.'

'I suppose we'll just have to wait until you're dead, then,' came another voice.

Frith's heartbeat quickened.

He would know that voice anywhere. Mainly because it was the voice of the man who had quite probably just tried to have him murdered.

He was from World and his name was Snearing, a beautiful illustration of exactly how he sounded. God only knew why the Castle had chosen him as an agent. He appeared to think exactly the same thing about Frith. If he was surprised that Frith was still alive, he was doing an admirable job of hiding it.

Supposedly, World and Angle Tar had stopped trying to kill each other a hundred years ago. Supposedly they now worked together in a facade of diplomacy. Angle Tar kept its walls up, shutting off the outside world to its citizens while maintaining trade with other countries on the sly. World left it largely alone, waiting for the day when that tiny island with its mad inhabitants would cave in and decide to join the rest of civilisation.

None of this stopped the spying game, though. World spied on Angle Tar and Angle Tar spied on World. Secret, dangerous dealings would always exist. Men like Snearing would always be trying to prevent men like Frith from continuing to play the game.

And the other way around, of course.

Frith's hand was itching. So badly. Like a fire was burning it; maddening. It begged to hold a knife again. He waited patiently until the feeling ebbed.

Derger had turned away, apparently bored of the conversation, and was chatting jovially to someone else. Frith listened to their shifting and overlapping voices, not for the words but for what lay underneath the words. He was good at listening. He liked very much that he was good at it. It had saved his life more than once.

There were several World agents here, as always, but then World had so many more countries and citizens under its bloated belt. China was noticeably absent, as was the Hispanic Federation. Smaller nations like Angle Tar had just one agent each, and they always came.

The talk around him was shot with nerves. It usually was before the Castle showed up.

He wondered which of them would come this time.

The Castle was still a mystery to Frith, even though it was now several months since he had been recruited by them. They claimed to be unable to show their true bodies, which is why they liked to meet in Life, where they could cloak themselves in whatever form they liked. He felt uncomfortable around the squid avatar they sometimes insisted on using. The girl that looked like a ghost was the most unsettling, though. He thought they had chosen those forms to provoke the exact reaction that they did; that somewhere in their strange, anonymous brains, it amused them to see people so afraid of something that wasn't even real.

It bothered Frith more and more that he still didn't know for sure what they were, but he was strongly starting to suspect that they didn't even have bodies, as such. That they were all mind.

There was a short intake of breath from further down the table. He looked for the source.

There she was.

Ghost Girl avatar, in all her glory.

She was grey, and thin and odd, her mouth a shadow slash, her eyes like mine shafts. It wasn't that she looked like a ghost, more that she looked how you might represent a ghost. Frith couldn't describe it better than that.

'Hello,' she said, in World. It wasn't exactly troublesome for Frith, who spoke the language to perfection. It just irritated him that the Castle had picked that language to talk to them all in.

Various mumbling variations of hello echoed meekly around the room.

Frith bit back a laugh.

The Castle avatar went methodically around the table, taking reports from each agent. She always did it like this.

The first Castle meeting they had ever been called to had been run by her. In it, she had given them an analogy she seemed to be very proud of.

She said that the Castle was the web.

Frith and their other chosen agents were the spiders.

The Talented were the flies.

Finding and catching Talented was not just Frith's job. It was his passion. Some of the agents called them Dreamers because of how their ability usually manifested; but to Frith the name sounded weak. At least one Talented he had met in his lifetime did a hell of a lot more than dream.

The Castle had chosen well when they had chosen Frith. How exactly they had decided on their agents was still a mystery, but he would never be able to forget the way they had approached him. He still had the nightmares.

He suspected that they made sure of that.

It had been several months ago now. He'd just got back from a short trip to World and another 'under the carpet' job for his government. Officially he was a minor diplomat. Only a few people knew what he did unofficially.

He hadn't been sleeping well. All he knew was that he woke often in the darkest part of the night, that pocket of time where he felt exposed and vulnerable, as if somehow, while he'd been asleep, the world had changed on him and left him behind. He didn't quite remember what it was that woke him, only that he had been dreaming of the past again, of graceful pillar trees and spotted sunlight and a laugh that reminded him how cruel and awful life was. He had these periods, sometimes, and nothing would do except to wait through it, patiently, until the dreams faded back into his head and left him alone. It was just a phase and it would pass, as always.

And then, one night, *she* was there.

The girl who looked like a ghost.

She had been watching him, that much he knew; that way that you just *knew* in dreams. She'd been skirting around the edges of him, watching his dreams unfold, and god knew what she'd seen. She'd squatted in corners, her thin arms draped over her grey legs, watching.

Finally, in a dream one night, she had started to talk to him.

She knew things.

She knew things no one could possibly know about him. That was the first reason he believed her.

The second reason he believed her was when she took him to the Castle.

She led him like a child, taking him by the hand and pulling him through, stepping from here to there. And then he saw it.

It was a place, she had assured him. Maybe not a place in the sense that he thought of places, but real enough. Just real in a different way.

It was a huge, echoing stone building, that shifted when you tried to look at it, really look. It was filled with rooms. Thousands of rooms, millions of rooms, rooms within rooms, twisting, turning, choking or wide as a boulevard, rooms that led you to black places, tiny cramped places where the things no one ever wanted to find or remember or think about were hidden.

Rooms that led you to a banquet hall with blood on the

62

flagstone floor and dishes of greased chicken and rotting fruit on the tables. Upturned glasses of wine dripping onto the cloth.

Rooms made of infinity mirrors that showed you yourself, endlessly repeated, again and again and overlapping and stretching all the way for ever until your mind cracked with trying to understand it.

Rooms draped in velvet, with that desk in the corner that you remembered hiding under as a child, that desk with the hidden drawers that could only be opened with a tiny key, that desk that seemed to contain secret worlds. Rooms he'd never seen before, fairytale places and strange. But there were also all the rooms he'd ever been into in his life; bedrooms and dining rooms and parlours and gambling rooms and bathrooms and half-remembered rooms and rooms where bad things had happened that he'd managed to forget and ones in which nothing much had happened at all.

This was the Castle.

It showed you the past, and the now, and the what might be. It showed them all together in the same place until it was hard to know when you were. It showed you other worlds, other times, other and other, until you started to lose all sense of yourself in time and place, and years could pass out there while you stood in a room, frozen and alone.

All this Frith knew, when the Ghost Girl led him to the Castle. She didn't have to explain any of it. He knew. And he also knew, not one tiny piece of him doubting, that there was something loose in it.

Something awful.

63

Something to end all worlds.

The only thing that could stop this thing, the Ghost Girl told him, was the Talented.

He needed to help her. He needed to find every Talented he could, recruit them, make them loyal. He needed to make an army of people who could fight this, before It came and it was all too late.

He said yes.

Frith was the first Castle agent to be recruited. But when he got a message calling him to a meeting in Life, and his avatar walked into that simulated boardroom, he realised just how busy the Ghost Girl had been. How many others, he was silently relieved to note, had been as affected by the dream as he had. How many others like him that she had managed to persuade to her cause, by worming into their minds and showing them a nightmare.

And that, one day, unless they could stop it, that nightmare was going to become real.

CHAPTER 6
WORLD

WHITE

Several days after his argument with Jospen and Cho, White sat in his room, surrounded by the detritus of his life. Clothes spilled over everything, mostly rejected. They would draw too much attention. He had a small bag packed at his feet.

In it was a battery-powered toothbrush, an ancient thing that had cost him a lot of credit and taken quite a while to find. There was also a skinsuit, which he would wear under his normal clothes – it was hard to get used to the bizarrely changeable weather in Angle Tar, and he had grown up in regulated environments. The skinsuit would cool him down if he overheated, and warm him up when it was cold. He couldn't imagine how Angle Tarain coped. In the winter, when the air was full of knives and snow fell often, their solution appeared to be to wear more and more layers of clothes until they were bundled up into balls, which hardly seemed practical if you moved about outside as much as they did.

He had also packed innocuous trousers and jackets, shirts and a style of soft boot that they tended to favour there.

There was a body gel, very much in World fashion at the moment, that would help keep him clean until he could find a more permanent solution to the problem of hygiene. There was a little money that he had managed to pick up on visits there, at first because he'd found a piece or two on the ground and had been curious as to what it was; and later, after reading up about money in Life, for more practical reasons.

He took a steady breath, trying to swallow the uneasy lump in his throat.

Jospen was right. What would he do in Angle Tar? How would he survive? Would he be able to find somewhere to live, some way to earn more money? There was no plan, there was no nothing. It was impossible to plan. He didn't know what people without technology did with their lives. In World, everything was answered for you. Everything was assigned to you. No effort required. In Angle Tar, it seemed that you found your own way or died. At least most people had a family who started them off. He would have no one. He would be all alone, drowning in a culture that still thrilled and terrified him in equal measure with how alien it could be.

Angle Tar wasn't part of World. It wasn't connected to Life. It had closed its borders a hundred years ago, declaring it illegal for anyone to visit, but neither laws nor lack of transport could stop someone like him. That was what made him so dangerous.

If he wanted to, he could easily read up about Angle Tar in Life. He could look at topography, and climate. National dishes, key historical moments. Holographic renderings of a typical street scene. Every fact he could ever wish to know was there, and for most people, that was enough. But his childhood dream visits to Angle Tar left impressions that had scored burning marks across his heart and secret soul, impressions he could call up any time he was bored, upset or lonely. The dreams managed to sustain him for a while; but gradually, he found that they weren't enough any more.

And then White discovered that he could do a lot more than just dream.

He called it slipping, not knowing what else to call it. He called it that because when he had practised and practised and learned how to do it well, it had a particular feeling of slipping through a thin crack as if his skin were supple and greased. Sometimes it was harder than others, especially if he wanted to go to a place he had never been to before. Then he had to squeeze himself through the air, edging carefully through, one limb at a time, feeling like his lungs would burst with the pressure. Ever after it became easier and easier for him to slip, as he thought of it, to that same place, until it was almost like walking forwards and simply finding yourself there. In prison, they had called it Jumping. He'd never heard of anyone else who could do what he did, but his captors had seemed to know all about it.

The first time White had Jumped, he had been eleven years old. He wasn't even too sure how exactly it had happened. All he had done was think, for a while, about the Angle Tar of his dreams, and how to get there. He had thought very hard and very long about it – how it had started, what everything had looked like, the sounds he had heard. He had felt a tugging at his belly, inside the core of him. He had stood up, felt himself vibrate like a flicked wine glass, and pushed his way carefully through a crack in the air, a crack that he couldn't see but that he felt with every atom of his body.

A moment where everything was black, and endless.

And then, on the other side of the crack, he had stepped out to find himself several streets away, still in World, alone and very confused.

It took him only a second to understand what he had done. Though his mother had never mentioned such an ability, it seemed logical to him that if your mind could visit other places when you were asleep, your body would eventually be able to do it while you were awake. He supposed ending up where you actually wanted to go took a lot more practice.

He had walked home, using Life to navigate. Found his house and gone inside, where he was a little surprised to discover that no one had missed him. His father was working, and his brother and sister were still jacked into school, whereas he had already finished for the day. His mother, as usual, was asleep upstairs.

So the phenomenon passed unremarked, and when he managed to do it again a month or so later, he didn't talk about it, because he had learned a long time ago that the things he could do were the subject of not a few ugly, heated arguments in his family, linked to a knotted feeling inside him that made him sick. He didn't want to feel like that. His mother still insisted he practise dream-focusing techniques with her, but he never shared the progress he had made.

So was his free and secret time spent. He experimented alone, testing, pushing. It seemed, for now, that he could only focus a Jump to places he had already been to, either in real life or in his dreams. If he wanted, he could travel to school with a Jump – not that he had dared to do that more than once. But simply thinking 'China' and trying to move did nothing.

It didn't matter though, because Angle Tar was what he wanted. It was hard to concentrate in lessons when he knew that night he might be in a place that fascinated and glittered like a jewel. He realised that most World people did not feel the same way as he did about that odd little nation, a country not important enough to make Life news unless one of its ambassadors had done something quaintly hilarious at a political function.

When White started to tentatively practise Jumping his entire self to Angle Tar and not just to visit it in his dreams, he bolted whenever he saw someone and hoped that they hadn't caught a glimpse of him. Angle Tarain didn't augment or body decorate – they all looked the same. White was too young to have done anything to his appearance when he had first started dream-visiting Angle Tar, but by the time he could comfortably Jump there, he had had his skin pigmented to a smooth, marble white and his dark hair was artificially extended to his hips. In World, his appearance was considered demure and rather boring. In Angle Tar, he stood out. He had exotic features, and World clothes were outrageous in comparison to theirs. He did his best with the most innocuous clothes he could find, and kept to the darker streets, huddling close to buildings in an effort not to be seen.

People spotted him, of course. After a while, he became used to watching city crowds from a side street. He had a great many odd looks tossed his way, but nothing compared to what he got if he wasn't in the capital city, where people were a little more used to oddness.

In between Jumping there, he learned and learned, with the rabid feverishness of someone who cared nothing for anything else in his life. In school, where before he'd been an object of vitriol, now he was a ghost, and it suited him fine.

When White turned eighteen, however, his game of a second life had become deadly serious, and his visits to Angle Tar were a secret no longer.

World knew.

The arrest was quick and brutal. Jospen was right – they had waited until White had declared adulthood and could be legally taken without reprisal by his family or anyone else. They knew exactly where he was. They knew where everyone was every minute of every day through implant tracking, and they had been watching him for a while, ever since they had found out what he could do.

They took him in the middle of the day, as easy as anything. He had skipped school and was intending to spend the afternoon in Angle Tar, when someone tapped him on the shoulder from behind and asked in a quiet voice if he could spare a moment of his time. A moment turned out to be several weeks, in the end. It had been well over a month since they had let him go and he still couldn't sleep through the night, broken with the fear that he would wake up to find himself back in that bare, bleached room.

His heart sank over and over, a sickening roll in his chest. He wouldn't think about what he was doing, because it was too late for that. It was all too late. Too late when they had tortured and humiliated him, and made him feel like he was defective and disgusting. But even long before that, when his mother had first talked to him about what he could do, aged five. When his teachers had looked at him that way. When he had been born. He was like a virus, a small bacterium that World's immune system was trying to reject. They didn't want him here. So he would go.

The countryside was out of the question – they were far more suspicious and isolated than city people. He couldn't quite bring himself to choose a place with no people and too much space. He would go to Parisette, their capital city, from the first. He knew the street patterns fairly well by now.

He looked around his room one last time. There was nothing out of it that he would miss. Outside of Life, it was grey, just like everything else. He jacked in and sent messages to his mother, brother and sister, messages they might pick up almost instantly, which is why he had done it, to force himself to go now and not put it off again. The messages were short notes telling them that he loved them and not to worry.

His mother was upstairs, still lying in her bed. Supposedly she was meeting with a counsellor in Life right now. There was something faintly ridiculous about a Life addict having to meet in Life to be counselled about it.

The house was quiet.

He concentrated, steadying his breath. It had become easy to find the way to Parisette now, to a particular spot in an alley. It stank in there and was usually full of rats, but it was a safe place from which to emerge. He had used it so many times that he thought of it as his alley. He felt it in the air, pushing forwards slightly to make sure. Standing, he took up his bag and slung it over his shoulder.

'Jacob.'

Startled, he looked back.

His bedroom door was standing open, and framed by the doorway was the thin, angular shape of his brother, Jospen.

'What are you doing here?' said White. 'You're supposed to be at work.'

'Where exactly are you going?'

White struggled between the truth and a convincing lie, then gave up.

'Where do you think?' he said.

'You can't just leave. You can't just abandon everyone.'

White shifted the bag on his shoulder, defensive. 'Look, I'm an adult now. I'm supposed to leave home now anyway, and find a job, and a house eventually, aren't I? It's better this way. You know it is. I'm sorry, okay? But you'll be glad when I'm gone. You will.'

'What about Cho?' said Jospen, his voice edged with anger. Was it? Or fear? 'What about Mama? Don't you have *any* loyalty?'

He was actually trembling. One arm disappeared behind his back, as if he was holding something he was trying to hide.

White felt the first trickle of fear.

'Jospen,' he said. 'What's going on? What are you doing?'

'I can't.'

'You can't what?'

Jospen brought his hand around and pointed something small and metallic at White's chest.

'I can't just let you go. They won't just let you go, Jacob! Why are you being so stupid?'

'What –' said White, before a tiny, white-hot flare on his shoulder caught his attention.

He turned his head to look.

There was something sticking out of his shoulder.

There was a little dart sticking out of his shoulder.

That wasn't supposed to be there.

He tried to bring his hand up to brush it off, but his arm, incredibly, weighed more than a building.

His hands were giant poles of meat, telescoping off for ever.

His legs were thin like razor cuts. Far too thin to hold up his body. Just how had he been walking around all this time?

He fell. He fell into the stars. The sky opened up beneath him, black and black and black.

Something banged against the side of his head.

And again.

And again. And then it melted away to a terrible, surging roar.

* * *

He opened his eyes.

He thought he opened his eyes.

Sound battered viciously at his ears.

'Stop shouting,' he tried to say, but had no idea if the words had even left his mouth.

The noise wavered; faltered.

'He's awake,' said a voice. 'He shouldn't be awake.'

'Well . . . the dart's empty. It's all in his bloodstream.'

White strained. Shapes blurred, focused.

Everything was all wrong. Everything was made of vertical lines.

He was lying on the floor.

'He's awake?' said a tentative voice. Jospen's voice.

White sent frantic signals to his body.

MOVE he said to his legs.

'Er . . . he's moving. Someone give him another shot, please.'

Oh no. Oh no no not again.

PANIC, ordered his mind.

He pushed everything he could feel outwards.

'Stop him!'

'I can't –'

'Hold him down!'

Thighs came into his vision. He bucked. He was hauled up, leant backwards against a body who hooked their arms over his, while someone else tried to push his legs to the ground with their hands.

Police uniform.

Police.

Prison.

GET UP GET UP GET UP

He could hear himself. Incoherent. Screaming no.

Jospen was against the wall, hugging his arms close, staring.

'I'm sorry,' he said. 'I'm sorry, okay?' He kept saying it.

I'm not going back there.

You're not going to make me go back! You can't make me! I'll die before you make me!

He screeched in his utter fury. An explosion against everything that had ever, ever existed to stand against him.

He felt the pressure on his legs release suddenly. His arms were free.

'What's wrong with you all?!?' screamed a man. 'Hold him down!'

White's eyes locked with his brother's.

Then he Jumped.

A moment of nothing, of in-between places. A vast void of empty, yawning black.

A moment where he thought he was dead.

Then he squirmed forwards, and found himself crouched in the back end of an alley.

Its smell hit him like a punch.

Noise and light and life. His Angle Tar alley, his escape.

The cobbles were wet and slimed against his hands. He didn't care.

They couldn't find him here. They couldn't follow.

Safe.

White put his back against the wall and curled into a ball, his whole body pounding.

He didn't have his bag.

He didn't have his bag. They had taken it off him, and he had left it behind.

His heart sank.

He had nothing.

But at least he was safe.

He closed his eyes.

CHAPTER 7
ANGLE TAR

FRITH

When Frith first saw the most fascinating person he had ever met, it was in an interrogation room. Frith tended to meet a lot of new people in these kinds of rooms. He enjoyed interrogation in the same way that he enjoyed the rest of his job – a lot of it was dull, but the interesting bits made up for it.

Occasionally, someone would end up here who presented a challenge for Frith, or a curiosity in some way. It had become rapidly apparent that the young man they were currently holding was both.

Frith had been sat outside the room for over an hour, watching him. He couldn't have been more than seventeen or eighteen, but held himself the way someone much older would. His skin was a beautiful, impossible kind of white underneath the grime, and his dark hair would have been long and striking if it were clean. At the moment it was pinned loosely back in a ragged, dirty plait. He was a lot less strange-looking than some Worlders Frith had met, but a Worlder he definitely was.

Frith walked into the room.

'Good evening,' he said.

The Worlder didn't stir.

'I understand that you were arrested for assaulting a guard. And that you demanded to be brought to a government building for interrogation.'

Silence.

'I'm told you can speak Angle Tarain quite well, even if you choose not to reply.'

Silence.

'When you were taken in this morning, you refused to give your name. Would you care to tell it to me?'

Not even a flicker. Frith folded his arms.

'You're foreign, of course. I am sure you would have known, before coming here, that skin augmentation doesn't exist in Angle Tar. But you chose to keep your skin colour. That means you didn't expect to stay here long.'

It was the merest movement, but Frith saw it.

'Ah, I'm wrong. Then perhaps you kept your skin because you're proud of your differences. Stupidly proud, one might say. Because you'll keep them even if it means that you're persecuted for them.'

The Worlder turned his head and looked at Frith.

'A victim of persecution, and you come to Angle Tar. The one place that will not tolerate difference.'

'There are many places that will not tolerate difference,' said the Worlder. His voice was hard and cold, burred with disuse. He was obviously homeless, but hadn't been for long. The clothes looked too new and he was slim, but not on the wrong side of thin.

The accent was familiar. Frith tried to place it. Eastern

World, for sure. Some New Europe nation, perhaps. Maybe even as far East as United Russian and Chinese Independents.

'You wouldn't be the first to leave, you know,' Frith remarked. 'You wouldn't even be the twentieth. Plenty of others have come before. From Germany, from URCI, any number of World countries. All over the place.'

There. A twitch on URCI. Frith smiled inwardly.

He sat on the other chair.

'May we talk frankly?' he said.

For a long moment, the Worlder was still. Then he nodded, once.

'So. I'm wondering what your reason is for coming to Angle Tar. You must understand why I need to know. Foreigners don't officially exist here. When they do, they are accepted for a reason, for a purpose. They can give us something that makes them valuable. What do you have that makes you valuable?'

'Nothing,' said the Worlder.

'That's not quite true, is it?' said Frith. 'Otherwise you wouldn't be here. Because you knew what would happen if you didn't at least try to blend in a little better. You knew what would happen if we caught you.'

'You did not catch me, I walked in.'

'Yes, you did. By the rather surprising method of deliberately attacking a guard. I wonder why.'

The Worlder gazed at the table top, his mouth in a stubborn frown.

That was all right. He didn't have to speak. His body talked for him.

'You can relax,' said Frith. 'I'm not threatening you. I'm

sure I don't have anything I can do to you that's worse than what you've already endured. Right? Prison, was it? I've heard they're very good at torture in World prisons.'

The Worlder flinched.

Frith leaned back.

'I'm going to make a guess about you now,' he said. 'I hope you'll be suitably impressed. Would you like me to tell you something about yourself that I could not possibly know?'

'Yes,' said the Worlder.

Frith clasped his fingers together and stared at the tabletop for a moment, assembling his performance. Sometimes he did like to show off. It was a bit of a weakness. But in a situation like this, where he held all the power, it couldn't do that much harm.

He'd known the Worlder's secret within minutes of laying eyes on him. There was a good reason for being so desperate that he'd committed treason by leaving World. The boy obviously had a healthy distrust of authority, and a whole lake of arrogance in that silent face, which he clearly tried to use to cover his fear and his youth. A surging restlessness. More than that, though. The Worlder's whole body thrummed with his secret, somehow. You couldn't always see it as easily as that, but on this one it was obvious.

'You,' he said, pointing at the Worlder, who looked at his outstretched finger as if it were poisonous, 'can do something. Something that is so frightening that some would like to lock you away for ever, and so valuable that others would like to study you for ever. And you were certain that here, in Angle Tar, you could use it as a bargaining chip to help you get what you want. Perhaps you thought you'd find only simple people here who'd believe that you were some sort of magician, rather than just an ordinary boy with an extraordinary talent.'

The Worlder closed his eyes.

Frith watched him patiently.

Silence pressed inwards, rolling around the room in slow, syrupy waves.

'Well?' said Frith, enjoying the game. 'Am I right?'

I've got you. I've GOT you.

The Worlder pressed back into his seat, as if he was afraid. And then he disappeared.

No warning. No gathering of himself, no concentration on his face, nor momentum in his body structure. No signs to read.

Just a gentle pop, and a big load of nothingness where his shape had been.

Frith watched the place where he had been sitting for a few moments, as if it was patently obvious that the Worlder was just tricking him.

Oh brilliantly done, and who's got the power now, yes, you showed me, yes, very good you little trickster, now come back and stay put. Come back.

Come back.

When he didn't, Frith said a short, sharp, 'Fuck.'

Frith never swore.

It was several hours later before White reappeared in the room.

Frith had gone, but the guard on duty completed an

impressive full body jerk and stumbled back, hitting his elbow on the wall behind him.

They stared at each other.

'Grad HANG me,' the guard swore, his voice trembling angry. He opened the door and banged it shut after him, giving White a rapid backwards glance, as if to make sure that he was still there and the whole thing hadn't been a hallucination.

White was left alone.

He sagged, sitting back on the same chair. He resisted the urge to clutch the table edge and rest his forehead against the splintered wood. He couldn't afford to look weak, or show how afraid and tired and alone he really was. Not for one second. Not with this Frith man, who seemed to pick him apart as easily as breathing.

He stared at his dirty hands.

It had been three weeks.

No money. No change of clothes. No body gel or skin-suit.

Three weeks of misery on Parisette streets.

He was dirty.

He was humiliated by his own smell. He couldn't wash. The best he had been able to manage was splashing himself with hurried cups of water from the ponds in the public gardens he slept in at night; but they were full of plants and fish, and often made him feel almost as grimy afterwards as before.

He was starving, too. He'd held out for two days; then, in desperation, resorted to Jumping into eating houses and shops at night to steal food. It was the first time he'd ever tried to move such short distances, but he found it easy enough. Sometimes he could be bitterly glad that at least his talent was not going to waste. But he still felt furtively guilty about stealing food, and did it as little as he could stand.

He had all the time in the world to think, on the streets. Seconds and minutes and hours rolling into days and for ever and ever. His brother's face often flashed, unwanted, through his mind. He tried to imagine killing Jospen for what he had done, but couldn't bring himself to do it. All he managed to feel was a dull, incredulous pain.

By day he wandered the city, achingly lonely, longing to talk to someone for more than a sentence or two. Longing for someone to do something to him, anything to make him feel like he was here and still a part of the real. When he grew too tired to keep moving, he would sneak into an abandoned building. There was a particular district that had more empty buildings than not. It was a haven for the homeless, but the buildings were regularly cleared out by groups of Parisette guards. He had learned to run when this happened. People here were afraid of the guard. Police were the same everywhere, it seemed.

His instinctive distrust of the other homeless he found himself bedding down next to made him feel ashamed. Some of the people who lived on the streets of Angle Tar were frightening; some were as sad and strange as ghosts. They mostly gave him a wide berth, caving into that natural fear of foreigners that everyone here seemed to have. Some of the older ones tried to speak to him sometimes, though, as if they were too desperate to care where he was from.

But he couldn't face them; just tightened up and turned his head until they stopped trying and left him alone. The guilt over it gnawed insistently at him.

Ideals were all very well when you had a warm place to live and enough food to make yourself sick on; but everything melted away in the face of this endless, dull nightmare. It wasn't living. It was existing. He had no reason to be. No one wanted to notice him, so no one did. It felt like he was fading out of the fabric of the world.

So he made a decision.

It was the only way, and he knew what it would cost him. He didn't agonise over it. Maybe that would come later, when he could afford it to. So he had gathered his courage, gone up to a Parisette guard, smiled at him, and then taken a wild swing at his face.

It had seemed like a good idea at the time.

The door opened.

White tried to sit upright.

Frith walked into the room, gave White a cursory glance, and folded his arms.

'That was an over-dramatic little trick you pulled,' he said, his voice pleasant.

White said nothing.

'You look awful.'

'It is very hard here,' said White eventually.

'You've only been gone six hours. What happened to you?'

White shook his head. He couldn't explain it well. He'd had a sudden connection with Frith, a connection that had lasted an entire conversation. To have that taken away, just as suddenly and by his own doing, had been more than he could bear. He had planned to stay away for an entire day, or even two to show off, but hadn't been able to face it.

'Disconnection from Life takes its toll. I've seen it before. You should have prepared yourself for that before you decided to come here,' Frith remarked, not unkindly.

'That is not the problem,' snapped White, before he could stop himself. 'I have no addiction to Life.'

'I understand completely,' said Frith. 'When you visited before, you always came with the knowledge that you could jack in, as you call it, and go back to that sea of voices and presence. Now you've made the decision to be here, and now you're starting to realise that you will never have that again. Ever. You'll now have to spend your time alone with yourself in your mind, feeling like you're in a box that you can see out of, but no one can see into. Feeling that no one will be able to touch you, to know you, any more. Just like the rest of us poor Angle Tarain, in fact. What have you been up to the last few hours? Did you go back to World?'

'I cannot,' said White, dizzied by Frith's change of gear. The speech had unnerved him completely. It was as if he had told Frith everything already, as if the man could pick him up and flick through him until he found the page he wanted, and read exactly what he needed to know. 'They will know as soon as I am back in World.'

'Yes, through your implant, I presume. But if your implant has told them of your previous visits to Angle Tar, why didn't they arrest you earlier?' said Frith.

'How do you know that I have come here before?' said

White, his skin prickling. Did they have their own kind of tracking system here?

'A guess. Tell me.'

'Information from . . . the machines that track our implants . . . it takes time to be collected. They could not know I left World until I already came back. But they knew, after time. That I visited here. When I was in prison, they gave me a better implant. It tracks only a few people more accurately. People they want to watch. It will tell them to a minute when I go back to World. They will send people to find me.'

'Do you still have your implant?'

'Of course,' White said impatiently. 'I will die without it.'

'No you won't.'

White opened his mouth, and then shut it again.

'You won't,' said Frith again, casually. 'I've met Worlders who have had it removed and continue to live just fine. I'm afraid that's just what you're told. There are doctors in your nation that specialise in the removal of implants. Illegally, of course. But it can be done.'

'You are lying.'

Frith spread his hands, a smile on his face. 'For what possible reason?'

White couldn't reply. But he had no reason to trust anything this stranger said.

He didn't sound like he was lying, his treacherous mind whispered to him.

He tried to force calm, press it on himself like a plaster, covering up his wounds.

'If you are nervous about the implant,' White said,

'I think it does not work outside of World. You have nothing here it can use to . . . power it.'

'Good god, I know that,' said Frith cheerfully. 'You're curiously persistent in believing that you're one of the first from World to seek asylum here. The only reason I'm spending time with you is because, I'll admit, you're the first in my personal memory to offer something so useful to me.'

'I can be useful. If it means you will let me stay here.' White paused a moment, gathering his courage. 'But I will not spy on World for you,' he said. He had already anticipated where this might lead, and there was no way he was going to let himself be used for that.

'That's an interesting statement. Let me ask you something in return. What is the last bargaining chip you hold?' said Frith. 'In other words, what will prevent me from compelling you to do whatever I want?'

White felt his heart give a panicky leap.

'If you make me a spy, I will go back to World,' he said.

'You just told me you can't.'

'There are people. They live outside Life systems, outside the city domes. I will go there.'

'If you believe that removing your implant will kill you, you must also believe what your government says about no one being able to survive off grid.'

White clenched his jaw stubbornly.

'I have heard of some who do,' he said. 'They hate Life. They say we are too dependent on machines. They live in the old cities, the ones abandoned when the dome cities were built.'

'I presume you're talking about Technophobes.'

The word sounded strange coming from an Angle Tarain mouth.

'You needn't look so surprised,' said Frith, sounding almost reproachful. 'I realise we seem a bit out of the way, but we do know things here.' He shifted. 'It must have been quite a hard life for you, growing up in such a place.'

White bit back a scoff. He needed no one's fake pity. 'Many people have hard lives,' he said, contemptuous.

'Still. They don't like you because you can't be controlled. Because you don't need Life. You don't need *them*.'

White was silent.

'So they arrested you for no reason,' came Frith's soothing liquid voice. 'What charge did they give?'

'It was all lies. They wanted to know if I had been talking to Technophobes. That was all.'

He subsided. Frith was silent, watching him. Listening. No one had listened to White in a long, long time. He felt himself open up.

'The charges said that we had ties to terrorists. People with my . . . ability, they say we help the Technophobes, because they think we hate Life.'

White searched, trying to force out his thoughts with unfamiliar words.

'Life makes travel unnecessary. Makes exploration unnecessary. Yet I travel. I *want* to explore. I am dangerous, because I cannot be . . . kept in one place. They arrested me for no reason. I was doing nothing. I was hurting no one. But they kept me in prison. No one did anything about it. They starved me. They drugged me. Like. Like I was an animal.'

88

The room was silent. White felt a wave of tears threaten underneath his eyes and bit on the inside of his cheek sharply to will them away.

Another room; another prison. A sickening fear fluttered through his head; that his life would always be like this. That there would always be people finding ways to keep him penned. Controlled. Docile.

'Let's take a break. Would you like some food?' said Frith.

White nodded. A treacherous tear escaped, tracking down his cheek, and he brushed it off angrily.

They ate together in the interrogation room. The meal was extremely good, but anything would have tasted incredible right now. The sensation of hot food sliding into him was a very obvious, natural one that he had craved in the last few weeks.

He felt watched, and studied. Guards stood at every corner, surrounding the two eating in the middle of the room at their rickety wooden table. Occasionally a pair of eyes would slide to him. He tried not to make any noise as he ate, and resisted the temptation to shovel everything into his mouth at once.

Frith speared a soft cream-coloured vegetable on his knife and mashed it on his plate with the flat of the blade.

'How do you call that?' said White.

'A pomder, in Angle Tarain. In high speech it's called *pomme de terre*; and high speech, for your information, is the one that no one speaks any more, except the most inbred of aristocrats. You have a tendency to slip into it, which won't endear you to the common man in Angle Tar.'

Frith paused. 'Though pointing out that Angle Tarain has more French words in it than anything else never goes down well, either.'

'It is the way the Angle Tarain language package that I bought taught it to me,' said White, fighting a sudden rush of embarrassment. 'I do not speak correctly?'

Frith laid down his fork. 'Actually, you speak extremely precisely. The way the old Empire of France would've had you speak, when they still ruled us. But things have changed. Now only rich people like to be reminded of those times, as it was only the rich that benefited from being part of the Empire. Nowadays, anything remotely French coming out of your mouth will get you a smile and an invite from the aristocrats, but a dirty look from everyone else. Let's move on, anyway, and talk about what will happen next.'

White spiked a pomder from the dish and nibbled on it while his heart dropped to his feet. In a way, he was grateful to Frith for being so direct. It was the balance of power that he had come to understand in prison. Hating the person who had control of you, loving them when they were kind to you; hating yourself for doing it.

'You'll stay here in Capital,' said Frith. 'I will be directly responsible for you. Don't worry, we'll treat you well. You'll have a place of your own to stay. Money. Food. Clothes. Not citizenship, of course. And there's no need for you to spy for us, if in return you give us every piece of information you have on whatever we ask about World. I'm also going to enrol you in our Talent programme.'

'What is this?'

Frith leaned back, wiping his mouth with a tissue. 'Did

you think we had no one with your ability here? Witness my lack of surprise at your little trick.'

'So you already have many people here who can do what I do.'

'No, we don't. We have many people who may have something of it, but without training, no clue about the full extent of their capabilities. You'll train with the other Talented. You'll show us what you can do.'

White was silent. He forked a piece of meat and chewed, aware of eyes on him.

Frith pushed his plate gently away. 'There are students in our training programme who can look into other places, travel into other countries, without leaving the comfort of their own rooms, through their dreams. There are some who can spy on others without them knowing anyone is there. They move their minds, somehow. I know the symptoms of Talent, and I know what to recognise. But in all the time I've been running the programme, I've only ever met one other student who can Jump the way you did today.'

White put his fork down, instantly curious. 'I have met no one else,' he said. 'Who is this student? Will I meet them?'

'His name is Wren. It's quite extraordinary, what he can do.'

White filed the name away. Perhaps he would be introduced to this Wren at some point. Perhaps train with him. Would Wren be better than him? He felt a stab of jealousy and tried to ignore it.

'Do you understand the Talent?' said Frith. 'How it works, where it comes from?'

'A little. Do you have Talent?'

'In many areas; but not in that one.'

'How did you find out about it?'

Frith took a sip of wine, and chose to ignore his question.

'You'll work hard, please,' he said. 'I need to prove that what I'm doing is the right decision. You will prove it. Look at me.'

White raised his eyes like an obedient puppy. Frith was watching him, his face expressionless. He would not refuse that face. It was the face of his future.

'You understand how important you are.'

'Yes,' said White.

'You understand what that means.'

'It means if I ever try to leave this country . . .'

He left it hanging.

Frith shrugged. 'We don't have implants here. But we do have other ways of tracking you. And quite a lot of spies in World.'

'Listen,' said White. The reverse had occurred to him, suddenly and sickeningly. 'They know I am here. The police, they tried to catch me when I left to come here. Will they try to. To do something?'

'Please don't worry about that. You'll be quite safe here, under my protection. And frankly, they'll soon forget about you. It'll become mired in bureaucracy and back and forth, and then they'll be distracted by a million other things. Yours is a very chaotic nation. Too much going on. They'll stop caring about you.'

White was surprised to find that he felt hurt. He knew

that Frith was right. It should have been relief he felt. Relief that they wouldn't care enough to come after him for his betrayal. But it stung him, very deep down inside, in a hidden and shameful part of himself that still desperately wanted their approval for what he was, wanted to be accepted and loved for what he was.

He saw now that such a thing was just not possible in World. But maybe it was possible here, and maybe he had done the right thing. And maybe he could be himself, and be happy.

So White looked into the face of the man before him, and accepted his offer.

He felt a cold hand grip his heart. But there was no choice, he told himself. No other choice.

CHAPTER 8
ANGLE TAR

RUE

It was a shoveller bird that woke her.

It had flown in through the open sliver of her window. She had been dreaming about Til. No strange places, this time.

Rue lay, listening to the bird buzzing and beeping. She heard someone moving about outside, and memories of the night before started to ooze through her sleepy content. She threw the bedspread back, startling the shoveller, who hastily winged his way outwards. She watched him go, sorry.

'You up now?' said Fernie, appearing at the window. She had on her floppy weeding hat that always made Rue laugh and cringe at the same time.

'What time did you get back?' said Rue, pushing her feet into her raggy slippers. Avoiding Fernie's eye would arouse suspicion. Looking at her too much would be out of place.

'Late. Not much later than you went off to bed, though, right.'

Rue shrugged. 'Didn't feel sleepy. Thought I'd wait up for you a spell.'

'Hm. Come outside and have tea. It's a goodish day, and we'll be to the market in a stretch.'

Fernie and her hat disappeared. Rue shuffled to the kitchen, re-examining the last few minutes for any hint of self-betrayal. The smell of fresh mint tea drifted through the air. She poured herself a glass and wandered outside. It *was* a goodish day, and unwittingly Fernie had given Rue the perfect opportunity to talk to Til. He'd be in his usual place at the market, selling the morning's freshly baked breads.

Her toes scrunched in the bare earth as she watched the horizon and sipped her tea. Fernie's generous backside was wiggling as she worked a herb border.

'What we on for today, then?' said Rue.

'You,' Fernie emphasised, 'will be learning your herbs. We'll be making up some fresh mixes for quite a few of my jars are nearly out. Mayhap a square of soap or two. I can show you how it's done, if you like.'

Rue made a non-committal grunt. When it came to the everyday practicalities, she could not rouse as much enthusiasm as Fernie seemed to expect her to. Doubtless she'd get the local soap maker to do hers when she became fully fledged. She didn't see the reasoning behind doing everything yourself.

'Will you go back to the Woolmaker's?' said Rue, trying not to sound hopeful. She liked having the house to herself.

'We'll both be going tomorrow,' came the muffled voice. Rue rolled her eyes, playing with the sodden mint stalks at the bottom of her glass. 'I know as how you don't care much for the babies part of the job, but you've to learn and appreciate. You'll understand when you see the kit and know you've helped bring it into the world.'

An image of those blood flowers floated through Rue's mind and she made a sour face. There was no appreciating that.

'Would she have died if you hadn't been there?'

'Who's to say?' said Fernie. 'Maybe she would have got better on her own.'

Rue chewed on one of the mint stalks, watching Fernie work. 'You're too generous,' she said. 'You saved her; she would've bled to death if she'd've been on her own.'

'There'd be some who'd argue 'twas Tro saved her. Or Buc who decided to spare her.'

'Tuh. No one really believes in them.'

Fernie turned, still squatting. She sat back with a sigh, her heavy skirts rumpled up around her stockinged legs. She looked both comical and sweet. Rue felt a rush of affection for her.

'You ought to be careful who you say such things to,' said Fernie. 'And how loud you say 'em.'

'Gods are worthless,' said Rue. 'Never around when you need 'em, always underfoot causing trouble when you don't. Ain't that one of the first things you ever said to me? No one ever sees them, anyway.'

'Or maybe they're deliberately choosing not to be seen. I never told you not to believe in 'em, just 'cause I don't. Just don't trust 'em, that's all.'

'If one came round here,' said Rue, 'I'd tell him to be off and that we didn't need his help, thank you kindly. We've been getting along quite well without him so far.'

Fernie laughed. 'He wouldn't think much of that.' She pushed herself to her feet and swept off the hat. 'Get some clothes on. It's market time.'

It was busy today. Most of the customers were young, the older folk having come in the early morning to avoid the worst of the heat. Rue steadily avoided gazing straight to the bakery stall and kept her eyes forwards, her insides churning uneasily. She both hoped and dreaded that Fernie would send her over there to get some bread. She didn't, more often than not – she liked to bake her own. Did they have any left in the house? Rue couldn't remember and momentarily hated herself for forgetting to check before they left.

Her shoes kicked up the gravel and sand mixture scattered across the village square flagstones. She trailed around, trying to appear enthused whenever Fernie turned and asked her opinion.

Where was he? At his stall? She'd risked a glance, but couldn't see him there. Maybe he wasn't tending today. Fernie was engaged in a mock argument with Shard the furniture maker and didn't look set to leave his stall any time soon.

Rue wandered nonchalantly away. She started to cross the square, making her way towards Til's stall. She'd only taken a few steps before she felt someone at her side and turned quickly; but it was only some boy, and her heart fell.

'Hello Rue,' said the boy. What was his name?

'Hello,' she said vaguely, still moving. She wasn't going

to stop and have everyone think she had something on with this boy.

'What you doing?' said the boy.

'Looking round the market.'

'Yeh.'

Silence ensued. Rue noticed that a handful of similar boys were standing in a group not far from them; watching and grinning to each other.

'So, what you doing tonight?'

'None of yours,' said Rue. She had intended it to be offhand but it came out sharp. The boy blushed.

'Nope, none of mine,' he agreed. 'Just wondered is all. If you'd be free.'

Rue stopped. 'For what?' she asked, though it seemed obvious.

'To meet me.'

'To do what?'

'Anything you like.'

It was Pake. That was his name. He was stocky, shaped by farm work. About her age, she knew. Nice eyes. Decent manner. But that was all he had. There was no magic there.

'Um,' she said, trying to think of the right combination of words that would get her out of this. 'Well. I'm real busy.'

'You can just tell me a time, then.'

Don't be a coward, Rue girl. Don't string him along. Just say it.

'Um. No,' she said, and then shut her mouth firmly, stopping any more vague excuse words coming out that might make him think he could still worm a meet from her.

He waited for a moment, and then smiled, nervously.

'No?' he said.

Rue shrugged. 'No,' she repeated.

'Oh,' he said. 'Um.' He took a step back.

Rue felt her face bloom crimson in mortified sympathy. 'Sorry,' she said. 'I just. Um. Sorry.'

Pake turned without a further word, his eyes away from her.

He went back to his group. Rue spun hurriedly on one foot and started walking, hoping she wouldn't trip or look stupid, feeling their glances landing on her back, over and over, like birds pecking at a seed.

Where was Til? She needed him to be right there, so she could stop the horrible feeling that everyone was talking about her as she walked. As she approached the bakery stall she saw that it was busy as always, but there was no sign of Til. She looked helplessly about.

Women milled in front, chatting, laughing, and cooing. Then, like a puppet, Til sprang up from behind the wooden table, loaves in hand. She worried for a moment that he wouldn't see her, but his eyes fell on her straight away. He nodded, turning back to the woman in front of him. Of course; she would have to wait until he'd managed to get rid of his customers before they could talk properly.

They did like to hang about. Rue watched them impatiently as they flirted and laughed. Til wasn't as silent and brooding as she remembered. She dawdled until the last woman finally left, and moved up to him before anyone else could approach.

'What do you need?' said Til.

'I just wanted to see how you are. I mean, after last night.'

'I'm well, thanks. Your advice was good.'

Rue smiled tentatively, hoping for more, but Til merely looked at her.

'I'm sorry,' she blurted. 'I measured it wrong. I'm really sorry. It was stupid.'

Til said nothing for a long moment. Finally he shrugged. 'Don't worry. It wore off quick.'

'Oh . . . good,' said Rue. 'If you're going to tell Fernie, could you let me explain to her first?' She tried hard not to sound shaky. 'I'd rather I fessed, if that's all right by you. I don't want her thinking that I didn't have the guts.'

Til shrugged again. 'I weren't going to say anything, unless you wanted me to. What breads you looking for, then?'

'I didn't come for breads. I came to talk to you.'

Til laughed, sounding awkward. 'Why?'

Rue knew her face was flushed and it made her angry. *Why?*

'Because of what happened, is why. I don't . . . I'm not. I don't feel bad towards you, it being my fault and all.'

'Glad you don't, Rue. And anyway, I told you your advice was good. You said to talk to her, so I did.'

Rue floundered. 'You did?'

'I did.'

'What did she say?'

'None of yours,' he said easily. Rue gave him a proper look. He was light in manner and seemed boyishly happy, at odds with his usual mysterious reserve. Her heart sank, heavy with misery.

'Well, and so it went right with her, then,' she said, trying for casual.

'Early days, but . . .' Til grinned. It was a beautiful boy grin and lifted his whole face so that it shone. 'Sure you don't want some breads? I made some Noisy Surprise.'

'No thanks,' said Rue. 'Fernie makes her own mostly and we've not run out.'

Another customer had approached and was waiting for them to finish. Rue took the opportunity to leave as fast as she could.

As she walked away she prayed no one was looking at her, because she knew that her face had fallen to the ground.

CHAPTER 9
ANGLE TAR

WHITE

'Ignore them,' said a voice.

White looked up.

The boy smiled.

'They're not used to foreigners, that's all,' he said, sitting across from White with his breakfast plate balanced carefully on his hand.

'They do not bother me,' said White. He turned slightly away from the tableful of students goggling at him.

'They don't?' the boy asked, amused. 'They would me. My name's Wren, by the way.'

Wren. The Talented student that so impressed Frith.

White watched him crack open an egg and dig his spoon enthusiastically into the shell. Wren had a nice enough face, sandy hair, and a soft round body that spoke of good living and no hard work, but he was quite ordinary-looking. Except for his eyes. His eyes were different. Expressive. Shifting through amused, fierce, then excited, all in a moment.

And his Talent was obvious. He carried it like a cloak around his shoulders. It hung proudly from his frame. He was definitely not shy.

But then, none of these students were.

White unenthusiastically stirred his oatmeal. Frith hadn't really prepared him for the staring part of it all.

After saying yes to Frith's offer, and making his choice, such as it was, in that tiny interrogation room, White had stared at his plate until someone had entered the room and quietly cleared it away, and then brought in dessert; pears baked in sugar, so soft each spoonful melted on his tongue.

As they ate, Frith had told White all about the university where he would be studying. It sprawled across a goodly section of Parisette's fashionable East Quartier. White remembered seeing it from the outside – a haphazard, village-like place surrounded by a smooth wall too high to climb. Frith gave him a map of the campus, a huge piece of stiff cloth paper that folded into pocket size with careful creases, buildings labelled with tiny, curling script and colour coded according to area of study.

He described the lessons White would have. He talked about the respect that White should show his tutors. He told White to be a silent, empty glass, to learn and to absorb and only speak when spoken to.

He would be reported on, said Frith, just like every other student in the group of Talented he would study with. They would monitor his progress, so he should try his hardest to impress, but not to show off. Frith said that he could take White straight to his new home on campus, if he liked. White could stay there tonight, and start his lessons in the morning.

He knew he was supposed to find it too fast, too

overwhelming, all at once. Lessons in the morning when he hadn't even slept in a bed for weeks. He was supposed to ask for more time. He was supposed to widen his eyes and stammer that it was too soon. He was supposed to look puzzled and wonder why they weren't going to put a guard on him at all times, afraid that he might try and run back to World at any moment.

But these were pointless thoughts. A guard certainly wouldn't be able to stop him going anywhere he liked. They knew that he would never go back to World, not now. And how prepared would a few more days of nothing make him?

Better to start tomorrow. Better not to give himself time to think. So White nodded and looked serious and said that was fine. He thought he caught a ghost of admiration in Frith's eyes, and felt the comforting warmth of approval.

Frith got a maid to draw White a bath, a completely new experience for him. It sat, a giant tub in the middle of a bare, tiled room. White was alone, but felt like the room watched him somehow as he slid uneasily in. He scrubbed and scrubbed at his skin, marvelling at how black the water turned as weeks of dirt bloomed within it. But the water was heavily perfumed, the smell clinging to his skin even after he was dry and dressed in new clothes. By now it felt impossible to keep awake, but Frith was waiting for him outside the room. He was handed a heavy mantle coat and told that they were leaving.

The journey was dark, too dark to see much outside their coach window. Ghosts of buildings drifted past as they rattled through the streets, unformed in the sparse street lighting they had here, all tall irregular lamp posts that threw everything into shadow more than they did relief. He only realised that they had arrived at their journey's end when the coach stopped and Frith said, 'Here we are.'

They stepped out of the coach.

'Some of the students might still be awake, even though they shouldn't be,' said Frith, opening the door of the building in front of them and ushering White inside. 'So let's go and say hello. Nervous?'

'No,' said White. His heart squeezed.

In truth, he hadn't been at all sure what to expect. How old were the other students, here? Maybe they were more advanced than him. Knowing and mature, giving him an imperious glance before dismissing him as a child.

Or maybe they would be embarrassingly younger than him, all noise and rabble, and he sticking out above their heads like an idiot.

They were quite a mix, as it turned out.

There were several of them still awake and lolling by a huge hearth in what looked to White like the social room of the house. Their faces turned towards him as he heard Frith say, 'Good evening. I've brought you a present.'

Some looked as young as twelve. Others close to adulthood. They were silent.

'He's a new student, and his name is White.' Frith paused. 'Just White.'

He could actually feel the entire room's humming interest go up a notch.

'As you may be able to tell, he's not Angle Tarain, but

I'm sure you'll treat him the same way as you do each other. He'll start tomorrow with you.' Frith smiled at them all. 'Be nice.'

One or two of them grinned, brazen. The rest didn't take their eyes off him.

Please, don't leave me here.

'We should get you a room,' he heard Frith say, and thanked him silently. 'Let's go.'

White tried not to look grateful that he was fleeing. He felt stares tickling at his back.

It had been that way since; the staring and the whispering. The other students all seemed to find White utterly fascinating. None of them would talk to him; they looked away if he challenged their gazes. He hadn't yet said a word in class. He didn't want to seem frightened, but neither did he consciously want to give them another reason to stare once they heard his accent and strange way of speaking.

He hadn't seen Frith again, though the evening after his arrival he'd walked into his bedroom to discover a package of clothes in his size. Cream shirts with oversized cuffs, waistcoats with matching indoor jackets that reached his knees, and a pair of softened leather boots.

There was also a stiff purse containing coins sitting on the bed, together with a brief note from Frith explaining that he should go into the town and buy whatever he wanted, and that he would get a small amount of money at regular intervals.

But White hadn't yet dared to venture beyond campus. He would, he promised himself. It wasn't cowardice. He'd slept on those streets, hadn't he? It was just absurd to be afraid of going back to them, now he was safe and warm and fed.

In World, he at least had been able to go home after a day of school and escape from his peers' babble, and mock fights, and laughter. Here, when they finished training for the day, he went back to Red House with them all; back to the squat, dusky building where the Talented students lived together on campus. He ate with them. Studied with them. Endured their whisperings. Locked himself in his small bedroom when it became too much.

Which, frankly, had so far been most of the time.

'There are all sorts of interesting rumours flying around about you,' said Wren, through mouthfuls of egg.

White tried to clamp down on a sudden flare of nervousness.

'Such as?' he said, pushing his food around on his plate.

'Oh, that you've had to run away from your country because your government wanted to kill you. That you fought off a dozen guards when they tried to arrest you, blasted them with your mind. That kind of crap.'

Well, actually, White wanted to say. That's not too far from the truth, in fact.

'That is stupid,' he said instead, with an effort.

'Yeah, I know. But I've heard that you're very Talented. Maybe even the most Talented they've found. Do you think that's true?'

White stared at the tabletop, irritated. What kind of a question was that?

'I do not know.'

'Oh stop it, Wren,' said someone else. White looked up. A girl had sauntered up to their table and was in the middle of sliding into place next to Wren, who put his hand out and gently lifted her long hair back over her shoulder, so that it wouldn't spill in her food.

She glanced shyly at White, her eyes barely touching his before blinking away.

'I'm Areline,' she said. 'I'm sure you don't remember all our names yet.'

White hadn't remembered her name, but it was extremely hard to forget a girl as lovely-looking as her. No wonder everyone perpetually tossed envious glances Wren's way.

'How are you finding it so far?' she said.

White shrugged.

'Well . . . weird, of course. It was weird for us when we first got here, too. Being trained in something we don't even know how to describe. I don't even know what the Talent *is*, really.'

'But I think you do, right?' said Wren, watching White. 'I think you know a lot about it.'

He can see it on me, too, White realised. He can see it like I can.

White felt his curiosity grow.

'Perhaps,' he said.

'We've got a free hour after breakfast, before our first lesson,' said Wren. 'Why don't you show us what you can do?'

'Wren, leave him alone.'

'What?' he protested. 'For fun, that's all! He'll have to

show everyone in our next Talent class, anyway. Mussyer Tigh said so yesterday.'

White took a gulp of his coffee. He knew this game. Normally he would ignore someone like that until they took the hint and left him alone, but this was Wren. Frith's favourite.

'Why not?' he said, standing up.

They stood in Red House's communal study.

Areline had draped herself over a couch, and pretended to be reading. White thought he could feel her eyes on the back of him.

'So,' said Wren. 'Can you Jump?'

Areline tutted.

'Of course,' said White, starting to enjoy the game. The circling. 'You cannot?'

Wren laughed. 'Well, not everyone can. Not yet.'

'No one can,' said Areline. 'Apart from Wren.'

Is that a challenge?

White folded his arms.

'Let's start with something easy,' said Wren. 'You can hook, right?'

'Hook?'

'You might call it something different, where you're from. It's when you send your mind out into the black, to find a place to go. But you anchor part of yourself here, so you don't get lost.'

White understood immediately. He had never heard someone else talk about it before; it gave him a surprising shiver of pleasure. Someone who knew what it was like to have Talent like that. Someone who would understand him, and know him.

Wren took his hand. White pulled it away in surprise.

'Don't be silly,' said Wren with a laugh. 'I need to touch you, that's all. So we can do it together.'

'Do . . . what?'

'Hook,' said Wren, glancing at Areline with a roll of his eyes. She had given up pretending to read and was watching them both avidly.

'I have never . . . done that with anyone else before.'

'No?' said Wren. 'Can't pretend I'm not relieved. I'll lead. Close your eyes.'

White hesitated. People closed their eyes when they did this? Maybe he had been doing it wrong. Maybe he was about to find out, right now, that he didn't know a thing about the Talent after all. That Frith had been mistaken about him.

Wren had his eyes closed.

White did the same.

After a moment, he felt something brushing insistently against him. Not his body. His mind. It was a strange sensation. A warm feather stroking gently on his brain.

It was Wren.

They were in the blackness. The nothing that existed between places. The dark that you had to cross whenever you Jumped. White had only ever been there for microseconds. He had never paused in it, too afraid to linger. Afraid that somehow, if he stayed there, he would get lost and confused, and never find his way back.

Yet here he was, standing in it with Wren.

It was like a dream. He could feel Wren next to him, but wouldn't afterwards be able to say if he'd actually seen him or heard him when he spoke.

Wren tugged at him, trying to get him to follow; but he suddenly had a better idea. He clutched tight to Wren and pulled him *his* way. Wren resisted for a moment; then let himself be moved.

The blackness was sucked backwards, stripped roughly away by light and air and the smell of living things.

They moved through it and stepped out into the real.

'Er . . . this isn't where I wanted us to go,' said Wren, looking around with puzzled eyes.

'It is my bedroom.'

'Which bedroom?'

'In Red House. Mine. Upstairs.'

Wren turned and stared at him, until he started to feel uncomfortable.

'You're trying to tell me you Jumped us a *few feet?*'

White shifted, embarrassed.

'Yes,' he said. 'Is that . . . unusual?'

'Gods, it's impossible! At least, I thought it was.'

White folded his arms defensively. Now he felt like an idiot for trying to prove himself. He had gone too far. The expression on Wren's face was too close to the ones he remembered from childhood.

'Do it again,' said Wren suddenly.

'What?'

'Come on. Jump us back to the study. I want to see it properly this time.'

Wren held his hand out.

After a moment, White took it, and pulled him back.

They came out into the study, inches from the spot they had, moments before, been standing in together. Areline clapped her hands, her eyes shining in delight.

'I think I'm going to like this one,' said Wren to Areline, putting his arm around White's shoulders. 'You won't *believe* what he just did.'

White felt a pang of happiness deep in his belly.

He would be all right here.

CHAPTER 10
ANGLE TAR

RUE

The sun shimmered and winked at her as she walked through the village. It bounced off a piece of glass in the dust and tickled her eyes. Or maybe it was a glass fairy, trying to catch her attention.

She let that fancy unwind for a moment more, before letting it go reluctantly.

All fantasy had to end sometime.

It hadn't been so in her childhood. She'd grown up on a farm, where hard graft and good food was supposed to give you all the satisfaction you needed. They hadn't cared much for the child Rue's insistence on chasing sprites through the long grass, or coming back from the stream and swearing she'd seen tiny freshwater mermaids, or her tendency to sit still and go blank for hours at a time while she was supposed to be sweeping out the kitchen.

A city family might have worried about her mental state and sent her to doctors under a cloud of shushing secretive privacy. The farmer had neither time nor money enough to care about that sort of thing, so learned to let her alone about it, then shout at her when she hadn't done her chores.

It didn't make any difference.

The gods knew she didn't *like* to get into trouble. Just if the alternative was never dreaming and so never getting shouted at, she'd take the dream and the consequences every time. She knew that it wasn't quite daydreaming, what she did. It felt too thick and cloying for that.

When she was older, she stopped seeing mermaids, and sprites, and tree boggarts. But she still had the memories of them. She knew that either they'd been real, and she just couldn't see them any more, or that she'd made them real for herself, and then forgotten the trick of it. That loss of magic pained her deeply, more than she could allow herself to think about.

They first started talking about witch's touch when she was twelve.

It began as a silly thing. One of the farmhands had liked to tease her. He was brown and muscled and she hated him with all her heart, because when he teased others joined in, and their laughter was as humiliating as the time when she'd been slapped around the legs as a child for being back home three hours late from crab-picking at the rock pools.

'You had me worried to DEATH!' screamed the farmer's wife as she'd done it.

Every time that stupid boy made a joke at her expense, that slapping flashed like a burn on her mind, and she felt herself grow hot. So she said what she said out of nothing more than pure wrath.

'It don't matter *anyway*,' she had said. 'It don't matter a bit what you ever say to me, cos tomorrow you'll be pra'tically dead.'

114

'Oooh,' the boy whistled. 'You heard that, din't you all? You heard, she's going to kill me. Best be on alert, then!'

General laughter. Rue wanted to scream.

'I didn't SAY that,' she shouted. 'I said you'd be pra'tically dead, not that I'd kill you. Why should I lift a finger when you're gonna be all lumpy and bloated like a rotted old fish? And serve you right!'

The laughter swelled, and she'd got up, meaning to storm out the room in a graceful, icy sweep. But her feet had got tangled in the forest of chair legs, and she'd stumbled to a crowd of hooting, and the whole thing was a mess.

Of course, the next day, when the boy was bitten by a snake while collecting hay and swelled up like a balloon from the poison, things took a bit of a different turn.

She couldn't say exactly how or why she'd said what she'd said, you see. She just felt that it sounded right when it fell out of her mouth. She had the image right there, as if she'd dreamed about it not long ago and still had a ghost of it in the back of her head.

And it couldn't exactly have been her fault. Only fate had taken the boy to that particular field at that part of the day when he could have been any number of other places, with Rue in the house with the women all day and nowhere near him. Fate had made him step on the snake's hidden tail, a tail placed just so in order to cause everything that followed.

Things changed after that.

People treated her funny, and kids pointed and wouldn't talk to her any more, and sometimes the farmer's wife would come home after selling cheese and meat out at the

115

town, sigh loudly, and complain that two people had come up to her and asked if Rue could tell their futures for them.

She couldn't, she didn't think. It wasn't like she normally walked around looking at people and just knowing what they'd be doing the next day. It had just happened that once, and she had no idea how to do it again.

It wasn't too long before they heard a hedgewitch was looking for an apprentice. She hadn't been at all sure about going for something like that, but what she did very firmly know was that farm work wasn't for her. It was hard to tell who was the more relieved when Fernie chose her – the farm or Rue.

She looked up to find that she'd reached the oak meadow at the back of the village. As she came down the last of the cobbleway, she saw a few figures crowded around Old Stumpy in the middle of the grass.

Old Stumpy was a famous meeting place for the young of the village. Struck by lightning not three seasons before in a particularly tempestuous autumn, it had been discovered in the aftermath, lying across most of the meadow like a corpse in a tangle of enormous, broken limbs. It had taken most of the day to clear the meadow and chop the rest of the tree down to its present three-foot-high trunk. No one lived close enough to have heard its death above the more general noise of the storm that had caused it – everyone with sense had barricaded themselves in for the night and sealed every nook and cranny of every door and window as best they could against the fury outside. It had been a mainstay of the oak meadow since before Chester, the eldest inhabitant of the village, could recall, and he reckoned it was about seven or eight hundred years old when he'd been a child. Back in its more magnificent days, it had been known by the nobler name of Baron. In its death it had been changed to the wildly witty Old Stumpy, and though it now existed in reduced circumstances, it still served the same important purpose in keeping the village alive, namely by facilitating the meeting, romancing and procreating of its inhabitants.

Rue stopped short. The unmistakeable outline of Pake was amongst the small knot of people there. She felt a blush creep up her neck. It wouldn't do to go near enough so he could shout something at her, and have them all join in like a pack of barking dogs. She'd rejected him in front of his friends. Rue knew enough about men to know that they took that kind of thing badly.

And she cared enough about appearances to hesitate, and more than she would admit, for she liked to put on an air of careless apathy around people of her own age. It had earned her a reputation for arrogance, which she professed to enjoy. It had also made her lonely, without really realising it.

She struck out a path towards the edge of the wood – far enough away from his group for them not to bother with her; close enough so that she didn't look scared of them.

She heard their voices tail away as she got halfway through the meadow.

I'm not going to look at you.

She felt her shoulders hunch under their stares, and flattened them down.

A few seconds and she'd be clear.

I'm not looking.

And there was the tree line, and there was safety. She slowed, relaxing.

Then she heard a voice behind her, clear on the air, say, 'She ain't very pretty, is she?'

She passed into shadow, her feet crunching on dry nut husks, and the trees crowded around, solid in their comfort.

It had stung. It had. But it didn't matter. None of them mattered. She kicked a pine cone out of the way with a vicious little flick of her foot, and immediately felt like a petulant child.

She was an outsider here, her home having been another village a way down the coast. Some said Fernie had had a whole county's worth of girls to choose from when she went looking for an apprentice. And Rue knew what being an outsider meant in places like this. It was almost three years since she'd first arrived, but it still wasn't enough to integrate her with anyone her own age here. She hadn't been to the village school; she hadn't grown up with them. And she was apprentice to the hedgewitch.

She knew what was said about hedgewitches. They kept to themselves. Never mixed with the common folk. They fancied themselves special because of what they did. They were arrogant. Weird. Bad-tempered. She understood the reasons why. Fernie had explained that being able to birth babies and help the sick and know how to do things that other people couldn't gave you power. And power always made everyone twitchy.

Rue passed a patch of deep yellow flowers nestled

underneath a craggy tree. Just Butter flowers; no good for herbing, but nice in soup and salad. She'd have been tempted to pick some for tea if they hadn't been sat underneath a Pestler tree. Fernie always said Pestlers were mean. Probably make the flowers taste bitter just to get you back for taking what was theirs. You never picked the plants or broke the branches of a Pestler tree. She'd always made fun of Fern when she started talking like that, saying they were all living things and had characters of their own. In the privacy of her own head, though, she thought it sounded mysterious and right. Pestlers always made her nervous when she walked past them.

Pake's face flashed through her head, earnest and coy.

Maybe she should have said yes to him. Things would have got a lot easier for her around here if she had, that was for sure. Pake was no pack leader, but he was well liked.

But he's not what you want.

Her experiences with boys so far had been less than satisfactory. They did nothing to dampen the dreams she sometimes had, which she kept locked in her mind and only revisited on her own, when she felt ugly, or boring.

In Rue's dreams, when men touched her (not always a specific man, merely a presence), it was electrifying, almost frightening. It was being possessed, and giving up everything, and not being afraid to do that. It was being gripped by a man who could properly see her, see all the things she hid from the world, could guess the pieces of herself that no one else could guess. If she could find a man like that, he would rule her. But she hadn't yet, because no man had

119

yet passed the tests she set them. Because they were ordinary, and she knew that. Ordinary people couldn't measure up, and she was beginning to wonder if the whole world was just ordinary, made up of people just like the ones she'd met in her life so far, people that would never measure up.

And what was the point, she thought, of settling for that?

She came to her favourite clearing. It was packed with blood herb, which Fernie had that morning directed her to gather. She could stay here a while, just to relax, and still bring back enough to satisfy her mistress a little later.

Rue liked the feel of dry summer soil on her skin. Sitting in the clearing, protected from the worst of the prickling heat by the cool, silent trees that stood sentry duty around her, she traced patterns with her fingertips and felt herself slip away on the gentle wave of bird hoots from above.

Things were better like this. Simple. Sometimes she thought it would be best to live in a forest and have the world fade away, doing what it liked in her absence. Sometimes it seemed such a stupid, impractical idea; other times it was the only thing that sustained her.

She unravelled a stuffed champig left over from last night's supper, peeling it delicately, laying the greased pieces in her mouth and sucking until the vegetable's juices ran down her throat. She let her gaze wander around the clearing, thinking of nothing much and enjoying it. After the last of the cold champig had wormed pleasantly down her throat, a comfortable lethargy started to seep through her.

Fernie wasn't expecting her back for another hour or more. She could probably lie down. Just for a moment.

She stretched out on the grass, spots of sunlight dappling her skin. It was warm, and hazy, and gentle. She closed her eyes.

And then opened them.

Oh gods, the light had changed. It was no longer cool and yellow green, but a foreboding shade of dusk. Panic charged her and she sat up, wondering how long sleep had overtaken her.

It took a moment, but then realisation sank into her, relief and apprehension rolled up together. It was a dream.

More than that, it was another one of *those* dreams; it had to be.

She stood in an unfamiliar landscape. It was a street, she supposed. Buildings lined each side of it, sat close together, uniform and seamless. The ground under her feet was smooth and grey. The stone, if that's what it was, that made up the walls of the buildings surrounding her, was grey. She looked up at the sky. It was clouded, she decided, though it looked too neat, like it wasn't made up of clouds at all but simply painted a mottled off-white colour. It felt like a place that didn't quite exist, as if it was waiting for its final injection of life.

She lingered for a while, hesitant to move. There didn't seem to be anywhere to go to. Everything was bare, and still, as if the whole world were contained in a glass jar. She was outside of the proper world where everything existed, in a strange nothing place where no one liked to come.

It's the skeleton.

This place is dead and this is its skeleton.

But then something flickered at the edge of her sight.

It came, slowly and slowly, moving around the far corner of a building, antlers first.

It was almost a person.

The antlers grew naturally out of its forehead, a set of graceful, twisting bones. It had hair, pushed back and hanging long behind its ears. It was hard to tell whether it was male or female. Its face was angular and sharp with huge doe eyes.

Walking beside it was a boy with a tail and tufty cat ears. He had a button nose and the sweetest face, an unreal kind of sweetness.

Sprites. They must be sprites.

More joined them, walking along the street as if it happened all the time. Some of them had glittering blue-green-yellow-gold scales for skin. Others strange purple eyes and hair that looked more like fur.

Or gods, or animal spirits. Spirits wasn't right, though; they looked so real. They looked like they smelled and sweated.

Rue watched them mingle, fascinated. They didn't even look at each other as they chatted, instead throwing their laughter and words casually out into the air, seeming for all the world like they were talking to themselves. She didn't understand the language. They didn't seem to see her at all, as though she were just part of the fabric of their background.

They lived here. Breathed here. This was normal. This

was their home. What *was* this place? Things that looked like that had fascinating lives, like ancient gods, of course they did. Nothing looked like that and had a job or ate biscuits and slept like normal people.

How could she become one of them?

A cry of surprise came from somewhere in the crowd. A man with tiny white feathers carefully sprouting from his neck was pointing straight at her.

Several turned to look.

They can see me.

She woke.

Light hit her face, and warmth slid over her skin.

She was in the woods. Her woods. That faint, grey world with its strange people lingered with her for a moment, then faded like a ghost, bleached out of her by the smell and sound and brightness of the real.

Rue rubbed her face, her confusion melting away.

Just another dream. She was used to it. It would pass, as always. Definitely just a dream, as there was no way anybody looked like that in real life. Another fantasy world conjured by her mind for her to escape to for a little while, that was all.

She shook it off, getting up from the ground.

Fernie would be waiting.

CHAPTER 11
ANGLE TAR

WHITE

'This is ridiculous,' said Wren, and threw his history book across the room.

It bounced off the wall and landed in a sad flump, its pages curled.

They both watched it.

'It is not the fault of the history book,' said White.

'No, it's the fault of the stupid class. A book is a book. But Mussyer Dronerie actually manages to make history physically, painfully dull.'

'His name is Mussyer Fromerie.'

'Gods, White, it's a joke. You know? Drone? A dull noise? Forget it.'

Wren leaned his head back against the side of the bed.

Even after a few weeks of getting used to him, White found Wren hard to keep up with. Areline thought it funny to compare them both; said they couldn't be more different. Wren was the one who sparkled with energy and wit. White was silent and dull, and he had already known that about himself. It was just tougher to deal with when he was constantly sized up against someone so very opposite to him.

Wren led the pack. Mussyer Tigh, their almost useless Talented tutor, had all but given up trying to control him in lessons. He bated the rest of the group, taunting them with jibes about their abilities, but doing it in such a way that it charmed instead of irritated. Even White, infected by Wren's confidence, found himself voluntarily showing off. Occasionally classes descended into a Talent contest between them both, surrounded by voices and faces urging them on.

Every so often, White caught Wren's face frozen between a broad smile and something else. A twist of the mouth that could be anger. But Wren was his friend; someone who had rescued him when he hadn't known he'd needed rescuing. Someone who irked him and pushed him and made him laugh and had shut the door so firmly on his loneliness, he had trouble remembering the taste of it.

He had his moods, though, and this was one of them. An urgent, spiky restlessness. Usually he disappeared when it came on him, and sometimes for hours on end. When White asked him where he went, he always said that he'd gone into the city to explore for a while.

'We are supposed to read this section on the Territorial Wars by tomorrow,' he tried, watching Wren's expression carefully.

'Hang the Territorial Wars. And hang what's written in that stupid book. And hang whatever Fromerie says about them. It's all opinion, anyway. Just because it's written in a book, doesn't make it fact. History is written by the winners. Didn't some famous person say that?'

White was silent. He actually loved reading about history, but he'd heard this rant before, from his sister Cho. She'd always been passionately dismissive of Life and its endless information banks, saying that no one should believe a word on there. Which was patently ridiculous, considering that was where the entirety of World got its information from. To say it was all lies was to say that World and everyone in it just didn't work properly. More than that, it flirted a little too much with radical speak. The sort of things that Technophobes and conspiracy theorists spouted. Cho had had a habit of making some very questionable friends. Sometimes he wanted to know how she was. But then he reminded himself that he couldn't afford to miss her, or worry about her.

'It'd be as useful for me to ask *you* about the Territorial Wars, actually,' Wren said. 'We could compare notes. You could tell me what you were taught, and I could tell you what I was taught, and then we could see which was the more unbelievably stupid.'

White shrugged. Cho still floated about his mind. He wondered how school was going for her. 'All right,' he said absently.

'Actually, I've got a better idea. Why don't you tell me about World?'

Cho disappeared from his mind. His bedroom came sharply back into focus.

'Oh, sorry,' came Wren's voice. 'Sorry. If it's hard, you know, we don't have to talk about it. I just thought it might be interesting.'

White shifted, uneasy, though trying hard not to look it.

'It is not a problem for me,' he said. 'What do you wish to know?'

Wren mused for a second.

'Do you have cherries there?'

'Cherries?'

'The little sweet dark red fruits on stalks. We had them at breakfast the other morning.'

'No. Or at least, not where I am from.'

'You have machines that make your food, don't you?'

'Machines is not the correct word, but I do not know a better one.'

Wren grinned, his eyes dancing wickedly.

'What are the girls like?'

White closed his history book, resigned. 'What do you mean?'

'What do they look like? Are they loud, soft, do they wear dresses? Are they beautiful?'

'They are all those things. And they wear many styles.'

Wren sighed. 'That's not quite what I meant.'

White could see he was disappointing him again, so he forced himself open, just a little.

'I was never good with them,' he said. 'So I cannot tell you much. They all found me too strange. I did not . . . like the same things other boys my age liked. I did not talk the same way. I avoided everyone because of my . . . talent. I did not change my hair every month or try face horns, or wear clothes that everyone saw on GameStars. So girls did not talk to me.'

'GameStars?' said Wren. He seemed utterly fascinated.

'A Life thing. A . . .' White searched, his hand circling

wildly. 'An entertainment. These people, they play games. Other people watch, and vote, and such. It is hard to explain.'

He saw Wren's body strain forward a little.

'What's Life like?' he said, eager. 'Do you miss it? I heard you can get really addicted.'

'I am not addicted!'

'Sorry.'

White squeezed his hand into a ball; the left one, the one Wren couldn't see. He dug his nails into the palm until his flesh stung.

'No,' he said, his voice mercifully level. 'It is fine. I know someone who is addicted. It is a very hard thing.'

Wren said nothing, and the moment grew heavy and awkward.

'Our cities are very different to yours,' White started, with an effort.

Wren looked up. 'Really? What are they like?'

'Yours are . . . haphazard. The streets, they make no sense. Your cities are like wild plants, confusing and illogical. Ours are structured, carefully planned. They are easy to navigate. Your maps make no sense.'

'Oh god, map-making here is as much storytelling as it is fact,' said Wren. 'You just have to learn your way around.'

'Well, I know that now. When I first came here I was very lost. Also, you do not have domes here.'

'What on earth are domes?'

'Environmental domes. I . . .' White searched. He was sure 'domes' was about the best translation. 'They are invisible, but they sit over a city. They protect us from airborne disease, from weather. Like a shield.'

'Weather?' said Wren, amused. 'You don't have weather?'

'Not like this. Not all this wind and rain. And the air! It smells so strongly here. The air inside a dome is pure. Nothing can get through a dome.'

He felt the words pouring out of him, eager to have someone to confess his dislocation to. Explain why he was so different here.

'You take so long at meals, also,' he said, spreading his hands as if he held a pot roast. 'People work for hours, so many hours, just to make a dinner! Your furniture is heavy and dark, and impractical. The buildings are all so different. They sit beside each other as if they should make sense together, but they look odd. And you walk *everywhere*. You walk so much!'

'Are you telling me you *don't* walk? How do people get where they want to go?'

'We have Life,' said White simply. 'We do everything in Life. We shop, work, meet in Life. We do not have transport between places. There is no need of it. But you have horse coaches and trains. It is so . . . so different.'

They stared at each other, tangled in mutual fascination. White could feel Wren's excitement, a pulse from him.

'What about you, and your life here?' said White.

Wren laughed. 'Gods, mine is dull as that history book. I grew up in a little city by the sea. Nothing ever happened there. Save sometimes you could see the foreign trading ships at the docks. No one except the sailors and merchants are allowed down there – they have heavy security, and fences, and walls. But everyone knew there were foreigners. We even had a handful of foreign settlers in the city, from different parts of World. So I suppose I grew up knowing more than most about what was beyond our boring old borders. And I remember thinking about the hypocrisy of what we were taught in school, that everything outside of Angle Tar is a mess, full of backwards cultures. And yet standing there in our midst, walking along our streets, were people who were so clearly more advanced than us, who could tell you about the fantastical things they'd left behind, things that you could only ever *dream* of. They'd only tell you if you got them drunk enough or paid them nicely, of course, and if you went where no one would see you breaking the law and shop you to the police. And some of them did get arrested, sometimes.' He paused. 'Worth it, though,' he decided. 'What? You're looking at me strangely.'

White shook his head. 'Not strange. But it is strange that you think that is boring.'

'Nothing like your childhood, I bet. All the incredible things you had around you.'

White considered. 'They were just normal things,' he said at last. 'Angle Tar was the thing that was incredible to me.'

'Even now?'

'Still.'

'You poor fool,' said Wren fervently.

White laughed.

Wren stared at his lap for a while. 'I used to wish with every piece of me,' he said, 'to find a way into those docks. I used to sit for hours, trying to make it so reality was different, or that I were in a reality where I was on one of those ships, bound for World. And I used to get so angry that it never came true. What's the point of a reality you can't change?'

'You could not Jump then?'

'No. I wasn't like you, Jumping before I could walk.'

White heard a sharpness underneath the joky tone, and kept silent.

'I could go back,' said Wren, faraway. 'I could try and Jump onto one of those boats. Leave here for ever.'

White couldn't keep the astonishment out of his voice. 'Why?'

Wren looked at him sidelong. 'We're not very different, you know,' he said. 'Not even slightly, actually. We've just approached the same thing from opposite ends. Except you got to escape. You got to go to your dream place. I haven't, not yet.'

'No,' said White flatly. 'Because it is not a dream. It is just a place.'

'So's this, White.'

'You are not listening! I left because they put me in prison for what I am. They would do the same to you. You would have to hide yourself. Never being able to relax. Can you know how that feels? Never being your true self, for one moment, because if you do people will hate you for it? Here, at the least, I have that chance.'

Wren was watching him, a thoughtful smile on his face.

'You really don't know Angle Tar at all, do you?' he said. 'But you will, don't worry. I'll teach you. I'll show you its secrets. Then maybe you'll change your mind.'

131

He had to bite down on his tongue, clamping his teeth to stop himself from shouting. Wren didn't know. It wasn't his fault. He probably thought the prison stuff was all exaggeration. He wouldn't believe until he saw. That was human nature for you.

But to have his pain reduced to nothing more than a knowing smile on an ignorant boy's face, a boy that grew up surrounded by love, and colour, and safety. It was almost too much to take.

Wren shifted beside him.

'Listen, White,' he said. 'Listen to me.'

His voice was so changeable and gorgeous, a song that sang everything he had inside him. He was practically quivering. His hand had come out, maybe to touch White's shoulder. But he held it back, as if he sensed he was bringing too much to the surface all at once.

'Don't you want to change the world?' he said. 'People like us were born to change the world. It's filled with shit. It's filled with people who did the things they did to you. It's filled with stupid pointlessness and ignorance and so much mundanity, it makes me want to scream. Don't you feel it too? You must feel it.'

He did feel it.

A desperate ache in him.

'Don't you want to change that?' came Wren's low voice. 'Snap everything out of its ordered way? Make . . . make people *see*?'

White leaned his head back.

Wren made it all right to think like that. He urged and pushed and prodded the world, pulled out the bits he didn't like and scorned people who weren't like him. He wouldn't back down and he wouldn't sit quietly somewhere until he died and he would never settle. White admired him for that.

Yes, maybe it was stupid, and arrogant. But around Wren, yes. He did want to make people see.

Yes. He did want to change the world.

CHAPTER 12
ANGLE TAR

RUE

It had been a busy few days. People did get tend to get ill with annoying regularity.

No more dreams, for a while, at least. Rue suspected she was too tired for them. Fernie was working her hard, and she practically fell into her bed every night, waking up heavy-headed each morning from a sleep that felt more like being unconscious.

In the mornings, Fernie had Rue doing chores from the moment she crawled to the kitchen. Rue was beginning to wonder whether she was being punished for something, and a horrible sickly thought began to form in the back of her mind: that Fernie knew what had happened between her and Til. But then, Fern had always been the sort to have it out, not keep it bottled up inside where it could do much more harm.

The whole thing was making her jumpy, and the fact that she hadn't even been near the village square for a while was starting to irk her. She needed information.

She skirted the kitchen, furtively checking the bread basket, and then each cake tin in the cupboards. She was in luck. They were running low, and Fernie was currently holed up in her workroom, overseeing a potion mix or two. She wouldn't have time to cook today, and Rue's baking was mediocre at best. So when Rue asked her whether she should go off to Til's bakery and buy some bread, Fernie absently said yes.

But as soon as she did, Rue grew nervous. Her bid to find out what was going on with Til started to seem like the machinations of a silly child, not the inscrutable, poised woman she wanted to be.

She knew she didn't love Til, or at least not the kind of love that was worth going stupid over. It was just that he was the only man worth wanting around here. The reality of him probably wouldn't be the same at all. She knew that. And the thought of being a baker's wife day in and out made her shudder.

Besides, witches didn't marry.

Or at least, none that Rue had ever heard of. Certainly Fernie never had, and she seemed to think that sort of thing an utter waste of time. She obviously hadn't at one point, though. Rue had heard tell that she had a son, though no one seemed to know where he was now. Fernie wouldn't talk about him.

Rue trudged along the track to the village. The sky was brooding along with her. There would be a big storm tonight. Her room ceiling always leaked in heavy rains. Fernie had promised to have it fixed but never got round to asking Mussyer Ofton, who had a long time ago done the cottage roof, whenever they saw him in passing.

She reached the square, and her jaw dropped.

Til's bakery was closed and dark.

In the middle of the day.

Rue stood on the step and peered inside. He hadn't opened all morning, that was clear – the floor was still swept clean from the night before.

Rue wandered around the square for a few minutes, unsure; then walked into Beads, the nearest open door.

She loved Beads, more than she would if Fernie weren't so disapproving of it. It was full of city silks, sparkling buttons, velveteen ruffles and meandering ribbons of butterfly lace draped artfully across display tables. The proprietor, Jennet La Damm, was rather old, wore far too much make-up and liked nothing better than gossip. Rue didn't care for her a whole lot but adored her shop. The deep woven baskets packed with beads were her favourite – you could buy a small bag of them for a few centimes. Rue liked to plunge her fingers into the baskets, wrist deep, and feel those beads shifting and pouring like oversized sand grains around her hand. Damm had harped at her on several occasions for doing it, but she wasn't the only one who did.

There were three women huddled close to each other and chatting, with Damm the middle one holding court. They stopped when Rue came in, and gave her a triple-headed stare.

'Your pardons,' said Rue. 'I was wanting to visit the bakery, but it seems closed.'

Their faces transformed with a sudden excitement and they exchanged sly glances, but said nothing.

'Never mind, then,' said Rue, turning to leave. Hang 'em. She'd find out from someone else.

'Well, and so you've not heard then?' said Damm.

Rue shrugged, burning up with curiosity.

'Well, it's the biggest scandal,' Damm continued, her eyes sparkling. 'At first it was nothing but whispers, you know it. This one saying they'd seen him and Mussyer Forthrint's daughter, you know the one, with the blonde hair down to her bum, well, they'd seen 'em down by the copse in the mornings together. It was dismissed by most but I was the only one who thought there might be some truth to it. I seen the way he's looked at her before and they were friends in childhood, of course. Well, and so, the talk started coming in fast about who'd seen them where doing what, though they were clever enough not to give a clue of it in public –'

'I seen them a couple of nights ago,' interjected one of the other women. 'She was coming out of his garden at three in the morning!'

Damm was not pleased.

'And what were you doing walking past Til's garden at three in the morning?' she demanded of her interrupter.

'I seen them,' said the second woman stubbornly, but she had turned red.

'What you see and what you dream is two different things. Now, and so. Her husband gets to know of it after some days of this, and there's such an almighty screaming and shouting from their place one night that you wonder it doesn't wake up the whole village. And he'd cracked her one or two nicely, for wasn't she sporting a big shiny bruise or two the next day on her face?'

'She was!' the third squeaked. The second had forgotten her sulk and was nodding eagerly.

What a bunch of bitches, thought Rue savagely.

Damm grinned, wide as a frog, as she talked. 'Didn't stop them, did it? If anything they stopped caring about hiding it. Everyone was seeing them after that! In the woods past Old Stumpy, people visiting her house during the day and her answering the door all flushed and badly dressed, them proper *looking* at each other in public.'

Damm leaned close. Rue could see the cracks in her lipstick.

'It was last night, they left. They tried to make it secret but the husband caught her in the middle of leaving and Til and him nearly fought it out in the street! Still, they're gone now. And who knows who'll run the bakery, as how it was all in Til's name and him with no sons?'

'Give him time, he may be back in a year or two with one,' said the second woman with a cackle.

Rue wanted nothing better than to throw up.

She muttered something and backed out of Beads, the three women bunched together before her and chattering like birds. They had never looked so happy, and she loathed them for it.

And it was all her. She had told him to talk to that woman. *She* had told him to. And then she had given him dagger weed and made him reckless and hot.

She covered her mouth with her hand. It had probably been that night. He said he'd talked to the woman the next day. What if they'd done more? What if he'd gone around and coaxed her out of the house? He would have grabbed hold of her and forced her down, just like he had started to do with Rue.

She flushed.

'Stupid, stupid, STUPID,' she muttered viciously as she clomped back to Fernie's house.

Everything was stupid.

Those repulsive women in Beads, who had no lives of their own but fed from the lives of others like insects.

This dreary little village, with its gossiping and secrets and scandals. They couldn't see how brave and how romantic it was. All they could see was the nastiness of it. No doubt it was the most exciting thing to happen round here since the local pig farmer had accidentally left his pen open at market and the loose creatures had caused a riot in the square.

So Til and that beautiful woman had gone off together now, hadn't they. And probably to the city. They would live a beautiful life, wouldn't they. It'd be a little apartment, setting themselves up at first. Beds hung with fluttering curtains. Silver-backed brushes and crystal perfume bottles and gemstones flashing at her throat.

They'd love each other. They'd love while Rue was left behind, growing old and fat like Fernie, treating back pain and gummy feet and keeping petty little secrets. Becoming nothing to no one.

And it was all her own fault.

No, she thought.

No bloody time for pity, Rue girl.

First chance I get, I'm out of here.

CHAPTER 13
ANGLE TAR

WHITE

It was getting hard to remember life before this. He'd forgotten how comforting routine was, and how days slipped into weeks so easily when you were in it. The murky, anxious dreams he'd kept having the first few nights, of URCI police breaking into his bedroom in Red House and dragging him away, eventually disappeared.

He had always liked discovering. Here there was a whole wealth of culture and strange viewpoints and history and mannerisms to consume. And books – real *books*. Made of paper. Extravagant, costly objects, thousands upon thousands of them, just lying about the place. His free time, when he wasn't with Wren and Areline, was spent at the university library. He could hide away in one of its little study rooms, tucked away in the back, round a crooked corner and closed off from the world. He could lose himself for a while, and be left alone, and only catch the occasional stare from a passing 'normal' student. The Talentless, Wren called them, grinning as he said it.

There was Areline, too.

Wherever Wren was, she inevitably appeared. Beautiful and coy.

Wren adored Areline, it was clear. It was less obvious how she felt about Wren. White had made a joke once, about how girls interfered with studies, and stopped you from learning as quickly as you might. Wren had laughed at that, but Areline had been hurt and annoyed with both of them. She was hard to fathom, sometimes.

White felt uncomfortable with her when Wren was not there. Wren made it okay for them to talk to each other. Somehow, when he wasn't around, it felt like the air moved more slowly between them. That they were doing something they shouldn't be.

So when he found himself alone with her in Red House's study, the rest of the group either out on the town or lounging in their own rooms, he had started to grow nervous. They had never been alone for such a long time before.

Wren had gone off earlier in the evening, on one of his mysterious jaunts into the city. He never took anyone with him, and had so far never bothered to explain exactly what he did other than 'walk around'; but Areline seemed not to care, so White followed her lead, wanting to say nothing that might offend either of them.

So they sat, alone together, in silence. Areline was curled like a cat on the opposite couch to White, scribbling in a notebook. Occasionally she would look up and smile at him.

She knew that she had lovely lips, and she knew just how to use them.

Finally, when their eyes had caught a third time, she closed her notebook and got up, floating towards him.

'What are you doing?' she said.

'Reading,' said White. He showed her the book.

'Good god, that looks boring.' She plopped onto the couch next to him. Her hair had swung backwards and brushed against his shoulder; a feather touch.

'History,' he said. 'Your history, in fact. It fascinates me.'

'Really? It doesn't me.'

'It has survived much, this country.'

She leaned over to him, her arm solid against his. He caught a sudden scent of raspberries. He tried very hard not to tighten up as she pressed against him. She would feel it, and ask him what was wrong.

She read a passage from the book. Or pretended to read it. Her eyes weren't moving.

'When is Wren back?' he said suddenly.

It worked. She moved away from him, her face uncertain.

Finally, she shrugged, with a little smile.

'I don't know,' she said. 'Sometimes he's gone for hours. It won't be for a while, anyway.'

Silence descended. An unwelcome thought surfaced in White's head.

Don't you know where this is going?

Don't you honestly?

He hadn't dared dwell on it.

'White,' she said suddenly, and then stopped.

'Yes,' he replied, trying to concentrate on the book. Straining to listen to her tone, for any desperate indication of what she wanted, inside her.

'Can I ask you something?'

142

'Yes,' he said again.

Stop saying yes like a robot in that stupid voice.

Areline cleared her throat. 'Would you like to go to dinner, sometime? Just me and you.'

His heart crashed alarmingly in his chest.

'What about Wren?' he managed.

'Just suppose Wren was not a concern,' she said. 'Just suppose that was so. What would you say if I asked you to dinner then?'

White couldn't deny the fact that the thought had occasionally lurked in the dark corners of his mind.

What it would be like to be with her.

But no. Just . . . no. He saw Wren's face in his head. It wasn't worth the hurt.

'I would say no,' he said, without thinking.

She recoiled, as if he had shouted at her.

'You don't . . .' she started, and then fell silent. He snatched a glimpse of her face and saw in horror that her cheeks were red.

'I am sorry,' he said. 'I did not mean to . . . hurt you.'

She said nothing.

They sat in excruciating silence. Every second that ticked by, the silence gained weight. He tried to think of something to say to lift it. He tried thinking of ways to explain. He had a friend now. He didn't want to lose his friend. She was lovely; she was. He would if things were different. Really.

But it was just words, and the words he chose in this language were always curt, or wrong. He couldn't speak properly. He couldn't express what he needed to. So he kept silent. Easier that way.

He forced himself to look at her. She was screwed tight into the corner of the couch, hiding her face in embarrassment.

He reached across, touched her arm.

'Areline,' he said. He hated how his voice sounded. Awkward and boyish.

'Yes?' she replied, her voice low.

'Are we still –'

– friends, he was going to say, but a faint popping noise distracted him.

Wren had just appeared in the middle of the room, a delighted grin on his face.

'Ha!' he said. 'I did that from just outside the front door!'

His gaze settled on them both.

The grin dropped, disappeared. His eyes grew dark.

White took his hand away from Areline's arm.

'What's going on?' said Wren.

'Nothing!' said Areline. 'I thought you'd be away for a while longer?'

It had meant to come out as chatty, but all it did instead was make her look enormously guilty. Wren was silent.

White felt himself closing up, wanting to be away from this. He fought against it. If she couldn't act normal and show Wren that there was nothing to be suspicious about, then he would.

'So where have you been?' he tried, but it sounded hollow and sickly.

And Wren's face was growing darker.

'Out,' he said. 'Around. Leaving you two alone with each other.'

'Wren, what are you talking about?' said Areline.

'Nothing!' he said. 'Nothing.'

And he smiled suddenly.

Areline had recovered some of her energy. She slid off the couch and moved to him, taking him by the hand and talking her head off about a dance class she had had that day. She walked around him, and he admired her, and laughed; and they fell into easiness.

White watched them.

But when her back was turned, Wren glanced at White. His expression was black.

CHAPTER 14
WORLD

FRITH

The meeting with the Castle had started off so beautifully this time.

This time, Frith could not wait for Ghost Girl to get around the table to him. He sat twitching impatiently at each agent's report, until her eyes had finally shifted to his face.

'Frith,' came her faded voice. 'Your turn. I think you have something interesting for us.'

Yes. Of course they knew, didn't they. The day he found out how they knew would be a happy, happy day.

'Yes, I do,' he said. 'Good for me. Less so for my esteemed World colleagues, I think.'

He could swear he felt shoulders go stiff around the table, though no one moved an inch. He swallowed a shark grin.

'I've found a new student. He's been training with us for about six weeks, and shows an unprecedented level of Talent. More than Wren, or anyone else involved in the programme. He can do things I didn't even think were possible.'

A resounding, crashing silence, which told him acres more than noise.

He looked around the table and couldn't resist. 'Your loss, my gain,' he said.

'Oh shut up,' Snearing hissed. 'You gloat like a child.'

'You were the ones who let him get away from you. I can hardly be blamed for it.'

'What's this?' said another agent. 'Explain.'

Snearing opened his mouth.

'He calls himself White,' said Frith. 'He's from World. URCI, I believe. The local secret police got wind of his abilities and arrested him. They tortured him for weeks, clinging to their rather silly belief that the Talented are joining forces with your Technophobe terrorists and gathering into some sort of anti-government army. You might want to do something about that, by the way,' he remarked to Snearing.

Who looked about ready to pop. God, it was easy.

'They let him go when they couldn't find anything concrete to connect him to the Technophobes. And then they let him escape,' said Frith.

'*Let* him, you prick?'

'Well. You did try to get him back, so points for that. Luckily for me your police can't even manage to stop an eighteen-year-old from dancing off into the sunset.'

'Why didn't you prevent this?' said someone else, to Snearing.

'Oh . . . come *on*,' he snorted. 'Those provincial URCI idiots wouldn't bother to tell central government if the country was on fire. I had no idea they'd arrested a Talented! By the time I found out, they had already screwed it up!'

'Enough,' said Ghost Girl. 'Frith. You said this boy's Talent is unprecedented.'

God, yes. You have no idea how unprecedented. And he's the only one who even understands a tenth of how it works. He's a damned goldmine. He's my goldmine.

'Yes,' Frith said out loud. 'He needs to be controlled and studied. Carefully handled.'

'All the more reason you should give him back to us,' Snearing said. 'You don't even have the facilities to deal with something like him!'

'Frith is capable,' said Ghost Girl. 'We wouldn't have chosen him otherwise. In fact, it sounds like his programme is accelerating a lot more quickly than yours.'

Snearing actually shrank in his chair.

'Diplomatic issues,' he muttered. 'But I have people in place everywhere now. I'm getting it approved. I'm very close to getting it approved!'

'It must be approved in every World country by the next time we meet,' said Ghost Girl, looking around the table. 'You're all wasting time.'

Frith watched Snearing squirm. A sublime memory – one that would sustain him for a while to come. In truth, Ghost Girl's support of him had come as a surprise. He didn't like to be surprised.

It had been a while wrapping up, this time. Some agents had moderate success stories to supply, but in the end, he had come out on top. Ghost Girl dismissed each agent by name, and one by one they disappeared. Snearing glowered at Frith as he left.

Eventually, Frith was left alone with her.

She watched him. He could practically sense her prowling around him, weighing him up.

'What do you think of him?' she said, at last. 'This . . . White.'

Frith thought. There was something in him curiously reluctant to say anything definitive about White. Anything that might increase his chances of being taken away from Frith, just when he had found him.

'I don't know,' he said, at last. 'He seems extraordinary. And the other students are in awe of him. He charms them, in his own strange way. And they're a little afraid of him.'

'But what do you think of him?' Ghost Girl repeated. 'What is he like?'

Frith cocked his head. Strange question, coming from her. She had never shown that kind of interest in his recruits before.

'He's . . . lonely,' he said. 'Closed off. Understandable, really, from what I've been able to gather of his life so far.'

She appeared to think for a moment.

'You must keep him,' she said. 'You must keep him within arm's reach at all times. You mustn't let him get away from you. Don't give him any kind of way out from you.'

He wanted to ask why. But he knew she wouldn't answer. He did it anyway.

'Why is he important?' he said.

'If he's as powerful as you say, then he is certainly important. We need him.'

Even through the mask of her black avatar eyes, he could swear she was holding something back. Not lying, exactly.

Just not giving him everything. But then, that was nothing new. She never answered questions about herself, and neither did any of the other avatars. She never told him more than she had decided he needed to know.

It was beginning to grate on him.

'We need the powerful ones,' she said finally. 'Because It's coming. It's coming and they can stop it.'

She watched him a moment more.

He felt a gentle thrill of fear. He hated her for being able to do that to him. He hated her for bringing him this knowledge, the heart-freezing certainty that somewhere, in a stone building that seemed to represent all worlds and all things and life and matter and everything that ever was, something was trying to break free. Something that meant death.

Because It's coming.

He couldn't deny the power those words had over him. Over everyone who attended those meetings. Even now, after a predictably dull two-day journey back to Angle Tar, they still slithered in his brain at odd moments.

He was tired. He was always tired after these trips, wallowing helplessly in the repetitive nightmares that plagued him after a Castle meet. He wondered if the other agents went through the same thing.

The nightmares were always in the same place. In them he woke to find himself in a cold, gloomy stone room with four blank walls. A room in the Castle.

It had no door. No window. No way out. A horrible, urgent need to do something saturated him until he felt like he was drowning. A need to stop whatever it was prowling outside the room from getting in. Desperately scrabbling around for help, for a clue. Always nothing.

Then the despair, sliding up his back and across his shoulders and clutching at his heart.

They were hard to shake, these dreams. He would wake up, his skin dry and prickling, convinced he was still trapped there in the stone room. It took a disturbingly long time to clear the fog in his head and forcibly shift himself back to the real.

So preoccupied, he finished the last leg of his journey home, stepping down from the university coach and opening the front door to Red House.

And then he felt it.

It was early evening. Classes had finished for the day. The place should have been swarming with them: opening and shutting doors, bellowing at each other. He should have heard the echoes of raucous laughter. There were twenty so far this year – a good number. They made a lot of noise.

But as he walked through the front door, he felt it descend on him like a fog.

He made his way through the foyer, down the hallway.

Past the bedrooms, every door closed. Not a sound.

Into the dining room. Nothing.

Off to the side, into the communal study.

There, by the fireplace, sat Mussyer Tigh. In the opposite chair was a girl, hunched and still.

Tigh looked up. His face was serious.

'Frith,' he said. 'We've been waiting for you. They said you'd be back this afternoon.'

'Train delays. Where is everyone?'

Silence.

'Frith,' said Tigh again, awkwardly. 'Something's happened.'

'I'm aware of that,' said Frith. 'Why don't you explain exactly what it is?'

'It's really . . . I mean. It was really unexpected, I mean. If we'd known about it, of course we would have done something. It was always –'

'*You* tell me,' Frith interrupted, pointing to the girl. It was Areline, one of this year's Talented group. The beautiful one. The shining star of the class. The one the boys loved and the girls wanted to be. Some of her loveliness had been shocked out of her now, though. Her face was puffy and blotched.

For a moment, she wouldn't speak. He could hear Tigh's intake of breath, a preparation to bluster his way through. No patience for that. Frith's anger was rising and he fought to hold it back, choking it grimly on its leash.

'Areline,' he said, his voice soft and warm. 'Take your time. Tell me what happened.'

'It's Wren,' she said, her voice blurred. 'He's gone. I think it's my fault.'

'No, no. Don't blame yourself, child,' said Tigh. His eyes blinked to Frith mid-sentence. Frith hoped that the expression on his face was enough.

It was.

Tigh fell silent.

'Where has he gone?' said Frith.

'He. He left. He said he was never coming back. He took his bag and he left.'

Frith looked at Tigh.

It took a moment. His stupidity was maddening. He lumbered awkwardly out of the chair and stood to the side as Frith took it and sat down.

Frith leaned forward, his hands clasped loosely between his legs.

'Tell me the story,' he said to Areline. Slow and soft was the way; even at the same time as a voice inside told him to shake it out of her. He ignored the voice.

'He and White. You see. They've . . . they started fighting.'

Surprise. The two most Talented boys in the class. Competitive, naturally.

'We were friends, in the beginning, the three of us. Wren really liked him. I mean . . . I think he did. It's because . . . before White, Wren was the best, I mean he could already Jump. I can't even do that. Only Wren could Jump. But then White came. And White can do things I've never even heard of. None of us have. And he's . . . secretive, you know?'

Frith resisted the temptation to sigh.

He knew where this was going. He could hear it in her voice every time White's name came out of her lovely, swollen little mouth.

'Wren didn't like him, even though he pretended he did. It's obvious, really. He was jealous. And Wren and I . . .'

She stopped.

'You were seeing each other,' said Frith. The kindness had gone out of his voice.

'Yes. Well, I mean sort of. I mean, we'd gone out to dinner a few times.'

She fidgeted.

'But then White came, and I . . .'

'. . . wanted White more than Wren.'

'You don't have to say it like that,' she muttered.

'Mussyer Tigh, would you be so good as to fetch White for me? Doubtless you know where he is.'

Tigh left without a word. Frith kept his eyes on Areline, watched her gaze track Tigh to the door.

'Areline.'

She looked back at him with an effort. 'Um. In class today, they fought. I think Wren tried to pull him into a Jump or something. I'm not sure. It was bad. They both sort of half disappeared. It looked really odd.'

She stopped, and gulped. Her expression rippled, like she was about to vomit.

'Really odd,' she said. 'Gods, it was. Like they turned inside out for a moment.

And then they came back. White seemed fine. Just shocked. But Wren . . . he had blood all over his mouth. I think his nose had bled. White said he didn't hit him. He screamed. He *screamed* at White. He called him some things I've never even . . . Then he said that we were all pathetic and that he was wasting his time here, and he was going. I tried to stop him, but . . . he pushed me. He actually pushed me away from him.'

Her hand went to her chest. She looked close to tears.

'We looked for him,' she said. 'But he's gone. He used to disappear sometimes, in the evenings. He said he knew about the city's secret places. I think he's gone.'

The door opened, and Tigh walked back in, White shadowing him.

Frith stood.

'Thank you, Areline. Tigh, be so good as to take Areline back to her room, will you?'

'I think I should stay.'

'There's really no need,' said Frith pleasantly.

White was watching him, his body tense. He never once looked at Areline, even when she stopped next to him on her way past and put her fingers timidly on his arm.

Once they were alone, Frith smiled at White.

'Are you seeing Areline?' he asked.

'No!' said White, shocked. 'She is with Wren!'

Frith took a step forwards. White moved back. He looked ready to bolt. His eyes were dark, wary.

'Calm down,' said Frith. 'I'm not going to hurt you. I just want to know what happened.' Sometimes, the boy was so hard to read. He fascinated Frith because of that, like an exotic bird.

'Areline told you, did she not?'

'I want to hear you tell it.'

White stared at the carpet.

'Wren doesn't like me,' he said, at last.

'Why?'

'Because of Areline.'

'That's not the only reason, is it?'

White glanced at him.

'Why else, White?' said Frith. Now we would see how self-aware the prodigy was.

'I suppose because he wishes to be the best.'

'But you're better than him.'

White said nothing.

'Well? Are you or aren't you, in your estimation?'

'Yes.'

'Much better?'

'I do not know.'

'What did he do?'

White shifted uneasily.

'He . . . attacked me,' he said at last, reluctantly.

'Details, please.'

'He pulled me into the nothing. I thought he was pulling me into a Jump, but he stopped in the between place. He . . . hit me. He tried to leave me there.'

Frith sighed.

'Come here,' he said.

White stiffened. The hunted look faded back into his eyes.

'No.'

Frith folded his arms. 'What are you afraid of?'

White's mouth curled downwards in misery.

'That you will put me out on the street again,' he said.

For a moment, just a moment, Frith felt an urge to wrap his arms around White; anything to take that look of crushed pain away.

He pushed the urge down.

'White,' he said. 'This was not your fault. But you should have told me that you were having problems with Wren.'

'You are never here!' White blurted. 'I did not wish to burden you. I thought it . . . I thought it unimportant.'

'Nothing is unimportant where you are concerned. Sit down.'

White hesitated. Then moved to the chair.

The way he moved. Wren moved just like that, Frith had noticed. Carrying themselves like eels slipping through water. He wondered if they had ever noticed how alike they could be.

'Mussyer Tigh's reports on you concern me,' said Frith.

White tightened, staring into the fire.

'They concern me because what I see in them is a student who knows more than his own tutor.'

He had expected White to react favourably to this, but his eyes didn't move.

'But you already knew that, didn't you?' said Frith.

'I would not presume.'

'Let's presume for a moment.'

White worried at his lip with a tooth. 'Yes,' he said. 'I suppose I had hoped to find someone here to teach me something new. But . . .'

'You haven't,' said Frith. 'And frankly, White, I haven't yet found anyone better equipped to teach the Talent than you.'

White, to his credit, took his time with an answer.

'What?' he said eventually. 'What? What are you saying? You would like me to teach here?'

'What if I was?'

White watched him. Their eyes were locked.

Believe me. Believe every part of me, thought Frith. *Come on.*

'Teach? Teach everyone . . . here? No! Mussyer Tigh, he . . .'

'Tigh isn't even Talented, White. He was the best I could do at short notice, that's all. He'll be moved discreetly to another department. Don't worry about that.'

White shook his head over and over.

Frith's mind worked. He had to keep White. By any means necessary, Ghost Girl had said. He had to keep him here. More than that, he *wanted* to keep him here. Keep him close.

White was special.

'Look. I don't have time to care about finding the best person for the job,' he said. 'What I need is the most Talented person showing everyone else how to do what he can do. As far as I can tell, that is exactly what has been happening already. They flock to you, White.'

'They hate me!'

'No, they don't. Areline is half in love with you, as are the rest of them. She's just less cautious about showing it. Much to her regret now.'

'What of . . . what of Wren?'

'Wren will be found.'

White looked away.

'I did not mean to,' he said. 'He tried to hurt me.'

'So you hurt him back. It's the way of the world.'

Silence.

Frith felt his patience drain to its end, at last.

He stood. 'I'm tired, White. And now I have to spend the night looking for an over-emotional teenage boy. As for you. You have nowhere else to go, do you?'

White flinched at that, though he didn't deny it.

Frith sighed.

'So. It's really quite simple,' he said. 'I want you to teach here. Say yes, so I don't have to worry about it any more. Go to bed. Get some sleep. We'll talk about the details tomorrow.'

Frith watched White's face, working through some internal struggle.

Five seconds was all he would give him to make up his mind.

It took four.

Three days later, Frith was given a small, plain envelope that had been left in the communal study at Red House. His name was printed in careful handwriting on the outside.

Then he opened it, and saw who it was from.

It had to have been Jumped there.

There was no other way it could have found its way here from World so fast.

The message inside was written in a flowing, cursive hand, and it read:

One for you. One for me.
Snearing

PART TWO

PART TWO

What if all the world you think you know
Is an elaborate dream?

Trent Reznor

CHAPTER 15
ANGLE TAR

RUE

'What an exceedingly rude young man,' said someone above her.

Rue looked up at the man's voice.

It was the day of the monthly fair, where several villages from around the area congregated in her village square. Stalls with local produce from across the way, boulangers and charcuters and patissers, farmers with animals and meat to sell. Puppet shows for the children and a small travelling theatre usually added to the noisy throng, and today was no exception. The fair tended to attract all sorts of people who weren't local, and this man seemed to fit neatly into that category.

Rue had been sitting on the stone wall that bordered the square, waiting for Fern to finish up with a gaggle of children she had been treating for food poisoning back at the house. It was surprisingly cold for this time of year, and she'd been alone, wrapped in her flimsy beaded shawl and trying not to shiver, when it happened.

A boy had been meandering towards her sitting place, someone she vaguely recognised as one of several brothers who lived in the middle of the village. He wasn't even her age. Fourteen, if that. And as he'd sauntered past, he'd smiled and called her a 'witch whore'.

The words had fallen out of his mouth like he'd been remarking pleasantly on the weather. So casually in fact, that she hadn't at first understood what he'd said. It was only when he'd walked too far for her to hurl a pithy insult at him that it had registered.

It happened, occasionally. She kept out of the way of any villagers her age, these days – easier than getting into fights, with her spitting and hissing like a cat and looking stupid. Fernie told her to rise above it, which was the most ridiculously impossible advice she'd ever heard.

But she tried. She'd threatened a hex or two, which usually sent the younger ones running. It stopped her from doing what she really wanted to do, which was tear all their ignorant, ugly faces off.

She shrugged, regarding the stranger. He was quite slight, and older than usually caught Rue's attention. He had curling hair and a pleasantly non-descript face. Definitely too old, though. She wondered how she would politely disentangle herself from this one, and then decided that she wouldn't be so polite about it if he pressed.

'He's just a boy,' she said. 'They're stupid. They don't understand much.'

'And you're looking for a man,' said the stranger, with a faint smile.

'Not your sort of man,' Rue said with what she hoped was a derisive sniff. To her surprise, he laughed.

'I should hope not. My sort of man is definitely undesirable.'

'You town?'

The man spread his hands. 'It's obvious, isn't it? I've had everyone looking at me like a mark; the poor city fool with pockets full of money and no sense in how to spend it.'

'City, is it?' said Rue with a spark of interest. 'I've met city folk before; well, but only old Mussyer Hodger, and he left his city twenty years ago to come here, got some woman in trouble and booted out to the countryside by her family is the rumour, though you wouldn't think it to look at him.'

The man smiled widely. 'I can see you're the person to talk to around here.' He gestured beside her, and she realised he was asking her permission to sit with her on the wall. She smiled.

The man sat himself. 'May I ask your name?' he said.

'It's Vela Rue. And yours?'

'De Forde Say Frith.'

'How do you spell that, then?'

He told her.

'Four names?' said Rue, impressed.

'Actually the de Forde is just one name. My family name. It's very old.'

'Oh.'

'You don't recognise it?'

Rue shrugged. 'Sorry.'

'No, I apologise. I'm being ignorant of how the country works differently to town. I rarely visit.'

'You famous?'

Mussyer de Forde smiled. He seemed quite charming when he smiled. Rue was enjoying herself.

'No,' he said. 'Only to people who don't count. It's the

name that's well known. It would be nice, sometimes, to have a different one.'

'Oh, I shouldn't wish it,' Rue replied. 'I knew a girl a couple of villages over across the moors, and her child name was Rainsplat.'

Mussyer de Forde gazed at Rue, his eyes round.

'Her mother lived in a boggy area, see,' said Rue. 'So when it rained it made a splatting sound. She said it was her favourite noise. So she named her baby after it. Course the poor girl insisted everyone called her Rain. Mostly she got called Splat.'

'She would have been crucified anywhere else,' said Mussyer de Forde.

Rue smiled hesitantly, unwilling to admit that she hadn't understood the word.

'So you've your two names, Vela Rue. Are you studying to get your third?'

'I'm to be a hedgewitch.'

'Really? That's quite an ambition.'

Rue shrugged. 'It's the only thing worth wanting to be.'

'You wish to help people.'

Rue only smiled in reply. It was one thing to boast, it was another to give away all her secrets.

'Or perhaps you just wish to be more powerful than other people,' said Mussyer de Forde, looking out across the square.

Rue watched him for a moment. 'That's a nasty thing to wish,' she said in her most neutral voice.

He laughed. 'Now you're testing me,' he said. 'It's all right to wish for more power, Zelle Vela. Some people are built that way. Out in the country, with limited options, it's natural that many of those would gravitate to hedge-witchment. A hedgewitch is the most powerful and respected figure in the community, save the Mayor.'

Rue rolled her eyes. 'The Mayor's the fattest one with the most farmland,' she said. 'But hedgewitchment, you can only do that with talent. I was picked out of hundreds.'

'Really?' said Mussyer de Forde in admiration.

Rue felt the past few words catch up with her and blushed. 'Well, not hundreds. But there were lots of us. And Fern said I was the only one there with potential. Fernie's the witch around here. She does this village and the two other villages on the hills. Across the border it's another man.'

'I would love to meet her, but I'm sure she's much too busy.'

'Mostly,' Rue said, 'but she'll be here in a minute to take a turn round the fair; she always does if she can. You could meet her then.'

'I'd be delighted,' he said.

When it came to it, Rue thought Fernie might have been mad with her for introducing her to a stranger. Fernie was a little cold with him and didn't invite conversation. But when Mussyer de Forde suddenly (and quite bravely, Rue thought, considering how the meet had been going thus far) announced that he would love to visit them both at the house at a time suitable, Fern agreed.

He would call tomorrow afternoon.

'Didn't you like him, then?' said Rue, after he had gone off into the throng of the fair.

Fern sighed. 'You are a forthright little thing, aren't you?'

'Sorry.'

'Don't be. You don't have a way with strangers, that's all – I was just surprised that you'd made friends with him so fast.'

Rue decided not to be irritated at Fernie's inference, as she rather fancied it a compliment that usually she wasn't friendly with people she didn't know.

'Maybe,' she said. 'But he's from the city, he says. I thought it might be interesting to talk to him.'

Fernie only smiled vaguely in reply, and changed the subject.

As it happened, Rue didn't have much time to dwell on the Mussyer, as she was busy until late into the night. Fernie had two visitors that evening, and insisted on keeping Rue with her throughout both meetings. The visitors had taken quite a bit of persuading, but Fernie was clever at it. Firm, unyielding but understanding, making Rue out to be quiet and secretive. Not the sort to blab, in other words. Fernie's reputation was enough to seal it, with the added realisation of each visitor that they wouldn't get what they'd come for until they agreed to include Rue.

One was straightforward enough – an embarrassing ailment that could only be whispered about under cover of darkness. The remedy had already been made up. The recipient was duly awed. No one ever realised that their problems were as common as mud. The second was a woman from the Flats who claimed she was so much in love that she was dying inside. Rue almost believed her – the woman was haggard and frail, and only in her thirties.

Fernie stayed up late to counsel her, and Rue soon grew bored. The only thing that consoled her through it was her silent determination never to cause herself such ludicrous misery.

In the morning, Fernie had her go to a farm over three miles away to collect a package of pickles and jam that was owed. It was a tediously long trip, but after the first half hour she grew into it, sucking in the pleasure of being alone and unfettered. And she would still make it back with plenty of time to spare before Mussyer de Forde was due to come by.

On the way back, she started to feel the first pangs of real hunger and stopped at a blackberry bush to eat her fill. She had well over an hour before the visit, she was pleased to note as she approached the back of Fernie's cottage. She needed to give her purple-stained fingers a good scrub, tidy her hair and wash the mud off her boots.

It was the voice that stopped her. A man's voice. She'd gone through Fernie's back gate without thinking; only visitors used the front door. She walked through towards the kitchen, and then she heard it.

'. . . not just you, Zelle Penhallow,' said the man through the kitchen door. 'They are all required to do it. I've already visited every informant in this district and not one of them has anything of worth to offer. She's mine by law, and you know it.'

Rue halted outside the closed door, caught.

There was a long silence. Then came Fernie's voice, and Rue felt odd hearing it. She'd never once heard Fernie speak with such a tone: bitter and flat.

'I'm aware of the law, Mussyer de Forde, but don't you

169

pretend that what you're doing's for the law. And I know what I've found. I knew it a long time ago when she first came to me. And you can't bring me up for that neither, for if you hadn't visited out of the blue, I would never've told you about it and you would never've known, so there we are. But when you're here, I know I can't lie to you and I hate you for it.'

'I know you do,' said Frith, sounding amused rather than angry. 'I admire you for it. But I don't understand why you don't want to give her up.'

'Because I know what'll happen to her if I do. She's a good girl, if a little flighty, but she'll grow out of that. She's got the head for hedgewitchment.'

'You mean to say, she's arrogant enough for it,' said Frith. 'In which case, you're correct.'

There was silence.

Rue stood, heart beating fit to burst. They couldn't be talking about her. They couldn't be.

'I'll not give her up to you,' said Fernie in a low voice, though she sounded like she had no fight left. 'The gods only know what you'll do to her.'

'I'm not really sure what you're so upset about,' came Frith's voice. 'All we want to do is educate her. Give her a once-in-a-lifetime chance to be part of something greater. Teach her to be powerful. Teach her about the world.'

'Oh, will you indeed? You'll tell her all about it and what it's like? You'll tell her about what happens to people like her in a world that ain't ready for 'em? Will you tell her about Oaker?'

More silence. Rue held on to her breath.

'You'd better come in, Rue,' said Fernie in a louder voice. 'I know you're there.'

Rue's stomach rolled over. She pushed the door open and crept in.

Fernie and Mussyer de Forde sat at the kitchen table together as if they'd known one another for years. It was clear now to Rue that she had been played by this man, that he and Fernie were just about the oldest acquaintances you could have, thick as thieves in fact; and wasn't that interesting and just a little bit humiliating?

'You know each other, then,' she said. 'Don't you?'

'Not really,' said Fernie, looking tired. Mussyer de Forde was leaning back in his chair, alert and serious. 'We've only met once or twice, a long time ago.'

'So tell me,' said Rue, her voice coming out unsure. How was she supposed to be at this moment? What was the right reaction?

'Why don't *you* explain it?' said Fernie, tossing her head to Frith with an angry glance.

He seemed only too happy. He rocked forwards, fixing his eyes on Rue. She tried to stare back, to show him what would happen if he lied to her, to show him she was strong and hard and could take it.

'Sit, please, Zelle Vela.'

'No.'

'Very well. I come from the city, as you know.'

'Oh, so that was true, was it?' Rue said.

'Certainly. I work for the university in Parisette.'

'Where's that?'

'You know it as Capital.'

'Capital City?'

'The very one. The biggest and most powerful university in Angle Tar in the biggest and most powerful city. We have a special department for the development and training of what is called Talent, in general terms.'

Rue digested this.

'And I have it,' she said finally. 'Talent?'

'It's possible. It would take a lot of testing and development to see whether you really do, or to be more accurate – whether you do over a certain level of ability. A lot of people are Talented, but almost none of them can do what we're looking for.'

'What is it, this Talent? What does it do?'

Mussyer de Forde held up a hand. 'First, before we can discuss anything further, I need your consent.'

'For what?'

'To take you to Capital for testing.'

Rue looked at Fernie, who was gazing steadily at the flagstone floor and wouldn't raise her eyes.

'Fern?'

Fernie didn't blink.

'Zelle Penhallow knows you have to make this decision on your own,' said Mussyer de Forde smoothly. 'I would like you to think about it. I'll be here for another two days, I'd say. You have that long.'

'If I say yes,' said Rue slowly, 'you'd answer all my questions before we get to Capital?'

'Yes, I would.'

Rue looked at him closely. His face was open.

'And this testing . . . how long would it take?'

'It's hard to say. Several months. Longer, perhaps.'

Rue's mouth fell open. That was long. That was a long time. No wonder Fernie looked unhappy.

'Why would it take so long?'

'I'm afraid I can't discuss it.'

'But you think I have something special, something really rare.'

'No. Your mistress does.'

Rue looked at the older woman and saw a stranger. She'd always seen someone round and wise, and kinder than she ought to be, and sometimes annoying, but there, always just there and real. Now she looked like an old woman Rue had never met before.

'Fern?' she asked. 'Why didn't you never say anything?'

Fernie shook her head. Her lips were thin and tight.

Mussyer de Forde stood up. 'I'll leave you alone to discuss things. Zelle Penhallow knows what she can and cannot talk about. You may ask her anything you wish but she may not choose to answer. Don't think her being hard with you – I'm the cause. There are some things she is not allowed to say. She'll let you know where I'm staying, for your decision.'

Fernie tossed him a look of pure contempt. Rue felt momentarily scared seeing it. He had bowed his head and now turned to leave.

'Good evening to you both.'

He closed the kitchen door gently.

Fernie sighed, massaged her cheeks.

'Sit down, dear,' she said.

Rue sat.

CHAPTER 16
ANGLE TAR

RUE

Mussyer de Forde had been silent for some time.

Rue was not inclined to rouse him from his thoughts. The past day of travel through endless landscape and crowds of people had shown her how small she was, and she felt glad to be going towards a place where she might mean something again.

This coach was the final leg of their journey to Capital City. They had taken a public coach from her village to the train station, which was many miles up the coast and further than Rue had been since she was a child. The station was a short squat building on the outskirts of a provincial little city, long and low, and filled with dirt and sound and people, always so many people.

Then the train, which she had taken once as a girl and had vaguely frightened memories of, her recall clouded by painful levels of noise and steam. In the end, it had been quite ordinary, though she loved the way the landscape slid past and around her, as if she flowed through it, and sat within the natural order of things. Fernie had packed her a substantial lunch and she had offered some shyly to

Mussyer de Forde, but he'd had none of it, professing himself too tired to eat.

After many hours, and several more stops at crowded platforms, they had left the last of the southern vegetable plains behind. The vista outside Rue's window shifted gradually, until the few scattered and huddled farm buildings had changed into a never-ending array of walls. And tall, how tall! There was nothing past a second-floor hay barn in the villages she knew.

The train station in Capital had been an airy, beautiful building with the highest ceiling Rue had ever seen, but she hadn't been able to pause much – the crowds had swept them along. Mussyer de Forde had hurried her through, stopping outside the station at another coach. This one was far grander than the one that had taken them from her village to the train, though, all that time ago. It was not a plain black but a gleaming blue, with an image of an eagle clutching a key painted in lovely detail on its side. In spite of the swathes of people milling about, there were only three or four getting onto this coach, and, noticing her confusion, Mussyer de Forde told her that it was a university coach, reserved for university teachers, students and staff only. He flashed a key he kept on a chain around his neck to the driver, and they boarded.

Fernie had told her a little about Capital City. Though claiming to never have been there, she had described it in some detail to Rue. They had sat at the kitchen table together, as they had done so many times before, eating, talking, working. Only this time would probably be the last time, and for who knew how long?

'I know you'll go, so it's no good pretending you're still thinking about it,' Fernie had said.

'Fern,' Rue protested.

'No, it's fine. Look Rue. I know you . . . I ain't doing this right.' A sigh. A pause. Then: 'You're young and headstrong, and you can do something that most people don't even know exists. I don't know how strong you are in it. I pray not very.'

'You pray?' said Rue, unable to stop herself.

Fernie waved a hand irritably. 'It's an expression. Stop interrupting, be a good girl for once.'

Rue fell silent.

'Now,' said Fernie. 'You know I'm sorry about the whole thing. You don't know how much. I should've told you what I long suspected. But I didn't want you to have it, Rue. The Talent. It brings nothing but trouble. But it's no good telling you that either, as you don't care right now, and why should you? You've been given an adventure, and you'll never be right in your life if you don't go to Capital and let Mussyer de Forde poke around inside your head and do his stupid tests. It's all right. I'll get a prentice in training to help me out once in a while. I'll get Mewan's girl from the Flats to come over once or twice a week, something like that.'

'Deer? She's messy in her prep work and she don't know any of the local herbs,' said Rue. She wanted to protest to let Fern know she cared, but not enough so that Fern would see sense and make her stay.

'Deer's more advanced in her training than you are and knows what she's about, and don't think I don't know what

176

you're doing,' said Fernie. 'I'll be fine, and you'll be fine, and Deer'll do, and you'll be back before you know it.'

Come back to this? thought Rue. Only if I fail.

She was determined not to fail.

It wasn't in Rue's nature to lie and say she didn't want to go, and Fern saw it plain as day, written all across her body. But still, she felt awfully guilty about being so eager to leave and do something Fernie clearly disapproved of.

But then again, Fern had kept the truth from her, hadn't she? Rue could be angry about that, if she wanted to be. She wondered when the old witch had first known what it was she had.

So Rue went to Mussyer de Forde by herself, to the small cottage where he was renting a room over in the next village, and he smiled when she said she wanted to go with him and told her to call him Frith.

They left a week later. Her last image of Fernie had been of her stood on her doorstep, framed by the rounded weight of her cottage, looking at Rue sitting in the coach. The coach had started to move and Fernie had gone inside almost immediately, firmly closing her front door. Rue had felt a small rush of sickness then. Fernie was her weight. Fernie looked after her and told her when she made mistakes and tutted when she said something wrong and guided her. She was deliberately discarding her only protection, leaving behind the only person who cared about her.

But Rue was determined not to be the sort of girl that was cowed by adventure, now that it had finally come and found her. She would prove herself.

The university coach was getting busy. The last stop they

177

had halted at had taken on several new passengers, and some of their clothes had been so outlandish, Rue had had to force herself not to stare. Frith had caught her open-mouthed gaze, nevertheless. She'd expected him to be angry but he'd smiled secretively at her.

No one was talking to anyone else, and so there they all sat in utter silence. The outside world began to intrude over the creaking and rumbling of the coach, and Rue listened keenly. There was a lot of shouting, words she tried to catch as they went past. There were brief snatches of smells she half recognised. It had begun to rain, and she watched people totter past with enormous shades held over their heads, jostling each other for space. Sometimes they even walked in the streets, and more than once she'd seen someone dance hurriedly out of the way when a coach had come rumbling up behind them. There was a lot of joyous swearing and shaking of fists. At first it had made her nervous, but as it seemed so much to be the way strangers interacted here, she presumed it normal and began to enjoy each short drama when it happened. Frith had apparently gone to sleep. Rue supposed that he found all this completely regular, even wearisome. But how could you sleep with such a racket going on?

There was a busy shuffling of people for the next hour or so, alighting from the coach and heading off determinedly into the rain. Rue wondered if she should wake Frith – they were almost the only people left. But in the strange manner he'd displayed over the last few hours, almost as if he could read her mind, he beat her to it and spoke without opening his eyes.

'Nearly there, Rue. Look out of the window and you'll see a yellowish tower poking up from the general mess of buildings we're heading towards. That is the university tower, and those buildings will be your home for the next few months.'

Rue peered out, trying to dredge up the required expression of excitement at what she would see. In truth, now it came to it, she felt a little nerve-sick. What if it all went wrong? What if it turned out she had less Talent than a cat?

No, she told herself. You're special, you know it. Stop this.

The yellow tower was obvious right away. It rose up magnificently from a sprawling nest of low buildings that surrounded it like a garden. All in all, it didn't look how she'd imagined. She'd thought of a series of grand monuments, pristine white, mysterious. Apart from the tower, the university appeared to be a clustered collection of mismatched buildings on a hill, albeit surrounded by an impressive wall. She would have been more awestruck if this had been the first thing she'd seen on leaving the countryside, but a day of travelling had rapidly hardened her.

The entrance gates were standing open and their coach rattled on through. Rue looked about as they went past – there were two small posts on either side with two plump, bored-looking guards stationed there. They moved on from the sprawling front driveway and started to roll down the side of the main layout.

When they alighted a few minutes later, it was in front

of a squat set of houses made of red stone. Frith had confirmed that everything they had passed was part of the university. Rue couldn't imagine a place so big. The red stone buildings, she was told, exclusively housed all those students who had specifically been recruited to study the Talent.

Despite his promises to the contrary, Frith had in fact told her very little of what exactly the Talent was on their long journey to the city. He'd evaded her ten thousand questions with an easy manner that should have provoked her but hadn't.

What Rue had managed to ascertain was this: the Talent surfaced in people at a young age, and to varying degrees. It was rare, and very hard to spot. In most of those with Talent, the ability was surface only. In a tiny handful of people it manifested more strongly, but it was almost impossible to test. In fact, Frith had said, there was only one man in all of Angle Tar qualified enough to decide how much Talent an individual had, and his name was Mussyer White. It would be he whom Rue and others like her would be having lessons with in order to test her.

What was the Talent, and how could you tell who had it? Frith had smiled at her awkward attempts to ask this in different ways and merely said that he couldn't speak of it because he didn't know; but that she would, soon enough.

They got out of the coach together and he took her up to the front door, which was opened before he had knocked. A woman with flickering, blinking mouse eyes peered at them both.

'Mussyer Frith!' she said. 'We weren't expecting you 'til tomorrow.'

'I'm a constant surprise,' said Frith. 'This young lady is special; I collected her myself.'

The mouse woman looked Rue up and down. 'I'm sure. Room fourteen, is it?'

'If it's vacant,' said Frith easily. 'Now I shall have to leave you, Rue. This is Zelle Penafers Hannah. She runs Red House, your new home. She'll look after you while you're here, and give you your itinerary and map. Everything you need.'

Rue felt a little abandoned but was determined not to show it. She smiled and bowed to the mouse woman, who did not acknowledge it.

'Until we meet again,' said Frith.

'When will that be?'

'Not for a few days, I'm afraid. Work we must. You'll be fine.'

He climbed back into the coach, and she watched it rattle away. As she turned back to the open doorway, she found the mouse woman had disappeared.

Good beginning, she thought, bending to pick up her battered luggage bags. She lurched into the hallway and thought better about kicking the door shut, bumping it with her side to swing it closed.

'Zelle . . .' She thought back. 'Penafers?'

Silence. It was a long hallway lined with doors, all of which were shut. She stood for a moment.

Fourteen, wasn't it.

She walked carefully along, looking at each door as she passed. Four. Six. Eight.

The lighting in here was terrible. Half the lamps weren't even lit.

Twelve. Fourteen. This was it. She grappled with the handle, hoping it wasn't locked. It swung open easily.

The first thing she noticed was that it was quite small. The second thing she noticed was that, compared to the hallway, it was quite bright. The third thing she noticed was that there was a girl with a very minimalist attitude towards clothing reclining on the narrow bed.

Rue dropped her bags. They made a series of thumping sounds as they hit the floor.

'Oh,' said the girl. 'You must be a new one.'

'I'm sorry, I've the wrong room.'

'No, I don't think so. It's been empty for ages, and it's the smallest one, so no one wanted it.'

Rue tried not to stare. The girl was wearing a dress made of very thin material, so thin that it looked like she wore nothing at all. It clung to every cave and corner of her flesh and stopped short of her knees. Her hair was very fair and frizzy, so that it stuck out in wispy waves from her head, and she was knobbly slim.

'You're quite pretty, aren't you?' she said. 'Allow me to enquire after your family name.'

And she was aristocratic. Only aristocrats spoke like that.

'It's Vela. My familiar's Rue. What's yours?'

The girl broke into a short stream of giggles. 'Oh my,' she said. 'You're from the country, aren't you? I wasn't sure at first but your dress, and that accent. Oh my.'

Rue stared at her in irritation. 'Why are you in this room, then, if it's not yours?'

'It's quieter in here. I come to read.' She did have her hand on a book.

'Why do you read with hardly no clothes on?'

The girl giggled again. It was starting to grate. 'Well, what do *you* wear to bed? Woollen pyjamas?'

They watched each other. The girl broke first. Rue felt triumphant.

'You don't look Talented, but I suppose that's a good thing.'

'You don't look Talented either,' said Rue.

'No one does, that's the point. Did you really just get here?'

'Yes.'

'You'll have History with us tomorrow, then. You've missed half the autumn term already. That will be a lot of catching up.'

Rue shifted on her feet, aching for the girl to leave. 'I shall cope, I'm sure.'

'Can you hook yet?'

'What?' said Rue, annoyed.

'Hook, you know? I can. But I suppose I have an advantage, my brother is Talented as well. He taught me some of it last winter, when we finally found out I had been accepted here. I cannot wait to Jump for the first time, though.'

Rue listened to this with resentful curiosity, trying to comb out anything useful she could from the babble. The girl must have noticed her strained expression, because she smiled.

'You don't know what the Talent is, do you? Well, why would you. I only know because of my brother. I'm surprised you weren't told on the way here, though. A recruiter picked you up, didn't they?'

Rue shrugged.

The girl slid off the bed, clutching her book. The thin nightgown ruffled briefly upwards to the tops of her thighs.

'My family name is Pralette. My familiar is Lea, though. Only Mussyer White insists on calling me Zelle Pralette, as if he still lives in the last century, so please don't call me that.'

'All right,' said Rue, warming to the constant chatter, despite herself. It was better than no talk at all, and listening was easy enough.

'You should come for breakfast at eight. It's in the dining room. You're too late for supper but you can go to the kitchen and eat anything you like. You wouldn't be able to do that in other university houses but we're treated quite well here. They're a bit afraid of us, I think. Sometimes I like that, but other times it's a bit annoying. And it makes me feel sad.'

Rue didn't quite know what to say to that. For the first time in her life, she began to understand what it might be like to talk to someone insistent on being truthfully blunt at every opportune moment.

'All right,' she said. 'Where's the dining room, then?'

'It's just down the corridor, but don't worry, I shall knock on your door and take you with me in the morning. All these doors look alike. And then I shall take you to class. Mouse hasn't told me I should but she won't worry herself about it, I am sure.'

Rue was delighted. 'You mean Zelle Penafers? She does look like a mouse!'

'She's useless,' said Lea airily. 'I shouldn't think on her at all. She's not afraid of us, she just thinks we're all pointless. I shall complain to my father about her, I think. He's on the university board, you know. Some people think that's why I got a place here, but I've been showing Talented signs since I was little, so.'

Rue had time to wonder at the oddness of someone who said she wanted peace and quiet to read, but created so much noise instead, as Lea stepped delicately over her discarded bags and whipped out of the open door.

'I shall collect you in the morning,' she sang as she walked off.

Rue watched her go, then hauled her bags inwards and closed the door.

The room wasn't bad, all things considered. It had a mismatched look which might have perturbed some people, but that Rue liked; the furniture was solid and there was a decent-sized grate. She wondered where the bathroom was and how many people she was sharing it with. Then she sat on the bed, and thought about her situation.

It was an odd one, there was no denying it. She was far from everything she had ever been sure about in her life, far from the faces she knew and the sights she'd seen a thousand times. She was in a room, in a house, in a place, in a city. *The* city, in fact, Capital, a place she'd only heard of and as a child decided was populated with giants and fairies, so unreal had it seemed to her. She was here because she might be able to do something only five other people her age could do. Five other people they'd been able to find, at least. Frith had told her that there were only six new Talented students that year, including herself, which was quite a low figure. Sometimes it could be as much as twenty.

And she still didn't know what the Talent was. All she could think about it was that it seemed to be to do with the way she dreamed, the way she thought, and the way she saw the world. It didn't seem like much of a skill, more an accident, but she supposed the skill was what she was here to learn. And then what? Would she be put to work? Being Talented seemed to be a very valuable asset. What could she do with it?

She sighed and lay down on the bed. Would anyone care about her here? Not that it mattered. It never had. She cared for herself and that should be enough. Perhaps she would think about her favourite collection of dreams, though, and see if she couldn't revisit one of them tonight, and comfort herself.

When she woke, it was to the sound of furious knocking.

'Rue! Rue!' blared a shrill little voice outside her door.

She looked around. The curtains were fastened shut, but the crack of light on the floor told her it was morning. She sat up, horrified.

'Rue! Rue! Get up!'

'Wait!' she called, her voice crackling with sleep. 'Wait a minute! I'm not . . . I'm just getting dressed!'

'I thought country folk were used to getting up early,' said Lea through the door. 'My nanny was from Rochelette and she always woke up at half past five, even if she'd gone to bed two hours previously. She said it was ingrained in her.'

Rue hopped about frantically to the background stream of words from the corridor. Lea's voice was actually quite musical, if you ignored what she was saying and listened to the rhythm of it. Rue hadn't washed, hadn't even undressed! It didn't matter. She needed Lea and would have to make do. She ran the tap and splashed her face with cold water, then peered at herself in the mirror and fluffed her hair.

'Come on, come on, I'm hungry,' Lea wheedled. 'It's eggs today and if we're late they'll all be gone. The boys are pigs.'

Boys! And me looking like a truffler's backside!

Rue sighed, stepped back, and opened the door.

'Did you even get undressed last night?' said Lea in delight. She was looking smart in wide pants with a perfect crease and a crossed blouse in the style that all the women in Capital seemed to be wearing, from what Rue had seen yesterday.

'I fell asleep,' said Rue crossly.

'Well, you look terrible, but that never matters when you're pretty. Come on.'

She bounced off and Rue followed. The entire way there Lea didn't stop talking, even though she was in front of Rue and half her words were lost. Rue looked around as they traipsed along, trying to memorise their route.

It turned out that they had to leave through a back door and cross the vegetable garden to get to the dining room. The garden was hemmed in by walls on all four sides, and looked lovely. She wondered if they grew medicine herbs here. Lea wouldn't pause for anything, though, saying in a determined fashion that she was a 'real demon' if she didn't get to eat in the mornings.

The dining room was small but quite grand, big enough to seat a hundred people at least. The tables were solid, varnished trewsey wood, from what she could tell, and the light was bright and pleasing. It was odd to see so much space and realise almost no one would be using it that year. Three of her fellow students were huddled together on the table nearest what she presumed to be the kitchen door, and there was one dark-haired girl who sat on her own at another table, her hands wrapped around a steaming bowl and her eyes focused on a book.

'That's Freya, sat by herself like a friendless prawn,' said Lea, not bothering to lower her voice. If the dark-haired girl heard her, she gave no sign of it. 'And the blonde one is Lufe. The fat one is Marches, and the thin bendy one is Tulsent.'

Rue stared at the three boys as they approached. She was resolved not to put out the impression that she was shy and nervous. They gave as good as they got.

The boy named Lufe had thick blonde hair that curled and flopped all over his head. He was the most aggressive of the three, openly looking Rue up and down with a lazy kind of smile she instantly disliked. Marches was hardly fat, though a good deal bigger than the other two. He seemed unconcerned about her arrival, as if he wished to give off an apathetic air. Tulsent she could barely read, as his glasses were so thick they obscured half his face. He did appear to be looking at her, but she couldn't be completely sure. One of his legs was drawn up to his chest in a most uncomfortable-looking position.

The thing that astonished her the most about them, though, was their age differences. Lufe looked almost like a man. Marches was perhaps her age or a little younger. Tulsent seemed barely out of his childhood. The dark-haired girl named Freya was harder to place, but she looked at least nineteen or twenty.

'This is Rue,' Lea told the others. 'Vela Rue. She got here last night.'

'Where do you come from, then?' drawled Lufe. He was definitely aristocratic. He and Lea could be brother and sister.

'From Kernow,' said Rue coolly.

'Never heard of it. Is that in the country?'

'Yes.'

'A country lass. You must be a polytheist.'

'Well, don't you know all the big words,' said the apparently fat one, Marches.

Lufe waved a hand airily. 'Just because you're thick as pig shit.' He swept his gaze back to Rue. 'So, are you?'

'No,' said Rue firmly, without a clue what the word meant.

'Yes you are. Grad and Buc and Threya and all that. All those made-up gods.'

'My family are polytheists, Lufe,' said Lea. 'Your point?'

'I think you just made it.'

Lea drew in a shocked breath. 'I'll have you know my family is one of the oldest in Capital, you ignorant prigger!'

'Come come, let's not fight,' said Marches, with a grin

that meant exactly the opposite. 'At least none of you are atheists.'

'Atheists are freaks,' Lea snapped.

Rue gave up trying to follow the conversation, and noticed Marches staring at her.

'So how Talented are you, then?' he said.

Lea sighed. 'Let's get some food.' She walked away without waiting for a response from Rue, who hesitated for a moment, and then followed her into the kitchen.

It was a homely place. The three stoves were familiar-looking cast-iron affairs, and a fire burned cheerfully in the enormous grate dominating the end wall. It was empty of people, but large dishes of food were set out on the counter tops in the middle of the room. Lea walked straight up to them and took a plate from a stack. She started ladling various spoonfuls of food onto it as she talked.

'Plates there, help yourself. There's a lot of choice today – sometimes they've only one or two things, I've no notion why that might be.'

'Must depend what they can get in the markets each morning,' said Rue.

Lea looked surprised. 'I never thought of it like that. I suppose you're right.' She gave Rue a sidelong look. 'Don't pay attention to Marches. He asks everyone that question, as if the Talent can be quantified so quickly. Actually he asks you as a test, not because he thinks you'll know the answer. To see what sort of person you are, you see. If you say you're very Talented, he knows you're cocksure. If you say not very, he knows you're meek. If you say you don't know, he knows you're uncertain of yourself.'

'There's no good answer, then,' said Rue, grabbing two warm eggs. They rocked gently around her plate as she moved.

'Quite. He just wants to make you feel stupid. He's like that. Tulsent is sweet, a bit young for all this. Lufe is just Lufe. Freya ignores everyone completely, and so everyone ignores her.'

Lea had somehow managed to fit three eggs, a huge hunk of broche bread, a slice of ham and a small pile of scones onto her plate. As Rue watched on in amazement, she picked up a spoon and ladled a torrent of jam onto the scones.

'So how did you know about the Talent?' said Lea. 'Do you have someone else in your family with it?'

Rue shrugged. 'Don't know. Never knew my parents. They put me on a farm when I was a baby. The farm owners never even saw who put me there. They were glad to raise me – they needed every hand they could get and only had two children of their own.' She picked up a scone and squeezed it before setting it on her plate. It had a firm crust but the middle was soft, springy sponge. She thought about dewberry jam but decided on apricot. As she ladled the jam onto her scone, she became aware that Lea had stopped talking, and was staring at her.

'What?' she said.

'You were an orphan?'

'Right.'

'I've never met one before.'

'Chances are you have,' said Rue, offhand. 'They're never talked about, but there's a few. Especially in cities, I'll bet. Not so many in the country, where big families are likely to adopt an unwanted kiddie and say nothing more of it.'

'How do you know all this?' said Lea. For once, she was in thrall to Rue, who walked back to the dining room not knowing if they should sit with the boys – it seemed wrong, somehow, to assume she would be included on her first day. So she chose a table next to them. Lea sat opposite her.

'Why are you sitting there?' said Lufe to Lea.

'Hush, I'm listening to something more interesting than you.' Lea focused her gaze on Rue.

'Don't know how I know, I just thought about it a lot, and I reckon that's the way it goes,' said Rue, starting to enjoy the rapt attention the higher born girl was giving her.

'So did they put you to work? Did you have to . . . harvest fields, or something?'

Rue laughed, rolling her egg to crack the shell. 'Gods, no! I'm not big or strong enough. Girls usually look after the animals, and the garden, vegetables and herbs. And the household chores. They hired men for the fieldwork. I wouldn't even be able to operate any of them field machines they used.'

'Animals, how lovely! That must have been a wonderful job to have,' said Lea, and proceeded to rattle off the names and types of all the pets she had had as a child. Rue didn't want to disavow Lea of the pretty picture in her head. Animals, in Rue's experience, were hard work, messy, demanding and disloyal. And only occasionally sweet enough to make it nice to keep them. She wondered where the egg had come from as she ate it. They must have chickens kept somewhere in the university. She wouldn't mind tending to them, if they needed the help. Chickens were silly but uncomplicated little creatures, and Rue had always enjoyed moving amongst them, feeding them their grain, feeling in their nest boxes for eggs, watching their fat bodies hop clumsily out of the way as she went past.

It wouldn't be so bad here, she thought. Lea was nice, and her room was nice.

It was a good start.

Rue had a dream that night.

She was walking along the corridor outside her bedroom, trying to remember where the kitchen was. The light was too dark for her to see properly, or perhaps it was that she couldn't open her eyes wide enough. She shuffled along, desperately hungry, feeling the walls with her fingers.

There was a glimmer of light up ahead, and when she got to it she was relieved to find that it spilled out from underneath the kitchen door. Someone had left the lamps lit, and the place was warm and bright.

Rue crept to the massive ovens, opening one of the doors and flinching as it creaked. There were the few scones left over from that morning's breakfast. She took out two and crossed to the enormous table squatting in the middle of the tiled floor, placing them on the top while she looked for the jams.

'Hello,' said a voice behind her.

Her heart stopped. Please don't let it be one of the boys, she begged silently. How would it look, grubbing for food in the middle of the night? Lufe especially would enjoy that so much he probably wouldn't ever forget it.

At first the owner of the voice seemed hidden to her, a disembodied sound. Then she noticed something moving forwards from a shadowed corner, over by the pantry doors.

It was a boy, maybe a couple of years older than her – maybe even her age, though it was hard to tell. The light must have been a little funny in here, because his eyes shone like knife blades catching the light. But the more she stared at him, the more she realised that they were coloured that way. Like twin silver mirrors.

Her mouth fell open.

He was slim and willowy. His face was a little odd, something in the way the features were arranged deeply unfamiliar. As he moved past the kitchen lamps, his eyes reflected the light.

'Don't be alarmed,' he intoned as Rue stared at him. 'I come in peace.' Then issued from his mouth a series of wild choking sounds that she finally began to understand was laughter.

'Who by all the gods are you?' she said in glowing astonishment.

'By no gods,' he said. 'Just myself, and all the fun that comes with that.' His voice was ordinary, and strangely jarring coming from such a body.

He made his way slowly towards her as he talked, moving quite abnormally. She later realised that it was how a cat walked, picking up its paws and placing them down with fastidious care. It looked bizarre when it was done on two legs.

'You don't make much sense,' said Rue, still too shocked to process anything much.

'Maybe I will in the future,' he commented, then collapsed onto a chair by the kitchen table with an oily gesture. He stretched out a hand and picked up one of the scones she had put on the table, tearing it apart with his slender fingers and throwing small pieces into his mouth. He did it with an air of intimacy, as if the two of them had done this countless times, sat up late together in the kitchen eating scones. Rue had no clue on how she was supposed to act.

'Who are you?' she asked again, instead.

'Patience, girl,' he replied. He didn't spare her a glance.

They sank into silence. Rue tried to pull upwards out of her confusion, but the more she fought, the easier it seemed to give up.

She watched him eat the last of the scone. He turned his head and his mouth filled her vision, curled at one end in a faint smile. She watched his lips open and words fall out.

'I come back for the food,' he said. 'Sometimes it just doesn't compare.'

'Are you a new student?' Rue managed.

'No, not new,' he said, his tone careful and amused. 'But I do know this place. And I wanted to tell you something. I wanted to tell you that they'll kill you, you know.'

'What?' Rue managed, unsure if she had heard him right.

'If they can't use you, they'll kill you, to make sure no one else can have you.'

He looked at her. His strange silver eyes gleamed.

'Be very careful,' he said.

She woke.

CHAPTER 17
ANGLE TAR

RUE

'Mussyer White is the only Talented tutor in all of Angle Tar, did I tell you that before? I've got your lesson plan here, look, but I had to basically pry it from Penafers Mouse, as if she can ever rouse herself to care one centime for any of us. Are you listening?'

Rue fiddled with the hem of her dress, trying to look like she was listening. She was used to hours alone, in relative silence, with time to think about whatever she liked. She was used to moving around all day, not sitting still in a classroom and having knowledge pushed into her head for hours on end. She was definitely not used to someone like Lea.

Dam Penafers, their absentee house mistress, was supposed to make sure they didn't wander off into the city at night, keep them on a tight rein, and chaperone them if they wanted to go shopping, but she was often nowhere to be seen, and the other Talented tended to come and go as they pleased. Rue was too nervous to do this much, but Lea had coaxed her out more than once during the day, when they had no lessons to fill the long hours. They spent their time trailing around clothes boutiques, Lea spending money freely on clothes that draped over her thin frame with artful grace. More than once she had offered to buy Rue something, but that was an offer Rue felt uncomfortable about taking up. She knew the girl was rich and wouldn't care, but that was almost the reason Rue didn't want Lea to spend money on her. It seemed obscene that you could do that without even noticing the difference to yourself. Rue's pocket money was coming from the university's own coffers, something she was acutely aware of. So she refused Lea's generosity, even though it was joyless going on a shopping trip with someone when there was no end result for yourself.

'. . . He'll be teaching you personally, you know,' continued Lea, apparently mildly put out at her lacklustre response. They were sat together on Rue's narrow bed. 'You're incredibly lucky. We all are. Mussyer White only teaches Talented, and he teaches us one on one, not in a class together.'

This got her attention. 'Why's that?'

'It works better, so he says, if you and he are alone. He can focus his energies into one person at a time only.'

This sounded a little bit nerve-wracking. Alone with a tutor that she had heard all sorts of strange things about. A tutor that would tell her what this thing was inside of her. This hunger.

'What's he like?' said Rue.

Lea touched her mouth with a finger, a smile curling upwards like smoke. 'Weird.'

That meant weird in a good way. She felt her curiosity unfurl a little more.

It was usually impossible for Lea to stop talking. Sure enough, she giggled, shook her head, and continued.

'I don't know. You think he's horrible at first, but he's so different. And powerful, you can feel it. I heard he's the most powerful Talented in the whole world.'

Powerful. He'd be imposing, then. Commanding. Or maybe wise, like a wizard. Long beard and startling eyes and magic spilling like water from his fingertips.

'What's he doing here?' said Rue.

Lea's voice dropped to a dramatic murmur. 'I heard he had to flee his country on account of his Talent. He hasn't even been in Angle Tar that long. A year or two, at most.'

As a rule, Rue had learned to believe exactly a tenth of what Lea came out with, and disregard the rest. But this Mussyer White certainly had an effect on his students – even Lufe spoke of him with a noticeable degree of awe. She wanted to impress this impressive man.

And then she yawned, suddenly.

'What's wrong with you, anyway?' came Lea's voice, irritable. 'You're practically lolling on me.'

And I'm not hanging on your every word, which annoys you no end, thought Rue.

'I'm tired,' she said out loud. 'Keep having these dreams.'

'Ooh, you'll want to write all that down. He asks you about your dreams every lesson, and gets awfully cross if you can't remember all the details. Dreams are the key, so he says. You know that, right? I mean, I know you haven't had a lesson with him yet but you know about the dreams, of course.'

'Course I do,' said Rue, irritated. She was currently strug-gling with an impasse concerning the Talent. She burned to know more, but couldn't bring herself to ask Lea or any of the others about it, because then she'd look ignorant. They already thought her backward just because she was from the country. She wouldn't prove it by asking questions that would make them laugh at her.

'Well, you'd better remember as much as you can, then. He'll ask you on your very first lesson, I don't doubt.'

Rue folded her arms. 'Well, and so, when *is* my first lesson?'

'In half an hour.'

She sat upright, squalling.

'Sorry,' called Lea, watching Rue as she scrabbled around the room, trying to make herself look decent. 'It's in your lesson plan, look. I've got it for you here and everything.'

Twenty-seven minutes later, Rue was walking as fast as she could along a corridor, glancing every few seconds at the map Lea had given her and looking desperately around for the right door. The building that Mussyer White taught from was hidden away at the back of several others. You could only find it by twisting and turning through a series of obscure rooms and then walking across a small, forlorn courtyard with cracked paving stones to another set of rooms and endless, endless corridors.

Eventually, she came across a black painted door with a small, neat plaque fixed about eye level.

Talent theory and practice

That was all it said.

She raised her hand, hesitated; knocked. No time for shyness, she was already nearly late. She listened for a moment, but heard nothing from inside. She opened the door a crack.

'Come,' said a voice from beyond the gap.

Rue slipped in through the doorway and stood, trying to make sense of the room. It was freezing in here, and far too dark. Why weren't the lamps lit?

She looked about for Mussyer White, but couldn't see him. She couldn't even make out the place to any degree, although there were vague bulky furniture shapes a good distance off. This part of the room nearest the door was bare and cavernous. It was a ground-floor room, which meant its floors were stone instead of wood, like the rooms in Red House.

'Come to the table,' said the voice.

It was a hard voice, and suited the room. Well, he was probably old and cold and dusty, wasn't he? That would be about right, considering the other tutors she had met so far.

She looked about, hoping that the table he meant was where the only source of light was positioned. She could see an enormous lamp, even from here, which gave out a strong but oddly dark colour, throwing everything into shadow and strange shapes.

Rue started to walk, feeling her anxiety grow. Instantly she disliked this White, for she understood his first trick; to make visitors walk to him across a bare and barren floor, with bad lighting and a dim, forbidding appearance, increasing their nervousness and fear of him. She had reacted the exact way he had wanted her to, and she did *not* like to be manipulated.

He was hunched over the end of the table farthest away from the lamp, a vague figure with his head lowered, appearing to look over papers strewn in front of him. The shadows his body cast against the wall behind gave him an insectile shape.

'Name, please?' he said, turning over a paper.

'Vela Rue,' said Rue. Was he even going to look at her?

'Ah. Yes. The one Frith found himself.'

Rue was silent.

'What you will understand from the commencement of our lessons,' he said in his strange, jangling voice, 'is that I do not appreciate time-wasting nor laziness. Whilst a student under my supervision you will work as hard as is possible for you to do. You are here to learn from me and I am here to examine you for latent Talent that I am informed you possess. If you do have such of worth to offer, we will see how far I can coax it from you. Do you comprehend my terms? A simple 'yes, syer' will suffice.'

During this speech, the man at the table had not once looked up. Rue felt her cheeks flush with the slow build of anger and embarrassment.

'You've certainly an odd way of talking,' she said.

White finally turned his face and gave Rue the full beam of his gaze.

Gods. He was so *young*. He looked as if he could pass for a student himself. No one had so much as mentioned that to her. Was it a mistake? Had she got the wrong room?

'But you're just a boy,' she blurted. 'Are you . . . are you supposed to be my tutor?'

He continued to stare at her, unreadable.

'You possess neither maturity nor manners. This is a good beginning,' he said at last, his voice drier than bone dust. 'Sit.'

She took the chair beside him, flouncing as much as she dared. He had bent over his papers once more and she studied his profile, determined not to be cowed. His face seemed chiselled from stone, his nose long and his skin smooth and luminously pale. He could not possibly be any more than nineteen or twenty. His hair was very dark, thin, and draped freely over his shoulders, a lacquered fall of silk.

Rue waited, watching him read. After a moment that lasted too long, he shifted and leaned back. It was strange the way he moved, as if his bones were built differently to hers. His eyes were black in the dim light. He was . . . exotic. Unlike any other boy or man she'd seen before.

'Vela Rue,' White stated. 'Vela to denote your approach to adulthood, Rue your birth name. Rue a country name by origin, meant to symbolise a relationship with nature. But Rue being the common plant name, not its proper form. Perhaps to denote humility.'

Rue couldn't possibly see where such an odd series of statements was going. She opened her mouth as if to interrupt, but White was staring off into the middle distance, as if talking to himself.

'I wonder,' he continued in his stilted manner, 'about origins. About how much they can affect a person. Whether a mind that has not been expanded from an early age by vigilant learning could ever hope to absorb the teachings it must to grow. The problem with Talent is that it is an art, a beauty, and a science all in one.'

You strange, rude little snob, thought Rue. I bet no one ever puts you in your place.

'I can't follow your talk at all,' she said. 'You speak like you're reading something out loud and your words don't fit together properly, and you've a horrible accent. If you put such faith in learning, how about getting on with some?'

White was icily silent. After a long, long moment, he stirred.

'Our lesson ends for today,' was all he said.

Rue waited.

White had moved back to his papers.

Rue waited.

'Perhaps you misunderstood,' said White eventually, still reading. His hand came out, and for one moment Rue thought he meant to hit her. His fingers flicked upwards.

'Get out.'

Rue stood, stumbled, turned and walked.

'Grad take him!' Rue spat. 'He's nothing but a stuck-up lump of brown ice!'

'Yes, indeed,' said Frith smoothly.

They were sat together in the common room of Red House. Rue hadn't seen Frith since the day he had dropped her off at the front door, but he had called in unexpectedly that evening for tea. Lea was nowhere to be seen and the boys had gone to play some dull aristocratic sports game or other with carved sticks.

She was glad to see Frith. It took her away from stewing about her encounter with White by herself, which was never as satisfying as doing it with someone else.

'He's just a baby! He's my age! I mean to say that it's rich the way he talks, as if he were forty years older than you and knows everything there is to know about everything!'

'He is slightly older than you, in fact,' said Frith. 'But I take your point.'

'What's a boy his age doing being a teacher anyway? That's just about the most ridiculous thing I ever saw. I could teach, if we're talking about having kiddies being teachers now. I could teach about a lot of things.'

'I'm sure you could.'

'He's rude. And he can't even speak properly! He has this horrible accent and he says his words all mixed up!'

'You didn't happen to mention that charming sliver of thought out loud, in front of him, did you?'

'So if I did.'

'Rue. Please think for a moment about the way your accent is received in the city. Your rather hit and miss grammar and the words you use that no one here has ever heard of.'

'And so? I'm not changing one slice for anyone,' snapped Rue.

'I'm glad to hear it. But think of what people say about you, based solely on what they hear when you open your mouth?'

Rue sighed loudly. She'd already seen where this was going. 'That I'm rude and ignorant.'

'And we know this to be both unfair and untrue,' said Frith. Rue watched him. If anyone else had said that, she would have slapped them for laughing at her. But Frith never looked like he was lying.

'So, think,' he continued, 'Mussyer White's mode of speaking makes you perceive him as odd and cold. But he can't help the way he speaks, any more than you can help the way you speak.'

Rue was irritated by this sensible reasoning and tried to ignore it.

'But why does he speak like that?'

'He had to learn our language. Some people are easy with adoption, others are not.'

Rue felt a grudging stir of interest.

'Where's he from?' she said.

'He's from URCI.'

'From where?'

Frith looked at her for a moment, tapping his chin with a finger.

'It's a country in World. What do you know of what lies outside Angle Tar?'

Rue shrugged, stalling. She hated appearing stupid, and she knew that he didn't ask her to make her look so. But still.

'Not much,' she said at last. 'They used to tell us at school that a lot of it was just wastelands, and they were all a bit backwards in other countries.'

'It's not *quite* like that,' said Frith. 'Their way of life is simply very different to ours.'

'Our history teacher's said some things.'

'Such as.'

'He said that everything I'd learned was wrong. That Angle Tar is some small country that no one cares about.'

'It's not quite like that, either. But you must understand,

Rue, that you will never get the truth as you want it about this. Everyone has their own idea of the world and how they want to see it. Your history teacher tells you how he sees it. I tell you how I see it. Both are true. You will decide how *you* see it. Facts can be wrong, and one person's opinion influences everything.'

'That's complicated and annoying.'

'Such is life. So. Tell me what you think of the world as you have seen it so far.'

'In my dreams?'

'If you wish.'

'Grey . . . and waiting, like the skeleton of a place instead of a real place. And people fall down. Something attacks them all together and they all fall down.'

'What?'

Rue stopped, feeling suddenly foolish and a little scared.

'Please, go on,' said Frith, seeming only interested.

'They . . . They have something I don't, and when they get attacked they fall. I don't fall. I watch them fall around me. And there's nothing there. Everything is grey. I feel like they're there with me but somewhere else at the same time, as if they can see things that I can't.'

'Yes . . . that's quite accurate,' said Frith after a pause. 'How interesting that you see it that way. You'll learn about that place, and others too, soon enough.'

Rue shifted nervously.

Frith smiled. 'You'd best just ask me,' he said. 'Never be afraid of asking questions, even if you don't get your answer straight away.'

Rue played with a fingernail.

206

'Why do they tell everyone there's nothing much outside, then?' she said at last. 'If there is?'

It's not nice to be lied to, was what she wanted to say out loud with a cold edge to her voice; but she didn't dare, not to Frith.

'Have you learned about the Territorial Wars in your history classes yet?'

'No. I mean, I think we talked about them one time when I was younger, but I stopped school young, see. Because of the prenticeship.'

Frith spread a hand. 'When you learn of the Wars, you'll understand why.'

'I spose it's why it's illegal to travel outside Angle Tar, and all. I always got told that it's because it's really dangerous.'

'It is,' said Frith. 'The world is a dangerous place. And the beauty of you, and the others like you, is that you'll never have to leave Angle Tar to see it. You can make your mind travel thousands of miles from the safety of your own room. You can dream.'

Rue digested this.

But it was all so vague. Her dreams felt real when she had them. But were they? Was she living two lives instead of one? What did her dreams mean? Her Talent? What about those beautiful creature humans, with silver antlers and rainbow-coloured fur and neat, perfect bodies? She burned to know. She burned for secrets.

'So,' said Frith. 'As Mussyer White possesses likely the most knowledge on the Talent of anyone in Angle Tar, and his first impression of you was not, shall we agree, the best, try to consider this for your next lesson: he holds the keys to your potential. You cannot afford to lose him as a tutor if you wish to be all that you could be. Powerful, and special. Be a little more polite.'

'I'm already special,' she said boldly, then flushed at it.

'Yes, you are, my dear. But not powerful. Not yet.'

Rue smiled.

CHAPTER 18
ANGLE TAR

WHITE

White couldn't remember the last time he had felt so apoplectic with rage. And all over a girl he didn't even know.

He was not an emotional being, displaying his insides for everyone to see and judge – he preferred to keep his secrets. He tolerated the behaviour his demeanour and his youth caused from other university staff because he knew, according to the standard social expectations here, that he deserved them.

When Frith had asked him to become a tutor, it had been his golden ticket. He could stay. More than that, his stay had been made more official. And more than that, he had been given a purpose. A direction.

It hadn't been without some uproar. He was to be the first ever foreigner to teach at Capital University. Not only that, but some of the more creakingly old staff had protested at how young he was. It was a farce, they said. There had been a petition. Nasty things said, but only over brandy and cigarettes in the head tutors' studies. Nothing overt. Petty things said under petty breaths and all with a veneer of politeness. That was how things were done here.

Frith had handled it. It was to be expected, but not worried over, he said. And he had been right. White still wasn't sure exactly what Frith did, but whatever it was, it carried weight. The petition had gone away. The grumblings had stopped.

And White had hidden himself, curling his life up into a ball, pulling his radiance inwards, building cold and careful walls so that no one could notice him or find fault. He could eat in his rooms instead of having to go to the tutors' canteen, and he could turn down the mandatory invitations to the social balls and the dances and the whiskie and card nights. He went only to those he couldn't possibly get out of, and then only because when Frith asked him if he was going and he said no, he would do anything to avoid that raised brow that his answer got him. It didn't do to displease Frith. The man with the power, who could take all of this away from him in an instant.

They had had an uneasy relationship, to begin with. But over time it had grown into something of White being his subordinate, his charge and responsibility; and just maybe even something of his friend. He would visit White in the evenings, sometimes, ostensibly to hear him report on the progress of his students, but often just to drink, and to talk. He was the only person White spent any kind of time with, and only because at first he felt that he couldn't possibly refuse Frith's visits. And then because it was tiring, deliberately being lonely all the time. Sometimes it was good to have someone, anyone to talk to.

He had made his peace with his life here. It wasn't perfect, but it was a life. It was fine. Everything had been fine, until that girl had walked in his door.

It had only taken her minutes, but she had done what he'd sworn no one would do again; make him show the world how vulnerable he really was, inspiring in him an emotion so profound, he had trouble stopping himself from visibly trembling when he thought about her.

That little country *nothing*.

She was supposed to have behaved as expected – raw, young, nervous. She was not an aristocrat – they were born knowing they were better than everyone else, and acted accordingly, Lufe being a case in point. Rural students were always timid and overwhelmed. Not this one. So she was Talented and therefore naturally a bit wild, but even taking that into account, he had expected a measure of respect.

When she had walked into the room, he felt that he had been right. She moved uncertainly, looking suitably awed, and there had certainly been nothing that struck him as out of the ordinary. True, there was something in her face that was immediately pretty and quite sweet, but all in all she was a country girl in over her head.

But when she opened her mouth, the bored, lazy insolence in her tone had shocked him, so much so that he hadn't reacted. When she looked at him, her eyes barely concealed a whole year's worth of contempt. For someone she didn't even know. He ran silently through all the cutting remarks he should have made, just to watch her face change.

But instead all he had managed to do, like a bratty little child, was order her from the room. He had ordered her out and out she had gone, as if nothing had happened. He had watched her leave incredulously, and it had not been until much later on that his shock had turned to rage.

There was a knock at his door.

'Come in,' he said, pouring himself more Grenadon and diluting it with water. Everything just so on the platter, the water jug sparkling in the light, calmed him somewhat.

Frith eased his way around the door and shut it, making his way to the empty chair.

'I presume you have heard about it,' said White. He tried for casual, but it came out mangled.

'I heard a version of it. Would you care to tell me what happened?'

White took a sip of the Grenadon, giving himself a moment.

'She was rude and ignorant,' he said eventually.

'Aren't they all?'

'No,' said White, 'they are not. Because they understand the privilege of having a place here.'

'Rubbish. Some of them are here because their father is well connected in government and Eldest Pride and Joy hasn't quite yet worked out exactly how he's going to waste his inheritance and his life.'

'I talk about the poor ones,' said White with delicate emphasis.

'The poor ones expect little in life and are therefore amazed when they get an opportunity such as this,' said Frith cheerfully. 'Now, the Talented ones . . . that's a different story.'

'Rudeness does not equate to Talent.'

'No. But Talented are often rude. Or lacking in social graces, if you prefer.'

White was silent.

'Let me put it this way,' said Frith. 'What was it exactly about her manner that offended you?'

White tried to push his irritation aside, like a grown man should be able to do. He tried hard not to show the immaturity of the adolescent he worried was still inside him.

He thought about Rue. 'She was arrogant. She should have been eager. She mocked me. What good is a tutor who allows his pupils to do that?'

Her face flashed in his mind. Her pretty eyes, narrowed at him.

'Not much good at all,' Frith agreed. His face was utterly neutral.

Even White, who thought he now knew Frith more personally than he knew anyone else, had trouble a lot of the time working out how Frith felt at any given moment. He was reactionless to a casual observer, and it seemed like a natural thing, but White thought privately that it had probably taken a lot of practice for Frith to acquire that level of skill in thinking one thing and demonstrating another.

'This conversation is theoretical, in any case.'

'How do you mean?' said Frith.

'I mean that I could not stop teaching her, if I even wanted to.'

'There is always a choice,' said Frith. 'In this case, you could continue to teach her, or tell me that she possesses no useful Talent, and so stop teaching her.'

And there it is, thought White. Said in the friendliest of plain ways. Teach who we tell you to teach. Tell us if we have mistakenly seen Talent where there is none. Stop teaching if we agree. Don't develop any free will. Or personal agenda.

'You're currently the only one here who can teach them,' said Frith. 'That's why we need you so much. But your situation means that you are more indebted to us than we are to you.'

'I am aware of that. I am always aware of that.'

'Very well,' said Frith. He unfolded himself from the chair. 'I have dropped in on our impolite student and impressed upon her the importance of manners. But perhaps you could also try something.'

White waited.

'Vela Rue is after the truth in any given situation. If you wish to gain her focus, tell her what you're really thinking.'

'I do not understand.'

Frith leaned on the doorframe.

'Instead of being silent or dismissive when something is not going well or she speaks out of turn, say what you are thinking out loud.'

'But that,' said White, 'is what you do when you are trying to anger a person.'

Frith smiled. 'Try it.'

Rue pushed open the door, saw the same dimly lit view as before, and just managed to stop a short sigh escaping into the room beyond.

She could feel her heart pounding in her chest, and she grew annoyed at herself.

He was only a tutor.

'Please come to the table at the end,' said the irritating voice that had been echoing in her head for the entire week.

Rue began to walk. This time around she gave the surroundings her most penetrating stare. It was so stark. Apart from her tutor's table and chairs, lamp and bookcases pushed in to the far end, there was nothing of anything much in the room at all.

'Why is this room so empty?' she asked when she reached White. 'Wouldn't it be better if you had a smaller room, if you only teach one student at a time?'

She was determined not to be embarrassed or angry by what had happened before, and tried to appear as she always did. She thought her voice sounded a little cooler than usual, but otherwise she had done all right.

White was sat in his chair, the lamp throwing stripes of shadow across his face. It was difficult to read his silence.

'The nature of the Talent means that we require much space to work within,' he said eventually. 'Please sit.'

Rue sat, folding her hands on her lap.

She realised he would think her rude, but she couldn't help staring at him. Everything about Mussyer White was unsettling. His face was the face of a marble statue. He avoided eye contact, but would occasionally favour her with a glance, and whenever it fell on her it was so intense that she felt as if he had actually touched her, not just looked at her; but the way he would touch a piece of furniture, not a living thing. His disinterest was what galled her the most.

He talked in his stilted fashion about what was expected of her, about what she would learn and how grateful she would be. Remembering what Frith had said, Rue tried to concentrate on the words, the keys this strange boy-man held to power.

He talked about hooks, about what he called 'like-to-like' threading and resonance of place. A hook was a feeling that you created out of yourself, a thing that was inherently you. With it you reached out to another place and gripped yourself there, and then used it to find your way back to where you had started. Resonance of place meant that you would more often be able to find another place that was similar to the one you knew best, that felt like your child-hood home, for example. Like-to-like threading meant that you could move yourself more easily between places that were similar. If you were sat in a room made of stone, you could find another room made of stone somewhere else, much more quickly than you could find a meadow, or a street.

Gradually she began to understand what the Talent was.

It was moving.

It was peeling apart all that stood between you and a thousand miles, and treating it as nothing more than smoke. It was easier, apparently, to move your mind across distances, which is why most Talented people dreamed of other places they had never been. It was much harder to move your entire self to another place, which was the thing that they were really looking for, and that hardly anyone could do.

His words were complicated and fascinating and Rue thrilled to hear him talk like that about something she possessed. But he spoke with a dryness, even a disdain she found bewildering. What he spoke of, to her, was nothing less than magic, yet he seemed to have little taste for it. Perhaps it was because he was jealous? Perhaps he couldn't actually do it himself, only teach it? That would certainly make her mad if she were in his position.

'Now,' said White, 'I would like you to tell me in detail about your dreams of the past week. We will be talking of these in every lesson, and so you may wish to become familiar with noting them down yourself to report them to me.'

Rue thought about it.

'I had a dream about carrots,' she said at last. 'I kept trying to eat them but more would come up on my plate. I started feeling sick.'

'I think we can ignore that dream,' said White. 'Carrots do not tell us much of interest.'

'You said all my dreams. I don't know which ones are important.'

She waited to see how he would take this.

'That is true,' he conceded eventually. 'I ask you to tell me all of them because you would not know which is of importance. I apologise.'

Rue grinned, delighted. 'I accept your apology.'

White shifted, looking uncomfortable. 'Your dreams, if you please.'

'I'm sorry about the carrots,' said Rue. 'I said it to annoy you.'

'I know,' said White. 'Your dreams, if you please.'

Rue sighed.

As Vela Rue had opened his door, White took a breath and ran through the mechanics of his behaviour one last time.

It was a general assumption that those with Talent were all the same and therefore understood each other on some cult-like level unattainable to ordinary people. This attitude he knew too well, but it was simply not true. People were people, which included the Talented, and were as varied in temperament as any other set of individuals.

Frith was not in any way ignorant and couldn't be accused of lumping all Talented together in such a fashion, but even he had sometimes assumed that they would understand each other and band together.

That was, of course, before all the trouble with Wren.

That whole thing was a knife in his heart. A continual ache there to remind him of how unaccountably, humiliatingly stupid he had been. Frith had never gone into the specifics, but after the first week of searching for the boy had turned up nothing, he had stomped into White's room in a frighteningly foul mood one evening and told him flatly that Wren had defected to World.

It was easy to isolate himself after that. No more friends who could hurt. No more girls who could cause such trouble. No more disappointments and no more reasons for him to lose the precious gift of being allowed to stay.

It was something that neither of them cared to dwell on, and he was grateful that Frith had never since brought it up as ammunition against him. But the fault for what had happened lay with White, and he accepted it as a man should.

So Rue would be handled carefully, and White would do his best to heed Frith's advice.

It was almost a shame about her spiky personality. There was something almost ethereal about her, as if she had one foot permanently stuck in another time, and she had the kind of unspoiled lovely face that the city women tended not to have. Life moved more easily for pretty women, and if Rue were possessed of a graceful, demure deportement she would soon find situations opening up like flowers for her, instead of the constant series of arguments she appeared to be in.

White watched her reach his desk, and then say something unconsciously rude about the size of his room. He held his temper in check. The encounter proceeded on firmer ground after that as he expanded on his basic theories of the Talent, growing more confident the more he talked.

They all started out this way. Like an eager sponge, greedily soaking up little pieces of validation of themselves – that they were special, that the Talent was special. But when Rue told him about the carrot dream, he became confused. Did she mean it, or was she playing with him? Mindful of Frith, he chose the former for safety. When he apologised, she smiled, and the most extraordinary thing happened to her face. It wasn't just a smile, but a smile directed to him. He felt an unexpected sharp wave of happiness for managing to make her smile. Then he felt embarrassed; then angry about being embarrassed. The girl was like some sort of emotional conductor; why was it so difficult to be normal around her? Did she emit an airborne chemical designed to upset people?

When Frith came by his rooms that evening, officially for a drink but mostly to check up on how the lesson had gone the second time, White gave him the reassurance he needed and said nothing of the discomfort he felt around Vela Rue. What was there to say?

Their lessons continued, and he continued to be baffled by her. She was Talented, of that he had no doubt. Her dreams were nicely varied, which spoke of a goodly amount of raw ability, but how Talented she would become would depend on how disciplined and focused she was. Which, at the moment, was 'not very'. She much preferred to pick at him and his private life than concentrate in their lessons together, and his disquiet mounted until he began to grow nervous moments before each time she was due to walk through his door.

She was a young thing, a silly thing. But sometimes she wasn't. Sometimes she would say something and her face would catch the dim light just right, and he would be utterly caught off guard at how wise she seemed, just then. Her body seemed to emit nothing but energy, energy; passion, raw passion; until he was exhausted just being near her. Areline hadn't affected him like this. No one had ever affected him like this; not even Wren.

It wasn't until the first dream he had about her a few weeks later that he realised what the problem was.

It began harmlessly enough. White felt that he knew, by now, which dreams were caused by the Talent and which were just dreams. This one seemed like it was just

220

a dream, but calling it that diminished the effect it had on him. It stayed in his brain for days, echoing round and round again, destroying his ability to concentrate on anything else.

In the dream, he was with Rue, and they were in his classroom.

They were discussing Ancient Theory, something that was not usually included in their lessons. He was expanding on the now defunct branch of psychology, and she kept asking him questions in a quiet, serious fashion that was completely opposite to her usual playfully complicated manner. In dream logic they could of course communicate perfectly; his grammar was not bizarre, his accent normal and not cause for odd looks and mockery.

He told her of the old masters, now obscure, who postulated such things as parental influence on behaviour and the unbelievable theory of Elektra and Oedipus. Rue expressed amazement and laughed. Then she told him quite suddenly that she had never known her parents. Which was odd, when he thought about it afterwards, because she had never told him that before (why would she?) and he knew nothing about her previous life at all.

He asked her how she felt about that, and laughed at the joke. But she hadn't understood it and looked only puzzled.

How I feel about you? she said.

Wait, that's not what I meant, said White.

How do you want me to feel about you? Rue continued.

I want you to see me as your teacher.

But that's not how I want to see you, she said.

They carried on with the lesson, but White could see her heart wasn't in it.

Is something wrong? he said at last. *You know that you can talk to me if you need to.*

Unthinkable outside of the dream. He would never, ever ask her to tell him anything of a personal nature, even if she wanted to. That way lay danger. A student was a student, not a friend.

I can't talk to you about it, said Vela Rue. *You especially.*

Why not? What is it about me that stops you?

I think about you, she said.

And then she added, *Not as a tutor.*

She was blushing and looking at the floor.

And then he couldn't remember how he felt about that because the next thing was that she was underneath him and he was kissing her. She was pressing upwards against him. The flagstones were hard and cold against his knees. He was ripping at her clothes. Her skin was hot. He pinned her arms down, grinding them into the ground, and pushed his face into her neck. She was rippling and whispering something over and over in his ear.

When he woke immediately afterwards, his heart was trying to climb out of his throat and his skin glistened with sweat. There was a long lump in his bed next to him, and for just one terrifying, incredible moment he thought that it was her. A brief examination, however, revealed it to be his pillow, which he had apparently been attacking.

The sensation of flat, rigid stone and her wriggling body on top of it stayed with him for days after the dream had ended. He would be teaching, or walking, in the middle of a sentence or a drink, and that feel of her would flash suddenly in his mind. He would remember every second of it, trying to prolong it, trying desperately to get rid of it.

People would talk to him but they sounded muted, as if he was cut off from them by a wall of glass; trapped in a dark, hot bottle of his own making. In the bottle he could be with the dream, as long as he wanted. He could watch her underneath him again and again.

And that was the beginning of White's fall.

CHAPTER 19
ANGLE TAR

RUE

It had been a busy dream life for Rue these past few weeks.

Since her first dream featuring the silver-eyed boy, she had had several more. Each time she had one, they felt so real, and she felt so tired the next day, that it was as if she hadn't been sleeping at all.

He seemed apart from her, as if he was just a visitor to her head, and now that she knew she had this phantom ability lurking somewhere inside her, she wondered if he weren't somehow a product of that instead of her normal dreams. Mostly, he lurked in the background, catching her eye as she wandered around the landscapes of her mind, one blurred face in a crowd, or a figure whisking behind a building when she turned to find him.

In one dream she had, she found herself in the kitchen of Red House again, and there they were together, sat like old friends at the table. This time he had a bunch of grapes and picked them off their stems one by one, eating with obvious relish as they talked.

She tried to quiz him on who he was, but he wouldn't tell her his name. When she asked where he came from, though, he talked of a place that sounded both beautiful and impossible. In this place, he said, people were never hungry. Food was never scarce, and appeared magically when you had the right token to make it do so. Everyone lived together in beautiful cities, and their souls were all connected as one living creature, and no one could ever be lonely. People thousands of miles from each other could talk and touch with their souls while their bodies stayed put. Everyone played games with hundreds, thousands of other people at the same time, and everything was easy. He called this place Life, and said that it was the only place worth living in.

She was more accustomed to the strangeness of his beauty now. He couldn't be real because he looked, smelled and moved perfectly, as if formed from an idea and not the messy horror of birth. When she woke from seeing him, she would lie in bed for a time, staring up into the darkness and thinking about him and the things he told her, desperate to extend the dream. Then she would sigh and turn over. Perhaps if she went back to sleep, she could return to that place and that moment, and see what happened next. Perhaps if she slept for ever, she could live there inside her head, inside her favourite scenes, for as long as she wanted.

In dreams, nothing was ordinary. There was no clothes washing or banality, dull people with their dull conversations, no humiliation, no wrong decisions or maliciousness. No boring boys with their boring ways. Everyday people in her life became extraordinary in her dreams.

She'd even had a dream about Mussyer White. The kind of secret dream she was used to having about men. White had told her, in his peculiarly emotionless fashion, that such dreams were an expression of her body's need and nothing more, and she could see the sense of that. So she tried to forget it. The next lesson she'd had with him after the dream had been nerve-wracking beforehand; but then he had behaved in his usual cold, uninterested manner and she had gone back to being irritated by him, as quick as thought.

The silver-eyed boy was surely more of the same; a beautiful, flirtatious dream she'd conjured up to keep her loneliness at bay, in the way that her mind often did. So she never spoke of him to White. He would think her disgusting, she was sure, if all she ever talked about were dreams like that.

Tonight, it was to be her third dream spent entirely with the silver-eyed boy, rather than merely seeing him out of the corner of her eye. And it would be the last time they ever met in Red House kitchen.

When she realised where she was, she looked around expectantly. The kitchen had become her favourite room, partly because of him. Whenever she was there in the mornings, she imagined him hiding in the pantry, or even walking around, watching the whole Talented group as they helped themselves to breakfast, as invisible and insubstantial during the day as a ghost.

But here, in the soft and dark hours, he was real enough. His eyes had their strange gleam under the lamplight.

'Hello, Rue,' he said.

Rue smiled.

'How are you this evening?'

'Well enough.'

'Bored?'

Rue shrugged, running her fingers along the table top. 'I suppose.'

'You must be,' he said, taking an apple from the huge bowl in the centre of the table and tossing it up and down. 'Last time you said that you never get to see anything in your lessons with White. All he does is talk.'

'I know,' said Rue. 'It's just chat. I thought I was to learn about how to do things with the Talent, but he just talks, as if he thinks I'm useless at practical things. At everything.'

Somehow, she knew, her anger towards White was something to do with the dream she'd had of him compared to the reality of him, and how those two sides could never exist within the same person, and how stupid that was, and how stupid she was for wishing that it could.

'I can teach you.'

Rue laughed and tossed her head, trying to appear unmoved. 'You can?'

'I'm extremely Talented, Rue. How else do you think I can appear to you, and talk to you like this?'

Rue felt her heart beat quicken, sure he would at last tell her a great truth about himself. No matter how much teasing and tugging she had done before, he had spoken of his life in the vaguest terms, and had never explained who exactly he was. She waited, patient, eager.

'Have you ever wondered how much of our time together is a dream and how much is real?' said the silver-eyed boy.

'It feels real enough. I've always had a bit of trouble

telling the difference between my Talent dreams and real life, though. Now they say it's because my Talent dreams *are* real.'

He smiled, his eyes gleaming in the gaslight. 'Clever girl. So if I tell you that this is real, and that I'm really here, in the kitchen with you now. And then I tell you that we're going to Jump together. What would you say?'

The languor of his presence faded. He was fired up, excited. He tossed the apple up again and caught it deftly.

'What?' she managed.

'Jump. We're going to Jump together. Now.'

'But. I can't. I haven't even got past the hook yet. Mussyer White said it would take months to even think about a Jump.'

'White,' said the silver-eyed boy, 'is an idiot.'

Rue was shocked into silence. She watched him put the apple back in the bowl and come around the side of the table towards her. He looked less like a cat and more like a spider tonight.

'But –'

'No, listen. I've been looking for someone like you. Your Talent could blossom and unfold to give you the most amazing power. Don't you want that? You won't get it with White. He's holding you back. Think how astonished everyone will be by how quickly you progress. You'll be top of your class. Envied and powerful. I can show you how.'

Rue hesitated. It sounded good, his promise. It also sounded terrifying.

The silver-eyed boy leaned forward and grabbed her arm. His violent movement panicked her.

'No, I'm not ready!' she said.

'Of course you are,' he sang, and laughed. Sometimes his laughter frightened her. His hand had fastened around her wrist. She made a half-hearted attempt to pull back, but he gripped tighter. She saw his knuckles slide and twist.

'But they said I could die if I tried to do it without learning properly!'

'That's just what they tell you,' he said, hauling her close to him. 'Anyway, there's always a chance you could die. We spend every minute of our lives almost dying.'

How profound, she had time to think sarcastically, but then he was crouching with her pressed in his arms, and all further thought vanished. The feel of his body pressed against her should have been making her belly squirm, but her attention was caught by the odd sensation coming from his fingertips on her skin. The flesh felt as if it were billowing like sheets hung up in the wind, and where his skin met hers she could feel prickles, as if he had suddenly sprouted stiff spines of fur.

Her arm began to thin.

She gazed at in horror It was definitely thinner. The thinness rolled slowly up to her shoulder, across her chest, creeping along like ground fog on a dark, weighted night.

And then the pain began.

It was like being forcibly squeezed into a gap between two stone walls that would fit the width of a knife. The silver-eyed boy was pulling her into it and she could not stop him. He tugged until she was screaming at him to stop because she was sure he would wrench her arm off. She could not fit through that gap – it was impossible. Her chest had collapsed and her hips were shattering into tiny shards, and the shards ground against each other like crushed glass. She could feel the inside of her stomach pressing against the bones of her spine. Her heart stopped, too squashed to beat.

And then she was on her hands and knees, and the floor below her was warm and hard. Her throat rippled and she vomited.

'You're alive!' said a delighted voice above her. 'Did you know that this proves you definitely have Talent? If you didn't, you'd be dead. A Talented can't Jump an un-Talented, you know. It's a shame.'

She felt him crouch beside her.

'What a rare, marvellous creature,' he cooed, rubbing her back. His flattery had the desired effect. Instead of trying to strangle him for what he'd done, Rue immediately started to feel better. Her body seemed intact and not misshapen in any way. She looked down at her arms, both of which were fine – in any case they were propping her up from the floor without much direction. A small puddle of vomit kept flitting into the corner of her vision, despite her best attempts to ignore it.

'Sorry,' she said, shamed.

'Don't think on it. Most Talented people have that reaction the first time they Jump. We'll clean it up quick as thought,' said the silver-eyed boy. He unfolded upwards and brushed his hands off, pulling something from his tunic.

'I'll get you some water, too,' he said from behind her. She sat on her haunches for a moment, until she was fairly sure she wouldn't vomit again. Then she stood up. Her stomach rolled, but the worst seemed to have passed.

'Where are we?' she said.

'A place you've never been before,' he teased. When she turned, he straightened up. The vomit was somehow, mercifully gone. She tried not to show that she had noticed – she didn't ever want to mention it again. Worlds would collide before she alluded to it again.

He handed her a small glass of water and she gulped it, looking around and wondering where he had got it from. Wild, gleeful curiosity took over.

'Where've I never been before?' she said.

'Iceland.'

'Is it made of ice?' asked Rue, delighted. The room they were in was smaller than hers, but otherwise unremarkable. The walls seemed much smoother and more lightweight than stone, and were painted an odd, glowing sort of pink. For a place made of ice, it was very warm.

'Almost. It's a very cold country, overall,' he said. 'Not that it matters. Everyone lives together in a warm city, protected from all the stuff outside.'

'Whose room is this?'

He waved a hand. 'It doesn't matter. We'll only be staying a few minutes, anyway. I've timed it beautifully, but the owner of the room will be back in a while.'

Rue started to feel uneasy. 'Won't they be mad that we're trespassing?'

'They will never know, my sweet. Take a look around.'

My sweet? Rue didn't quite know what to make of that.

231

But he was watching her, so she let it be, and turned around to explore their surroundings.

It was a disappointingly dull kind of room, except for the ethereal warmth. There was no fire that she could see, but when she touched a hand to each wall, she could feel a gentle glowing heat coming from it.

'This is what I really wanted to show you,' said the silver-eyed boy, pointing to a small black box sat innocently on a desk top. 'It took me a while to find someone else with one of these. People don't really need them any more.'

'What is it?'

'A gateway to another world,' he said, smiling. 'I promise. In that box is a whole other place, invisible until you access the box. We call it Life. In there is how everyone's souls meet. It's what makes things beautiful. Life is full of everything you could ever want. It's like an endless dream.'

Rue stared at it.

'It doesn't look like much,' she said at last.

'The most powerful things often don't.'

'Will you show me the invisible world in the box?'

He laughed. 'Not this time. But soon, I promise.'

'Do you go there often?'

'To Life? As much as I can. There are people that rarely come out of it.'

'I wouldn't neither,' Rue mused. 'If I had that instead of just this.'

She turned away and wandered about, running her fingers across everything she found.

'Do you live in this country?' she said.

'No. This is far away from where I live. Iceland is closer to Angle Tar than I am, in fact.'

Rue looked at him sharply. He was leaning against a wall, watching her.

'How come I don't know about it, then?' she said.

'Angle Tar doesn't like to talk about what lies outside of Angle Tar.'

Rue shook her head.

'What is it?'

'I don't know,' she said. 'People keep telling me about that, in my wake life. But then everyone always said before that they were all wastelands and not worth much. Who am I supposed to believe?'

The silver-eyed boy came forwards, stretching his arms wide. 'Does this look like wasteland?'

'No, it looks like a fairytale,' said Rue. 'Boxes that have secret worlds in them and walls that give off heat.'

'This place is real. And I can show you all the other places that are just as real as this one, and as amazing, and long before they will ever allow you to leave Angle Tar.'

Rue said nothing.

'There is so much more in the world than Angle Tar,' he said, as he came closer. She thrilled whenever he came closer to her with that little smile on his mouth. 'There may even come a time, one day, when you think of Angle Tar as a small place, and you'll wonder how you ever fitted in there.'

'Will you show me more things like this?' said Rue.

'Yes. And soon.'

Her eyes came onto the black box, sitting calmly on the table in front of her.

Did it really hold another world? Perhaps there were more worlds, other worlds she couldn't see, or smell, or hear. Worlds without end and of infinite variety, everything you could ever imagine existing somewhere, just waiting to be tasted.

She would find a way to get to them all; to see them and be in them and feel them for herself. She would have adventures. A wild and passionate life. Her years stretched before her, blank and promising. She would fill them with everything.

And if Angle Tar wouldn't help her, maybe the silver-eyed boy could.

CHAPTER 20
ANGLE TAR

WHITE

He rolled over, sheet sweat-soaked and twisted.

Gods, he prayed with a fervour that shook him, please get rid of it. Please cure me. I'm sick. Any god will do. Help me.

The dream would linger all night and for at least two more days, as usual. This time it had been more abstract. Flashes of skin and her open mouth, and her head turning, turning. Every time his attention wandered, he would find himself running his fingers over the freckles on her arms in his mind.

He groaned and pressed his face into the pillow hard. There would be no more sleep. But he would not think of her. He would not indulge and encourage himself by picturing her lying next to him, or thinking of how she might look if she were here, with him, in his bed, talking to him in little whispers.

It was as if his skin itched constantly, and no amount of scratching could relieve it. The more he scratched the worse it became; maddening and constant. He couldn't concentrate on anything for more than a minute or two, because she was always there, waiting for him to come back.

'Stop this,' he said again, trying to cut through the mist of her with his voice. 'Stop it.'

It was Tuesday, the day, the best and most nerve-wracking day of the week. Rue's weekly lesson with him would be this afternoon. No wonder he couldn't sleep.

'Today we will further the hook,' he said.

Rue sighed theatrically. That used to annoy him. Now it did something else.

'It is tiresome, I know it,' he said. 'Tiresome to learn, to take you from your busy hours of doing what you do.'

'What I do?' she said, with a teasing grin. 'What do I do? You won't know what I do. It could be very important.'

'No doubt it has much to do with frivolous fantasising,' he snapped. Inside he cringed at himself. What was he becoming?

Her face fell, and he knew he had hurt her, which made him angry, so he tried to shake it off.

'Focus,' he said, aware he was speaking mainly to himself. 'Close your eyes and let us begin.'

She did, obediently.

'Now we have five minutes of reaching inside. Start breathing.'

'I'm always breathing,' she murmured. 'If I weren't, I'd die.'

'Stop playing and concentrate.'

He watched her.

It took half an hour, this time, which was an improvement. But slowly, so slowly, inch by inch. Almost as much as they gained they would lose, and Frith was going to be unhappy.

'It is imprecise,' White said to Frith once. 'It is not a skill you implant. It is most probably linked with brain development, personality traits, factors of environment. You cannot control with precision how someone develops. So you cannot control this. It is a confused, intricate human thing.'

Frith had looked at him for a long moment. White was afraid that he knew what Frith was thinking. *Then what good are you?*

White had become nervous. 'It can be honed, as with any skill,' he had said, trying not to appear defensive. 'But it takes time, and it depends on the student. Some will understand precisely from the start and develop fast. But then they will reach a certain level and go no more. The unpredictable ones are those that are usually the most Talented.'

'Like you,' Frith had said softly.

White saw Rue's eyes twitch. And there it was.

'Where are you?' he said, his voice pitched as gentle as he could make it.

'A room. It's wood everywhere. It's pretty.'

'Are you alone?'

'Yes.'

'What can you see?'

He ran through the requisite questions, noting everything that she said as meticulously as he could. Questions about the environment around her, what anything man-made looked like. What the people, if she could see any, looked like. How it smelled. How it felt. How she felt. What she could hear. Every little thing, so they could attempt to work out where she was and if she could see or hear anything of use.

Truth be told, it was dull, always dull. Always the same questions, and it took so long. It was always rooms such as this one, with the newer Talented. It was easier for them to Jump their minds to places that reminded them of the one they were in.

Rue had to search to answer his questions; it took her a full minute, on occasion. Almost as if she couldn't see properly. The light was too dim, or their vision was blurred. It took them a long time to be able to see in a mind Jump the way they saw normally.

Her voice had a curious quality to it when she used the Talent. Dreamy and languorous. Seductive. He thought often about reaching in and kissing her when she was in this state, knew that he never would, and so felt safe in letting himself think of it.

He sighed. It had been three hours, almost. He should bring her back.

'Zelle Vela,' he said. 'Find the hook now. I need you to find the hook.'

She was still for so long he thought she'd gone to sleep.

'Can't feel it,' she said eventually.

'You know what it feels like, reach for it.'

'Can't feel it.'

White watched her. 'The hook, Zelle Vela,' he said, keeping his voice soft. 'You will remember what it feels like.'

'Can't find it.' Her voice had lost some of its sleepiness. He thought he could hear nervousness.

'It is thin,' he said, as if reading from a textbook. If he showed any emotion at all, she would hear it and start to panic. 'It vibrates with the frequency you have given it. It is familiar, it feels as if you are coming home. You will want to stay away from the feeling of home, but you must embrace it. There will be another time to explore, always another time. As you find the hook, you are overwhelmed with tiring sensations. It is time to come back now, and you are too tired to stay out there in the world.'

Rue stirred. She looked more crumpled and faded this time around, a good sign that she had thrown more of herself into the mind Jump. He noted it down to mention in his report later. Her eyes opened and she almost slid off the chair.

He wanted to put his arms around her. She seemed worn, and very tired.

'It is time to rest, an hour at least,' he said, standing up. She looked at him, muzzy.

'Come,' he said, more sharply than he'd intended. 'I have another lesson in a moment.'

'Who with? I thought you said you didn't have one 'til the evening.'

'It is the evening. Our lesson today has been three hours.'

Rue looked around stupidly. 'Oh,' she managed. 'I'm getting longer. Is that good or bad?'

'Neither,' said White. He could have lied, but had taken Frith's advice to heart. It appeared, miraculously, to be working.

'Oh! I'm late,' she squealed, as her eyes fastened on his wall clock. 'Threya take me, and I've to change clothes.'

'You should be resting.'

She ignored this and gathered up her bag and coat, giving him a glance he thought – hoped – was shy.

'Don't you want to know where I'm going?' she said.

'No,' said White, though he did, and desperately.

'I shall see you next week, then.'

She hurried out of his door, and he watched her go.

Rue ran across the gardens, banging the back gate closed and bursting into Red House.

'You should hurry,' said Lea, floating past. 'Marches and Tulsent have already gone ahead.'

'Don't go without me?' Rue pleaded, springing into her room.

At breakfast that morning, Lufe had led the way in suggesting that the group go out to the town together in the evening, in the spirit of friendship. They were to dine at a favourite tavern of his, and he would be paying. When Rue had protested at this exuberant display of generosity, Lea had laughed and told her it wouldn't even make a dent in his weekly allowance.

Rue picked up the dress she had decided to wear. It was old-fashioned, she supposed, but it looked good on her. She pulled it on and checked her face in the mirror. Not bad. A little tired-looking, maybe.

Lea and Lufe were waiting for her in the corridor. Lea looked lovely, far too lovely for her own good, according to Lufe. He teased and taunted her mercilessly as they walked, but she would have none of it. Finally he went up ahead in a huff, to find a carriage.

'He's just annoyed because he thinks I'll attract some rich man and go off with him,' said Lea gleefully.

'Why does he care?' said Rue, though she could guess.

Lea gave her an impish look, but said no more.

They travelled to a less dainty and more raucous part of town than Rue had yet seen. Still respectable, but wild enough to have a good time, as Lufe put it. Lea was provoking some admiring stares, which she did nothing to dissuade. Rue fancied she caught a glance or two tossed her way, but she supposed she was like a robin next to a swan walking along beside Lea in her finery.

When they reached the tavern, it was noisy, smoky and packed. Lufe being Lufe had ordered a table in a private booth near the back, and Rue was glad of it. The dividing curtains kept out the worst of the noise.

She slid in next to Marches, who was already sat with a blinking Tulsent beside him. They both looked really young, here. She supposed they all did.

'I'm starving,' announced Lea, as she slid into the booth. 'Let's order everything they have.'

And so the evening went. Rue had never been out to dinner before, unless you counted the spring and harvest dances at the village, and really then it was more a case of wolfing down what food you could find on the ramshackle tables laid out in the square in between dances. This was different. You were sat, eating, drinking, talking. Close together like conspirators. You could feel that people looked at your closed-off booth as they passed, perhaps in envy or curiosity. It felt nice, and strange. It was easy to get on with people when food kept coming, and wine kept flowing.

Rue started to enjoy herself.

'The midwinter ball is soon, and I must have a dress for it, for I still haven't found one quite right,' said Lea, in between mouthfuls of hot chicken drenched in lemon oil.

'What's that, then?' Rue asked, swilling her mouth out with wine. She had chosen spiced beef baked with soft, fat apricots, and her tongue was on fire.

'Only the biggest event of the year,' said Marches. 'I shall be in peacock blue.'

'You're to be a fat, blue peacock for the night?' said Lufe, feigning polite interest. 'That's quite a statement, March. Will you manage it?'

Marches tossed him an oath so explicit that Rue snorted wine through her nose.

'S'a yearly tradition at the university to mark the culmination of the midwinter festival,' said Tulsent. His words were slurred. The poor boy probably hadn't drunk more than a glassful of alcohol at a time before this. Rue looked at Lea, and they both started giggling.

'Yes, and it's bloody important in fanning the flames of your social calendar, if you understand my meaning,' said Marches. 'All the students worth knowing will be there, as well as important government people, scouting for potentials. It's just about the only bloody time the bloody Talented get to mix with other people.'

'You say bloody a lot when you're drunk,' observed Lea.
'Shut up.'

'Do you have a dress for it?' said Lea to Rue.

'I don't know.'

'I'll check your wardrobe. If not you'll have to hurry out and get a suitable one. They all go this time of year – the seamstresses will be booked up so you'll have to pick up a ready-made. I can't wear ready-made, it never sits right on me, but you have that kind of figure that anything looks good on, so you'll be all right. We'll go shopping tomorrow. I'll take you to the best ready-made shops or you'll never find anything decent.'

'Good god, girl,' roared Lufe, thumping the table. 'You talk enough for all of us!'

'I'm not sure what you meant by social calendar,' said Tulsent to Marches, whose mouth split into a wide, evil smile.

'He means you need to pick out anyone you might want to bed, Tulsent,' said Lufe.

'Oh.' Tulsent blushed.

'Hush,' said Lea. 'Don't scare the poor boy.'

'I'm not scared,' Tulsent insisted, still scarlet.

'Oh really,' said Marches. 'You may act the harlot, Lea, but your good family name would never allow casual dalliance. I bet a hand up your skirt is as far as you've got.'

Lea laughed in outrage. 'You pompous cock,' she screamed.

'And you,' Marches pointed at Lufe. 'You, syer. I would reckon that you've had half the maids in your house.'

Lufe only smiled lazily.

'As for me; it's been a while, I'll admit. But there was a young lady of my acquaintance who did enjoy a game or two in the back bedrooms while our parents held parlour parties.'

'What complete lies,' said Lea. 'If a girl has laid a hand on you other than to deliver a slap, I'd be astonished.'

'I do enjoy a slap,' mused Marches.

'What about you, my country dear?' said Lea to Rue, who up until now had been laughing hard at the turn of conversation. She swallowed her wine and pressed her lips together. Let them think what they wanted.

'I'll bet she's had thirteen farmer's lads, all together,' announced Marches, to gales of laughter.

'D'you speak from experience?' retorted Rue with a raised eyebrow.

'Give us a number, then.'

'Less than a million and more than nothing.'

'Definitely more than nothing. At least one I know of, anyway,' said Lufe.

'What's this? Say it!' Marches demanded.

'What? What do you know?' said Rue, puzzled.

'I said I know of one of your conquests, at least,' Lufe repeated, a strange smile on his face. It took her a moment to realise that it seemed painted on, like smiles did when they came from anger.

'Lufe, hush up,' said Lea.

'What's going on?' said Rue.

'I know what he's talking about,' said Tulsent suddenly.

'Tulsent, hush!'

Rue looked around the table. They all knew what he was talking about, except her.

'Tell me right now,' she said, growing angry. 'For I've not been with anyone here, and even if I had, I'd want to know how you think you might know about it. So you tell me.'

'There's nothing to tell,' said Lea impatiently. 'They're just playing with you.'

'I wouldn't have guessed you liked them older,' said Lufe, and hissed when Lea punched him on the shoulder.

The table descended into silence, and the noise of the tavern crowded back in. Rue looked at them all, again and again, but none would meet her eye. Lufe started whispering in Lea's ear, and she started giggling. Marches decided to lecture Tulsent on the merits of gambling. Rue was left to finish her dinner by herself.

The evening wore on, but with Rue on the outside of it. If it had been a joke, as Lea had said, it was an unfathomable one. But it seemed too serious for that. The atmosphere was of a step too far – something said that shouldn't have been. And not one of them would look at her properly again, not even Lea. They were tight as clam shells, and no amount of prying would shake them open.

So Rue became angry, and bored with their game, and when they reached Red House, and the rest of them had to plunge Tulsent into a cold bath to revive him from his semi-recumbent drunken state, Rue left them to it, and went to her room, alone and hurting.

CHAPTER 21
ANGLE TAR

RUE

Rue was lonely.

Since their falling out, the other Talented had been giving her an extremely wide berth, which irritated her no end, but also wounded her. Lea stuck to Lufe's table in the mornings at breakfast, and Rue was left to sit by herself, as Freya did, ostracised and alone. She was still bewildered about what had happened that night, but as none of them were keen to talk to her about it, and she would *never* bend for them because she would bend for no one, they seemed stuck in this for evermore; and her bewilderment had turned to hurt anger.

Frith had become important to Rue, because she had no one else to talk to. When he dropped in on Red House of an evening, which was infrequently, he would bring them all presents of gingered chocolate and quiz them about their day. He would chat to her, and laugh with her.

So when he had mentioned the midwinter ball, she'd nearly fallen over with excitement, thrilling to hear his tumble of anecdotes from last year, and the year before. Women outdoing each other with more and more elaborate hair. Thirty-seven different meat dishes. Stone fountains that ran with champagne instead of water.

The ball was so important that they had a tutor, Dam Joya, come in to Red House to talk to the Talented about it as a group. First she addressed the boys, giving them outlines on what kind of shirts they could and could not wear; which dances they were allowed to ask partners for and which they could only partake in if they were married or of a particular social class; which drinks were safe and which were for hardened constitutions only. Then she turned to the girls. Rue sat astonished as she listened.

You could not wear pearls if you were under a certain age. Any shade of red was declared too womanly, white too young, and dresses in the latest fashion were the only possible choice. You could not dance with a man unless he requested it, and you could not take a drink unless he gave you one. She wanted to ask if you were even allowed to talk but the tutor was a stern, stiff-backed old crock and provoking her was tiresome rather than fun. The others in the group were either not listening or looking bored.

'This is completely pointless. Can I be excused? I've been taught this stuff since I was three,' drawled Lufe.

'Well, I haven't,' Rue retorted. 'I want to listen.'

'That's because you're a country nothing.'

'Silence, Mussyer Troft,' snapped the tutor. Lufe shot her a rebellious glare, but said nothing else. 'To continue. Only unmarried women of courtable age can agree to a request for the Stinging Dance, the Barter Fanning or Rabblers. Only married women can dance, with their husbands, the Lifelong Ribbon and Tea Cupping. And anyone, within

247

reason, can dance the Mixer together. Within reason being that – unless he is related to you by blood – you absolutely do not dance with a married man. Ever. And now we will learn the steps to the set dances. Up you get.'

There was a collective groan.

The night of the ball eventually came, and not fast enough.

Lea had suddenly decided, in the spirit of the evening and because she couldn't possibly have a boy as her chaperone, to be friendly with Rue again. Rue wanted to snub her but couldn't summon the energy because excitement kept washing it away; and most of her anger was at the boys. Especially Lufe. She'd decided to ignore his jibe about 'liking them older'. There was no sense to it, none at all. The only older man she even knew here was White, and *that* notion was simply ridiculous. So she'd had a dream about him, once; but so what? It meant nothing. Lea seemed anxious to be her friend again, so Rue left it alone.

They dressed together, chattering and laughing. Lea exclaimed when Rue pulled out her dress, as Rue had known she would, but laughed when she saw it on and said that it suited her very well.

The ball itself was in the university's main reception halls, reserved for occasions such as this. None of the students had been given carriages, unless they lived far away, but fortunately Red House was quite close, and it took them only fifteen minutes to get there, or it would have if Lea hadn't insisted on walking at a decorously slow pace. Her reasoning had been that she didn't want to arrive looking flushed. Rue privately thought that men quite liked a flushed-looking girl – it denoted passion, and all that came with that. But Lea would have declared her coarse if she'd said such a thing out loud, so she kept it to herself. She didn't want them to fall out again.

When they arrived, they joined a stream of people making their way slowly indoors. Music and light spilled out into the dark, frosty evening. Everywhere was laughing, sparkling chatter. Rue grinned.

'So are you pursuing anyone this evening?' said Lea, pulling Rue's linked arm closer to her.

'I don't know what you mean,' said Rue, putting on a haughty voice, and was glad to see it made Lea giggle.

'Just watch out,' she said. 'Some of the boys have the morals of a dog.'

As they entered, Rue allowed herself to think about it a little more. She didn't really know anyone, apart from the Talented group, and she wasn't the slightest bit interested in any of them. But there would be plenty of others there tonight to look at, and maybe dance with. She hoped she didn't muck up the steps and embarrass herself.

The halls were grand indeed. Ceiling-to-floor heavy curtains, chandeliers of intricate silver as far as she could see. Each set of double doors was open and pinned back, so you could see through into the next room. The crowd was swelling. Everyone was in their finest. Sparkling jewellery flashed on the women. Complicated lace collars and heavy velvet adorned the men. It was beautiful, and Rue stood for some time, watching everything with her mouth open before she dared enter.

Lea, predictably, scampered away from Rue as soon as

they had passed through the entrance hall, presumably to find Lufe and giggle at him uncontrollably. Rue was a little annoyed about finding herself in a sea of strangers with no one familiar to anchor herself to. Where was Frith?

She stood for a moment, uncertain. There was a great rippling world of people before her, and not one of them had given her a second glance. Should she wander slowly around the room with an arch air, and let people know she was the sort of interesting girl who preferred her own company? Would that make them stay away from her? Neither did she want to appear eager or too pleasing – that was not the kind of impression people should have of her at all.

Rue set out, determined to find Frith. As she searched for him, she found her gaze locking with so many strangers by accident, that by the time she'd looked down in apology and back up to search again, an entire group of people had been missed out. If only they wouldn't all move about so much.

The air glittered and snagged her eye as she walked slowly around. She soon realised it was the light catching the droplets of liquid people were sprinkling on their shoulders, for luck. She wished she could do the same but had not yet found the source of the drinks everyone held in their hands.

'Where's your chaperone?' said someone standing next to her.

Rue turned. The owner of the voice swung forwards to face her. It was a young man, possibly her age, and dressed quite finely. Not a poor student, then; but she knew there were hardly any poor students in the university. The only poor ones here, who had their education paid for them by the government, were exceptionally gifted in some fashion. Like her, she supposed. She hoped.

'Did you manage to dodge her? Good play,' he said.

'Actually, she dodged me,' said Rue.

'And left you alone at your first ever ball? Appalling.'

'How do you know it's my first ball?'

'It's a look you have. Virginal. Also, your choice of dress. A pure swan amongst preening peacocks. Would you like a drink?'

Rue thought about this. The boy was confident and nicely built, and therefore normally no hesitation needed. But somehow he wasn't quite what she was waiting for.

On the other hand, she was friendless and wanted a drink.

'I don't even know your name, though,' she said for politeness.

'Ackery Shay,' he said promptly.

'Vela Rue.'

'Shall we?' He offered his arm.

Rue hesitated for a moment, then took it.

Shay steered and chatted at the same time. His voice was smooth and sure, and he pointed out the most expensive dresses and people of the most interesting reputations as they sashayed past. He was pretty and had rescued her in an easy fashion from the embarrassment of being alone at a social ball. But he was younger than she was really wanting, and his manner too nice, somehow.

Shay procured her a drink, promising that it was mainly

251

made from apples and amongst the weakest of the array on offer that evening. She wanted to explain that country girls were quite used to such drinks, but Dam Joya's frowning face flashed through her mind with a cry from her beaky mouth of 'decorum!' So Rue smiled instead. The drink was pleasant enough; it had a crisp, sweet taste, something like mead but less syrupy.

A dance had begun in the hall next to them and Rue manoeuvred a reluctant Shay to watch it. After a minute or two she realised what it was.

'This is Tea Cupping!' she said, pleased with herself.

'The dullest dance known to the civilised world,' Shay agreed. 'Let me show you the gardens.'

'Wait, I want to watch it. I haven't learned this one.'

'Thank the gods for that. It's a marriage dance.'

Shay let her be for a while as she gazed at the dancers, trying to work out the steps. When the dance ended, he touched her elbow.

'What would the next one be?' said Rue.

Shay shrugged. 'A mixer, most probably. Come with me to the gardens.'

'Aren't you going to ask me to dance?'

'Oh, I'm a terrible dancer. And it is very hot in here, don't you think?'

It was quite hot, of a sudden. Fresh air and cool darkness became more important than dancing in bright lights. When Shay took Rue's hand and led her away, she didn't protest. She dimly remembered Dam Joya saying something about hand-holding in public, but couldn't raise enough energy to care about whether it was good or bad.

After much weaving and walking, and feeling progressively warmer and more uncomfortable, Rue became aware that Shay had stopped their quick march and was in conversation with someone.

'I apologise, syer,' Shay was saying. 'I didn't know you were her tutor. Nevertheless, unless you're also her chaperone, I'm a bit confused as to why you feel you should step in.'

'I am not her chaperone,' said the other. 'But I *am* her tutor. You will relinquish Zelle Vela to me and find another girl to do what you like with.'

The other man's voice was deeply familiar. Rue peered over Shay's shoulder to get a look at him, and her mouth fell open.

It was White, and he looked angry.

Shay was trying not to back down. 'Who else do you tutor, syer? I'm afraid I've never had the pleasure of knowing your reputation.'

'It will stay that way,' said White. 'Leave.'

'I can complain.'

'To whom? Will you tell them why I stopped you and what you were going to do with my student?'

'If you are not a relative or a chaperone, you can't interfere,' said Shay, though his voice was small. Rue felt a spike of irritation. He had lost his handsomeness and was now only a silly young thing who buckled in the face of authority.

'I don't need a chaperone,' she snapped. 'I don't need anyone.'

She shook off Shay's hand and stalked away. Two men deciding what she should and shouldn't be doing! She would find a dark room somewhere and sit down, away from all this. Then she would find Frith.

'Stop, Zelle Vela,' said White behind her.

'Leave me be,' she retorted, but stopped. It was very hard to disobey White. She could tease and delay, but eventually she would do whatever he said. She hated that about him.

'Where are you going?' said White. He moved around to face her.

'I'm going to find Frith.'

'Mussyer de Forde is not here,' said White.

'But he told me he would be!'

'It was his plan. But he received urgent business and left to attend it this morning.'

Rue tried not to let her dismay show. An evening alone here? Who was she to talk to? Who was she to dance with, if another Shay did not come along?

'Why do you want Frith to be here?' said White. He was watching her.

'Because I don't know anyone else. Frith was to introduce me to people. I wanted to dance. I wanted to feel normal, not as a freakish secret that has to be kept hidden away. And a boy come to me and treated me normal, and you come and ruined it!'

Rue knew she was going too far, being malpolite and petty, and everything that made her tutor angry with her. She didn't want it to be like the first time they had met. She still thought about it with severe embarrassment. But she couldn't stop herself.

White had gone quiet. Rue became horribly aware how

254

loud her voice might have become in the midst of the crowd.

'If you wish to find the boy,' he said, 'I will not stop you.'

'Then why did you?' said Rue. Inside her head a voice filled with alarm kept telling her to shut up.

'He was taking you to the gardens. Do you understand what that means?'

'Oh, of course I do,' Rue snapped. 'I'm from the country, remember?'

White looked taken aback. 'Then I made a mistake,' he said. 'I thought you were troubled. In trouble. I saw him give you Esprit to drink. Perhaps you have *that* in the country, also.'

'Don't know. What is it?'

'An amouriser.'

'Oh. Well, he didn't need to do that.'

White's face flickered.

'You know, I *can* do that if I want, with whoever I want,' said Rue. 'Just because you see everyone as silly children, doesn't mean they are. I'm an adult in the law's eyes. So you can't tell me what to do.'

'You are correct,' said White. 'Do as you will.' He turned to leave.

'Wait! Why do you care what I do?'

'The reputation of my students reflects upon me,' was his sharp reply.

Of course. How stupid to think that it could be anything else. Rue stood her ground and gave him a defiant look, but it was an empty gesture and she knew it. However she felt about him, she did not want him thinking of her like that. She wanted him to like her.

She hated that about him, too.

She watched White walk away. The more she knew him, the more confused she became about him. His stiff and formal behaviour was so much a part of him that no amount of provoking could dislodge it. He obviously disliked her teasing manner but made little attempt to correct her behaviour, which only made her do it more. She knew nothing about him as he volunteered no information whatsoever, and whenever she questioned Frith on him, Frith smiled and said she should ask White whatever she wanted to know.

She had never seen White in public before. It was quite extraordinary how much attention he attracted. She watched people turn their heads as he walked past them. No wonder he never went out much. She knew his lily-white skin was put about as a birth defect, but she wondered how many people actually believed that.

It was funny how people looked at him, as though they were trying to make it seem like they weren't, as if he was just another face in the crowd. But he wasn't; he could never be that. Not here. As he stopped in the middle of the hall and turned back, she saw them all hurriedly avert their gazes in case he caught them watching him. Which was stupid, because only someone very drunk or unaware would have missed those collective stares.

It was then that Rue realised White was walking back towards her. Inexplicably, her heart jumped. What was he doing?

As he reached her, he bowed his head shortly.

'Zelle Vela,' he said. 'Would you please join me in the next dance?'

'What?' said Rue, astonished.

'Dance. You mentioned you wish to dance tonight.'

'With you?'

White gave her one of his silences.

'Yes,' he said eventually.

'But that's . . . is that allowed?'

'I am unmarried,' he said. 'And a viable chaperone. Of course it is allowed.'

Rue waited for more, but he said nothing else.

'Er,' she said. 'I accept.' She strained to remember the correct reply. 'With thanks.'

White held out his hand. She stared at it.

'The next dance will start soon,' he said. 'We must go to the correct hall.'

Rue was paralysed. Touch him. Touch him as if he were an ordinary person and not her odd, daunting, enigmatic tutor.

Touch his hand.

They had never touched each other, not once. Not even accidentally. She'd wondered if it was because he found physical contact repulsive for some reason. She'd even teased him about it once. He had given her a White silence, and then changed the subject.

Yet here he was, offering his hand out to her.

'Come,' he said. 'We must go.'

She slid her hand into his. It was warm. His fingers curled around her palm and held it tight. Then he was walking, practically pulling her along. She could see faces turned towards them, rivers of people watching. She prayed she wouldn't trip.

When they reached the dance hall, couples had already lined up in their places. The pattern they were standing in was unfamiliar.

'Wait,' said Rue. 'Which dance is this? I won't know the steps!'

'I will lead you,' said White. There was a place open near the back of the set – in truth it was not very busy. Many people had migrated to the food tables in the dining hall by now.

White led Rue in front of him and stood her there. They waited for the music to start.

'I'm nervous,' said Rue. She could feel the stares of the dancers around them, like hot sunlight on her face.

'Ignore them. You will be perfect,' said White.

Before she could react to this, the music started. White stepped forwards and took her hand.

'First it is a box step,' he said, above the noise. 'You know it?'

'Yes,' said Rue. The box was easy, the first thing she had been taught. Most steps were built on it, she remembered.

'Four box, two linked, three box, and then change sides,' said White.

'All right,' said Rue. The steps were easy enough. She tried to concentrate on her feet, but her worry about the dance was nothing in comparison to being close enough to smell him. She watched the creases of his shirt, for safety; it was too difficult to look up into his face.

'Why are you here?' she blurted suddenly, as they moved through a link. She was conscious of his hand on her back as he guided her through it.

'To socialise.'

'But why? You don't go out around the city much. I've never seen you. Frith says you hardly ever go out at all.'

They passed, and then moved through the second link.

'Frith is the one who encouraged me to come out. To remove the mystery, so he said,' White replied, his voice dry.

'So people will get used to you,' said Rue.

White said nothing.

'Does it bother you that people treat you different?'

'It does not.'

'It doesn't bother me when people do it to me, neither,' said Rue.

'Yes it does.'

Rue did look up at him, then. 'Why do you say that?'

'You have spent this evening attempting to be as everyone here. Did you not say to me earlier that you wanted to feel normal?'

'That's not the same thing,' said Rue, momentarily forgetting her nervousness in outrage. To her everlasting shock, White was smiling.

'Yes it is. If it comforts you, we both lie. I would like to be treated as normal. But I also think to myself that I do not want to be anything like everyone else. It is hypocritical, and human, to feel both of these things.'

Rue thought about this. 'Why did you come here?' she said. 'To Angle Tar?'

The smile dropped from White's face, and Rue was sorry to see such a rare and magical thing go. Now he was himself again.

'I'm sorry if you think I'm rude,' she said. 'I know you don't like me much because of that.'

White looked as though he was about to open his mouth, but the set broke to change sides, and when they came back together to start the first box, he said nothing. Rue's heart had fallen into misery. Just when she thought the rest of the dance would be spent in silence, he spoke.

'I came to Angle Tar because it is so different,' he said. 'There is not another place like it in the whole world. That is a valuable thing.'

She wanted to ask him what it was really like outside of Angle Tar. What it was like in this strange-sounding URCI place. If they really did have boxes out there with whole worlds in them. If anything the silver-eyed boy said was true.

'Do you know a place called Iceland?' she said.

White looked at her. 'What do you know of Iceland?' he said.

'It's full of snow. They have things there that can make food out of air.'

'You have not told me this dream.'

Rue squirmed. How to get out of this? 'I had it last night,' she said. 'For the first time.'

'We must speak of this in your next lesson in detail.'

Rue looked away.

She had to keep the silver-eyed boy to herself.

The more she dreamed about him, the more she realised

that he was something more than her. Something outside of her. She supposed it had to be a Talented thing, but she was afraid that he represented a defect in her, somehow. No one else in the group saw strange silver-eyed boys in their Talent dreams; or if they did they weren't telling. So neither would she. White didn't need to know every little secret thing about her, did he?

'Syer,' she said.

'Yes.'

'In this dance we don't change partners.'

'No. It is not a mixer.'

'What's it called?'

White paused. Rue watched him, puzzled. He seemed uncomfortable.

'It is called an Intentional,' he said.

'Oh. Why?'

'I am not sure.' White looked away from her.

'What's the last step?' she pressed, aware that of the dances she had learned, there was usually a last step different from the rest.

'A two-turn round, and then finish.'

A moment later, they moved into it. White was extraordinarily good at dancing for someone who never socialised at balls. Rue wondered if he had had private training. When he led her he did it smoothly and she had no trouble understanding where he needed her to go. They turned once, and then again, circling back. Then he took both of her wrists in his hands and pulled her gently towards him until her arms were resting up against his chest.

'What are you doing?' she said, suddenly afraid.

'This is the last step,' he said. When she turned her head, she saw that he was right; the couples either side of them had pressed together in a similar fashion. Then she saw the man nearest to her lean down into the girl in his arms and kiss her.

She looked back at White, a horrified blush creeping across her face.

'Are we meant . . . to do that?' she managed.

'Of course not,' he snapped. 'It is optional.' His face was turned outwards, away from her.

Rue had never felt so awkward in her entire life. This was some kind of nightmare. She was standing so close to White that their bellies practically touched. When would the stupid music end?

Thankfully, a moment later, it did. Before they broke apart, though, she realised something. Her palm had been resting on his chest, and she could feel his heartbeat underneath it. It was pounding so fast she thought he might suddenly collapse there and then in the dance hall, but when she looked up into his face he seemed the same as ever.

Then he stepped away from her, and it was over. He bowed his head, and she remembered that she should do the same. Before she could say anything more, there were people all around them, swarming across the floor now that the dance had finished. Lea had appeared out of nowhere, and Rue could see just behind her stood the rest of the Talented group – none of whom she had seen all evening.

'Threya take us! What by all the gods were you *doing* with him?' squealed Lea.

'You were watching?' said Rue. Her voice sounded whispery and weak, and she cleared her throat in annoyance.

'Rue, half the *university* was watching.'

'I think it's disgusting,' announced Lufe.

'It's just a dance,' Rue said irritably. 'I was all alone and he offered to dance with me. It's the sort of thing he'd do to seem proper.'

'You were dancing an Intentional, Rue.'

'So? So what's that?'

Lea giggled. 'You don't know much, do you?' she said.

Lufe was smiling in his predictably superior fashion.

'Oh, Grad suck your bones,' said Rue, in high temper. Her pulse was still racing, and White had disappeared. What was she supposed to think about all this?

'Well, there's no need to be so rude. I want another drink, anyway. This is boring now. Lufe, get one for me, will you?'

'I've got you three already. Find another boy to be your garçon.'

Rue turned away as they started to argue. Marches had wandered off, and Tulsent stood to the side, looking awkwardly at Lea and Lufe.

They'll end up getting married for sure, Rue thought wearily.

She needed to get out of here.

She searched the corridors leading off the halls until she found a room thick with quiet and only a small, dim lamp for company. She sank down into a stuffed armchair, curling her legs under her, and stared at the paintings on the wall opposite until her eyes ached.

If only he would come in right now, as if he had been searching for her in every room. Then she could ask him what had happened. She could pin him down, alone, and demand that he tell her why he had done that. Why he behaved the way he did. Why and why.

Then, of course, he would kiss her.

She closed her eyes.

CHAPTER 22
THE CASTLE

FRITH

When Frith opened his eyes, he saw a stone wall.

Stone walls only ever meant one thing.

Oh no, his heart whispered, and sank miserably, hiding itself away.

He levered himself up from the floor. The air was freezing. His skin furred protectively. The ground slabs were hard and cold against his palms.

As usual, there was no door to the room. Just four blank and bare walls.

This is a dream, said his mind. Remember?

I know that. But.

No. Listen. You've just been to a Castle meet. You always get these dreams after a Castle meet. You know this.

But it didn't matter that he knew. The stone room was diseased, infecting him with fear.

'Frith,' came a familiar voice.

He looked around.

Ghost Girl stood a few feet away, her hands clasped primly before her.

This was strange. She wasn't usually in this dream. The

only other time she had been was in the first one he'd ever had. The one that had convinced him to work for her. The one he had carefully locked away in a part of his mind that he never wanted to visit, ever again.

'We need to talk,' she said. 'Away from a meet.'

It was so hard to keep control in this place. He felt like a child again, swallowed up in the dark, waiting to be eaten.

'Do we have to talk here?' he said. The whine in his voice dismayed him.

'Yes. This is the Castle. This is the only place we can meet outside of Life.'

Silence.

'All right,' he managed.

The girl stretched out a hand, her little fingers stroking the wall. She stroked as she talked, as if it helped her think.

'When we first came to you,' she said, 'we showed you what was going to happen to you. What was coming. We asked you to help us. You said yes.'

Frith's heart was pounding. God, it was so difficult to *think* straight in here.

'I did.'

'It's been a while now. Your programme is going well.'

'Thank you.'

'Yours is a small nation compared to World. We know this. Despite your disadvantages, yours is the programme we are currently the most interested in.'

'You flatter me.'

'It's because of White, Frith.'

Frith felt an icy thrill run gently along his skin.

'He's —'

He stopped. Tried again.

'He's doing well. He's progressing each student I send to him at an extraordinary rate.'

'I know. We've been watching him,' said Ghost Girl.

He couldn't stop a sudden dark wave surfacing on his face. 'You've been . . .'

'Watching him.'

Ghost Girl's black holes for eyes were fixed on his face. 'Are you keeping him close?'

'Yes.'

'Because you didn't keep Wren close. You lost him.'

That was too far, even for her. 'I didn't lose him. World has him now. Snearing has him. He's still in the programme, then, isn't he? Besides, you told me to let him go!'

'No. I just said not to stop him if he wanted to leave.'

God, she had a politician's love of carefully chosen words. Frith remembered the conversation with her very well, just after Wren had had his tantrum and gone to World. She'd all but ordered him to stop trying to find Wren. At the time, he'd thought she was trying to smooth the situation over and stamp out any potential retribution between agents.

But occasionally, he wondered if she'd had a different motive. He wished he knew what it was. He wished he knew all her secrets. He was so powerless.

'It's different with White,' he said. 'He has nowhere else to go.'

Her little frame rippled. 'Yes he does. All that's stopping

him is fear. You must give him good reasons to stay here, Frith. Don't drive him away.'

'I'm not going to!'

Silence.

Frith gathered his courage around him, as if it could protect him from the cold and the fear like a cloak.

'You don't tell me why I have to keep him close,' he said. 'All you say is that he's powerful. He's dangerous. But you tell me nothing more about him.'

She lowered her hand, watching him.

'He's the key,' she said at last. 'The key to what's coming. That's all you need to know.'

'I realise that. When I found him, I could see how import-ant he was to you. You think your avatar is so anonymous, but you might as well have screamed it out loud. He's what you've been waiting for, isn't he? Why? Because of what he can do?'

She stood by the wall like a statue.

'If you don't want the assignment,' she said quietly, 'I could have him taken away from you and given to someone else.'

Frith felt his heart skip in fright. He fought from showing it.

'I won't let you do that,' he said.

'Why not? It's all the same, surely. And if you don't feel you can handle him . . .'

'I didn't *say* that –'

'Then I'll give him to World.'

'They'll kill him!' Frith shouted.

Silence.

'Do you care for him, Frith?' came her little voice.

It shouldn't have unbalanced him, her needling. But here, where everything was a hundred times itself, he was a spinning top, unwinding, wobbling wildly.

'You owe me,' he said. 'I do your work for you, in the dark, stumbling blindly towards something I'm not even sure of. You don't tell us who you are and how you know the things you know. Are you Talented? Where are you from? Are you all Worlders? Another nation? Which one? China?'

But she said nothing at all.

He spread his hands. 'Is any of this even real?'

'Yes. In a sense,' she said. 'Not in a sense you'd understand.'

'Try me!'

'You're wasting time.'

'How the hell should I know that? Sometimes you say It's coming in the next few years. Sometimes you say it could be as long as twenty. Tell me. *Make* me understand!'

Outside the room, there came an ominous, deep-bellied, rolling boom.

The sound of buildings falling. Felt, rather than heard.

Frith's insides squeezed.

'Don't bring It here,' he pleaded, whispery. 'Why are you bringing It here? To scare me?'

'We don't have control over It, Frith. It roams the Castle, looking for a way in. We can't let It find a way in!'

Another boom. Closer.

Oh god. Oh no.

He didn't want to see It again. Once had been enough.

Another boom.

He sank to the floor, clenching every muscle he had to stop himself from leaping into full-blown panic.

You can't frighten me into doing what you want!

'We don't have the luxury of playing nice, Frith,' said Ghost Girl, as if he had spoken out loud. 'Everyone will die. You *know* this!'

The walls of the room actually shuddered.

Frith felt a moan trickle out of his throat.

'Stop this,' he said. 'Stop.'

She was still talking, but her words were getting lost, sucked into the gaping roar of sound outside.

'Tell me the truth about White!' he shouted. 'Stop tricking me!'

No, you don't.

No one controls me.

But she did. She did it with fear.

She had moved closer, bending down to his crouched figure, her thin, bony arms resting on her knees.

The booming was closer, and impossibly loud. His ears tried to shut down.

'It isn't real!' he screamed. 'None of it is! It's just a dream!'

'If you believe that,' came her tickling voice in his ear, 'then we're all dead.'

He didn't believe it. He knew it was real.

In his soul, he knew.

But they couldn't keep playing him like a harp, and they couldn't play with White's life like this, and they couldn't threaten things. Not any more.

He'd never had anyone of his own, and White was his.

Outside the room came a wet, bone-crunching roar.

'Frith, listen to me,' said Ghost Girl. He thought he could hear something in her voice. Urgency. Fear?

Wake up now, Frith. Wake up. God, wake up.

'Frith, listen to me!'

He buried his head on his knees.

Wake up wake up.

WAKE UP WAKE UP!

WAKE

The roar had gone, cut off mid-fury.

It was dark.

It was warm.

It was his room.

He had curled in a ball in the midst of his bed. He unclenched.

His body was shaking. He stopped it.

They couldn't be angry with him. He was doing what they wanted, after all. He would continue to keep White close. He would watch. He would know what White did before he did it. And whatever plan they had for White, Frith would make sure he was there to protect him from it.

He sat, clutching his bed blanket, thinking madly.

He had to find out everything he could about them. He had to know what they didn't want him to know. So he hadn't had much luck gaining information so far, but then he hadn't even spoken to the only people who knew anything about them – the other agents they had recruited.

Which meant that now he had to try like hell to forge some sort of alliance with World, and with that awful bastard Snearing, to see what they knew. For now, they were his only source of information.

And if the Castle brought him more nightmares, trying to screw him into his place with terror, well, then.

He just wouldn't sleep.

That was all.

CHAPTER 23

ANGLE TAR

WHITE

It had been a long, tiresome day.

Lufe had been especially troublesome in his lesson. He had been moody and snappish, thoughtlessly rude, as if White had done something to offend him. It didn't help that Lufe knew he was progressing much more rapidly than the rest of the group.

White sighed. He would go to bed early tonight. He would make sure his reports were ready. He would plan the rest of the week. When everything was done, then and only then would he allow himself to think about her, and the night of the ball, and the feel of her underneath his hands for the first time.

It was a stupid thing to have done, certainly, asking Rue to dance. But explicable. Within the boundaries of acceptable behaviour. When he wondered what Rue's reaction to it had been, he found himself sliding anxiously away from pursuing that line of thought, as if he didn't have the courage to contemplate any possible outcome. All of them, good and bad, scared him.

He set out from his classroom, locking it behind him.

He would take the long route back to his rooms. It would give him time to think. He would eat in his rooms tonight, instead of the tutor's dining hall; that meant sending through on the messaging service as soon as he got back, to get something in time from the kitchens for later.

The night air was frosted and thick. White liked the university about this time. The streets were quiet – students were elsewhere in the town, drinking or gambling or temple-visiting. Some of them might even be in their rooms studying. There was a low-level hum of life, of people moving about and lights shining through windows. He liked it. Liked to enjoy it from a distance.

It was at moments like these where this life he had chosen came into its own. There were other moments that made him think about just leaving. Not to go back to World, of course, but to find somewhere else new and accepting. Then he would shake off the illusion and see it for what it was. A life was a life, wherever he would be. And if he was honest, he didn't have the courage to start all over again.

He didn't miss the technology of World. He didn't miss the stagnation of a culture that thought a lot of itself and consequently had decided that change was bad. Anything new startled them senseless, made them fear.

But Angle Tar was a place annoyed by its own backwardness, brash, needing to prove itself. It was ignorant, entrenched in history, origin, old ways and habits. It was also exciting and vibrant, embracing anything it could get its hands on. It was a patchwork place, made up of other cultures and influences, but it was proud of the fact, not ashamed of it, and claimed the result as its own; as 'Angle Tarain'. Despite everything, the invasions and the conquerors of the last few hundred years, the reins of rule that had held it back and in a way continued to do so, it still struggled against the leash, snapping its jaws. He found it comforting, that such a small, inconsequential place had that spirit.

He reached his door, unlocking it and stepping inside, feeling his shoulders relax. They were not much, his rooms, but they had become a home to him. They were filled with his possessions, his and his alone, and inside them he could be himself, just be, without eyes on him and without judgement.

With this thought in his mind, he came to realise that someone was here, sitting in his chair by the fireplace.

'Good evening,' said Frith. He rose to his feet and bowed.

White said nothing.

Frith had never been in his rooms uninvited before. Not once. It was a violation and he knew it. He knew it would upset White. Something was wrong. Frith must be angry over something White had done wrong, and he would punish him for it by reminding him of his place here.

'Good evening,' said White eventually, hoping his voice had come out indifferent. It was a small rebellion, but it was there.

'I'm sorry to come into your rooms unannounced. I had assumed you'd be back by now. So I thought I would wait.'

'It is not a problem,' said White. He hung up his

275

great-coat. A maid had been in earlier and lit the fire, and it was beautifully warm. 'Have you eaten? I was going to send a message now to the kitchens.'

'In fact, I have. But please carry on. I don't want to interrupt your routine.'

Frith sat back down. White crossed to the messaging plate and wrote his order, then took the chair opposite Frith and met his gaze.

'Would you care for a drink?' said White.

'Certainly. I'll get it, though, no need for you to get up again. Whiskie?'

'Yes. It is on the bottom shelf.'

White watched Frith retrieve the bottle and select two glasses from the top cabinet with deft hands.

'You are back from World earlier than you expected,' said White. Whatever Frith wanted, he was determined to take his time about it, and White was not going to let it hang like a cloud over the table.

'Yes,' said Frith. 'It went quite well, this time.'

'I suppose you cannot talk about what you were doing there.'

Frith gave him a sidelong glance.

'No,' he said. 'Not really. But you may want to know that I happened to see Wren there.'

White was silent. Inside his chest, his heart skipped, nervous.

'Why?' he managed, after a moment to steady himself.

'No one gets to defect to another country for free, White. He works for their Talented programme. I heard tell he's their little test rabbit. They prod and poke him to see if they can quantify what he is and how he can do what he does. You know, with science.'

Frith said the last word with a kind of mild amusement, that for him seemed to translate as downright derision.

'How is he?' said White quietly.

'Oh, quite ridiculous-looking. He's had his whole body changed, in the way Worlders love to do. He's all slim and narrow, and has silver-coloured eyes, of all things. God knows what purpose they serve. I suppose he's just trying to fit in.'

White watched Frith dip a lemon sugar cube in his whiskie glass and soak the liquid up before putting it into his mouth. He had the sweetest tooth White had ever come across.

They sat in silence for a moment. Frith selected another cube and dipped it into his glass. 'How did the ball go?' he said.

It was actually impressive, really it was. Every time it was impressive. There was no hint whatsoever that this was what Frith was angry about; but it could only be this.

'It was odd,' said White. 'But interesting.'

'You've said that about every social occasion I've sent you to,' Frith said, with a smile.

'I enjoy the formality of it,' said White. 'Everything has a rule that should be obeyed. I enjoy the structure of the evening, and when each dance comes I understand what is happening. It is the talking and drinking I do not enjoy.'

'Talking and drinking is the only way people get to know each other here,' said Frith. 'How did our Talented group fare?'

'As well as can be expected. Lufe was very comfortable in that context, but he comes from such a background. Lea also. I suspect they are having a relationship, or having something, at least.'

'No surprises. Freya?'

'Did not talk much, did not dance, complained to be taken home.'

'Her usual self. Rue?'

Now it had come to it, White found he couldn't hide it as well as he had thought. His throat constricted at the mention of her name, and he knew he had paused too long.

'Vela Rue was a little too easy in her choice of company. I had to intervene at one point to save her from an embarrassment. Thereafter she behaved properly.'

'White. You danced with her.'

Finally, there it was.

But there wouldn't be shame and there wouldn't be defiance. He would show Frith that his behaviour had been normal by treating it as such.

'I did. Lea, her chaperone, left her. She knew no one and expected to see you there. When she realised that you would not be, she became upset. A boy had found her; he was taking her to the gardens.'

'Was she refusing to go?'

'He was giving her Esprit and telling her it was a harmless drink. His intentions were unfavourable, in the least.'

Frith sat back. 'Then you were absolutely right to intervene. So why did you dance with her?'

The key was not to hesitate, but also not to let it all come out smoothly as if it were rehearsed.

278

'She was alone and upset. She said that she wanted to dance. She needed a chaperone and so I decided to be such. I am not sure what it is that I did wrong.'

Frith laughed and White felt a twinge of nervousness. When Frith laughed, it was almost never out of genuine humour. And if he laughed when he was angry, the person in the room with him would do well to make an excuse to leave.

'Either you are genuinely ignorant of what you've done, which I can't really believe, or you're attempting to play me, which has never been, is not, and will never be a good idea. White, how long has this been going on?'

If White believed enough in his own innocence, it would come across in his voice.

'Of what do you speak?' he said.

'How tiresome. You won't even give me the truth. Do you trust me that little?'

White felt a sudden flash of resentment. He knew that Frith had intended that, but he still couldn't stop himself.

'Trust you? How am I supposed to do that?'

Frith spread his hands. 'How? Well, let's see. When you came here alone, looking for help, for a reason to explain your betrayal of your country, did I turn you away? Did I treat you like a spy and torture you? Have I treated you since with anything but respect? When Wren betrayed us and you didn't see it coming, when you didn't tell me about what was going on until it was too late, when he nearly ruined *everything* for us, did I blame you? Did I punish you? Didn't I take care of everything?'

Frith sat back.

'And this is your response,' he said, with a sharp-edged smile. 'All this time, I've tried to prove myself to you, over and over. Did not one single thing I did mean anything to you?'

White listened to this speech with a mixture of surprise and irritation. He knew Frith was playing him with guilt. He knew it. But Frith seemed agitated; he wouldn't stop gesturing with his hands, which was unlike him. Hands had never been a part of his conversation. And what was the right response?

There wasn't one.

'Well, apparently not,' said Frith, after a moment. 'However, let us forgo our usual pretence, just for a moment, and then we can forget that we were ever so candid, and go back to normal. So listen to me, because I can see what you won't. You made a mistake at the ball, and now you must repair the damage. I'll take care of public opinion, but you must see to your students. They've lost their respect for you. They laugh about you behind your back. Do you see?'

White suddenly realised why Frith was so angry. It was because he hadn't known about it. He hadn't even considered the possibility of it. Who knew the last time someone had been able to fool him so completely? It wasn't triumph White felt at this realisation; it was relief. The jibe about his students should have upset him, but he found that he couldn't care much about it, if he thought about her and the way her waist had felt in his grip.

'You didn't know,' he said.

Frith, to his credit, shrugged it off beautifully. 'No, I

didn't. In all honesty, I hadn't thought it even credible. It's happened before, of course. Students and teachers. It's a time-honoured cliché. But I didn't think it would happen with you.'

'Why not?' said White, genuinely curious.

'Why?' Frith replied, and laughed. 'Of all the women you could pick, and there are some jewels in my acquaintance alone, why her?'

'I have no idea.'

'Perhaps you should think on it. Work out what it is that attracts you, so you can get rid of it.'

'What will happen if I do not follow your advice?'

Frith swilled his whiskie. 'You have to ask?'

White's heart pounded. He was pushing, hard, and something could break.

'How could you stop it?' he said. 'It is not illegal.'

Frith changed his line of attack. 'If this stems from unhappiness, speak to me. Tell me what has caused it. I'll do my best to change things for you.'

'I do not rebel,' said White. He struggled not to show amusement. 'It is very difficult for you to accept the only other explanation. Why is this?'

Frith did not respond. He looked around the room, as if appraising its condition. 'This is a nice apartment. But I know being stuck in the old alchemy tower by yourself bothers you, though you'd never admit to wanting company. I could have you moved somewhere else, somewhere bigger. Still quiet, away from the big living halls. There's a set near the research complex.'

'This is a bribe?' said White.

Frith looked at him. 'No, just an option. Please don't dismiss it.'

Silence fell.

'I don't want to sit here and call you stupid and tell you what you should already know,' said Frith, after a moment. 'But please, think. If you're not serious about her, you'll ruin her life and her reputation by dallying. If you are, you'll do the same thing. What do you suppose people will think about your relationship? Do you think they'll accept it? They can barely accept *you*. What do you think will be said about her? Do you see yourself marrying her? If you do, it won't be in Angle Tar. You can't even apply for citizenship, never mind a marriage licence. Perhaps you think you could leave Angle Tar together. But of course, you can't go back to World now. They'll lock you up without a thought as a treacherous spy; they may even kill you. And what do you think will happen to her then?'

'You have spoken much this evening,' said White, his voice thin with fury. 'You must be tired from dispensing such a lot of advice. I will bid you goodnight.'

Frith got up smoothly, as if all were normal, and bowed.

'I'm sure you'll think on it,' he said, his tone polite.

White tracked him to the door with his eyes. Watched him close it behind him.

What would his life be like, without Frith? Would it be better, without the constant feeling of unwillingly belonging so completely to another? Would there be someone else instead, controlling every part of his existence? Could there be someone else like Frith? White didn't think so.

Once, a while ago, White had wondered in a vague, fanciful sort of way how hard it would be to kill Frith. Just once. Then, by chance, he had seen him in a fight. They had gone together to meet a contact from World in a fairly seedy part of the city. The contact had promised some sort of vague exchange of information deal. The reality had been no such thing, and the situation had turned sour fast. The contact had pulled a rod, the kind of weapon inconceivable in Angle Tar, and there should have been no possibility of escaping that.

The impression White had had of a striking snake had never left him. Frith was horribly fast, but his true advantage lay in being able to predict exactly what you would do next. His ability was frightening. The contact had stopped before he had the chance to think about firing the rod.

Without Frith, White would still not be free. He'd heard that things had started to change after his departure from World, not least its covert acceptance of Talented people as useful rather than dangerous. Wren was proof of that. But they would always, always see White as a traitor and a spy.

Frith had a way of killing you with the truth. He used it as a weapon. White understood everything he had said already. Hadn't he used the same arguments with himself over the last few weeks to try and reason a way out of his ridiculous situation with Rue?

But it was too late for all that. It was too late the moment she had put her hand in his. If there had been a way back, it would have been before that, in the weeks when he was sure she felt nothing for him. Now that he was not sure, he clung to the hope like a dying man to a miracle cure.

Nothing he could come up with, nothing Frith could threaten him with, made him even consider the possibility of backing down. If she truly wanted him, he would do anything to have her.

It would be bad with Frith now. It would be bad because of so many reasons. Because White wouldn't obey. Because he wouldn't stay in his place. And because of a secret part of Frith's soul that he had revealed to White, not so long ago. They had never spoken of it again between them; gone and forgotten, as if it hadn't even happened.

But it had happened.

It had been a few months ago; the night before Frith had set off to the south west to recruit Rue.

White had been alone, as usual, sitting at his desk in his teaching room. His last student had just left for the evening, and the letter he had in his hands had been burning a hole in his pocket all day.

'Bad news?' Frith had asked. He stood in the doorway, lingering hesitantly.

White folded up the letter and put it away. It was from his sister, Cho. There might be a lot of trouble for both of them if her letters were ever intercepted. No need to panic and try to get it out of Frith's sight as quickly as possible – it would only draw his attention to it.

'You look very tired,' said White. It was shocking how much concern he could force into his voice. Or was it more shocking that he no longer tried as much to feel friendship towards Frith, because now it was second nature? Frith was his friend. His only friend.

'It was a long trip,' Frith replied, mashing the palms of his hands into his forehead.

'But successful.'

'I suppose you heard. She's older than I'd like, but already quite Talented, from what I hear.'

'Who found her?' said White.

Frith came forwards into the classroom.

'Sedar, my youngest recruiter. He has an old friend in Border City who is acquainted with her father.'

'Border City.'

'You'd know it as New Lyon. Colloquially it's called Border City, just as Capital should officially be Parisette. Or London, as some would have it. Take your pick.'

'There have been a few from Border City, have there not?'

'Second largest city after Capital – a higher probability.'

White watched Frith. He really did look tired.

'Not very many this year,' he said.

'No. There doesn't appear to be a reason for it, at least not one I can uncover and prevent. There's another I've just heard of. Another girl, apprenticed to a hedgewitch I used to know. She sounds promising, but the situation is delicate.'

'Why is this?'

Frith gave him a wan smile. 'The hedgewitch despises me. It will need some careful handling.'

White had a glimpse of Frith's past, a past he did not want to know about. It was one thing to try to puzzle Frith out based on anecdotes and stories – it was another to have it related from the man himself, when he wouldn't even be able to understand Frith's reason for telling him. Because there was always a reason.

'What about this one that Sedar has found?' White said, carefully attempting to sidestep. 'She will come?'

'God, yes. She can't wait to get away. Fortunately for us, her home life is less than satisfactory. Her father is a drunken idiot who might possibly have ruined her. You will see if there is anything to salvage.'

'Her name?'

'Tresombres Freya.'

'That is an old Angle Tar name, no? She must be aristocratic.'

'It's an Empire family. Unfortunately now fallen to disrepute and a faint sort of poverty. Their house is lovely, though. Almost as large as mine was, growing up. They live out of a tiny corner of it, and the rest of it is rotting away. It's a shame.'

White leaned back in his chair.

'Are you hungry? You may tell me of it over supper,' he said.

'No. Do you have a drink here?'

White leaned down and unlocked the deepest of his desk drawers. He kept a stunted bottle of flowered quintaine in there for fainting and vomiting emergencies – unfortunately not that uncommon, especially with students learning to Jump on their own the first few times.

'I have only one glass,' he said.

Frith produced a cap glass from his person in reply. White couldn't imagine what he was doing with it. There was no possible reason you would walk around with a cap glass in your pocket unless you were an alcoholic.

White poured. Frith talked.

'It was odd, at first,' he said. 'There we sat, attempting to tell this pickled fool what exactly the Talent is and why exactly he should let his only daughter go to study with us. It was much like talking to air. I didn't have to tell him about the compulsory law, he already knew, and that was why he was being so unmoving towards us. Loss of power, you see, over her. Unfortunately, Sedar became emotional and pressed the issue. The father had thrown Freya to the floor and drawn a knife before the poor boy could finish his outraged sentence.'

Frith took another pull from his cap glass. He had finished the shot in two swallows, and White silently poured another. It was becoming obvious that Frith had been drunk when he'd arrived here. He was, of course, the sort of man on whom drunk sat as normally as sober. His only tendency, which gave it away, was to talk. White was starting to suspect that when he drank, it was because he wanted to talk, and being drunk was the only way he could do it.

'What happened?' he said

Frith said nothing for a long moment. Then he shugged.

'A bit of a fight. The man managed to get the knife almost to my throat before I disarmed him. We left him tied to the kitchen table. The maid would find him in the morning.'

White watched him.

'That is very . . . unusual,' he said. 'That he got so close to you.'

'Yes, I suppose so. I reacted too poorly; I had allowed my mind to be somewhere else that evening.'

Frith fell silent again, staring at his cap glass.

'Will you visit the other?' said White, after a pause.

Frith looked up. 'I'm sorry?'

'The other. The one in the care of the hedgewitch.'

'Yes. Yes. I must do it. I'm going tomorrow morning.'
Frith stared into the fire.

White wondered. Frith had never hesitated in recruiting someone before. Neither had he ever mentioned some country hedgewitch with such apparent power. Frith had never been one to show his fear like this, or his weaknesses.

Out loud, he said, 'What is her name? The witch apprentice?'

'Vela Rue.'

'You are finding more commons, these days.'

'I suppose they were always there. My network is spread a little thinner in the country, as you might understand. It's more difficult to gauge out there – there are no recruitment halls, as there are in the cities. Communication is poorer. It's a very different life.'

'You sound like you know it well,' said White, trying to lighten the mood. 'I had thought you were from Parisette.'

'Well, yes, but our main house was out in the country, though that's not quite the same thing. But I used to summer in various backwater villages, on occasion. My mother had decided it would be good to broaden my experience of life. In other words, she wished me to live with common folk, to understand them better.'

White said nothing. He suspected the quieter he became, the more Frith would talk.

He was right.

'And so, one place she sent me to, I would have been about sixteen, was a little village in Bretagnine. Do you know Bretagnine?'

White shook his head.

'It's an area in the far south west of Angle Tar. Its original name, back before the French, was Kernow. The village was called Tregenna, a very old name. During the French years it was officially changed to a French designation, as with everywhere, but the locals completely ignored the new name and it remained Tregenna. And probably will for ever after.

'I had become used to these summers by now, if not happy about them, and I went for a month, which feels like a life-time when you're young. I lived with an old Kernow family – this family was particularly old, they could trace their lineage for many hundreds of years. If they had money they would have had the status of my own family, but they didn't, so no one cared. My mother always placed me with such families, her thinking being that I would at least be mixing with the very best sort of commoner.

'Poltern, that was their name. I helped on their farm – they had pigs, cows, chickens. Their produce was quite famous, locally – people visited most days to buy eggs, or dried ham, or milk and cream. It was very hard work. It was the first time I understood the gulf between those such as I and the rest of the population. How we depended on all these unknown people for our survival. That was the lesson my mother wanted me to learn, and I did.

'I took my books and studies with me to work on the

rare times when I had an hour or two to myself. They were not unkind, you understand. They were practical. In their eyes, you worked to live, and you lived to work. Books were distractions. Fanciful learning was pointless. It produced nothing of value. So they could not quite grasp my frequent need to be alone and read about subjects they had never heard of and couldn't care for at all. Most of the village was the same. The only person who interested me was the local hedgewitch.

'I'd never encountered one before. Our family had its own doctor, of course, and hedgewitches are ten a franc in the cities, but by reputation alone they're reserved for the poor or desperate. You know how they're seen.

'In the country it's completely different, I assure you. With your local hedgewitch rests the future health of you and your family. They help new mothers give birth, and are often last call for those on their way to death. They keep the village secrets, and know more about everyone than everyone else does.

'The Tregenna hedgewitch was called Penhallow Fern, and whenever anyone spoke of her it was with a variety of emotions, but it was also always with respect. To have such power over swathes of people naturally drew my intense curiosity. I tried very hard to find an excuse to visit her, but one does not visit a witch's house unless one has need, and I never did.

'Then I had a touch of luck, if you like. I was working in the cow stalls, clearing them out while they were to pasture. One was sick and wouldn't be moved from her stall, no matter how anyone tried, so I had to work around her as best I could. She stepped on my hand as I was shovelling hay on the ground, and had sat back to rest for a moment.

'The pain was intense. I kept screaming and brought a worker running, one of the Poltern sons. Hammet; that was his name. He was enormous – they all were, like men made out of boulders. He stood me up and forced me to walk the mile or so to her house, even though I cried and protested the whole way. I wasn't a brave child, I must confess. Eventually we reached this small cottage set back on its own. He hammered on the door, and it opened, and there stood this boy.'

Frith paused, then. The sudden silence was startling. White realised he had been leaning forward, fascinated, and sat back.

Frith poured himself another drink, took in a deep breath of its scent, sipped, and continued.

'This boy was about my age, I supposed, and even slighter than me. He was brown, nut brown, and had big, glittering eyes, like an animal. He looked us up and down with an amused face and asked us what was wrong. Hammet told him my hand had been crushed by a cow hoof, and the boy laughed. Have you ever been laughed at while in pain?'

Yes, thought White.

'It's a very humiliating experience. The boy led us inside and explained that Zelle Penhallow was not there at present, but that he could mend my hand, and what would we be offering as payment? Hammet said that the boy's mistress could have her pick of their newest crop of hens, if she wished. The boy agreed that it was a good price and then he sat me down. I'd only been half-listening to their exchange. I couldn't concentrate on much beyond the pain in my hand. But what I had heard made me want to strangle this cocky boy in front of me, treating my pain as if it were a childish phase I was having.

'He mended it, though. The boy. He made some highly dubious-looking pastes and rubbed them into my hand, while I tried my hardest not to cry with the hurt. He made me want to seem braver than I was, as if I could prove to him that he had no right to laugh at me. Then he sat, my hand resting on his. He closed his eyes and said nothing. I looked at Hammet, who shook his head and told me to stay there for as long as it took and keep quiet. The whole thing was a show, of course. The paste he had applied to my hand made it grow numb after a moment, so that it appeared he was doing it himself. Tingling and stinging at first, and then nothing. It was quite impressive, and so I was affected at the time. Hammet looked as though he'd seen a ghost when he saw me sit upright and regain my colour. I told him the pain had gone and he stood, babbling to the boy his thanks, telling him to bring Zelle Penhallow over in the morning for her payment. Then he pushed me out of there as fast as he dared. On the way home and all that evening I tried to question him on the boy, but he wouldn't talk.

'The next morning, they came together, the boy and his mistress. The witch herself was a pleasant-looking woman, plump and motherly. I could see why people would trust her with their secrets. I couldn't see why so many people were afraid of her, although I understood that people in a position of power always attract such feeling. She inspected my hand before choosing her hen; I suppose to satisfy herself that the boy had done a good job with it. As she went off to the yard with Mussyer Poltern I hung back, hoping the boy would speak to me. I asked him his name. He said it was Oaker. I made some passing snobbish reference to country families always choosing such simple names, with rarely any deep meaning or finesse. But instead of becoming angry the boy smiled and said that my name sounded very much like I'd inserted my head into my own backside. We instantly became friends.

'From then on, I wanted to spend every second I had with Oaker. When I wasn't with him I thought of him; each moment I could devote to him I did. He could not bore me, nor turn me away from him. I'd never met someone so fascinating. He spoke to animals as if they were his friends, and they in turn treated him with affection and respect. He commanded the other young of the village simply with his presence. Everyone wanted to be his friend. He was by turns charming or cruel to all of us, randomly doling out his affection as if he thought we weren't worth distinguishing between. Naturally everyone wanted to be the one to capture his special attention, so we spent our time fawning around him like dogs. Anything he asked me to do, I did. Some of those things were not things I'd have liked anyone to know I was responsible for, and I'm sure it was the same for many of his other friends. He had a way of persuasion. There was something about him, something mysterious, like a secret he kept that made him feel superior to everyone around him. He was afraid of nothing, and it intrigued me; I wanted to know why. What was this secret ingredient that made him so sure in every situation? Of course, I found out soon enough.

'Oaker had been favouring me of late, and we had spent some time together alone. I was in a constant state of nervous happiness, ready to do anything he asked of me. One particularly hot day he suggested we go to the river together for an hour or two. I met him at a secluded spot along the bank, an area I hadn't been before. I could see why it wasn't popular with anyone else. The grass was scrubby and there wasn't a lot of shade.

'After a time, when we had been swimming and eaten all the food we found, I asked him why he'd wanted to come here, hoping his response would be that it was to guarantee that we'd be alone. He just smiled and said he wanted to show me something. I must have looked wary, because he laughed at my face. After much teasing and playing, the end result was that he told me to sit still and watch him. And at first nothing happened. I watched, then started to grow bored and somewhat irritated by his behaviour. My eyes never left him, not once.

'He was there. And then he was not there.'

Suddenly, White understood. He understood, finally, how Frith had known about the Talent if he was not himself Talented, a question that had nagged at him ever since they had first met.

Frith had not looked up.

'It really was extraordinary,' he said, his tone brittle with forced calm. 'He was there. Then he was not. You're used to it, I suppose. For me, I confess, it still surprises me every time I've seen it. There was no apparent transition. His face was collected, still, as if he concentrated very hard. His bare arms were stiff, I could see the hairs on them raised, gold in the sunlight. He was there. Then he was not. My first reaction was to assume that I'd somehow become confused – that I had hallucinated him, perhaps, or that I had looked away, fallen asleep, lost time, and he'd left me there. I looked about, as if to see him walking away from me, further down the riverbank or back amongst the trees. And then I realised that I had felt the air shift when he had disappeared – I had felt it move into the space he had left behind, I had heard it rush inwards. My confusion turned to wonder, and then to amazement and delight. I waited for him to return – it was an incredible trick. He would explain it to me. He would appear back in front of me, laughing.

'I waited there for hours. I waited until the sun had started to turn red in the sky, and the Poltern boy Hammet had been sent all over the village, looking for me. But I had no patience for that. Instead of returning to them and allaying their fears, I got up from where I'd been sitting, unmoving and alone. I walked to the Penhallow house, knocked on the door. Kept knocking until the mistress herself answered it. Instead of looking at me astonished, as I'd expected, she sighed and let me in.

'"Where is he?" I asked her.

'"He came by not long ago, but now he's down in the village with his friends," she said. She saw the incensed look on my face and told me to sit down, but I wouldn't.

'"Let me guess. He disappeared on you and didn't come

back?"' said the witch, a strange, sad sort of smile on her face. My anger deflated and I sat.

"'He does this trick a lot, then," I said.

"'Tis no trick, I'm sorry to say," said the witch.

"'Am I supposed to believe that it's magic?"'

"'If the inexplicable is magic, then yes, it is. Others might claim him to be a demon or god of some sort. But he's just a boy, same as you."'

"'He's *not* the same as me," I said. "I would not play such a stupid joke on someone simply to make them worship me."

'She was looking at me with a depth of knowledge I hadn't felt from anyone in quite some time, and it made me uncomfortable. I wasn't used to being understood, not even then. But I was in a high temper, and when you allow emotions to control you, you lose control of everything else. In her face she showed me that she understood her son exactly, that she understood why I was so angry with him, why I had used the word "'worship".

"'Don't punish him," she said to me. "He's not as clever as you."

"'Does everyone know about this?"' I said.

"'Not at all. I take great pains to keep it secret, and he takes great pains to have it out there for all to see, silly cock. Those who do know are in debt to me. I keep their troubles and they keep mine; on such a backbone the life of a village turns. But he's convinced he's special and will have none of this secretive business."

""He *is* special," I said. "Are you trying to tell me that there are many people who can do what he does?"

"'He's not the only one I've met, if that's what you mean,'" was her obtuse reply. "But he's the only one round here for miles."

'And there, you have it – the seed that was planted in my head with her innocuous sentence that would grow over some years into something of a preoccupation of mine. She was very clever, that woman, perhaps one of the cleverest I've met. She could read me and I feared it.

'She told me that I'd be wise to put it out of my mind and make nothing more of it than what it was – a rarity that meant little. She could see what it could mean, and had done from the beginning of it, I presume. For her own reasons she wished it not to be used in such a way. She also took great pains to play Oaker down. I suppose it was obvious the impression he'd made on me; that he made on everyone young and impressionable. I was angered by her interference, by her accurate assessment of me, and wouldn't listen. She was correct on every point, however.

'When I found Oaker it was in the square, surrounded by his admirers. He saw me and a smile broke across his face as if we had that afternoon shared the most glorious joke. He called my name and I went to him, but stood my ground in front. He asked me what was wrong in a most patronising tone.

'"You left me on the riverbank," I said.

'"Grad take me, have you been sitting there all this time?" he exclaimed in his knowing fashion. "I thought you cleverer than that, you know it."

'I was going to tell everyone what he could do. I was so angry at him. I wanted to ruin his smug little life. He wouldn't see it that way at first. He would celebrate the awe it would inspire, but the awe would eventually turn to fear and mistrust. People would see him for what he really was.

'People would see the truth of him.

'I hoped that he might still be able to care about me. But of course everything his mother had said about him was right. He'd done his trick to bask in my heightened adoration, and couldn't understand why I was angry. So to defend himself, he mocked me in front of everyone. Called me names. When I thought of all the things I'd done for him, things that would irreparably damage my reputation, it was as if he could see them on my face and seized on them, speaking them out loud. His friends looked at me with shock, loathing, and pity. The pity scratched at me like a knife, as he knew it would. It was a fight, only with words. He'd scored the first wound, and if I let him, would deliver the killing stroke.

'So I did it. I said it out loud to all of them. I told them all what he could do, and they laughed at me. But Oaker did what I hoped he would do – he backed me up. And then he went further. In front of all of them, he disappeared again. It was as incredible as it had been the first time. One boy sprang up, burst into tears, and ran straight home to his mother, who he told. It was all over the village by the morning. It took less time than you would think for people to credit it. The son of a witch would of course have such tendencies. There would be questions asked about how he did it, what he used it for, why it had been kept secret. There would be fearful looks, hateful looks, suspicious whisperings. There would be judgement and blaming him for things that went wrong. It would get worse, and worse.

'But before it came to that, I'd written to my mother to send me a carriage home. After that evening in the square I never again sought his company or looked him out. He never approached me for reconciliation or apologies, and I knew, at last and for certain, that he'd never cared for me in the slightest, that my hopes on that score had been ridiculous, founded on my own imaginings, that he'd played on them as he did on everyone's, that he'd known how I felt and used it to his advantage. So I felt nothing for what I'd done, because it was a just punishment.'

Frith stopped, then.

White uncovered his mouth, which he had been gripping with his hand like some imitation of a woman's feigned gesture of horror. Frith seemed quite calm now, his earlier agitation dissipated. He looked up at White, who returned the gaze out of pride, but couldn't hold it.

'Why did you tell me this?' said White, giving in.

'The hedgewitch whose apprentice has come to my attention,' said Frith, 'is the same mother of Oaker I encountered all those years ago. So now you can understand my apprehension. She has no call to help me and may even do something foolish while I'm visiting there. I'm not sure. She's unpredictable.'

'Do I remind you of that boy?' said White, before he could stop the stupid, stupid words coming out.

Frith only smiled, and said nothing.

'What happened to him?' said White, while inside his head he shouted at himself to shut up.

'I don't know. I actively never tried to find out. But I will, I suppose, once I get there. He's never been recruited, even though I have a person in place down there, so I assume he either left the village a few years ago or is dead.'

Dead was such a casual word in Frith's mouth. White felt his skin prickle and willed himself to remain neutral.

The story and the message had been clear enough, though, and White had not forgotten it; no matter how much he had tried. He knew why Frith had told him. Somewhere inside his head, in a box he never opened, he knew.

And now, between them, there was Rue.

CHAPTER 24
ANGLE TAR

RUE

'Wake up.'

Rue ignored the voice. She had been having a very pleasant dream about being able to fly and was fairly certain the voice had nothing to do with it. In any case, it was not time to get up yet.

Or was it? She opened one eye, seized with middle-of-the-night panic that she'd somehow overslept and someone had been sent to see if she was all right.

Her clock was showing twenty past two, and there was no crack of light slicing across the floor from the gap in her curtains, so it was quite definitely the middle of the night. The delicate little filigree numbers on her clock glowed gently in the darkness.

'You have to get up now, Rue. We don't have much time.'

'Who's there?' she croaked.

'Who else would it be?' said the voice. She recognised it, she was sure, but it sounded rougher than she remembered. She turned her head, peering into the gloom.

There he was, a shifting shape at the end of her bed.

'Get up,' he said. The sharpness in his voice stung. He didn't usually talk like that, not to her.

'Go away,' she snapped. 'I'm sleeping.'

His voice became softer. 'I'm sorry, my sweetheart. But we only have a few hours and this has to be done tonight. It has to.'

Rue sat up, caught. 'What has to? What's going on?'

The silver-eyed boy would say nothing more. All he did was twirl about the room impatiently while she dressed. As soon as she had pulled on her winter coat, he had her hand.

'What's going on?' she said again, trying to stall him. He was making another Jump with her, she could tell. And again so quickly, giving her no time to prepare herself. It came easily to him. It was still frightening to her. He didn't seem to understand that.

'Rue, my love, I'm going to show you something,' said the silver-eyed boy. He was looking straight ahead, grasping her hand so tightly her fingertips were buzzing. 'Something you must see for yourself. And then I'm going to tell you a story. But you must make up your own mind about what you think of it all.'

Before Rue could make anything of this, she was pulled into the Jump.

When she came through to the other side, she thought it had gone wrong. Her nightmares about being stuck mid-Jump came back to her; trapped in an in-between place with no light, no sound, no heat and no life. A nothing that would go on forever. Lost and alone in the middle of it, on and on, and on. Until she died.

The darkness here was not absolute, though. As her nausea passed and her aching chest eased, the panic faded with it. Gradually, she made out differences in the black all around her; varying shades of shadow. The silver-eyed boy's hand squeezed her own. She was grateful for his comfort.

'Stay close,' he said in a soft voice. 'We'll need to walk a little. Don't be alarmed – we are somewhere real.'

They started to walk. The ground was solid and flat as if paved, but seamless, unlike the city cobbles she knew. It was not that dark, once you became accustomed to it. She could see enough now to know that they stood in a tunnel, though they were somewhere in the middle of it, for the light was the same whichever way she looked.

'Which country are we in?' she whispered. They seemed to be alone, but the air carried sound and their footsteps echoed alarmingly. The ceiling was high, too high to feel unnaturally close.

'An old one,' said the silver-eyed boy. 'This is one of a vast series of tunnels and halls built underneath a great city. They seem to go on forever, though they don't. They were built a long time ago as a place of protection for the people above ground, in times of war.'

'We're underground?'

'Yes. Don't worry. There's more light the further in we go, and I have light with me.'

'Put it on, then,' said Rue, attempting to be casual.

'Not yet. These tunnels were built by very clever men in great secrecy. There was a time when this country was threatened by everyone around it. It was small, insignificant.

Its neighbouring countries had built weapons, Rue, weapons that with one blast could destroy an entire city, kill everyone in it, and burn it to the ground.'

His voice had become stronger and echoed forcefully, expanding out from them in invisible clouds of sound. Rue was silent. Such a weapon was so ridiculous, she couldn't even conceive of it. He had shown her things she could accept, even as she marvelled at their existence. This she could not. Who would build such a thing? Someone who could destroy whole cities would be a god. They would also be the most reviled and feared person who ever lived. Why?

'These tunnels,' came his voice again, 'were built so that should such a threat occur, the people of the city could escape the horror above and live here in relative safety until the danger had passed. As they had no real defences of their own against such weapons, it was the only way they could think of to survive.'

'They would stay here? In the dark?'

'Well, and so the tunnels all used to be lit. But after such a long time, the lights don't work very well any more. The core generators are no longer powerful enough. Closer to the centre, most basic systems are still running, though.'

Rue ignored this. Sometimes the silver-eyed boy forgot himself and spoke to her as if she were his equal, using words and concepts she had no grasp on how to begin understanding. She tried not to resent it. She should be grateful that he could sometimes mistake her for being as clever as that.

'But you see, Rue, though this place is big, it's designed

to comfortably accommodate a small number of people. They had supplies, systems, medicines, comforts enough for only five thousand.'

'But what about the rest of the city?'

His voice sounded triumphant. 'So glad you asked. The five thousand chosen few were carefully selected on the basis of wealth, class and usefulness. These people were secretly tattooed with a special symbol on their heads, underneath their hair. If you had such a tattoo, when the threat came, you'd go to a specially designated entrance to the tunnels and show the gatekeepers your tattoo. Then, and only then, you'd be allowed to reach safety.'

She already knew the answer, but felt compelled to ask. 'What about everyone else?'

'If they knew of the tunnels' existence and managed to find one of the gates, they would not be allowed entry. If they pressed the issue, they'd be killed.'

Rue shook her head. 'That's ridiculous. Everyone else would die.'

'Of course. And there were a lot more people living in the city than there are now.'

'But why wouldn't they let them in?'

'Well, the richest automatically gained entrance. After all, their money had helped pay for the tunnels' creation in the first place. It was only fair, in their eyes. After that, it was a matter of those with the best genes. Those who came from the most aristocratic families, the purest of blood.'

'But why? That doesn't make sense.'

'It did to them. If they were going to lose the vast

majority of the city population, it made sense they would save only the best, to create future generations of only the best.'

'Why are we here?' said Rue. This country sounded awful. It was nothing like any of the incredible places he had taken her to see so far. Why show her this?

'You should know all sides of life, Rue. You should be shown what is kept from you.'

Rue struggled to keep up with all of this. They had been walking throughout the conversation. It was late. She was tired. Her mood was turning incredibly sour.

'Near enough,' said the silver-eyed boy suddenly. She looked around, surprised. The light was much brighter now, but it had been growing so gradually she hadn't noticed. 'Let's see how far we can get.'

He took something from his pocket that she couldn't see. There was a short pause. Then an explosion of fierce, painful light. She screwed her eyes shut and fell. Her back scraped the floor.

When she opened her eyes, they burned and she had to squeeze them into slits. She could just make out the silver-eyed boy standing straight with light spilling from his hand like water. It moved quickly, sluicing along the floor and crawling up the tunnel walls. Whatever surface it touched glowed brightly after it had left. The whole thing was over in seconds.

Now she could see everything. The walls were neatly constructed from something like stone, but there were no lines where there would be with brick. She could see how big the tunnel really was. She could see a groove halfway up the walls, like a deep cut. It ran as far as the light reached, and beyond. And she could see that they were not alone, and had perhaps never been since they first stepped foot in this place.

There were people, as startled by the light as she had been; some of them were on the ground. The rest were shielding their eyes, tears streaming down their faces.

'Who you?' said one boldly. He had moved forwards while everyone else had stumbled back. 'Who you, aye? You foreign. That why you down here?'

'I'm just a visitor,' the silver-eyed boy replied. His voice was pleasant, as if he were having a conversation with a friend.

'Visitor? What you say? No one visits.'

'Oh, your little place here is famous; in certain circles anyway. I wanted to show it to my friend.'

The man transferred his gaze to Rue, who looked away immediately, her cheeks burning. He was gaunt and his skin was a dirty yellow. His clothes were old-looking. She'd never seen the style before. He looked ill.

'We don't want visitors,' he said to her. 'If you not come to help or bring stuff, get out.'

'Rest assured, I have "stuff", as you put it,' said the silver-eyed boy. 'It's this pen I hold. I will give you the pen, which will make the light you just saw whenever you want it. It will also dispense a supply of medicines that will keep your family going for a very long time. But please don't think of trying to take it from me. You'll never understand how it operates, and you know it. If I don't authorise it, the technology will shut down and become useless to you. I

307

am willing to authorise it after our visit is over, and if I feel that we've been treated well.'

The man had listened to this in silence. His face twisted in a sneer. 'You fucken hoity types. You fucken well bred. Worse, even, you are. You're a foreigner dog. How do I know you tellen truth bout your pen thing? Don't know, do I. You fucken putan. You conn.'

This was all that Rue could understand. The man reeled off a string of words she couldn't begin to recognise, but guessed their meaning well enough. She looked at the silver-eyed boy in alarm, but he seemed calm. He waited until the litany had died down. He had put the pen away, but the light in the tunnel remained.

'Well?' he said. 'Do we have a deal?'

The man spat. Rue watched this in horror. Then he turned around and walked off. The others followed him. The few behind Rue and the silver-eyed boy lingered, waiting for them to move. She got up from the ground, her back flashing with pain.

'Stay close,' he said to her in a low voice. 'Don't worry. He wants the pen too badly.'

'Maybe we should go,' said Rue, praying her voice sounded steady. 'I don't want to upset anyone.'

'Don't be silly. I'll protect you. And I haven't told you the story I promised I would.'

'Did you tell him the truth? About the pen?'

'Of course. I never lie. The truth is always more interesting.'

They started to walk.

'These people living down here are outcasts,' he said, in

a low tone. 'Somehow they're different, broke the law, rebelled in some way, or generally made someone important angry. A lot of them are basically just poor, facing charges for unpaid debts, or homeless. Instead of prison or banishment, they choose to run. Some of them eventually find their way down here. They aren't exactly welcomed with open arms, but it's shelter, and protection, of a sort.'

Rue pressed close to him. Criminals. It made sense. It didn't make much sense why she had to visit them, though, instead of simply being told about them.

'Hello, dear,' he was saying. At first Rue thought he was talking to her, but then she realised he had turned his head and was addressing a woman behind them. 'Come up and walk beside me.'

She did, to Rue's everlasting horror. She was a scrawny thing, her lank hair twisted into rat-tails. She looked at Rue with the kind of gaze that would be considered rude anywhere else.

'Why are you down here?' the silver-eyed boy asked her.

'Prostitute. Law caught me. Said I could stay and be executed or leave and find somewhere else to live. Left, dint I?'

'Bravo. A logical choice. Who here is an atheist?'

Silence as they trudged along. Eventually, grudgingly, one man spoke from the rear. 'Me. What you gonna say about it?'

'Nothing at all,' said the silver-eyed boy cheerfully. 'Where I live, atheists are commonplace. It's the religious that's in the minority.'

Rue couldn't help herself. She turned around to look at

the man who had spoken. He glared at her. She'd been hoping to see something of Fernie in him, the only other atheist she had ever met. But he was nothing like her.

'I know an atheist,' she said. 'She said gods were pointless and no one should believe in 'em. It's not spoken of, as such, but there's nothing wrong with it, I don't think. People should believe what they want.'

There was a sardonic amusement in the atheist's voice. 'She ever get stones thrown at her in the street? Ever get her door kicked in and her stuff broken? Her family threatened?'

'No,' said Rue, feeling ashamed. 'It's better, where I'm from.'

'Where you're from?' he said with a sneer. 'You Angle Tar, ain't you?'

Rue swelled with pride. 'Yes, I am,' she said. 'You know it?'

Someone walking just behind her laughed, and she flinched. The atheist sounded even more disdainful, if it was possible, than before.

'Something wrong with you? Where d'you think I'm from?'

'I'm sorry,' said Rue, trying to placate him. 'I don't know where we are.'

'Rue, my dear,' said the silver-eyed boy. He sounded sad, and she turned to look at him. 'We're in Angle Tar.'

'What?' she said, and laughed.

'We're still in Angle Tar. We never left. Why do you think you can understand what they're saying? No one can speak Angle Tarain outside of Angle Tar. We're still here.'

Rue's stomach rolled over in fright. 'Are you playing?' she said.

'No, I'm not. These tunnels are right underneath Capital City. They've always been here, but no one knows about them, with a few exceptions. The city guard knows they exist, which is why our friend the ex-prostitute here was given the generous choice of leaving to find them, if she could. Better than death.'

'Not much,' said the woman, and a few amongst them cackled.

'I don't understand,' said Rue. 'Stop, wait a minute. Stop walking, I don't understand.'

'Rue,' said the silver-eyed boy. 'Listen to me. There are things you don't know about Angle Tar. Things they keep from you. You might think that because you're special and Talented, and because you're taught things that are taught to no one else, that they tell you everything. They tell you only what you need to hear in order to be loyal. They know, without doubt, that sweet souls like yourself would never pledge to work for a country that lies to its own people.'

Rue shook her head. 'Maybe there are good reasons. Maybe I don't need to know.'

He put a hand out to stop her. 'To your left.'

There was a door beside them, an ordinary-looking thing. On it was a small plaque with a series of numbers.

'The location,' said the silver-eyed boy. 'All the doors look alike. It can get very confusing, so of course they've all been given a location number. This one is plain-looking because it's the artisan's area. The people they had to keep.'

The door was opened by someone from the inside.

'People they had to keep?' said Rue. She did not want to go through the door.

'Indispensables. Builders. Tradesmen. Cooks. Other doors and areas were more lavish – inlaid with gold, that kind of thing. Now they're not, of course. Anything valuable was pawned long ago.'

They were filing through, one at a time; the door was open only a sliver.

'How do you know so much about this place?' said Rue, wanting desperately to doubt him.

The silver-eyed boy smiled before he moved through the door. 'Because I used to live here.'

Rue watched him disappear, shock freezing her. Someone behind her snorted impatiently, and she squeezed through the gap.

The room beyond was bigger than her old village. An enormous hall, divided into sections with walls, metal railings and curtains. So many people milling about. The ceiling was higher than she could believe. Powerful smells. Noise. Light.

'We're still underground?' she breathed.

The silver-eyed boy took her hand. 'Come on. The pen will count for a lot. Let's get some food.'

'No!' she said, horrified. She wanted to take nothing from these people.

'Hush. They have food to offer, and now they all know I've brought them something more precious than a hundred meals.'

It was the worst thing she could think of. But he took her hand and led her onward. There were tables with enormous cooking pots set on them, lined up. They reached the nearest. A vast man wearing a sweaty, stained shirt eyed them.

'I'm the man with the pen, in case you were wondering. Two bowls of your finest, please,' said the silver-eyed boy.

The serving man sniffed, but ladled a steaming liquid out into two bowls. Rue watched his arms as he worked. She couldn't help it; they were covered in spiky black tattoos.

The silver-eyed boy gave her a bowl and led her to a bench, pushed up against the nearest wall. They sat.

The silver-eyed boy cleared his throat. 'I've been lying to you, and for that I'm sorry. I'm not proud of it, but I have my reasons.'

The meagre soup Rue held in her hands was doing little to comfort her. The outside of the bowl was greasy and slid unpleasantly in her hands. One of the silver-eyed boy's arms was draped over her shoulders, hugging her close as he talked.

'My name's Wren. Draper Wren,' he said.

So finally, she had his name. Wren. She rolled it around in her mind. It seemed like such an ordinary name for someone so strange-looking.

'I'm from Angle Tar, originally,' said Wren. 'New Nantes. You know it?'

Rue shook her head silently, afraid to speak in case he stopped spilling his secrets.

'It's on the east coast. A small city. I grew up knowing there was something wrong with me, probably the same way you did. Only you like your differences. I didn't like

313

mine. Neither did anyone else, much. My parents kept sending me to doctors, who couldn't see what the problem was. Luckily, I was bright too. I held my ground and spent most of my teenage years begging my parents to send me to university. Of course, you have to have a lot of money, unless you're so special they'll take you on for free. I didn't know about the Talent, then.

'Anyway, this man came to our· school one day. Said he was recruiting for the university from the less wealthy areas, looking for the cleverest students who couldn't afford to get in. We could take a couple of tests, see if we were good enough. I couldn't believe it – like a helping hand from the gods, like all my years of praying and temple-visiting had finally been answered. My parents were nice enough people, but I couldn't be more different from them.

'Well and so, I signed up for it. We weren't given any indication of what they might be, so I sweated and studied for three days on any subject I could think of. When it came to it, one of the classrooms had been cleared of everything except two chairs, and the recruiting man was sat on one of them. He told me to sit on the other, and the tests began.

'All he did was ask me questions. But he kept asking the right questions, as if he already knew everything there was to know about me. He asked me about the dreams I had that no one else seemed to. He knew about the times when I was awake and felt like I was being pulled into another place. He asked me to close my eyes and try to do impossible things, like tell them what was written on the notice they'd put on the wall in another room a moment ago.

'It seemed fast, but when it was over I was exhausted. Then I noticed that I'd been in that room with them for over five hours, and I spent the rest of the evening in shock.

'It happened quickly after that. The man came back after a week. I was brought into the head tutor's office and told that I had passed their tests and was offered a place at their university, subject to certain conditions.'

Rue had drawn back while he talked and was watching his face. 'That you couldn't ask questions about what you were going to study until you'd said yes and signed the contract. And then even after that they wouldn't tell you really anything about it.'

'Exactly,' he said, smiling. 'I've heard other people's recruitment stories and they're always much the same. So only a short while later I'd left home and was taken to the university. Those first few weeks were the most exciting of my life.'

'Did you miss your parents? Do you miss them now?'

Wren looked at her, a brief frown flitting across his face. 'I don't believe so,' he said 'I don't think I thought of them once. I send them a card from time to time, but it's quite expensive to communicate in the old-fashioned Angle Tar way. Do you know physical post doesn't exist outside of this country? Hasn't for centuries. And the nature of my work now means I have to be careful who I talk to and what I say. But I'm sure they're fine.'

Rue wondered why she had asked him that. It wasn't as if she missed her adoptive family. She hadn't thought much on Fernie either, since arriving in Capital. It had all been too exciting. But now she wondered if Fernie thought of her much, and decided she needed to write a letter to her as soon as she could.

'I met others who had similar differences to me,' Wren was saying. 'I'd never before known people who dreamed the same way I did, or had the same mannerisms and thought the way I thought. At times it was unpleasant, like a mirror that shows you in a way you'd never seen before.'

Rue nodded, eyes gleaming. This was so right! Why had he never talked about this to her? It would have been comforting to know that this was something other Talented had felt, too. None of her group seemed to care about that sort of thing at all.

'And then I met Frith.'

Of course.

Stupid girl. There was only one place in Angle Tar that trained the Talented. Of course he would have been at Capital. She couldn't quite believe it, though. The thought of him there, amongst all the reams of ordinary faces and attitudes, just didn't fit.

Wren was watching her with a sly half smile. 'De Forde Say Frith. What an interesting character, wouldn't you agree?'

Rue shrugged, feeling inexplicably nervous talking about him. 'He's the one who recruited me.'

Wren looked surprised. 'So you really are special, aren't you? I've never heard of that before. But then he's quite the string-puller. Wants to do everything himself. Can't have anything happening he doesn't know about.'

That sounded accurate enough, though Rue had never considered those traits of Frith in quite such a negative light before. 'I like him,' she said defensively. 'He was nice to me when he didn't have to be. He's been my friend even though he's busy and important.'

'I don't doubt it. He was my friend, too. He has a way of making you feel like you're the only one he thinks is worth his precious time. Then you find out that he plays everyone he knows in exactly the same way.'

She watched him, searching for something recognisable in his face, something to latch on to. He talked about her life as if it were his own. He knew the people she did, the places she did. She wanted to know what had taken him away from here, away from Frith and the university and to a life she could not even imagine.

'There's someone else we have in common, you know,' said Wren slowly. 'The only one in this country with an ounce of decent Talent.'

Rue realised that she had been waiting for this, and hoping that he wouldn't bring it up. She would have thought it a relief to find someone, a confidante to whom she could spill her thoughts about White, before they threatened to burst her open. But not here. Not now. Not with Wren, this stranger.

He was looking at her expectantly.

'You're talking about Mussyer White, I suppose,' she said. 'Who else?'

He was silent, then, as if unsure what to say next.

'What do you think of him?' he said eventually.

Rue's heartbeat felt faint. She struggled to keep a sudden burst of aching emotion inside her and swallowed.

'He's all right,' she said. 'A bit rude.'

His face came into her head and she tried to push it away.

'He's a genius,' said Wren. 'He's also a bastard, and I swore once that I'd kill him if I could.'

Rue looked at him in shock. His jaw was stringed with tension, and he was smiling in that way that she'd noticed people did when they were angry. She'd never understood that. When she was angry, she was angry. She supposed she didn't have the control of herself that others did.

'Why?' she asked, knowing it was expected, but taken in by the drama.

'He ruined my life. But I can't hate him. Not now. I can hate him for what he did to me, but not for the turn my life took because of him.'

'What did he do?'

Wren sighed, as if it pained him.

You brought it up, Rue felt like saying.

'We trained together,' said Wren. 'I was in complete awe of him. He knew things about the Talent. No one understood it in the way he did. No one could fill you with such excitement about such a vague thing. He could tell you anything and you'd believe it; he was such an authority, even though he was the same age as most of us.'

Rue nodded silently. It was a perfect picture.

'I liked the fact that he was different to everyone else in our class. He didn't care about being rich or having fine clothes. He didn't think like anyone else. He didn't go out drinking with us. And his Talent was extraordinary. I'd been the most Talented one in the class until he joined, by far. But I didn't mind that he was equal to me. He acted like a catalyst. Made us all want to do better. Made us push ourselves. We were friends. So I thought.

'Then I met someone.'

Wren looked away from her and out across the hall. People had left them alone, preoccupied with their steady business of survival. She'd become used to the smell without noticing. The first man, to whom the pen had been promised, was nowhere to be seen.

'Her name was Areline. I'd noticed her before, but tried to put her out of my mind. She was aristocratic and I was from nowhere, with nothing fine to wear and no money to spend. She had her friends, people she'd grown up with who were not Talented, but nevertheless secured places at the university to study the mundane subjects. By secured I mean paid for, you understand.

'So, I'd put her out of my mind, but that didn't stop me thinking of her from time to time. That was one thing I could do without anyone knowing. She was queen of our Talented group, even if she was hardly ever there, always off out at parties with her non-Talented friends. But when she was, the whole group became exhilarated trying to impress her or get her attention. I found the whole thing embarrassing. I suppose she must have started to notice this. One day she stopped me as we were coming out of class.

'She told me I was to come with her that evening for dinner out in the city. Didn't ask – told. She did it sweetly enough, and did anyone ever refuse her? I doubt it. Mostly we were glad to be noticed. I said I'd think about it, but it was all a lie and she probably knew it.

'It didn't take me long to fall for her after that. We spent every minute we could together. I was shunned by the rest of the group, out of jealousy I suppose, but I didn't care. Areline was all the company I wanted. That was her name. Lasarette Areline. Such a beautiful, old name. One of the oldest aristocratic families in Angle Tar, so I'm told.

'It wasn't long before I'd noticed that White had started changing towards me. He was moody with me. In class he'd mock me in front of everyone, say things. I tried to ignore it, all the time thinking what I could possibly have done to offend him. I couldn't see it. I was blind, I suppose.'

Rue shifted uncomfortably.

'That year was strange. Frith was never there. Something was happening that he wouldn't talk about to us, and he kept having to make trips overseas. So things felt weird, anyway. And then . . . well.

'Areline and I were out one night together. She was all . . . quiet and withdrawn, and I couldn't get her to smile. She wouldn't tell me what was wrong, at first. But I kept asking her. And eventually, she said that the night before she and White had been in the communal study together. Once he'd seen that they were alone, he sat down right beside her on the couch. She said he was agitated. He asked her what she was doing with me. She laughed, puzzled, and asked him what he meant. And then White said . . . '

Wren stopped. His expression was stiff.

'White said to her, "if I asked you to be with me, would you say yes?"'

'Areline told him no. She said that she loved me. But he wouldn't accept it. He kept demanding an answer from her. She started getting afraid, and told him to leave. For a moment, she thought that he wouldn't. That he might even attack her. But he did leave.

'How her words scratched at me. I couldn't believe it. I couldn't believe he had betrayed me like that. We were supposed to be friends. He knew how much I adored her. And he'd gone to her, like that, frightened her, tried to steal her while I wasn't there, like a coward. Who knows what else he might have done?'

Rue felt a sudden surge of nausea hit her. It wasn't possible. It wasn't. That was not the White she knew.

It couldn't be.

'We had a Talent class the next day,' Wren continued. 'I couldn't stop thinking about what he'd done. How he must have been thinking that he'd got away with it. Mussyer Tigh, the tutor, had us practising Jumps in pairs. White and I always paired together, being the strongest two in the class.

'He and I were practising Jumps easily. We both found the class boring, truth be told. It was my turn. I was getting ready to go, sending myself out, you know. I was looking out into the blackness in between. There's nothing there to help you. You make it through alone, always alone. It's frightening, the first time you have to do that.'

Rue thought of the time, not so long ago, that Wren had pulled her into her first ever Jump without warning, and treated her fear like a childish fancy; but kept silent.

'So there I was, surrounded by the nothing. And suddenly, I could feel him behind me. He'd followed me into the Jump.

'He grabbed my neck. He kept saying that I didn't deserve Areline, and that I was a show-off, and that I would never, ever be as Talented as he was.

'I panicked, and fought him. I knew what he was planning to do. He wanted to leave me out there, in the dark. He wanted to hurt me. Maybe even kill me. I knew it instantly. He hit me in the face, but I still managed to haul us both back to the classroom.

'It really shocked him. He'd expected to win, you see. He'd expected me to be weak. It was such satisfaction, my dear. Such satisfaction, to see the look on his face when I got us back, and right in front of everyone.'

Wren's face had become alive in a way Rue had never seen before. She had no doubt that he felt every word he said. Every word. She never would have guessed that such smoothness could hide such pain. Such a boiling sea of passionate wrath.

But why now? said a voice inside. Why didn't he tell you this before? Why did he keep these things from you?

She ignored the voice.

'What happened?' she said.

He laughed bitterly. 'No one believed me. They hadn't understood what he'd tried to do. All they saw was the two of us disappear. I told them what had happened. I *told* them. But he told them, too. He lied. Said I had done to him what he had tried to do to me.'

'But what about Areline?'

'Her family were there before you could blink. They took her off. Out of the university and back to her home city. Back to a life she hated.'

322

'No!' said Rue. 'How could that be? How could they just take her off?'

Wren said nothing.

'Did you ever see her again?'

'No,' he said. That was all.

'But,' said Rue, 'what did Frith do? He didn't have you sent here, did he?'

She saw a slow smile creep across his face. There it was again, she thought. The smile that didn't mean happiness.

'Of course he did,' he said. 'No doubt he hesitated. Not out of affection towards me, but because he must always be looking to the future, when he has his army of Talented spies to do his work for him. But they're great friends, you know, Frith and White. They don't look it, but they are. Angle Tar's premiere Talented, and its most valuable spy. What a powerful pairing that is. So when White pressed Frith to arrest me, it was done in a heartbeat. He was jealous of me, and my Talent. I don't believe he'd ever met anyone with Talent equal to his own before, and he couldn't stand it. And he wanted Areline for himself.'

'But he isn't *like* that. I'd know if he was like that!'

Wren looked at her finally. 'Would you, really? And how would you know about what White gets up to? Does he impart his secret life to you? Does he tell you of his women?'

Women? How many was he supposed to have?

She felt her heart shrivel.

'Rue,' came his voice. She couldn't look at him. 'Rue, my love, listen to me. I know how you defend him. I know how he must have worked on you. He did me, and he

323

would have for ever if he'd not made such a mistake with Areline and shown his true self.'

Rue shook her head stubbornly. 'I've never seen a woman near him, 'cept his students.'

'And yet now you have me to tell you otherwise.'

She was angry and ashamed. There was no point explaining why; he already seemed to know. She couldn't stand the fact that anyone could know about her most secret feelings. That was her secret. If she couldn't protect her secret, how could she protect anything of herself? She hated being shown that she was still as stupid and as easy to lie to as a newborn. She hated being let down in such a fashion, by something as commonplace and boring as someone who appeared to be one thing and was in fact another.

She looked out across the hall again. The place was emptier, but there were still swathes of people milling around. Had he really lived here?

'So he had you arrested but they told you to escape,' she said.

'Not quite. A friend warned me about the arrest, so I managed to leave before they found me, and I came here. I'd known about this place for a few weeks. Rumours, you understand. The children of rich families often know, and like to tell others. So before I could be caught, I'd packed anything valuable and left. The tunnel gates aren't guarded any more. They haven't been for decades. If you know where to look and how to open one, you can find your way here easily enough. It's not as bad as it looks, to an outsider. When you've nowhere to go and the rain is falling horizontally, and you feel you may never be warm again, it can seem like a gift from the gods.

'You need to learn how it works, though. It's just like any other place where humans are packed together. People flock to groups for safety. You must belong to one of the major groups here or you'll get everything stolen. Some of the more colourful residents take a kind of pleasure in physical violence, and loners are their targets. If you hurt a group member, you're likely to expect similar retaliation from that group, so you join a group for the protection.

'I was part of the Fourexgee. This is their hall. The groups tend to be named according to the location sequence on the doors. I tried to explore as much as possible during my time here, but it's hard to get very far – you stray into other groups' territories and they, well they find ways to encourage you not to.'

Rue tried to imagine the life she would have here. Sleeping in one of the rows of cots that lined the walls. Lining up to suck down thin soup and hard bread crusts. Sitting, staring. Talking to prostitutes and criminals.

'Where do they get food?'

'Upside. That's what they call Capital; Upside, or the "overground city". They go out in small gangs and forage.'

'But that means they're in the city. I've never seen 'em. I've never seen anyone like this walking the streets.'

'Of course you haven't, Rue. As a university student you're encouraged to roam only the safest, richest, most beautiful areas of Capital. I'm sure you aren't even aware of the other areas. They make sure you aren't, because it's dangerous to go there, even with a chaperone. And when they raid the rich areas they do it now, when most people are asleep. You'll never see them upside, Rue. You're not supposed to.

'You have no idea what a horrible mess this country's in. Thousands of people starve because the rich are in charge and keep everything for themselves. Children die on the streets. Do you know how many babies die in the city, because their mothers can't feed them? One in five. One in five! No wonder people turn to crime. They're desperate. But no one cares. No one cares.'

Rue listened to this in horror. How could she not have known about any of this? Why didn't they tell people? Why didn't they try to help everyone, instead of ignoring it? It wasn't fair that she got to sleep in a bed and eat as much food as she wanted. It wasn't fair that she got money every month to buy herself things that she didn't need. It wasn't fair that Lufe had so much money he had to invent more and more ways to spend it all, when they were surrounded by people who didn't even have enough to survive.

She thought about the White and the Frith that Wren presented. She had been blinded by the flattery of Talent, of being told she was gifted and special. She hadn't seen what those two men stood for. She knew that Frith was not all he said he was, but everyone knew that. She knew that White was not an affectionate person, but she had hoped it was a front to hide his true emotional depths. Now she saw she had been deluding herself.

Wren shifted beside her. She felt the warm weight of his arm drop gently onto her back. For a moment, she wanted to push him away. He had ruined everything.

But she knew it wasn't his fault. She knew she should be grateful for the truth he had given her. The illusions he had shattered, just like that.

'This was a great nation, you know,' said Wren. 'A long time ago. The fact that makes me laugh the most is that it was famed for its tolerance. It would welcome people from any nation across its borders, any religion, any anything. So much so that it couldn't cope with the amount of people coming here, begging to be let in. You've never seen such a colourful place. So many cultures. Not always harmonious, but interesting.' He snapped his fingers.

'And so? It isn't any more,' said Rue tiredly.

'You should be proud of our history, Rue. They don't teach it any more because they don't want anyone going back to the old ways. Progression! Forward thinking!' he barked.

Rue said nothing. He could be curiously light in the midst of serious situations, and it irked her.

'Angle Tar was a great empire. The most important country in the world. But it made mistakes, and now it's nothing. It's backward and alone. In World, everyone is together, everything is shared. It's impossible to be hungry or lonely in World. You've seen. That's the way people should live.'

Actually, Rue hadn't yet seen. The box he had shown her all those weeks ago remained unopened, though he had demonstrated something called a food unit to her, on one of their dream visits. If everyone really did have a machine like that in World as Wren claimed, then that really was incredible, and right, and how everything should be, with no one lacking or hurting ever again.

The things Wren had shown her in World were impossible, and beautiful because they were impossible. She wondered what would it be like to be surrounded by that every day.

That magic.

Why didn't they have those machines in Angle Tar? Why wouldn't they want to eradicate poverty and misery? What kind of a nation would do that to its own people?

'Why do they lie to us?' she said. 'What's the point of it?'

'To make you stay. Imagine how Angle Tar would be if everyone knew of World, of the incredible way of life they could have, of the technology that exists. Imagine if you said to an Angle Tarain that he could talk to someone hundreds of miles away as if they stood in front of him. Or tell him he would never be hungry again, and give him a credit chip and a food unit. What would happen to this country, then? There'd be no one in it!'

'Why won't Angle Tar join World, then, if it's so much better?'

'Many reasons. Pride. Stubbornness. I don't know. Offers have been made but always turned down.'

'Where is she now, Areline? Did you ever try and find her?'

'Rue, how could I? Do you understand how difficult it is to get back into Angle Tar once you've left? Only Talented can do it. There's no other way. All borders are closed; the only transport that reaches this island are trading cargo ships from World. They'll let you believe that Angle Tar has nothing to do with World, by the way, but they'll happily trade with them. They're not even half as self-sufficient as they'd like everyone to think.'

'But you're here now. You came to me. You visited me so many times.'

'Yes. But I can visit you because I know Capital City. I lived there in Red House, remember? We can Jump to places we've been before. But I don't know where Areline is, I've never even been to her home city. I wouldn't know how to start.' A satisfied smile spread across his face. 'I'm learning, though. White isn't the only Talent expert. World has the tools and the means. You'll see.'

She knew she'd flinched when he said his name, and she knew he'd felt it.

She wanted to believe that she couldn't imagine White the way Wren had painted him, but it was actually quite easy. When she re-examined his behaviour at the ball, it became obvious that he really had danced with her out of some bizarrely misplaced sense of propriety. That the endless impatience he showed around her was because she irritated him, not because he was nervous. That he found her strange, and not in a fascinating way. That she was just a child to him, a student with little ability and less brain. What interest could he possibly have in her?

'It's late,' said Wren. 'We should get you back.'

She should have been surprised or worried, but could only feel enormously tired. She'd probably missed her first lesson of the day already – would they be looking for her? Would they care?

'We must go back to the area we started from,' he said. 'I can't Jump from here.'

'More walking?'

'I'm afraid so, my sweet. I'm sorry. I didn't think we'd be here so long.'

She looked up. 'Can we leave okay? That man wants your pen.'

'Don't worry. If I try to go without giving it to him he'll catch up with us soon enough.'

Wren was right. They hadn't even reached the door to the tunnel when he reappeared behind them, as if from nowhere.

'Had yer fun, dint you?' he said. 'Payment's due.'

'Of course,' said Wren. 'I've deactivated the authority tag. Now anyone can use it.' He took it from his pocket. 'The controls are easy enough. Watch.'

Rue watched the man's creased face change from deep suspicion to wonder. She shifted uncomfortably, wishing they could leave right away. To her left was the woman who had walked with them to the hall; the prostitute. She smiled at Rue, who felt bad for her earlier attitude towards her.

'Can I ask you something?' said Rue to her.

The woman tugged on a rat-tail of hair and shrugged. 'You can ask.'

'Do you remember him?' she said, shifting her eyes over to Wren, who was still giving instructions on the pen.

The woman laughed. She had bad teeth. 'Hard to forget someone with silver eyes, and so no.'

'I don't think he would have had silver eyes back then.'

She shrugged again. 'He knows a lot about how it is down here. If you ha'nt been here before, you wouldn't know.'

'Is this the Fourexgee group, in this hall?'

She nodded.

'Sorry,' said Rue. 'I just wanted to ask.'

'Ain't my business. I used to check up on everyone, I did, for safety. You can't feel bad for wanting to know the truth about people.'

This should have made her feel better, but it didn't.

Wren finished and walked over, taking her hand. The man who had taken the pen gave neither of them a second glance, but turned and walked off, his new prize clutched tightly in his hand. Rue watched him go. No one was paying them much attention; though she supposed they'd be followed again once they left the hall.

'Rue?' said Wren.

'Tired.'

'Come on. We'll be back to your bed in no time.'

They started to walk.

CHAPTER 25
ANGLE TAR

WHITE

White's next lesson with Rue was going to be totally, utterly normal.

He would not treat her differently. He would give her no cause to feel uncomfortable. He would do nothing out of the ordinary. And maybe, if he admitted it, he would be testing her, to see how she behaved. It was in line with Frith's advice, even though he tried not to care about that. And it was in line with his own careful nature. It was *not* fear.

When she arrived, it started as it always had, though his heart was hammering even more than it usually did around her, and his hands were annoyingly clammy. She walked down to his desk, looking around as if there would be something new to see every time. He had been careful that the light was at its normal level, and that he dressed and appeared as usual. He was confident in his voice, but not his eyes. He couldn't avoid her gaze, as that would be too telling; but he could limit it so that he caught her eye-line less.

'I saw Lea in the hallway as she came out,' she said when

she reached him. 'You've changed your lesson time with her. She never used to be before me.'

'You are correct,' he said. He was pleased with his voice; it sounded normal. 'She requested the change.'

'T'will be to spend this evening with Lufe,' she said, with a throwaway air. 'They're courting but no one knows it.'

'Then I wonder why you tell me,' he said, before he could stop himself.

'Don't know. What do you think about that?'

She was watching him.

He realised that he might not be the only one conducting a test. Everything could rest on his next answer – the trouble was, he didn't know which one would have the effect he wanted. He didn't even know what effect he wanted.

'I think that whatever my students may do in their private life is and should remain private,' he said. 'As long as it does not affect their work.'

She sat, folding her hands on her lap. 'I agree,' she said seriously, then fell silent. She was frowning.

White took a quick review. Was she behaving strangely? In truth, he couldn't tell. She was so unpredictable to him that he wasn't too sure what normal would look like on her. She seemed a little shy, but maybe she was tired.

'We should begin. Do you have your week list of dreams prepared?'

'Yes.'

'Please speak on them in order of importance. Do not forget the date.'

'I had one about the ball.'

His heart spiked. Her voice sounded defiant.

'When did you have it?' he said.

'The night after.'

'Then it is of little importance, just your mind reviewing events. Why did you place it first?'

'It's important to me.'

He was sure that everything showed on his face. Everything.

Concentrate.

'What of people?' he tried. 'What people have you dreamed of?'

She looked away, irritation on her face. 'Why does it matter?'

That was a strange reaction.

'It always matters.'

She brushed it off. 'I've dreamed of many people.'

He had no idea why he said what he said next. No idea whatsoever, other than the fact that Wren had been on his mind recently. It just came out.

'Anyone with silver eyes?'

Her face flickered in alarm. Just for a moment. Just right there.

His throat squeezed in fear.

'You saw him,' he said. His voice was flat with shock.

She said nothing.

No, no, no, this isn't happening.

'Tell me when,' he said, resisting the urge to shout at her. 'Tell me what he said.'

She shot him a thunderous look, and he felt a sharp pang of fear.

'You danced the Intentional with me,' she said. 'Someone told me what that means. Is it true?'

'Zelle Vela, please. The silver-eyed boy. Tell me of him.'

'They said that it's a declaration of interest. That if two people dance it, it means they like each other and wish to court,' she said.

White felt his heart shiver. He stared at her openly, and the longer he stared, the more dangerous it became. Her eyes were challenging him to look away.

He wondered if they were falling in love.

He wondered if this would be the moment he would look back on for ever, replaying it over and over in his head.

'Well?' she demanded. 'What do you say? Do you wish to court me?'

'Zelle Vela, stop.'

'Why? Do I behave improperly?'

'Yes.'

'Well, you started it,' she snapped, and then lapsed into silence.

'Why are you angry?' he said

'Why?!'

'Yes!'

Their voices were loud. They were arguing. It was rushing forwards, escalating, moving towards something frightening and unstoppable. He did not want this. He wanted her to sit there in silent encouragement while he told her everything he was afraid of; everything he felt.

Rue tried very hard not to speak. He was falling, spilling like dropped water. He was an open wound. He was waiting for her to make him admit it. Maybe he wanted to admit it. She watched him open and felt a sort of glee, a power over him that she had never had before. She sat back.

'You won't answer me,' she said. 'I don't want to be here if you won't even tell me the truth, and maybe I don't want to be here at all. So that's all there is to it.'

He gazed at her for a moment. 'Why do you not want to be here?' he said eventually.

Here it was, the opening she'd needed to play a card from her hand. This was where she would look back and know that this was the moment she could have stopped it. But she didn't want to. She wanted it out, like a poison. And she wanted to break his barriers, to hurt him and see him hurt so that she would know he was human, and could feel pain.

'I know about your history,' she said. 'I don't want to get better than you at anything, because I know what would happen if I did.'

His face was still. She watched intently.

Now she would know if Wren had been straight with her or not.

'What did he tell you?' said White. His face was carefully composed, but his voice had dropped to a thin, furious note.

'Things that haven't ever come up before. About a friend of yours who you betrayed, because you wanted his girl. And about how you felt threatened by him because his Talent was so good. So you tried to kill him. And then you ruined his life.'

White had frozen.

She couldn't believe it. Every word was true. He wasn't even defending himself.

'I actually thought that it was exaggeration,' she said. 'But I can see now that it wasn't. And I wonder if you even have any Talent at all? Is that a lie, too? Do you boss your students like you know what you're talking about, but secretly you hate us because we have something you never will?'

One moment he was there in his chair, behind his desk, yards away from her.

And then he was not.

It was that fast.

The sudden displacement of air in front of her made her hair whip back and her clothes billow. He was standing, his face inches from hers, his hands resting on the arms of her chair. He had her surrounded.

'Is this Talented enough for you?' he hissed.

Rue shrank back in her seat.

This close, his skin was luminous and his eyes freezing.

What he had just done was impossible.

Impossible.

And horrifying.

She could feel his breath on her lips.

Then he was gone again, reappearing in the corner of the room. He made it look like nothing.

Disappear. Reappear.

His gaze was on the far wall.

Rue was too shocked to speak.

'He lies.' White turned, agitated. 'But you will believe him over me. Of course you will! Do not believe what he tells you. I know what he is doing. He will take you away from me. Do not go with him. I implore you.'

He stared at her, but she couldn't see what she needed to see. The warmth, the wit and passion of Wren. She trusted warmth. She couldn't trust cold.

'Please,' he said. There was an urgency in his voice that frightened her. Everything he was doing was frightening her. 'Please. He will try to take you away from here. Do not go.'

'So tell me why I should stay,' said Rue.

White was silent.

'This place is full of liars. I've been in the tunnels underneath Capital. I know all the little secrets of Angle Tar. He showed me. The rich are rich and the poor stay poor, with no hope of anything. The travel law keeps Angle Tar ignorant of the outside world. To keep us stupid. We can't go to foreign lands, but foreigners can come here. Why don't anybody think that's strange? We're so backward, the rest of the world probably laughs at us. *Laughs*. He's shown me these amazing, incredible things. Things that change lives. But you won't never see these things in Angle Tar, will you? This country is stupid. This stupid, ignorant little island.'

His mouth was open, but he said nothing. He didn't even have the courage to shout at her, and tell her she was wrong.

'I hate lies,' said Rue. 'I really, really hate 'em. No one's ever thought me worth telling the truth to. People I trusted . . . they lied. You lied. Everyone here lies. Why should I stay?'

Still White said nothing. Rue felt a bitter triumph.

'You can't even give me *one reason*,' she said.

Somewhere very deep inside her, she knew that if he would only touch her, she might start to feel differently. She was crying out for him to touch her. To give her a reason. But he wouldn't. Because he was a part of Angle Tar, a part of inwardness, where passion and curiosity were sins, where expression was forbidden, where you couldn't even discard your belief in gods that had never helped you without fear of being targeted.

'Fuck you, then,' she said.

He had lost her.

She cared nothing for him. She didn't even care enough to appreciate what he'd done. What a monumental risk he'd taken. What a bad, horrifying mistake he'd made. He wanted her to go, right now, because it would be better if he never saw her again. He would burn her from him and start again. She could go. She could go and have her new life in World. He would never be enough for her anyway. He was nothing.

'Just get out,' he said. 'Just leave.'

Rue stood. She was trembling.

Dismissed, imperiously, just as it was the first time they had met.

Her fury came then, almost too much to bear. She wanted to twist the knife for what he'd done, for what he'd made her feel and how he'd played with her and then thrown her away.

'He makes me feel alive,' she said. 'You make me feel dead.'

As soon as it was out, she took it back. It was monstrously untrue. White made her feel panicked, alarmed, nervous, upset, awed, heart-poundingly hopeful; he made her feel more alive than anyone. But it was too late. His face had changed – his eyes were bruised with misery. She had managed it at last, and she felt nothing but shame at herself. She ran from the shame, slammed his door behind her and ran, away from the pain and the moment when he had been so close to her mouth he could have kissed her, the thought that made her feel like her heart would burst.

CHAPTER 26
ANGLE TAR

RUE

The next few days were a mess of churning wrath and shame. Rue couldn't bear speaking to anyone. Lea's chatter and giggles seemed to have amplified. Tulsent's nervousness made her annoyed rather than sympathetic. Lufe had been even more aloof and smackable than previously, if that were possible. Marches told one of his stupid arch jokes; she'd lost her temper and called him a fat, truffler-bodied cock. He had been so taken aback that he'd not spoken to her once since then.

She couldn't stand how ignorant they were. She ached to spill the secrets she had, to tell them of the tunnels, to expose White for what he really was. But she was afraid they would laugh at her. She was afraid, most of all, they wouldn't believe her; and she had no way of proving any of it. And then she would have to tell them who had shown her the tunnels, and who had told her about White. She couldn't bear giving away that secret most of all.

She was deeply embarrassed. That she would let a strange boy, whose name she had never even known until recently, invade her and turn her life upside down. She would have to admit that he visited her at night. It would give something very private of her away, and there was no chance she was going to offer such a group of selfish, amoral people as her fellow Talenteds such a weapon to hurt her with.

So she wrestled with it quietly, worried it was too obvious in her behaviour. But odd moods and phases were such a way of life with them all that it seemed no one had really noticed there was anything wrong.

And when she was alone, she thought of White.

She thought of the incredible ability he had; how he had appeared right in front of her, the immense skill and calculation that must have taken in that split second that he had chosen to do it. It made her feel very afraid, but to her private shame, it also made her want him more.

She thought of Areline, and wondered what White might have done to her. She wanted him to show up in Red House, like Wren had – to be that intrusive and bold. A shameful part of her wanted him to appear suddenly in her bedroom, while she was in bed. Maybe to watch her while she was asleep. To march up to her and demand of her, so that she could reject him again, or scream at him and say everything she really wanted to say.

But he never did.

Frith was nowhere to be found. None of the group seemed to know where he was, but they were used to him being away for long periods of time, and then turning up unexpectedly at Red House to catch up with them over a hot chocolate. Rue needed him badly. He would tell her what she should think.

She would ask him about the tunnels, and he would not know what she was talking about. He would laugh it off, at first. But as she grew insistent, so would he become more serious and promise to find out the truth, whatever the cost. He would tell her about White and Areline and Wren, hanging his head in shame and making her swear not to expose the secret. It would cost the Talent programme too greatly to lose him, Frith would say. Rue would swear.

This fantasy wound around inside her head at least ten times a day.

Wren had not visited her again, but he had left a note on her bed, which said that he would come for her Tuesday next. That he would take her away to World, away from lies and boredom and petty things. Everything in World would be extraordinary. Everything in World would fascinate her.

She sat on her bed in her coat, travelling bag at her feet. Wren had said in his note that everything she could want would be provided, and so there was no need to bring any of her clothes or possessions. Truth be told, she would feel strange and exposed without at least some of her things around her, even if they didn't fit in and reminded her too much of everything she had left behind.

She looked at her little clock. It would be left behind. Clocks weren't needed in World. She wasn't sure how that could be, but Wren said she would know soon enough.

He was almost two hours late. When he did arrive, Rue was disappointed. She'd never seen him arrive from a Jump before, but as far as she could tell, nothing much happened. He was not there, and then he was; just like White. The air popped gently around him, but that was it. He grinned at her, delighted.

'You're ready!'

'You're late,' Rue snapped, hoping she sounded annoyed rather than afraid.

'You're right, my sweet Rue, and I apologise. Preparations took longer than I thought.'

Her heart jumped.

'So this is really it, then,' she said.

He came over to the bed and sat beside her.

'Still time to change your mind,' he said.

'You're just saying that to be nice. I can't change it now. I can't stay here.'

They sat in silence for a moment.

'Where are we going?' she said. 'Which country, I mean.'

'Well – we'll be going to World. The part of World I live in is called North America South West.'

'Is it pretty there? You haven't taken me there yet.'

'No, I haven't. And if you mean by pretty – it's hard to explain. The real place isn't pretty, but in Life it's beautiful. The environment is controlled, you see. What you see, and then what you see in Life, are two very different things.'

Rue was silent, trying to unpick his words. He hadn't really seemed to answer her question.

'You know you can't take those with you,' he said, pointing at the bags.

She shrugged. 'I just want something of here. Just small things.'

'But Rue, clothes don't Jump. Nothing Jumps except people.'

She laughed. He didn't.

'Come on,' she said. 'You're wearing clothes.'

'Wearing them, yes of course. They're on you, they're part of you, they come with you. But your mind can't cope with taking separate objects along.'

'Why not?'

'It just can't, love of mine. It's enough to ask your mind to move yourself. No one can do it.'

'You brought that pen.'

'I'm going to tell you a secret, Rue. It took me four months of practice to be able to take that MediPen on a Jump. Four months, every day. The first few times I managed it, I mangled the Pen beyond repair. That landed me in trouble; those Pens are quite expensive to make.'

She allowed herself to wonder very briefly if White could do it.

And then she allowed herself to wonder very briefly if Wren knew the real extent of White's talent. If anyone did. Then she pushed everything about him away from her and stood up.

'Then let's go,' she said.

This was it. This was the end.

He had been watching Rue for days. He would leave his body where it was and use his mind to watch her. Just snatches of five minutes at a time. He couldn't bring himself to look at her for longer than that.

He watched her lie awake, blinking into the darkness. He watched her in Red House's study in the evenings. He watched her sit alone at breakfast.

There was something in White that felt immense disgust at what he was doing. He had promised never to do this again, never to be so intrusive on people when they were alone. Sometimes he'd seen things he'd rather not see, but most often it was just dull. When he was younger and stupid, he'd thought it would help him find out secrets and gain power over the people who could hurt him, like Jospen or Cho, or his mother. When he was older he realised how pointless it was; how it only gained him secrets that hurt him, too.

All these years later he had broken his promise, but he didn't care enough to stop. She was leaving. He knew it.

She packed a bag. He watched her from the corner of her room, panicking every time her eyes roved over the spot he was looking from, even though he knew she couldn't see him. He watched her sit at her mirror and brush out her hair. Line her eyes. Choose her best travelling trousers, and the beautiful white silk shirt Lea had made her buy. He watched her make every preparation to leave and did nothing.

But he would, he told himself. Before she went, he would do it. He would step out of his hiding place and tell her everything, every last detail. He would beg her to stay. Screw pride. Screw everything about him that had stopped him from kissing her months ago when he should have.

But she turned and smiled and a boy with silver eyes was there, and that was the moment White knew he would do nothing. She had chosen who she wanted, and all he would do now would be to ruin himself in her eyes. He couldn't bear that.

Wren did look incredible. His face had changed beyond

recognition. His body was lithe and smooth – nothing like the original slightly chubby boy that he had known, over a year ago. That had lain before him on the classroom floor, screeching curses with wild, shocking hate in his eyes. That had tried to kill him.

That had promised to take revenge on him.

He could see why Rue would prefer Wren. He was beautiful. He had been quite plain, before the modifications. Most people were, in comparison. But he'd always had the luminous quality of the extraordinarily gifted and ambitious. Now of course, his outer shell matched his inner fire. In Angle Tar, you were stuck with how you were born, which had always seemed unfair, when it was obvious that the more well-formed people progressed so much more easily to where they wanted to be in life.

He watched them talk.

He watched disappointment ripple across Rue's face as she was told she would be able to take nothing with her. Wren lied smoothly, without an obvious change in behaviour. He had always been good at lying.

You could take anything you liked on a Jump, as long as you could hold it in your hand. Your mind incorporated it automatically; it was as easy or as hard as taking yourself. The only thing you couldn't take was something alive that didn't have the ability to Jump. Anything that link-Jumped with a Talented died, unless it was another Talented. This White knew. His experimentation on this was a scar on his soul. One of many. He had an ugly soul.

And he knew why Wren had lied. He was cutting all her ties with Angle Tar, severing emotional connections, making sure she had nothing to remind her of here once she was in World.

White should say something now. Right now.

What would happen if he appeared right there, in front of Wren? Would he be afraid? What would happen if he told Rue, in a quiet, authoritative voice, of the lies Wren had said to her? What if he told her the truth about Areline, and who had really tried to kill who? Would she gasp in astonishment, step away from Wren, shake her head and say that she could no longer go with him?

She would be angry. Angry with herself at how stupid she had been. Angry with him for not stepping in sooner, for hesitating again and again to tell her how he felt. He would tell her he was sorry. He would bend on one knee and look up into her eyes. He would take her hand, touch her skin. He would tell her he loved her.

He enjoyed the fantasy for a moment more, then dismissed it.

She wouldn't believe him. He had no proof.

And what would he say when she asked him about the tunnels? He knew about them, of course. One of Frith's favourite evening conversations was the shredded social fabric of Angle Tar, and how messed up everything was. In White's opinion it was messed up pretty much everywhere you went; it wasn't as if World was doing any better on that score. But Rue wouldn't want to hear that. She'd want an explanation. He didn't have one. Life was not as neat as that.

He watched. Wren was the one who took her hand, who held it and drew her close. They Jumped.

White did nothing.

Nothing, nothing and nothing.

He went back to himself, alone in his room.

The fire had almost gone out. Embers glowed dully. His bed was unslept in. He hadn't moved from his chair all day. None of that mattered, though.

He waited.

And waited.

And eventually, Wren came.

He opened White's door, looking cautiously around. Saw him sitting hunched by the fire.

'Aw. You've been crying,' he said.

White watched him come closer. Felt every part of him scream to get up. To wrap his hands around Wren's beautifully slender neck. To squeeze. To break his face with a fist, over and over.

'Sorry I took so long to visit,' said Wren. 'To be honest, I was a bit nervous of coming back here, the first few times. For some reason, I'd thought you'd be able to sense me, or something. But, erm. Apparently not.'

He grinned.

White stirred.

His grin faded.

'Where is she?' said White.

'In World. Sleeping. In my bed.'

White couldn't stop pain surfacing on his face.

'You're such an idiot,' said Wren, his silver eyes narrowed incredulously.

White gazed at him. Wren's newfound beauty couldn't hide the horrible rage he clearly held on to. 'Why are you doing this to me? *Why*?' he said.

Wren sneered. 'Gods, White. It's just all about *you*, isn't it? And it always was. Everyone fawning over you like you're some kind of hero. Well, now I've found a place that understands what I can do. What I can give. The same place that rejected you. That stings, right? That must really sting.'

'I have never done anything to you. Nothing.'

Wren sighed shortly. 'Really? We'll go there, if you like. How about Areline?'

'Nothing happened. NOTHING HAPPENED. When she asked me to go to dinner with her, I refused. Did she tell you that I said yes? She lied!'

Wren's face flushed.

'It's not even about that!' he shouted. 'What about our plans? The things we talked about? I thought you were different. Someone I could actually respect. Someone who *understood*. I gave you my secrets! But you're just as bad as everyone else. You waltzed into my life and humiliated me all the time, fucking showing off to everyone! You think you're better than me. Don't you? Well, you're not. *I can beat you.*'

White gazed at him, furious. Bewildered.

Wren folded his arms, calmer.

'Well. It doesn't matter any more. In fact, you did me a favour. You really did. So I did you a favour in turn. She was holding you back. Isn't that what you used to say to me? Don't bother with girls. Don't bother with love. It only holds you back from your purpose in life. I used to think you were such a pompous cock, saying that. But you know – you're right. I came to realise that. You are. So I did you a favour, as a thank you. She's gone now.'

350

White flinched, his body aching to throw itself out of the chair and into that horrible smug face.

Wren smiled, held his hands up.

'Look, it was just an assignment, at first. They asked me to come back. Check out the competition. Maybe even recruit someone, if I could. I didn't know about your, er, special regard for one of them, not at first. But when I heard about it, I thought . . . well. What better way to pay you back a favour? What tickles me most, though, is that you didn't even know. Didn't even *know* that I was visiting her at night. And yes – it was always at night. And she's actually quite pretty with no clothes on.'

White's hand tightened on the pistol he had jammed into the seat cushions, and he pulled it free. Fumbled. Pointed it at Wren's chest.

It was a small, ancient thing that Frith had given him last year as a birthday present. He'd practised this earlier, a few times. Pointing it. He hadn't fumbled, before. But then, nothing ever turned out the way it should, when it came to the time that actually mattered.

Wren's jaw fell open, and his features spiked in fear.

'I'll Jump before you can fire,' he said.

'Try!' White screamed. 'Go on and try it! We'll see!'

There was a knock on his door.

'White?' came a voice from outside.

Frith's voice.

Wren was shifting nervously.

'I can do it,' he said. 'Don't think I can't.'

White kept silent.

If you just shoot RIGHT NOW.

RIGHT now.

NOW.

You'll get him. Do it.

The door opened, and Frith came in. And stopped.

Wren took his chance.

White's finger jerked on the trigger.

Too late. The noise made his ears shut down.

Wren had gone.

Frith stood, thunderstruck.

White threw the gun as hard as he could across the room. It smashed into the wall.

He covered his face.

He willed with everything he had that the world would fade away. Fade away and leave him alone in the dark, with only his own breathing for company.

EPILOGUE

That night, he wakes up in a cold, dank, stone room.

He knows it is a dream. He also knows it is unlike any dream he has ever had before. He knows that instantly.

This feels different. The inside of his mouth is tacky with sour thickness. His whole body strums with tension. He feels like he has been running flat out. His lungs struggle and heave.

He has never been to this place in his dreams before.

The room is completely bare. The walls are made of huge, thick blocks of stone, solid and real and sparkling with mica. In one corner, the corner he wakes up in, the dusty flagstone floor is covered with tangled, angry black markings, scribbled in something that might be charcoal. He looks around, then down to the markings. These are what he has come for, he knows it. He needs these. More than anything else in the world, he aches with his desperate need. But the more he stares, the more they waver and dance, senseless but lovely. They mean nothing to him, an alien language. Just a series of sharp, tilted lines.

There is a sound.

The sound makes his lungs squeeze.

He looks around again. Four smooth, unbroken walls. No door. How did he get *in*?

Something is prowling outside, shifting up and down the walls. The stone near his head hisses for a moment as the creature makes contact on the other side.

He flinches away from the wall. He knows what it is, but doesn't at the same time. It knows him, though.

It knows everything about him.

It moves in grid patterns, combing relentlessly outside the room, searching for a way in. It will find one, he is sure of it. There is nothing to do about this. The black markings cannot save him. He doesn't know the way out of the room. Even if he did, the thought of going near the thing outside makes him feel sick.

A flickering out of the corner of his eye turns him, every nerve screaming in alarm. But it is not the thing outside. It is a girl, standing in the room.

She is odd. Out of focus. Greying and blurry. Her eyes are huge, dark holes. She stares at him sightlessly. Her mouth is moving.

She looks like a ghost. He shrinks back. She raises her hands, palms outwards.

Please. No threat.

The question he wants to ask her is *where am I?*

And *what the fuck is going on?*

And *who the fuck are you?*

And *what the FUCK is that THING OUTSIDE?*

But nothing comes out as it should in dreams, and instead he asks, 'Why can't I see you properly?'

She stares at him for a moment too long, her eyes

flickering over his face. Drinking him in. He begins to feel uncomfortable under her black gaze.

Then she opens her mouth and tries to talk to him. Words splutter in and out of hearing, like a badly tuned radio. Her mouth works. Syllables blare out into the room but hang, unformed. He can't make out a whole word.

'I can't hear you!'

The thing outside is making more noise. It scratches against the stone. Then it does something heart-failingly awful. It starts to throw its weight against the wall.

It is really, really big.

Only really, really big things can make stones shiver and deserts of brick dust puff out into the air.

That wall won't hold long.

White feels a desperate, ridiculous urge to pee.

The girl is waving her hands at him. Her black hole eyes are wider. She mouths and mouths.

'I can't hear you!' White shrieks. 'I can't! What do I do?'

'– Castle!' she says.

'What?!?'

'– Castle! – It's coming!'

'I can SEE THAT. What do I DO?'

She rushes forwards and grabs his arms, desperate. Her touch is like bunches of sticks brushing against him, as wavery and insubstantial as her voice.

'– Castle!' she says. '– you must – because It's *coming*!'

'I can't . . .'

'– don't open – Castle! Because – coming!'

She takes a breath. He watches her mouth. The thing outside screeches, its voice wet.

'– kill you,' she says. 'It will kill you.'

The first stone smashes to the floor with a crash to end worlds.

'– kill everything. It will kill *everything*.'

White stares at her. The wall is crumbling slowly, battered and battered.

'Don't open the Castle!'

She is pleading. The thing outside is squeezing itself through the hole it has made. He can hear its body making squishing sounds as it grunts and heaves. The flesh coming through is thick, thicker than him, and long, long, long. Like a giant snake it comes.

With a pure and sudden burst of knowledge, White realises that the giant snake of flesh he sees filling up the room is only part of one of its fingers.

The girl flickers; disappears.

It reaches for him.

His ears shut down, overloaded with the thing's buzzing roar.

His imagination is filled with the sound of his own bones snapping as the room crumbles around him.

He wants it to be quick.

White woke with a mangled gasp in his throat.

It took a long, long moment to understand that he was safe.

That it had been a dream, and that he wasn't there any more.

What kind of dream, he had no idea. But it couldn't have been a Talent dream. No. Not possible. The thought of that room as a real place made him want to scream, scream, scream.

As he sat up, he felt streams of sweat pour in tickling rivulets down his chest.

It wouldn't leave him.

Every shadow was something disgusting and alive, come to eat and to chew. He lit his bedside lamp. It didn't help.

Huddled against the headboard of his bed, the ghost girl's words drifted round and round in his head.

Don't open the Castle.

It will kill everything.

In a strange bed, in a strange room, in another country, Rue woke from the same dream, alone and shivering with terror.

READ ON FOR AN EXCLUSIVE EXTRACT
FROM THE STUNNING SEQUEL TO
FEARSOME DREAMER
- COMING SOON . . .

WORLD

Rue

In her dream, Rue runs.

The dream is a game in a castle, but more than a game; and if Rue loses, she will die. The humming dread that drenches the walls of this place makes her neck clench and she can taste it, like blood on her tongue.

This place is death and the game is that she has to survive.

The floor is made of cracked, uneven stone slabs that make her footfalls echo so loudly, each separate noise a cacophony that she is sure will bring every horror this place has to offer right to her, to pounce on her like a ragdoll and tear her to strips that they can gobble down.

She comes to an enormous king of a door that stretches up into the rafters. When she touches the handle, it opens easily, despite its size. The room beyond is bigger than a church, with the same dusty walls and echoing space. It is bare, its floor made up of uneven slabs that slope steadily downwards toward a hole in the centre of the room. Like a wound it gapes, coloured in blackness. The slabs disappear into it as if they are being sucked inside.

There is only the smallest ledge of slabs up against the walls that don't slope downwards. She has a feeling that if she steps on any one of the sloping slabs, she will slide helplessly towards the crevasse and disappear into it forever.

Rue knows what lives in the crevasse. She has been here before.

She steps into the room. Her feet slide and slip. She shuffles along. The sense of danger grows so fast she can imagine very strongly that whatever lives in the crevasse is skittering, climbing up the sides of its hole, coming closer to the source of that smell it can smell, the smell of her and of meat. She is halfway across the room. If she doesn't hurry, she will die. Someone enters the room behind her. Rue screams a warning over her shoulder.

Don't come in! Don't come in! Find another way around!
She knows the newcomer has put a foot on the first slab.
Don't come in!

She can see it shifting its bulk from side to side as it heaves up the sides of the crevasse. The smell of meat is stronger now. Double the strength.

She makes it to the other side and wrenches open the door. The newcomer is halfway across. Something slithers out from the blackness of the hole in the middle of the ground. Broken pieces of slab tremble and shift. It moves horribly fast, scrabbling upwards in a massive rush.

I told you not to come in! Rue screams.

The newcomer looks up, her mouth hanging open in terror. She has long, thin dark hair which shivers wildly around her shoulders as she looks between Rue and the hole, rapidly, again and again.

Cho, Rue says, her voice clipped and gasping. *Cho, I TOLD YOU NOT TO C—*

Rue woke, fighting.

It was too hard to breathe. The screaming had taken away her air.

It took a while to realise that wherever that place had been, she wasn't there any more; she was here where things were real, and normal, and safe. The overwhelming sense of relief she felt brought tears to her eyes.

Underneath it there was the other emotion she confessed to no one; the one that made her want to go back into the dream, nightmarish though it had been. A slick, slimy kind of fascination to the place she had visited. A desire to know more about it.

It was the second time in a week that she had dreamed of that castle, each dream in a different room; but always that sense of sick-hearted fear to it. The whole place was wrong, so why did she want to go back there? Was it a real place; a dream caused by her Talent? Or was it something she had made up? She wasn't skilled enough to tell.

That girl, Cho. She was new this time. Rue had never seen her before. She didn't know who she was, or if she was real, a long ago memory of a name and a face that she had pulled from the back drawers of her mind and slotted into the dream. Some girl.

Sometimes, being Talented was, simply put, a pain in the arse. Since she was little she could remember dreams like this, dreams of other places and other people, real places she could not possibly know of but visited nightly, through no will of her own. Being Talented meant you could travel in your dreams, spy on people and places with your mind, and without them ever knowing you were there.

And if you were freakishly Talented, it also meant you could Jump your entire body between points, stripping away everything between you and somewhere else six feet or even a thousand miles away; treating distance and physics as a second's inconvenience.

Rue couldn't Jump yet; or at least not without help. She couldn't even control where she visited in her dreams; it happened randomly and without her input. She felt helpless, but there was no denying the thrill that rippled through her as she went to bed each night. Where would her mind take her? Would she learn a great, secret truth?

She stretched, feeling her back press satisfyingly into the bed, and then realised.

Wren was not here with her.

She felt a stab of panic, then annoyance like a soothing wave. She wouldn't be a stupid, nervy mouse. She would show everyone that she wasn't afraid of being alone in a strange place. He was probably out getting food, or doing something important. He would be back.

She turned on her side and switched off the bed comforter on the third attempt. Wren had shown her how to do it but she was still nervous of getting it wrong. At least here there were no sheets to wash her buckets of sweat from. Although the bed comforter mimicked the warmth and weight of sheets, it wasn't real in the same sense.

Rue lay, thinking.

The small room around her was a dull, metallic grey. The walls were grey. The floor was a soft, fuzzy grey. The bed she lay on was grey. The ceiling was actually white – Wren had told her why it was a different colour, but she couldn't quite remember. Something about how Life worked when you looked upwards. There were a lot of the last few days that she couldn't quite remember. Strangeness upon excitement upon strangeness had taken its toll.

Rue had come to realise that a lot of her reactions to things were considered, by general people, to be odd. It had taken a while as a child, but eventually she had realised why people pulled faces when she said or did certain things. So finding out that she had a mysterious, rare ability like the Talent had failed to surprise her one bit. Of course she did. It explained everything. It explained the fascinating, frightening dreams she had, that were rich and thick as velvet and felt so real that it was like living another life while she slept. It explained her constant itch, the craving she had to be away from here, wherever here was. To be doing extraordinary things.

So being recruited to train in the Talent at Angle Tar's premiere university seemed obvious to her. Why have such a skill, if it was never to be used? She had gone willingly, leaving her old life behind, her life of routine and learning and banality, and the dull ticking of hours and days and weeks.

And everything would have been fine if she hadn't met White.

He made it easy to leave, when Wren asked her to. He made it easy because when she thought about him she felt a burst of pain, and humiliation, and a horrible, embarrassing, overwhelming desire to be near him. To have him think well of her.

Want her.

But he didn't want her. He probably, all things considered, hated her. He thought she was a rude, stupid girl. And he'd done things that made her feel savage towards him. She had pushed, and she had broken something past repair, and part of her was glad, because if there was one thing guaranteed to make her lose her mind in rage, it was being lied to. It had happened too many times in the recent past. It would not happen again.

So she had left Angle Tar, and everything she had ever known. She hadn't seen it as treason, coming with Wren to World – but now she'd had time to think, she knew that Angle Tar probably would. It was illegal for Angle Tarain citizens to travel outside the country. To keep them ignorant of how amazing it was everywhere else, she had bitterly decided. It didn't make a difference, though. She had crossed a very thick, unyielding line.

Maybe, just maybe, that meant she could never go back.

And maybe you'll never see him again, said a small, treacherous voice in her mind.

She tried desperately not to let it feel so final. She tried to leave it open and vague. Surely they might make an exception for her. Surely Frith would allow it. He knew people in government – he practically was the government.

Frith would help her, if the time ever came. She was sure of it.

Right now, though, there was no space in her head for

dwelling on the past, waking up to that chest ache every morning as the memories of what had happened took hold of her again. She had to put it all away, grow up, and deal with where she was now.

When she had come out of the Jump from Angle Tar with Wren that first night, head spinning, the thing that caught her attention was the light.

She leaned against him and he held her, until the nausea passed and she could stand up straight. They stood on what was clearly a street, though it was starker and cleaner than any in Angle Tar. The buildings were flat and strangely angular, with smooth, colourless surfaces. The street itself was so wide, an airy stretch of space. Nothing like the tiny, penned cobbled mazes of Capital City.

And all the while she looked around for a source of light; but there were no street lamps to be seen. When she glanced up into the sky, she couldn't see the moon, despite the fact that there were no discernable clouds. But she could still *see*. It was dark, like it should be at night; but then it wasn't, somehow.

Wren was smiling. 'It's strange,' he said. 'I know it. But you're not seeing World how everyone else sees World. This is just the platform for World.'

'The what?'

'The platform, the basic "real" version. When you jack in to Life, you'll see it very differently. You'll see a sky filled with stars, and a moon. Over there, those long stretches of ground with nothing on them? In Life they're covered in trees. The buildings here, look. To you they're just blank, right? Well in Life, that one is covered in a ten-foot-high mural. And that one, there; it has an advert for Lost in Time, it's a Life game. It's got a train exploding on it. I mean, the train is actually exploding, right now.'

He threw his hands wide, and Rue looked around, fascinated. There were no trees anywhere. And there was nothing on those buildings. Nothing at all. But she could almost believe there was, if she watched him.

'I'll be honest with you. Out of Life, it's pretty dull,' said Wren. 'They whine about the sociological problems Life causes, but then they offer us the platform as an alternative. So our choice is trees and beauty and colour and amazing, *amazing* things. Or this grey nothing of the real. It's astonishing that they think that's actually a choice.'

An uneasy frustration crept over her. She couldn't see what he saw. She couldn't understand this place yet. She needed to know how it worked, and what it felt.

'Come, Rue mine,' he said, putting his arm about her shoulders. 'We'll take you home.'

She felt immense relief, and sank into his side as they walked.

'Where am I to stay?' she said.

'With me, of course.'

She stopped in surprise.

'It isn't like Angle Tar, Rue. There's no oddness involved in men and women of age living together without being married. And I live with many people; it won't just be us. You'll see.'

She had seen.

Wren's building looked just like every other building

around it. It was a wonder he could pick it out. It was an enormous building, too; a little more like the tall houses in Capital City that held twenty or thirty different families inside them.

'It smells funny, here,' said Rue, sniffing the outside air.

'No; it doesn't smell of anything. It's a relief after all the stench of Capital, right?' said Wren.

He was right. She inhaled deeply. That was what had been confusing her. There was nothing there to smell.

Wren walked up to what was presumably the main entrance, though the door looked just like a number of any others set into the wall that faced them. He pressed his face close to a flat, black decoration at head height.

'What are you looking at?' said Rue.

There was a series of quick beeps, a little like the noise of droning bees, thought Rue, cut up into slices. Wren leaned back. The door opened smoothly, disappearing into the wall rather than swinging in or outward.

'It's like a key,' Wren explained. 'Only you use your eye.'

'You use your eye as a key!?'

'We'll have to get you registered as quickly as we can. Until you're given citizenship, we won't be able to put your eye pattern on the door key.'

Rue didn't think much of that. Using your eye to open doors! She tried to swallow her fear of this strange culture and its magical way of living, tried instead to concentrate on the incredible things she knew it offered her.

'Where's the box? You said you had one,' she said, as they passed through a corridor much like the one at Red House, except it was coloured a uniform grey. He had

369

promised her another world in that box, and she had not forgotten.

'Patience, Rue,' said Wren with a grin. 'We'll get to it. It's in my room.'

His room had turned out to be quite ordinary. The box he had shown her before, or one like it, was there, on a thin side table that looked like it couldn't carry the weight of a chicken. Wren told her that it was made of one of the strongest materials in World. She'd considered testing his assurance by standing on top of it and jumping up and down, but didn't have the courage.

He had insisted she sleep for a while. Though she protested vigorously, it turned out that once she lay down, sleep overtook her almost at once. She didn't remember if he'd stayed with her or not. She hoped that he had, at least for a little while.

She shifted on the bed. It was warm in here, but she was much like a cat – a room couldn't be too hot. She had seen Wren touch the wall to control the temperature, but was too scared to try it herself until she learned the skill of it. Wren called it technology; which was, she supposed, their word for magic. At first she had been so struck with wonder she had wanted to spend hours playing with the things he had shown her so briefly, in just the way she had wanted to spend hours playing with every wonderful thing he had shown her in their dream trips together, all those weeks ago.

Magic was so commonplace here that it had infiltrated every part of everyone's lives. They had magic devices set into walls that made food. There were other things, Wren said, that made you almost anything you could think of. There was no skill or understanding to it – you asked for and you got. It was so normal that it had become boring for them. Would it become boring for her, the longer she stayed here? Wren thought so, but Rue didn't see how that was possible.

There was a lot she didn't understand, and Wren didn't seem able to tell her how things worked. Where, for example, did the food come from? Was the food device like an ordering service? Were there vast kitchens underground every block of houses in the district they lived, who received your order and then sent it up by pulley? But how could that be, because the food arrived hot if you wanted to, and how could they possibly know what you were going to order beforehand, and have it ready to go when you ordered it?

She knew these were stupid, childish ideas, so never voiced them; but when she quizzed Wren about the food devices, he spouted a lot of words that didn't translate into Angle Tarain and then became annoyed with her if she pressed.

That was another thing that had become very clear on coming here. She needed to learn the language they spoke here in World, as quick as she could. Then she could talk to some of the other people who lived in the house with them. They wouldn't seem so strange and distant from her if she could only talk to them. Wren had said there was a quick way for her to learn the language, but it took time to set up, so she had held tightly onto her patience and waited, meanwhile spending every day surrounded by people who chatted and talked with him and not her for hours and hours while she sat by his side, bored and trying hard not to show it.

World was a language that sounded both quite musical and a lot like a bad cough at the same time. No one spoke Angle Tarain in World. It was a quaint and pointless thing. So she waited and watched, while Wren laughed and ate and drank and sat her beside him with a protective air, but then mostly forgot she was there. She didn't blame him. It must be exhausting to spend every day having conversations with people and then translating everything that was said at the same time.

Wren maintained that he was viewed by his World friends and acquaintances as something of a curiosity, because he spoke two languages. No one in World spoke anything but World. No one in World needed to, because no one else in World spoke anything but World. It was a fundamental part of being a citizen of World. Wren was only allowed to retain his 'other' language, Angle Tarain, because of his job, he said. When Rue tried to quiz him on what exactly he did, he merely smiled mysteriously and said that she would find out soon enough.

In order to learn World, Rue had to jack in, as Wren kept calling it, to Life; that other world inside the box that teased her with its squat, ordinary presence on his desk. Although he had a box, it was not a common thing to be in possession of one, apparently; everyone else in the house could access Life automatically, whenever they wanted, and needed no kind of box at all.

So first, she had to be taught how to jack in. Second,

Wren needed to request and obtain a bio-code pack to buy the language for her so she could learn it; which was apparently what he had been doing the last few days. He said that his employers would pay for her to learn, and were also responsible for obtaining the bio-code pack (in Rue's mind, she equated bio-code pack with spell) and processing the odd request, in case of any questions asked – because who in World would need to learn World?

She lifted her feet in the air and examined them, wondering idly if she had the courage to get up and try to find Wren. She had no idea what time it was. Would he even be here?

Then she realised she was hungry, and that decided it.

She crept out of Wren's room. Much like Red House, her old university living quarters, everyone in this building lived in separate rooms but shared the 'communals' – the kitchen, bathrooms and the social room, where people ate and held parties. But the doors all looked the same, and everything was exact and placed just so; it made her shrink back from imposing herself so much on this place as to dare to move around in it, as if she belonged here.

She pressed on a random door, hoping it would open. It did, and beyond it, to her relief, was the social room. Two people looked up as she came in. Neither was Wren, though she recognised them vaguely from the past few days.

Rue stopped, embarrassed. She did her best to smile at them, though it must have come out crooked. One of them jumped up and returned the smile, opening her mouth as if to say something, then closing it as she remembered. She looked around at the other, who shrugged.

Pressing a hand to her chest, she said, 'Sabine.'

Rue understood well enough. 'Rue,' she said, pointing to herself.

Sabine smiled. She had glittering seawater coloured skin, and her hair was rolled into long, swaying tails, the tips of which grazed her elbows when she walked. She looked magnificent, and completely out of place in this dull grey room. Rue wished, wished she could look like her, and wondered when she might be able to learn how to change her skin and face and hair like that.

Her friend was a young man (or old, Rue reminded herself – augmentation made everyone look young) with fairly ordinary-coloured skin. He had chosen instead to change the texture of it – ridges and bumps had been carefully constructed to run the length of his face and neck, and presumably the rest of his body, in various patterns. He had a starburst of little bulbous ridges on his cheek. He also had a small set of six horns protruding from his forehead; five smaller ringed around a large one in the middle. He looked her up and down quite openly, and inside she rolled her eyes. Wren had warned her of it – every Worlder would find her simple, unaltered appearance strange, but for some it might even border on the offensive. Only Technophobes proudly displayed no augmentation whatsoever, and stuck out like a sore thumb.

'Technophobes are intensely annoying,' said Wren, when Rue pressed him about the word. 'They're a group of idiots who think Life is evil, or something. They have their implants removed illegally and go off-grid. They attack people for no reason. All kinds of strange things.'

In the meantime, Rue would have to endure the stares. She returned the young man's gaze directly until he dropped his eyes. Let him think she was rude – it was only a mirror of himself.

Sabine spoke. 'Lars,' she said, pointing at the man, who managed a cross between a nod and a shrug.

Rue ventured in a little further, then looked around.

In the study at Red House they had a huge array of books on shelves, a games cupboard, a wicker chest full of art materials. But this room was as bare as could be, much like everything she had seen so far in World. She looked around at the walls for the black square shape of a food device, but couldn't see one, and stood uncertainly. Even if she found it she wouldn't know how to work it; but she didn't want to ask these two strangers for help. How would she even get them to understand what she wanted?

Sabine was looking at her, as if trying to work out what she was thinking.

Lars said something, speaking unintelligible World with a bored sounding voice. Sabine answered him, and they talked for a moment. Rue slid awkwardly onto a seat near the door, not quite knowing what to do with herself.

Being around Worlders was strange – more often than not they seemed elsewhere. She knew that it was because they spent most of the time hooked into the invisible, tantalising world of Life, a world she wouldn't be able to see until she'd learned how to use the box.

As Talented, it was easy enough for her to understand that Worlders could see a place inside their head where they didn't physically exist. She wondered how easily non-Talented Angle Tarain would take to such a concept, and decided that most of them would probably find it impossible. But here, an entire culture revolved around the way her head worked. People would understand her without even knowing her. Rue loved that about World; more than the technology, more than the unfathomable things they did to their bodies, more than the incredible machines they liked so much to create that made their lives an effortless glide.

Sabine kept throwing Rue a glance, as if she was repeatedly considering trying to talk to her. Rue hoped she didn't. It was hard enough having to sit and listen without being able to join in, but when mime was resorted to, things became plain strange.

So there they sat.

She wondered if they both had a day off today, and where they worked, and what they did, and whether their parents looked as young as they did with all this augmentation floating around, and whether that bothered them. She was sure it would have bothered her if Fernie, her old hedgewitch mistress, had looked young and pretty. But thinking about Fernie and Angle Tar squashed her heart and gave her pain, so she moved on.

What did people do for fun in World? What would she do? Wren had said he would introduce her to his superior, a woman called Greta Hammond, who sounded much like Frith. She supposed if this Greta Hammond liked the look of her she might be enrolled in a school or training programme here, too, and meet another Talented group she would have to get used to. At least here she would have Wren, and she wouldn't have to make a start in this place all alone.

As she was thinking of him, he walked into the room, searched for her, and grinned when he found her. She squealed and ran to him, throwing her arms around his neck.

'Really,' he said with a laugh. 'I wasn't gone very long.'

'Wren, I can't wait to learn the language here.'

'Won't be long now, I promise you.'

Sabine asked him something, her eyes flicking between them. He answered, and they laughed. Wren moved out of Rue's arms and wandered over to the seats.

'What did she say?' Rue said.

'That Angle Tarain sounds like trying to gargle with water when your mouth is filled with glass balls.'

'Oh.'

'Don't take offence – we like to joke with each other. I told her that to us, World sounds like pigs mating.'

Rue barked a laugh and then covered her mouth in mock outrage. 'You're so mean.'

'I am, indeed,' he agreed.

'Where've you been? I woke and you were gone,' she said. It had meant to come out playful but sounded whiny, and she immediately regretted it. Wren shrugged evasively.

'Out, meeting people,' he said. 'Work. You'll understand, when you start yourself.'

'You mean when I start training. I can't work yet, I'm not old enough.'

Wren laughed, and draped an arm over her.

'Hungry?' he said.

LAURE EVE

Laure Eve is a French–British hybrid who grew up in Cornwall, a place saturated with myth and fantasy. Being a child of two cultures taught her everything she needed to know about trying to fit in at the same time as trying to stand out. She speaks English and French and can hold a vague conversation, usually about food, in Greek.

She has worked as a bookseller, a waitress and, for one memorable summer, a costumed bear for children's parties. She now lives and works in London in the publishing industry. Follow Laure at www.laureeve.co.uk or on Twitter: @LaureEve